THE INDUS STAR

A. H. WANG

ISBN: 978-0-9756360-2-2

www.AHWangAuthor.com

This book is a work of fiction. Except in the case of historical fact, any resemblance to actual events or persons, living or dead, is purely coincidental.

For any enquires regarding this book, please contact:
ahw@AHWangAuthor.com

DISCLAIMER

The Indus Star is book 3 of the Georgia Lee Adventure series. The series should be read in order:

Book 1: *The Imperial Alchemist*
Book 2: *The Golden Khan*
Book 3: *The Indus Star*

For my teachers,
past and present.

Map of India

HARIDWAR

PAKISTAN

•DELHI

NEPAL

•LUCKNOW

•VIDISHA

•JAMNAGAR
•DWARKA

•SURAT

•ELLORA & AJANTA

•MUMBAI

Arabian Sea

Bay of Bengal

•THIRUVANANTHAPURAM

SRI
LANKA

The only truly infinite thing is our ignorance.

—Carlo Rovelli

PROLOGUE

DHARA SHAH FIGHTS the crush of bodies making their way towards the Ganges River, pushing against the throng as she searches for the elusive godman. Her feet barely touch the ground as she is half-carried along by the mob.

Denied an interview with the guru she's sought for weeks, she has come to Kumbh Mela as a last resort. This is the largest human gathering in the world; up to fifty million Hindu pilgrims arrive each day for a ritual bath in the Ganges —the holy mother of rivers. The religious festival, held once every four years, is one of the most important in India, giving the faithful a chance to wash away a lifetime of sin with just a few dips in the sacred water.

Sadhus, swamis, babas, and yogis with long dreads and matted hair surround her, their faces and torsos smeared with ash, some dressed in saffron robes or white loincloths, and others not wearing anything at all. There is an irrepressible excitement in the air, an almost contagious, clamorous sense of exhilaration as they all make their way to the riverbank.

Dhara knows for sure the godman she is seeking must

have set up a tent in one of the encampments, most likely performing some feat or miracle to recruit new disciples unaware of his past and recent transgressions. But as she fights the surge of the sweaty, semi-dressed, enraptured horde, she realises that, in her blind desperation to chase the story, she has made a crucial mistake. There is no way she's going to find a man she's never met among all these people. This is literally the biggest assembly of spiritual guides in India, and all of their ash-smudged faces blend into one as she looks through the crowd.

Up ahead, a metal post appears like an oasis amid parched land, and as she is thrust forward by the merciless drive of the human juggernaut, she realises the pole is sticking out of a large bucket filled with concrete. She makes a ruthless leap for it, provoking the wrath of her nearest neighbours as she elbows her way over, and exhales with jubilant relief when she finally escapes the crowd.

Dhara clings onto the makeshift platform as the sea of bodies breaks around her and rejoins again, flowing past her little haven of an island. Several hundred yards ahead, an ocean of heads bob up and down as thousands upon thousands of holy men and ordinary citizens splash about in the Ganges like gleeful children.

Taking a moment to absorb her surroundings, she marvels at the scene before her, unable to fully fathom the sheer number of people present. Were she here as a tourist, she would have immersed herself in the spectacle of it all. Revelled in the wondrous, kaleidoscopic congregation. Even basked in the assault to her senses from the suffocating heat, the thick atmosphere of body odour, and the relentless cacophony. But right now, every person is an obstacle between her and the story she has promised her editor.

She makes a full turn, spotting an area to the far left, where the crowd is thinner and a patchwork of multicoloured tarpaulins has been set up for shelter.

That is where her godman will be.

She's just worrying about the impossible task of making her way there, when a commotion erupts at the bank of the river. Screams of terror ripple through the congregation. She spins around. Everyone is now fighting to get out of the water.

It takes her a moment to identify the one word being repeated over and over again within the escalating mayhem.

Blood.

She frowns, craning her neck to make out what is happening. Men and women with panic-stricken faces scramble to flee the river. Their bodies are covered in a layer of gore. People faint and vomit on the banks.

Her heart thundering in her ears, her breath coming in short bursts, Dhara's eyes dart about, frantically seeking the perpetrator of the heinous crime. She cannot see the source of the blood. Is it a psychopath on a killing spree? A terrorist attack? What could cause carnage on a scale like this?

Then her gaze travels further, beyond the horde of people jostling to escape the water. She freezes. Her mind struggles to make sense of what she's seeing.

A chill runs through her body.

The Ganges is at least a mile across from this bank to the other. And the entire river is running with blood.

What in the world — ?

That's when she feels the first drop of water land on her scalp.

Another on her shoulder.

Then another.

A stunned, eerie silence falls over the masses. Dhara lifts her hand to catch the raindrops in her palm. Her confusion amplifies as she fights to quash the rising panic in her gut.

Black. The rain is black.

Dhara looks up. With every moment, the downpour intensifies. Soon, a deluge of inky water descends from the sky.

Somewhere, someone shrieks about the wrath of Shiva.

Pandemonium erupts once more. The swarm of bodies wrestles and claws, screaming and yelling as everyone tries to escape all at once. Limbs flail in fits of hysterics. Those who fall are buried by the clambering crowd. Several pilgrims scramble onto Dhara's small island of refuge, each delirious with fear as violence breaks out among them.

Dhara gets shoved into the mob below. Try as she might to stay upright, there are just too many people writhing and twisting against each other. The throng surges behind her. She and some others tumble to the muddy ground. More fall and climb over them.

Dhara's breath comes in gasping stutters as an overwhelming weight crushes her. She cries out in agony as someone kicks her in the side. Another person steps on her back. She struggles to throw them off.

An elderly woman yelps as she falls beside Dhara. The frenzied horror in her creased features is heartbreaking. Before she knows it, Dhara is pulling her close, shielding her frail body with her own.

Dhara knows she and the old woman have little chance of making it out alive. She shuts her eyes in a fervent plea for a miracle that may never come. But in that final moment, the only thing that floods her mind is an endless stream of regrets: words unspoken, dreams uncompleted, and promises unfulfilled.

1

"I'm TELLIN' ya, Georgia, best way to end a drought is to jump straight into the ocean. No tip-toeing about it," Sarah says in her accented English, giving her boss her unsolicited opinion. "Always rip the Band-Aid off in one go, I say…"

Georgia Lee sips her coffee, tuning out her assistant and letting the older woman drone on. It's study break week, the university cafeteria is empty, and she is enjoying the rare tranquillity. She wishes Sarah would go bother somebody else about their dating life, but it's a wish she knows would never come true. So she tries to focus instead on the muted television screen across the room. There's a news report about a dreadful mass stampede in India, with hundreds killed and even more injured.

"I know you don't like dating apps, but let's be honest, it's not like you're settling down and getting married. You just need to get your head back in the game…" Sarah continues as she munches on a croissant, doling out advice with her mouth full.

Georgia rolls her eyes. Then she chokes on her coffee

when her gaze falls on the figure by the door. She splutters and coughs, reaching for a paper napkin.

"Shit. You okay?" Already dabbing at the coffee stains on Georgia's shirt, Sarah freezes when she sees the expression on her boss's face. Frowning, she turns to look in the direction of Georgia's stare. "What the f—"

"Buri." Georgia rises to her feet, knocking Sarah's hands out of the way.

Buri Myagmar marches into the spacious cafeteria. Several paces ahead of him, Indi trots, then gallops at full speed with her tongue lolling out. Her long strides eat up the distance between them and before Georgia can even blink, the German shepherd's front paws are on her chest. Indi lathers her cheeks with drool and affection, huffing hot doggy breath in her face.

"Indi. Hey. Hey, cut it out," she says as her hands sink into Indi's fluffy coat. She gives an involuntary laugh at the dog's ardent display of affection, then falters as her attention returns to the man advancing towards her. A sense of déjà vu overcomes Georgia as she remembers Buri's sudden appearance eight months ago, when she hosted a press conference to return Chinggis Khan's Spirit Banner to the Mongolian government.

Buri's thick eyebrows are knitted together as he watches the way his dog greets her. Georgia's eyes travel over him, noting the changes since they last met. He's cut his hair. The once long, dark locks have been cropped close to his head, revealing the curve of his skull and emphasising his sharp features. The style is now neat and orderly, just like everything else in his life. His scruffy beard is also gone and only a hint of stubble remains, outlining his strong jawline.

But it's the intense stare and the permanent scowl, characteristics that are an unmistakable part of his intimidating personality, that make him easy to identify.

He draws to a halt before her, and his canine companion

immediately sits down, looking up at her owner and awaiting his command.

"We need to talk," he declares. His voice is the same low timbre Georgia remembers, its vibration sending a tremor through her.

She stares at him, mouth agape, stunned by his mere presence and immobilised by his familiar earthy, masculine scent. Her heart hammers in her chest.

"What the *hell* are you doing here again, you grunt?" Sarah's sharp voice cuts through the awkward silence. She plants her hands on her hips. "I thought you fucked off back to Canada eight months ago?"

Buri's eyes do not stray from Georgia's as he says evenly, "I lived in Mongolia. And I'm American, not Canadian."

Sarah gives a dismissive wave with her hand. "Yeah yeah, same same. If you think for one second—"

"Buri," Georgia interrupts, finding her voice at last, "what are you doing here? I thought you went home, after we… after I… I…"

"I never left. Travelled around Australia instead."

"For *eight* months?" Sarah butts in.

Buri's nod is brusque, his expression shuttered. "It's a big country. Lots to see."

"Well, I'm sure you've seen it all now," Sarah says. "Time to say bye bye. *Adiós. Au revoir. Sayonara*—"

Buri reaches out and touches Georgia on the arm. The contact is startlingly gentle, yet it burns her skin. She bites down on her tongue to stop herself from flinching, but Buri drops his hand anyway, clenching his fist by his side.

"I need to tell you something," he says again.

Indi whimpers. She circles a spot on the floor near his feet before sitting down, then lets out a yelp.

"What?" Tendrils of anxiety grasp Georgia's heart as she notices the flash of emotion in his dark eyes.

"I think you should sit down."

"Oh for God's sake. Just spit it out already." Sarah crosses her arms over her chest.

For the first time since walking in, Buri turns and stares at the older woman. A muscle ticks in his jaw. At least a foot shorter, Sarah glares up at him, unaffected by the obvious tension radiating off his formidable physique.

"Anya Mihailovich is alive," he finally says, his eyes darting back to Georgia.

"What…?" Shock and disbelief coursing through her, the revelation has Georgia stumbling back into her seat. A million questions race through her mind, each one fighting to be the first out of her mouth. Her hands tremble and she clasps them together, trying to hold on to some semblance of composure.

"But you told me… you told me she was dead?"

"I never said that. I said she was missing. Presumed dead by her own people in Russia. That was the intel we got. With the crimes she committed, I assumed the authorities in Mongolia would have given her what she deserved."

"What happened to her? Where has she been all this time?"

"I don't know the specifics. Only that she was kept in a secret prison in Mongolia. She escaped six months ago."

"Six months? She's been free for *six* months?" Georgia's tone is almost accusatory. She can't help it.

Buri swallows, his Adam's apple moving up and down his throat. His expression softens. "I only heard about this on Monday. I drove down from Brisbane to tell you—"

"Where is she now?"

"I don't know. I came as soon as I found out. I was worried she might make contact with you."

Georgia shakes her head, unwilling to hear any more. Her assistant takes over, issuing rapid-fire questions at Buri, which he answers in a curt, clipped tone. Their voices are a blur as Georgia tries to process what Buri has revealed.

Dr. Anya Mihailovich, the Russian archaeologist, has

haunted Georgia's every thought and dream ever since she brutally murdered Georgia's best friend, Ethan Sommers. Her mind returns to her last encounter with Anya in the Mongolian royal tomb, and her gut clenches as she remembers how the psychopathic woman shot her in the stomach.

A conflicting mixture of guilt, grief, and rage courses through her. Georgia left Anya to an almost certain death when she allowed the Mongolian authorities to take her away. But at that moment, with her bloody gut wound still healing and Ethan's death fresh on her mind, it felt like justice.

Ethan was Georgia's childhood sweetheart. A man with whom she had a complicated past. And the man she hoped to have a future with. Anya ripped away Georgia's choice for that future, robbing her of the chance to make things right with Ethan.

The chance for happiness.

She looks up. Three pairs of eyes now stare at her, all waiting for her to say something. Indi huffs by her side, licking her palm then resting her chin on Georgia's lap. Georgia shakes her head again, as if the gesture would somehow clear her mind so she could make sense of this. She stands, wincing at the sharp scrape of the chair against the floor, and is about to make a beeline for the exit when she sees another man approaching them.

Bespectacled, with average height and build, the South Asian man's face is framed by a neatly trimmed beard and bushy eyebrows. Wearing a black turban that indicates his Sikh background, he is dressed in a white T-shirt and jeans. His boyish smile seems familiar, but she cannot conjure up where she has seen him before. His dark eyes are fixed on Buri's back as he walks towards them.

"Ben." He stops behind Buri, addressing the burly man by his American name.

Buri turns and takes in a sharp breath. "Harshan." He lets out an abrupt, startled laugh, his face betraying his disbelief.

The sound is so unusual from him it makes Georgia pause for a moment, storing it away in her mind.

"What are you doing here, man?" Buri's face is momentarily lit up with a rare smile as he envelops the shorter man in a bear hug, and then claps him on the back a couple of times for good measure.

It's disarming to see Buri this way. The surly, mercurial, ex–Special Forces medic is suddenly gone, replaced by somebody else entirely. Someone more... real. Georgia watches the reunion between the two friends with keen interest, and she's almost disappointed when Harshan turns his attention to her and Sarah, throwing an expectant gaze at Buri.

Buri clears his throat and introduces them. "Harshan Singh, meet Professor Georgia Lee." Then he blinks as he looks to Sarah, and his expression resumes its usual mien. "And... who are you again?"

Sarah glowers at him. "Sarah Wu, Georgia's assistant." She offers her palm to Harshan, who clasps her hand with both of his, offering her a warm smile.

"Dr. Harshan Singh," Georgia says, finally recalling where she's seen the man before. The renowned linguist has been making waves in the archaeological community lately with his groundbreaking work on the Indus script, one of the earliest forms of writing in the world, which has remained undeciphered since its discovery. "I've been following your work."

"And I, yours, Professor Lee," he admits with a hand over his heart, speaking with a blended Indian and American accent.

"Please, call me Georgia."

"Georgia." He beams, colour rising in his cheeks as he effuses, "What an absolute pleasure to meet you. I'm a big fan. I've read all of your published works. Your work in China, and the most recent discovery in Mongolia—"

"Harshan." Buri puts his large hand on the linguist's shoulder, repeating his question. "What are you doing here?"

Harshan's wide smile fades as he fidgets. He clears his throat. He adjusts his laptop bag and pushes his glasses up on the bridge of his fleshy nose. "I've come for your help on something, Ben. And since Professor Lee is here too, maybe she could give her expert opinion on what I need to show you."

Buri frowns. "You came all the way from India for this? How did you even know I was here in the first place?"

Harshan gives an exasperated shake of his head. "You're a hard man to track down. I had to call your brother, who told me that you'd be here with Professor Lee. I've been looking all over the campus for you both this morning."

Buri's face darkens. The sudden shift of his posture sends alarm through Georgia. She recalls he has a half-brother who is also in the military—a Russian language expert, if she remembers correctly. That was one of the very few details Buri has revealed about his family.

"Well, what's this thing you need help with?" Sarah chimes in. "What can be so important you had to fly all the way from India?"

In the corner of the cafeteria, one of the staff turns up the sound on the television. A few people gather around, their attention captured by the scene playing out on the screen.

The news anchor's voice echoes through the cafeteria space: "Citizens around the world are completely baffled. The waters of these major river systems—the Nile of Egypt, the Ganges in India, the Yangtze in China, and the Tigris–Euphrates—are all running red with blood…"

Video recordings of the rivers are shown in quick succession on the screen, the waters stained a rich scarlet hue like streams of blood from a deep, open wound. Thick, darker red streaks ripple through the water, the sight so chilling it sends tingles through Georgia's scalp.

"Authorities are urging the public not to panic as they investigate the causes, but already, farmers and fishermen dependent on these rivers are in upheaval. Rumours are running rampant among the locals, whisperings of curses and the apocalypse…"

Harshan's face is twisted with concern as he points to the screen, answering Sarah's question. "I've come for help with *that*."

2

———————

GEORGIA USHERS EVERYONE into her and Sarah's shared office and shuts the door. The room is already too small for the women, and now it feels claustrophobic with the addition of two more men and a large dog. But the expression on Harshan's face told her this is not a conversation they should have in public.

"Harshan, start talking," Buri says, looking around the crowded space as if he's unsure of where to place his bulky frame. After a few moments, he wedges himself in the far corner beside Sarah's desk, where Harshan has sat down and is now setting up his laptop.

Georgia stays near the door, placing as much distance as possible between her and Buri. Indi sprawls out in the centre of the room and stretches her long legs, apparently deciding it's now time for a nap.

Bringing up a few images on his computer, Harshan explains, "Two years ago, a stone tablet now known as TN-031 was uncovered at a Mesopotamian site in southern Iraq, fifteen kilometres from the ancient city of Ur. Etched on the artefact was the longest inscription we've ever found of the Indus script. This was a breakthrough discovery, because it meant we would finally have a chance of truly understanding the Indus Valley Civilisation. The text was sent to a few scholars around the world—including me—and we were all racing to be the first to decipher it."

"Okay, hold up." Sarah raises her hand. "Start from the beginning, please. I know nothing about the Indus Valley Civilisation or the Indus script."

"Right. Yes, sorry," Harshan says. He takes a deep breath, scratches his forehead as he thinks, then starts again, "For a long time, one of the greatest misconceptions of history was that civilisation began roughly six thousand years ago in a single place: the Fertile Crescent."

"The Cradle of Civilisation," Buri asserts. "Home of Mesopotamia and Ancient Egypt."

"Yes," Harshan says. "Everyone believed that writing began exclusively there, in settlements along the Nile and the Tigris–Euphrates. And a while later, the Yangtze in China." He grabs a pen and paper, drawing a rough map to illustrate his point.

"The same rivers on the news reports," Sarah points out.

"Yes. You are right. But that's something I'll come back to later." The distress returns to Harshan's face, and he fidgets with his pen. "Now, it wasn't until the late nineteenth century that a fourth, independent writing system from another early river valley civilisation was found. This previously unknown culture existed at the same time as Ancient Egypt and Mesopotamia, and it was the largest civilisation in the ancient world.

"That fourth writing system is now known as the Indus script, belonging to the Indus Valley Civilisation, also known as the Harappan Civilisation. Its territory was twelve times the combined size of Ancient Egypt and Mesopotamia, occupying a vast area of one million square kilometres and covering what is now Pakistan, parts of northwest India, and northeast Afghanistan. At its peak, its population was the largest in the world, reaching up to five million and spread over two thousand towns and villages, from the Himalayas to the Arabian Sea. But while the other river valley cultures flourished and are well known by everyone today, the Harappan culture vanished without a trace. It's one of the most puzzling mysteries of human history."

Harshan leans back in his chair. "We know very little about the Harappan people, their values and beliefs, or what their daily lives were like. But what we do know is this: Indus Valley wasn't like any other Bronze Age Civilisation of its time. While the other societies were governed by strict hierarchies, state-controlled economies, powerful religious institutions, and monarchies such as kings and pharaohs, we found no evidence of any of that in the Indus Valley. There were no palaces, no royal tombs or pyramids, no temples or ziggurats, and no indications of a state religion. The Harappans were ahead of their time, adopting a relatively egalitarian social and political structure. And they had advanced city planning skills and sophisticated sewage system technologies. They were highly organised, and the standardisation of weights and building materials across their vast territory reflected that. What's more, they appear to have been peace-loving people, because we've found no signs of warfare or slaves. The Harappans were more interested in business than conquests, and there's proof of extensive trade between them and Mesopotamia."

"Hence the reason TN-031 was uncovered in a Mesopotamian settlement," Georgia points out.

"Yes." Harshan brings up the British Museum website on his laptop. Keying in a few search terms, he quickly finds images of some Harappan seals.

Georgia peers at the small, flat square pieces of stone. They are carved with motifs of animals and human figures, and bear inscriptions similar to Egyptian hieroglyphs.

"Up until recently," Harshan continues, "the only examples of the Indus script we've found are on these seals. We don't know for sure what they are for, but we think they are stamps that may have been used for identification, or marks of ownership. As you can imagine, it's impossible to decipher an entire writing system with only a few characters like these. And without access to written records, it's difficult to truly understand a culture. TN-031 is the first artefact we've found that has more than just a handful of characters on it. What makes the discovery most astounding is that the Indus script inscriptions are followed by its cuneiform translations."

Buri inhales audibly. "It's the Indus version of the Rosetta Stone."

"Exactly. The Rosetta Stone was the key to decoding Egyptian hieroglyphs. Since its discovery, we have made leaps and bounds in understanding that ancient world."

"And you are hoping this TN-031 would do the same for the Indus Valley Civilisation," Sarah says.

"Yes."

"Okay." Sarah nods slowly. "But what's all this got to do with the bloody rivers?"

Harshan sighs. "Deciphering the Indus script is what I've been doing on the side. My main job has been supporting an archaeological team in Gujarat in north-western India. We've been excavating a submerged city off the coast."

"You're looking for the lost city of Ancient Dwarka?" Buri raises his brows with surprise.

"What?" Sarah asks.

When Buri doesn't answer her, Georgia explains, "It's believed to be the sunken city of Krishna, the Hindu deity. Some even call it the Atlantis of the East."

"Yes, but the area is also a well-known Harappan settlement," Harshan corrects, taking off his glasses and using the hem of his T-shirt to rub the lenses. "Dwarka is an ancient place and dates back thousands of years. Now, marine archaeology requires more resources and has some unique challenges, so work was done in dribs and drabs over the decades. There hasn't been a lot of significant excavation until the last year. In the beginning, all we found were shells and more Harappan seals. As we uncovered more of the city, though, we realised it could be the biggest Indus Valley site we've ever found. Until now, Mohenjo-daro in Pakistan was the largest and most extensively researched site, covering an area of seven hundred and fifty acres. We believe Dwarka is easily twice that."

He places his glasses back on his face and brings up another image on his laptop, showing a brick wall marked with inscriptions. "Last year, our lead archaeologist made a major discovery. During one of his dives, he found extensive etchings on the Granary wall."

"You're kidding," Buri says in a low tone.

"Exactly." Harshan widens his eyes. "What are the chances of two separate teams finding significant samples of the Indus script within a year of each other, when nothing had been found for centuries? Anyway, all of this meant my workload doubled overnight. With the progress I've already made on TN-031, I was able to translate some of the text from Dwarka. But the process has been slow."

He turns to Buri. "Do you remember the deciphering software we created together back in college, when we were writing our dissertations about decoding the Proto-Elamite script?"

Georgia studies Buri with keen interest. She's well aware of his talent and skills in linguistics, since she tried to get him a job at Sydney University eight months ago. But she still views him more as an ex–Special Forces medic rather than an academic. And since he is about as forthcoming as a dead clam, she knows very little of his past.

"What about it?" is all the big man says.

"I've been using it as the basis for my work on the Indus script. But I'm not as good at coding as you, Ben. Never have been. There's some kind of bug in the system, and as much as I've been trying to figure out what it is, I can't. I managed to decrypt a chunk of the text four months ago, but progress is now pretty much at a standstill." Harshan stares up at his friend, his expression hopeful.

Buri's brow furrows. "That was a long time ago. I can't even remember what was in the program. And surely there are plenty of computer geniuses in India who are much better at this than me?"

Harshan shakes his head emphatically. He points to the sketched map of the major rivers, and the anguish returns to his features. "This is sensitive material, Ben. I didn't really think too much about the content at first. Then, one by one, the signs started coming true. And now, with all the rivers running red with blood… I thought… It's not just me. My entire team is spooked. They urged me to come to you. We just can't trust anyone else with the text. We're worried it's going to cause mass panic. It's some kind of prophecy." His voice escalates and his breath quickens as he continues, "With all the media coverage of everything that's going on, we can't let anyone else see what we've got. People are going to—"

"Okay. I'll have a look." Buri places his hand on his friend's shoulder. "Just take a deep breath."

Indi gets up, suddenly alert. She makes the couple of paces over to Harshan and sits before him, letting out a soft whimper. When the Indian man looks at her with unease, she lays down before him in what little space she can find, placing her chin on top of his shoe.

"She's trying to comfort you," Georgia explains, her heart warming as she watches Indi's performance.

"Oh." Harshan frowns, easing his foot away from under the dog. He clears his throat, looking back up at Buri. "Look… maybe you'll understand better if I show you what I've got so far."

He wakes up the screen on his computer and clicks into a

file. The four of them crowd around the desk. Major sections of the text are missing, probably from the deteriorated engravings or the faulty deciphering software, but the message is abundantly clear:

[…] in the twilight of time, this foretelling be revealed:

Omens forewarn the Age of Man's demise,
Take heed, […] shall foreshadow the end,
And as more manifest, the swifter the final chime:

[…] from heavens fall,
While rivers of major cities flow with blood.
The Earth trembles and quakes with fury,
Its molten core spewing inferno in fiery wrath.
Rain black as man's heart descends upon us,
Fires […] drought […] storms […]
The world torn asunder, overturned and undone,
Then creatures of the sea rain from the sky,
A disease so foul spreads its wings through our realm […]

3

"As you can see, the message is alarming." Harshan's fear is so palpable, Georgia's own heart starts to race. "Last month, Mount Merapi in Indonesia erupted, blanketing villages in debris and molten lava. Some villages couldn't see the sun for days because of the ash. And only this week, we've had black rain in several places in India. One of the locations was Haridwar, where Kumbh Mela was happening. There were millions of pilgrims there, and when the Ganges became red at the same time, everyone panicked."

"We saw news reports of the stampede on TV." Georgia nods. "But let's not jump to conclusions here. All we've got is a few half-translated lines on an ancient wall from four, five thousand years ago."

"Yes, but for all of these things to happen at the same time? It can't just be coincidence. The *rivers of major cities* during the Bronze Age period were the Tigris–Euphrates, the Nile, the Ganges, and the Yangtze. They are all flowing with blood right now. *Simultaneously*." He stabs his finger at the map he has drawn for emphasis. "And like I said, I'm not the only one worried about this." He takes a long pause before giving Buri a pointed look. "I don't know if you've heard, but Dhara was caught up in the Kumbh Mela disaster."

Buri stills, his expression unreadable as he asks in a low voice, "Is she…?"

"She's alright," says Harshan. "She's got two cracked ribs, a broken arm, and some nasty bruises. But she made it out alive… thank god." Harshan sighs. "Even saved an old lady while she was at it. Dhara's tougher than you and I combined. But I worry about her."

"Who's Dhara?" Sarah pipes up.

"My cousin," Harshan replies.

But she's more than that. Georgia can tell by the way Buri averts his gaze, and by how Indi lifts her head again, watching her master carefully as she gauges his needs.

"Let's see what we can do about that software bug first." Buri changes the subject as he pulls up the other chair to sit beside Harshan.

"Yeah, you do that," Sarah says and grabs Georgia by the arm, dragging her out of the room.

Pulling Georgia down the corridor, Sarah speaks with a hushed, exasperated tone. "Listen, Georgia. All this Indus Valley mumbo jumbo has nothing to do with us. Why are we even letting them use our office?"

"Well…"

"I don't like this DIA guy," Sarah says, referring to the Defense Intelligence Agency in America. "Him and Agent Miller must be onto you, if they're hanging around like this."

"Buri's not DIA—"

"He works with them, doesn't he? Anyway, why would he bother coming all the way here again after you told him to bugger off eight months ago?"

"He never left the country. He came to warn me about Anya, as a friend," Georgia argues.

"I heard what he said. But I don't buy it. And that bullshit about him travelling around Australia? Nah-uh." Sarah shakes her head. "You shouldn't trust anything he says. I mean, how well do you actually know the guy? He's gotta be spying for the DIA, feeding information to Agent Miller about you. We have to get him as far away from you as possible."

Georgia frowns. "I've got questions for him. He can help me find Anya."

"What the fuck for? You need to let that bitch go. You gotta let all this Ethan stuff go. Anya's not your responsibility. Leave it up to the DIA dickheads to find her…"

But Georgia is already tuning her assistant out. Buri's unexpected appearance is shocking, but the news that he bears is even more so. She will not sleep well again until she has her answers.

What has he been doing over the past eight months? Why has he stuck around for so long? Like Sarah, Georgia doesn't believe in his excuse of sightseeing in Australia. She knows how attached he is to Mongolia. Thinking back to the last time she met with him, her heart squeezes with remorse. She wishes she'd handled things better between them. But lately, that seems to be a recurring sentiment in her life.

Eight months earlier, Sydney, Australia

TWILIGHT VEILED THE LANDSCAPE, *and overhead, a blanket of deepening hues unfurled in the sky. As the last remnants of a vibrant sunset seeped from the horizon, long shadows grew amongst the neat rows of tombstones, and the hushed whispers of willow trees were drowned out by the hubbub of squawking ravens.*

Georgia crouched down, barely registering her trousers becoming soaked in the moist grass. She placed her palm against the headstone. The cool surface was smooth and damp in the wintry air, chilling her skin. She traced the name etched into the stone with her fingertips, the letters perfectly cut into the black granite that reflected nothing in the waning light of dusk.

ETHAN SOMMERS
1982~2016
BELOVED BY ALL WHO KNEW HIM

Blinking back tears, she sniffled. The cemetery was empty, and the rest of the funeral attendees had left for the wake at Ethan's parents' place. It'd been a lovely ceremony with a large congregation, and it was clear Ethan was going to be missed by many, especially by those who had got up with grief-stricken faces to speak about him.

And all of it compounded the guilt weighing on Georgia's heart.

She'd stayed behind for a moment alone with him, and perhaps also to avoid having to talk to the others. That was almost an hour ago. Her tears had long since dried against her cheeks, leaving in their place an unbearable hollow in her chest. She rubbed at her sternum, knowing she ought to leave but could not bring herself to walk away.

"I'm sorry," she whispered, taking a deep breath as fresh tears threatened to spill over.

It had taken weeks for the Australian police to release Ethan's body for burial after they tried to build a case against the Russians. But Georgia wondered at the point of it all. Lev Ivanov was already dead, and Anya had been captured by Mongolian authorities for atrocities she'd committed on their most hallowed ground. So the people responsible for Ethan's death were gone, and the only thing the police had achieved was to prolong the agonising wait for closure.

Even so, Georgia couldn't shake the lingering unease that gnawed away at her. It was a relentless itch that nothing could satisfy, an unfinished business that hung in the air and weighed heavily on her mind. Thoughts of Anya had plagued her since Ethan's death, and at times she'd find herself fantasising scenarios of retaliation that could somehow match the pain the Russian woman had inflicted upon Ethan before his murder. Looking back, the few meagre punches she had thrown at Anya seemed like such a feeble attempt at justice.

Then Georgia would be overcome with shame. She'd never been a violent person. She hated guns and even martial arts. How could she possibly wish such cruelty on someone else, no matter what they had done? What would Charlie have said?

Charlie.

She sighed at the thought of her friend, her teacher, and the reason she was changed forever. Their search for the elixir of life in the mountains of Taiwan had ended in catastrophe—with his death and her newfound immortality. And now she felt the weight of responsibility on her soul, a burden she feared she could not shoulder.

She was not wise like her friend. Her powers of swift healing could bring so much to humanity, and yet Charlie had warned of the devastating consequences of sharing it. She wished he were here to guide her, because the one question that had circled her mind since they met was now louder and more persistent than ever.

Was the world ready for immortality? Or was it a curse she must protect at all costs?

Could she have saved Ethan that night by giving him some of the elixir—her blood?

Lost in her own thoughts, she hadn't even noticed the stranger walk up to her.

"Professor Georgia Lee?" he asked.

She looked up, startled. A middle-aged man in a navy suit, he had a generous belly and a thick neck strangled by a pale yellow tie. She rose to her feet, brushing off the grass on her pants.

"Yes?"

He fished out a business card from his wallet, handing it to her. "I was told I'd find you here. My name is Damien Brown. I'm Charles Jiang's lawyer."

Her bewilderment must have been obvious, because he explained, "I believe you would have known him as Charlie?"

Too shocked to reply, she took his card, her heart racing at the mention of her friend. She realised with embarrassment that she hadn't even known Charlie's full name. He was always just 'Charlie' to her; names had seemed irrelevant given how many he'd had in his long life.

"I'm sorry to disturb you like this, but it's been difficult for me to track you down." Damien reached into the inner pocket of his jacket, bringing out an envelope. "Charlie's recent death triggered a series of instructions that I've been carrying out. One of them was to pass this onto you."

She sucked in a tremulous breath. With hesitation, she took the packet from him.

"I'm sorry for your loss," Damien offered. Then he nodded at the fresh pile of dirt beside them and corrected himself, the pity clear in his hazel eyes. "Losses. My deepest condolences."

She barely registered him leaving as she stared down at the crisp, white envelope marked with embossed lettering — 'Brown & Allen'. At the centre was her name scribbled by hand. The sight of Charlie's handwriting made her heart bloom with nostalgia. She turned it over in her palms and was about to open it when a woman called to her.

"Georgia. There you are."

Flinching at the familiar voice, she snapped her head up. Her breath was caught in her throat as she took in the face she hadn't seen since the funeral of her own daughter, Jacqui. Incredulity and astonishment coursed through her, followed by a pinch of anxiety in the seat of her gut. She felt the invisible walls of her defences go up instantly.

"Mum," she breathed. "What are you doing here?"

The last time Georgia had seen her mother was seven years ago, yet the woman had not aged a day. Dressed from head to toe in black, her tall figure was adorned with an edgy, one-shoulder dress with a flowing chiffon skirt. The smooth skin of her cheeks and fore-

head was flawless, with only the faintest touch of lines between her eyebrows. Her dark hair, cut in a stylish bob, hung just below her angular jaw. Silky, artisan-crafted earrings dangled from each ear, and on her index finger she wore a chunky ring studded with a large onyx.

"What kind of a question is that? I wouldn't have missed this for the world. Ethan was like a son to me." Linda Chang raised an unimpressed, meticulously shaped eyebrow as she strode up to Georgia. "My plane from Melbourne was cancelled, and I couldn't get the airline to put me on another flight early enough for the funeral." She shook her head, muttering, "Boggles my mind, how useless some people can be."

Georgia frowned. She didn't remember her mother ever having much interaction with Ethan. He was just the boy who lived down the street, and Linda had always been more interested in his parents, Dale and Susan Sommers, who were well known to be strong supporters of the arts. Linda Chang sniffed out art collectors like a bloodhound, and this was no exception.

"Where are Dale and Susan?" her mother asked.

"At the wake, back at their house."

"Oh. Well, I'll head over there." She turned, stumbling a little as her high heels sank into the waterlogged lawn. Pausing to regain her balance, she stared at the tombstone and heaved a sigh. "Such a damn shame. I'd been trying to call Ethan since he was appointed the curator at the NGV," she said, referring to the National Gallery of Victoria in Melbourne. "I've been doing so well. And I landed a solo exhibition at one of the most prestigious galleries in Australia. Ethan would have loved my latest work. I wish he could have seen it. Maybe he would've even brought me new collectors."

Georgia tried to ignore the resentment bubbling up from the pit of her stomach. Linda Chang had always been this way, so why should she be surprised that her mother would only talk of herself at somebody else's funeral?

But this was Ethan's funeral.

The older woman shook her head, and the sorrow on her features actually seemed genuine. "I talked to Susan on the phone last week. Poor thing. Her heart is absolutely broken. You wouldn't understand, Georgia. You were only a mother for three years. That's not even close to what Susan and I have had to endure. Motherhood is a tiresome, endless string of responsibilities. All you ever do is give, give, and give. And what do you get in return? Nothing."

Georgia bit the insides of her cheeks until she tasted blood. The mention of Jacqui was a sharp prick to her heart. Yet she knew that the quickest way to get rid of her mother was not to engage with her monologues or tirades.

"You and Ethan were always close," Linda continued as she put a hand on Georgia's wrist, who recoiled at the contact but didn't dare to pull away. "I heard you were there the night he was murdered? My God. How could you have let it happen, Georgia? He'd always looked after you when you were kids. You could have at least returned the favour." She searched Georgia's eyes, then nodded as if coming to a conclusion. "I should've warned him long ago that he could expect nothing good to come out of being with you. I mean, look at how you've treated your own mother. No calls, no visits for all these years."

Georgia gasped, pushing down the sob that threatened to break free. She wrenched from Linda's hold and half-stumbled, half-ran towards the gate of the cemetery.

"Hey! Don't you walk away from me while I'm talking to you!" her mother yelled. "Georgia!"

Georgia's emotions boiled and raged within her like a thunderstorm. She barely held on until she got into her car and slammed the door shut. Only then did the sudden wail of despair explode from her throat. Tears cascaded in an unstoppable torrent, streaking trails down her face as her body convulsed with the intensity of her grief. The pain, guilt, rage, and sorrow swirled around her in a maelstrom, and this time she could not wrestle them into submission.

She didn't know how long she sat there as it all poured out of her; it seemed to last forever before she came back to herself, calming with exhaustion and the finality of defeat. Wiping her face with the back of her hands, she blew her nose on crumpled tissues. Numb and empty, she started the engine and drove away.

She didn't even know where she was going until she turned off the engine and realised that she was back at the university. It was mid-term break, there were thankfully few people around, and the parking lot was almost deserted as campus lights flickered on in the dark. She kept her head down and made a dash for her office, knowing that Sarah would have gone home hours ago.

She stopped short when she walked in the door. The sight of Buri sitting at her desk was like a kick to her stomach.

Several days ago, he'd shown up at the press conference where she presented the Spirit Banner of Chinggis Khan to the world. It was an important event, with reporters and scholars flying in from all over the globe to see the relic in person, not to mention the representatives from both the Australian and the Mongolian governments. It was also one of the highlights of her career, to be able to return something of such value and importance to its rightful owners.

Buri had explained that he'd thought long and hard about her offer to work together again, and had realised he wanted to get back to his linguistic roots. Against Sarah's loud protests, they'd made plans to meet and discuss job possibilities at the university, or through her contacts around the academic circles.

She'd forgotten that was to be tonight. How could she have been so stupid to think that she'd be able to have a meeting with him on the same day as Ethan's funeral?

He rose to his feet, flashing her a rare smile that faded just as fast when he scanned her face. "What's wrong?"

"Nothing." She averted her gaze, and saw that he'd brought dinner. It was there, neatly stacked in takeaway containers on her desk. The aroma of food and the thoughtful gesture made her stomach turn.

"Georgia?"

She squeezed her eyes shut, willing her emotions away.

"Hey, what's going on?" His voice was unusually soft as he stepped closer, touching her on the arm.

She drew in a sharp breath and raised her head. His dark, intense gaze met hers, and for one terrifying moment, she was convinced he'd look right through her and see how broken she was.

And how true her mother's words were.

She swallowed. What came out of her mouth was something she would regret for months afterwards.

"I think you should go back to Mongolia. There's nothing for you here."

4

_____

Present day, Sydney University, Australia

SARAH AND GEORGIA are still arguing in the hallway when the door to their office opens. Buri sticks his head out, staring at them as if he's heard everything they've been discussing. He doesn't mention a word about it, though.

Instead, he simply says, "It's done."

"You fixed it? The software?" Georgia asks, surprised. It barely took him an hour.

"There were a couple of bugs buried deep in the code. All Harshan needed was a fresh set of eyes."

Somehow, Georgia doubts it's as simple as that.

"Well?" Sarah asks, impatient.

Buri's expression is grave. "I think you should see this." He disappears back into the office.

Walking into the room, Sarah and Georgia step over a snoring Indi to stand next to Harshan, who's hunched over his laptop with a deep frown. He shifts aside to give them a better view of the information on the screen:

[...] in the twilight of time, this foretelling be revealed:

Omens forewarn the Age of Man's demise,
Take heed, for any six shall foreshadow the end,
And as more manifest, the swifter the final chime:

The detritus of man from heavens fall,
While rivers of major cities flow with blood.
The Earth trembles and quakes with fury,
Its molten core spewing inferno in fiery wrath.
Rain black as man's heart descends upon us,
Fires rage across the lands,
Crops laid waste by drought,
While cities crumble to storms of dust.
Then wind and wave shall batter the shores,
And the Earth swells with warts and tumours,
Which rupture and burst to create portals to hell.
Skies turn ebony and eclipse the sun,
The world torn asunder, overturned and undone,
Then creatures of the sea rain from the sky,
A disease so foul spreads its wings through our realm,
And men feast upon the flesh of their kin,
And bones of the dead rise from their graves,
Until the Lord descends to destroy the dark hearts of Men,
Scorching them to oblivion,
[…] bestowing a new chapter.

Yet within this darkness where all hope seems lost,
Redemption is possible, through […]

"Jesus," Sarah says. "That's grim."

The fear in Harshan's voice is clear as he says, "*Any six shall foreshadow the end*. We've already had four signs: the black rain, the bloody rivers, the volcanic eruption in Indonesia, and the ashes from that eclipsing the sun. And according to this, as more omens manifest themselves, the faster the end would come."

"Let's not jump to conclusions," Georgia says. "I'm sure there's a logical explanation for all of this. Volcanic eruptions happen from time to time. It doesn't mean the world is ending."

"What about the black rain? The rivers flowing with blood?" Harshan counters.

When Georgia fails to give him an answer, Sarah asks, "What happened to the end of the text?" She points to the bottom of the screen. "It says *redemption is possible, through…* what?"

"The rest of the inscriptions were cut off there," Harshan explains. "I just sent this to the rest of my team in India. There must be more information buried at the site in Dwarka."

Buri, who has been quietly scrolling through his phone until now, holds up the device to show the screen to everyone. "Look at this. Came up on my CNN feed."

He hands it to Georgia, who reads out the title of the article, *"Europe Burning."* Frowning, she continues, *"Wildfires are raging across the Mediterranean countries and parts of the Middle East. Unseasonal heat waves in these regions make it difficult to combat the blaze…"*

"That makes it five," Harshan whispers.

"Hold on," Sarah argues. "To be fair, this probably has more to do with climate change."

Harshan isn't convinced. "But—"

His laptop starts ringing a *Star Wars* chime, and an app appears, showing he has a call.

"That's my team in India now," Harshan explains as he presses on the button to accept the video conference.

Two separate windows pop up on the screen, one showing a middle-aged man with a full head of thick, curly hair and a neatly trimmed goatee. His dark brown eyes are deep and alert, shining with an intelligent gleam.

In the other window is a woman. North Indian, she appears to be in her late forties. With her light-coloured eyes, bright-red lips, and shiny black hair that reaches just past her shoulders, she is not conventionally attractive, but her sense of presence—even through a conference call—compels one to stand to attention. Around her neck is an elaborate emerald necklace, most likely antique. Georgia guesses it's from the Mughal period. The statement piece is stylishly matched with an amber-coloured silk saree.

"Madam-ji." Harshan ducks his head with his palms joined.

"Harshan," the Indian woman says. "I saw the latest decipherment you sent. Good job." Her distinct, British accent hints at her education.

"I had some help, ma'am," Harshan admits, turning to Buri. "This is my friend from college, B—"

"Buri Myagmar," Buri interrupts his friend, who looks at him with surprise.

"Your Mongolian name," Harshan murmurs, looking pleased. Turning back to the screen, he explains, "Buri's the one who found the bugs in the deciphering software." Then, looking at the others in the room, he gestures to the woman on the screen and says, "This is Madam Mallika Sharma, who is funding our excavation in Dwarka. And this is Dr. Faraaz Khan, the lead archaeologist."

"Is that… ?" Dr. Khan squints. "Professor Georgia Lee I see in the background?"

"Yes." Georgia smiles. "Dr. Khan, it's been a long time."

"It sure has," the older man replies. Then, addressing Mallika Sharma, he says, "Madam-ji, Professor Georgia Lee is an esteemed colleague of mine," then goes through her long list of academic accolades.

"Wonderful to meet you, Professor Lee," Mallika Sharma says with a smile, then gets to the point of the meeting. "So, I gather you have all seen the latest news of the fires in Europe. This is alarming."

"Yes," Harshan agrees. "That makes it five signs."

"Well—" Georgia starts.

"Could this all be a coincidence?" Sharma asks.

"Yes, of course," Dr. Khan says, pressing his lips together in thought. "And I don't usually entertain superstition, but what happened at Kumbh Mela has given me pause. We owe it to the victims and their families to look deeper into this. Something strange is happening."

Sharma is thoughtful as she muses. "Think about it, though: almost all major religions and cultures, at their core, speak of an end—a radical transformation of the world as we know it. In the Bible, it's the Book of Revelation. With Islamic teachings, the Day of Judgement. In Norse mythology, Ragnarök. These prophecies share common threads, omens that mark the end of days: conflicts, rampant immorality, environmental crises, the rise of false prophets, and so on."

She tilts her head, continuing, "And every tradition fore-tells a point where humanity deteriorates beyond redemp-tion, triggering a time of reckoning. Sooner or later, a change comes. Either by a conscious effort to transform for the better, or by complete obliteration: to wipe the slate clean for a fresh start."

Harshan points out, "And all of the omens pretty much describe the world we live in now."

Dr. Khan nods. "I think, though, we should find out more before making unfounded assumptions. There appears to be a part of the inscription missing. It must still be buried in the sediments at the site."

"Then we have to make this our priority. Figure out what's going on as soon as possible," Sharma says.

Dr. Khan nods. "We need you back here, Harshan."

"May I suggest we also bring Buri onboard?" the linguist says. "He was my dissertation partner in college, and his soft-ware skills are much better than mine. That is, if you're willing to help?" He looks to his friend.

Buri raises his brows with surprise, but says nothing.

Sharma gives her assent. "The more assistance we have on this, the better. I will compensate you well for your time, of course."

"While we're on the topic of more help..." adds Dr. Khan, "Georgia, I could really use a hand on site here."

"Oh, I couldn't possibly—"

Dr. Khan shakes his head. "I'm inundated with artefacts being uncovered every day, and I would appreciate a different perspective on some of our findings. The significance of this discovery cannot be overstated—it's the most monumental archaeological find in South Asia over the past century. Just imagine, we might soon unravel the mysteries of our ancestors—who they were, what they believed in, and why their civilisation ended."

"Time is of the essence, Professor Lee," Sharma cuts in. "For humanity's sake, I hope the recent events have nothing to do with what's written here. But after what happened at Kumbh Mela this week, you must admit it's unnerving to be reading about it in a prophecy made by a culture that disappeared for no apparent reason. Think about how the media is going to spin this when we reveal the team's findings to the rest of the world. It could cause an upheaval in the community, especially when so many lives were lost at Kumbh Mela. So before we announce our discoveries, perhaps you could take some time to join our team for a few days and give your expert opinion on what it all means? It could go a long way to help calm the public when the information is released."

"I've got my work here at the university—"

"I will make arrangements," Sharma says. "Let me give your dean a call now. I'm sure he wouldn't object to a funding boost in your department, and the recognition of having one of his professors work on such an important project. I promise to make this inconvenience worthwhile for you."

Sarah, who has been silent until now, sticks her face in Harshan's laptop camera. "I'm coming, too."

Georgia stares at her assistant, shocked.

"I'm sorry, but you are?" Sharma asks.

"Sarah Wu, Georgia's assistant." Sarah flashes her most charming smile. "I go where she goes. She needs my help with… assistant things."

"I'll have to bring my service dog," Buri chimes in. "She does the same things for me as Sarah does for Georgia."

Sarah glares at him.

If Mallika Sharma is confounded by the whole situation, she doesn't show it. Instead, she shrugs. "Very well. Now if you'll excuse me, I have a dinner to attend. Harshan, wait for my PA's call. He'll let you know the travel arrangements."

5

SARAH WU IS STILL STARING daggers at the Mongolian-
American scum, imagining her hands wringing his thick
neck, when her boss drags her out of the office.

"I don't understand," Georgia fumes. "I thought you
wanted to get rid of these guys and leave them to their *Indus
Valley mumbo jumbo*? Why did you involve us in the project?
What happened to *we need to get you as far away from Buri as
possible*?" She mimics Sarah's tone.

Sarah watches Georgia, noting the frustration on her
young, pretty face. The girl is a genius in her field, but she can
be so dumb with the day-to-day dealings in the real world.

"Sharma has a point," Sarah states. "Look, she's probably
on the phone now talking to the dean. And that means you
have no choice but to get involved." She pauses as she
remembers her boss's lack of interest in celebrity gossip. "You
do know who Mallika Sharma is, right?"

"No." Georgia crosses her arm over her chest, sulking.

"Oh, my God. This is why you need me around." With an
eye roll and a dramatic sigh, Sarah asks, "Ever heard of
Nikhil Sharma?"

Georgia thinks for a second. "The media mogul?"

"Bingo. Mallika is his daughter. Nikhil is the face of the business, but everyone knows that she's the one running the show. The Sharmas are one of the richest and the most powerful families in the world. They own half of Bollywood and a big chunk of the global media industry. Forget Mark Lambert, this is a bigger deal. Mallika's been on the cover of *Forbes*, *Time*, and a zillion other magazines as the most influential woman of the decade. She's a climate activist, a patron of the arts and culture, and she pours millions into archaeological projects all over India."

"So what? I don't care if she has money—"

"What do you reckon the dean is gonna do once he gets that call from her? He won't let you refuse the offer. Hell, he's probably sending Paul Flannigan down here to talk to you right now. And since you can't say no, that means I have to come with you, to protect you from the big hairy marmot." Sarah flicks her thumb at the office door.

Then she adds, "And you know what? This is your perfect opportunity to become indispensable to the department. It's gonna make everyone forget the China dig we lost last year. This project? It'll turbo boost your career."

The faculty's head, Paul Flannigan, suddenly jogs towards them down the hall, waving at them with enthusiasm as if sensing they are discussing him.

"See?" Sarah whispers. "Never seen him greet us with *that* expression before."

"Georgia. Sarah. How are you both?" Paul skids to a stop before them, a little out of breath. "I just got off the phone with the dean. He said—"

"Yes, yes, we know what he said," Sarah interrupts.

"Well, this is *great* news! Your involvement with the project in Dwarka! How wonderful!"

Georgia starts, "We haven't really decided—"

"This will bring our faculty to an even higher status. You are on a roll, Georgia! First Mark Lambert, then Chinggis

Khan's Spirit Banner, and now this? And all that funding!" Paul wipes at his brow, flustered. "When do you leave?"

"Well, I've still got my work here, and my PhD students—"

Paul gives a dismissive wave. "Oh, I'm sure we can figure all that out. Have one of the other professors step in. You have our full support with this. Anything to get you on that plane and on the ground in India."

"Uh—okay…" Georgia now looks bemused.

"Whatever it takes to secure Sharma as a long-term supporter. Wow her with what you do, Georgia," he continues, "and the dean and I will discuss your promotion, of course."

"And a raise, too?" Sarah suggests.

"Of course."

"And for me, as well," she adds.

"Uh… I'm sure we can figure something out."

"Good." Satisfaction surges through her, but she keeps a straight face.

"All settled then." Paul beams. "I'll be off to the dean's now. Anything you need, just call my assistant."

"But…" Georgia starts, but Paul is already gone, trotting down the hall from where he came.

The door to their office opens again, and this time Harshan comes out. He asks for the direction of the toilets, and Georgia offers to help him navigate the labyrinth of department corridors.

Sarah seizes the opportunity, striding into the room and shutting the door.

The DIA spook is still at Georgia's desk, pensive as he stares at the screen of Harshan's computer. He doesn't look up or acknowledge her presence.

"You're up to something, jarhead," she accuses, pointing at him. "And I'll find out what it is."

Georgia may have a soft spot for him, but Sarah knows

better. She just hopes that she'll be able to prevent her worst fear from coming true. The DIA would do anything to exploit Georgia's healing abilities if they find out, and Sarah would die first before letting that happen.

The big man ignores her, his fat fingers striking the keyboard.

"Hey." She walks up to him and pushes the laptop shut. "I'm talking to you."

His giant dog sits up, alert and watching.

The brawny dirtbag raises his gaze to meet hers, and the intensity of his scowl surprises her. But she doesn't waver. "Say something."

"Not a jarhead. That's for marines. I was in the army. And that was a long time ago."

"Whatever." She rolls her eyes. "Explain why you are here."

"I already did. I came to tell Georgia that Anya is still out there, alive. Figured she'd want to hear it from me."

"And you flew all the way here from Mongolia just to share that with her? You couldn't pick up the phone?"

"I told you, I never left Australia. I travelled around for eight months, seeing the country."

"Bullshit."

Buri shrugs and opens the laptop again to resume his work. "Believe what you want. I don't need to convince you of anything."

Seething, Sarah leans in. "You listen to me, GI Joe. Georgia is one of the most important people in my life. There's nothing, *nothing*, I won't do for her. And you? I don't get what the fuck it is you are after. But you and the army and the DIA arseholes have been hanging around for too long—"

"The DIA?" He suddenly looks up. "They've been here?"

She frowns. "What? I'm talking about *you*, you nitwit."

The relief in his features is obvious but brief. He shutters his expression and returns his eyes to the screen.

"Anyway…" Sarah resumes, so confused by his reaction she forgets momentarily what she was saying. "I don't get what you want from Georgia, but you're up to no good, and I am watching you."

"We leave at nineteen hundred hours," he says calmly, his gaze still on his task. "A van will pick us up from here for the airport. That leaves you just under five hours to get organised. I trust you'll relay this information to Georgia."

Sarah glowers at him, frustrated with his apparent nonchalance. "One wrong move, arsehole, and I'll be all over you."

But the man has already decided that the conversation is over. He continues typing as if she's not even in the room.

Huffing with indignation, she stomps to the door and slams it behind her.

6

Country New South Wales, Australia

TIM SLAMS his foot on the accelerator, gunning the engine as they race down the highway. His wife chews on her nails beside him, staring in horror at the rearview mirror.

"It's getting closer," Donna whispers.

The sky is an unrelenting furnace, radiating searing heat and blistering the black asphalt surface before them. But behind them looms a much greater threat: a towering wall of dust stretches across the horizon for as far as the eye can see, hurtling towards them at a breathtaking speed. It's hundreds of meters high, an immense, unstoppable beast barrelling over the land and swallowing up herds, buildings, and everything in sight.

"Mummy!" their five-year-old daughter, Tammy, cries in the back seat. Her eyes are wide with fear.

"It's okay, sweetheart," Donna reassures her with a shaky voice. "Everything's going to be alright. Here, put your mask on." She rummages through her bag and hands Tammy the respirator.

"You need to hurry, Tim." Donna looks at him.

"Trying." He grits his teeth, keeping his foot pressed to the floor.

A sudden gust almost rips them off course as he grasps the steering wheel with sweaty palms, fighting to keep the truck steady while willing in vain for the vehicle to go faster. The pickup is already pushed past its limit, and yet it feels as if they are barely crawling away from the approaching danger.

After a year of drought which decimated his crop and livestock, this sandstorm is like pouring salt into a gaping wound. Were he a single lad living on his own, he might have doubled down on the farm and tried to ride it out. But Tammy has asthma, and they're worried about what the dust will do to her poor little lungs. Worse, they're terrified that they won't be able to get her to the hospital in Sydney if she has a severe attack.

"C'mon c'mon c'mon," he chants, his eyes flickering between the road before him and the rearview mirror.

The distant rumble of the storm turns into a thundering roar, making his heart pound. He feels impotent as the enormous cloud of dust swells and spreads, engulfing them in a murky scarlet fog and blotting out the sun.

The bellowing wind slams into the truck, granules of sand pelting against the window and buffeting every inch of metal.

Tammy screams.

Tim's head smashes against the window as the vehicle sways violently in the wild gusts.

7

_____

Somewhere over the Indian Ocean

"OH MAN, I could sure as hell get used to this," Sarah says, leaning back on the plush sofa as she stretches out her legs, sipping on champagne from a crystal glass.

"This is too much." Georgia shakes her head as she takes in the interiors of the private jet, secretly delighting in the sensation of her feet sinking into the soft carpet.

The cabin is palatial compared to what she is accustomed to, decorated with a neutral underlying palette with accents of brown and copper trims. Four individual reclining seats are at the back, while a luxurious sofa large enough for eight dominates the centre of the space, furnished with ample cushions to ensure comfort and enjoyment. An enormous flat-screen TV sits opposite the lounge, and next to it is an old-fashioned record player. There are decadent floral arrangements scattered about, filling the air with a faint, pleasant scent. Everywhere she looks, she sees fine leather upholstery, elegant wood veneers, and sophisticated finishes.

"Does Ms. Sharma always send you around in a jet like this?" she asks Harshan.

"Of course not." Harshan grins as he sits down on the ottoman next to the couch. "She wants us to be in India as soon as possible. Using the jet cuts out time wasted in transit, immigration, and customs. And also the added complications of bringing a dog on a commercial airline."

"Well, no complaints from me." Sarah sprawls out on the sofa to get more comfortable, her mouth full as she munches on the pastry the flight attendant has brought for them. Indi trots over, sitting before Sarah with eager anticipation. Her master is in the cockpit, his enthusiasm for the private aircraft undisguised as he chats to the pilot.

"What?" Sarah frowns at the dog, pulling the plate of food closer to her. "It's not for you. Shoo."

But Indi just sits there patiently. She rests her chin on Sarah's knee.

"Uh-uh, that trick's not gonna work on me. Go on. Piss off," Sarah grumbles at Indi.

Georgia watches the exchange, amused as her assistant tries to rid herself of the large German shepherd who refuses to budge. Knowing better than to get involved, she gets up and walks to the individual seats at the back, planning to devote her time to researching the Indus Valley Civilisation.

She's excited about visiting the subcontinent again, having always had a keen interest in South Asian history. India is a vast and ancient land, a place rich with the depth of its past and the diversity of its people. As the world's largest democracy, it stands as a testament to the sheer magnificence of human civilisation, where a myriad of languages, ethnicities, cultures, and spirituality weave into a tapestry of unparalleled complexity. Whenever Georgia plans for a journey to India, she knows it will be a unique and enthralling experience. And with every trip, she is struck by a conflicting mixture of emotions as she witnesses the paradoxical coexistence of unity and cultural variety, tradition and modernity, unimaginable wealth and destitute poverty. India is a perpetual enigma to her, an ever-evolving kaleidoscope that beckons her to unravel its mysteries and embrace its wondrous contradictions.

"Do not feed my dog," Buri's deep voice booms from across the room.

Startled, Georgia looks up to see Sarah giving Buri a smug sneer as she hands another piece of pastry to the German shepherd.

"Indi," Buri snaps, and his canine companion immediately drops the food on the floor, jumps up, and follows her master with her ears drooping low. Buri's sour mood chills the atmosphere as he marches over to sit across the aisle from Georgia. Indi is meek as she licks the back of his hand several times, then lies down by his feet.

Georgia gives him an apologetic smile. "Hey."

He stares at her, and the intensity of his gaze makes her look away.

"Hey," he responds at last.

Searching her mind for something to distract him from the object of his annoyance, she says, "I never knew you were so close to getting a PhD in Computational Linguistics."

As Sarah has pointed out, Georgia knows so little about him. And if she were to be honest, her inherent trust in him troubles her.

"Who told you that?" he asks.

"Harshan."

He purses his lips, then reveals, "I was just about to hand in my thesis when 9/11 happened. I enlisted the next day. I always meant to go back to my studies, but..." He shrugs. "Life took over."

She nods, then changes the subject. "You and Harshan seem close."

His features soften with a ghost of a smile. "We were college roommates at Boston University. He's a good man. He taught me Hindi."

"You speak Hindi?"

"Some. Bits of Gujarati and Malayalam, too"

Across the room, Harshan's phone rings. He picks it up. "Yes, Dr. Khan…" His thick eyebrows shoot up as he listens. "Yes. Okay, sir."

He hangs up and reaches for the TV remote, turning it on and flickering through the channels. He stops when he finds CNN, where a stunning drone footage of an enormous sandstorm is being displayed.

"Towns across country New South Wales and even parts of Sydney are being swamped by the monstrous wave of dust," the news anchor says. "The combination of strong winds, dry soil from months of drought, and unstable atmosphere with low humidity has created this major sandstorm, where winds up to a hundred and twenty kilometres an hour blast through the region…"

"Oh my God," Sarah whispers. "I have to call my family." She reaches for her bag, frantic.

"This makes it six signs," Harshan points out, turning to Georgia and Buri. He pauses, then his face blanches as he says, "No, the drought makes it seven."

8

SARAH SPENDS the rest of the night on the phone with her husband and children. Thankfully, all of them are safe at their respective homes as they wait out the storm. She is unusually silent as they prepare for landing, something Georgia knows is never a good sign.

"Oh, fuck," Buri mutters as the plane skids to a stop on the runway in Jamnagar, the closest airport to Dwarka. He gestures out the window, demanding an explanation. "Harshan?"

Puzzled, Georgia looks out the window and is surprised by the sight of a crowd of reporters and photographers on the tarmac.

Harshan shrugs in bewilderment as the flight attendant opens the cabin door. A surge of dry, hot air rushes into the space, and all of them look outside, unsure of what to do. Disgruntled, Buri instructs the cabin crew to send their luggage to their accommodation.

"Leave everything here except your valuables," he tells everyone. He hands Indi's leash to Harshan. "You go first with Indi. I'll round up the back. Do not engage with the press. Whatever happens, just keep moving until you reach the van by the gate. Walk fast, but do not run."

The crowd rushes forward as they make their descent down the stairs, pushing and shoving to get closer to Georgia and Harshan. Microphones are thrust in their faces, and blinding flashes obscure their vision. Indi growls at anyone who gets too close, warning them off with sharp, vicious barks.

"Professor Lee, what's your take on the apocalypse predicted by the carvings in Dwarka—"

"Have your family and friends been affected by the sand-storms in Australia?"

"This is now the seventh sign. Doesn't that mean—?"

"Dr. Singh, what should families do to prepare for the end of the world?"

Georgia's heart pounds as she pushes her way through the throng. She keeps her eyes fixed on Harshan's back as she follows him, her mind in turmoil as she realises how much the press already knows, considering the Dwarka text was only deciphered twenty-four hours ago.

Someone has leaked their findings.

Irritated, she stops and turns to the reporter closest to her. "Look, all we've found is some incomplete writing from an ancient civilisation. What it says has nothing to do with what's happening now. Droughts happen in Australia all the time. Sandstorms, too. That doesn't mean everyone should freak out and think that the world is ending—"

A strong hand clamps down on her elbow. "Stop talking," Buri hisses in her ear, pulling her along. "You're feeding the vultures."

As they approach the black van, a woman suddenly appears from the rear, calling out. "Ben, Harshan! It's Dhara!"

Buri shoves Georgia into the vehicle before spinning around.

Already settled in the front passenger seat, Harshan

exclaims with delight and lowers the window, "Dhara! Get in, get in!"

The woman hops into the van with Buri, who slams the door shut and barks at their driver, "Go!"

As they pull away from the frenetic scene at the airport, Harshan turns around with a big smile. "Dhara. How are you feeling? I was so worried when I heard what happened to you at Kumbh Mela." His smile fades, concern creasing his brows.

"Getting better. Lucky to be alive, that's for sure," Dhara says. Her accent is American, with the slightest hint of something else. Tall and slender, she's wearing a black blouse and long khaki pants. Her left arm is in a cast.

Harshan waggles his head. "What brought you back to India, anyway? Thought you were happy in America?"

"I didn't tell you I changed my job?" Dhara says with a tinge of pride in her voice. "You're looking at the new chief foreign correspondent for the *Washington Sentinel*."

"Impressive." Harshan beams. He then motions towards Georgia and Sarah, who are seated behind Dhara and Buri. "This is my cousin, Dhara Shah. Dhara, meet Professor Georgia Lee and her assistant, Sarah Wu."

Dhara turns around to face them, giving them a luminous smile before offering her firm handshake. "I've read up on your work. It's a pleasure to meet you, Professor Lee. And you too, Sarah."

Georgia smiles in return, taking a moment to admire the young woman's features. Dhara's large, almond-shaped eyes are framed by thick, dark lashes. Her olive skin is smooth, her face radiant, marred only by faint bruising on her left cheek. Inky black hair, hanging to just above her shoulders, shimmers in the light. When she speaks, her soft and husky voice entices one to lean closer.

"Dhara and I both studied in America," Harshan goes on. "She was the only person I knew when I arrived. Well, that's until I met B—"

"Shouldn't you be resting at home, after what you went through at the Kumbh Mela?" Buri interrupts.

Dhara's laugh is warm and deep. "Hello to you too, Ben." She embraces Buri and plants a kiss on his cheek. "This is your dog?" She scratches Indi behind the ears, and the German shepherd's tail thumps with affection against the door.

Georgia blinks. She frowns at the pinch inside her chest and the prickle of jealousy crawling over her skin.

Dhara turns to Harshan. "Is it okay if I tag along? Mallika Sharma approved it. I called ahead."

Buri visibly stiffens. "You're working with Sharma?"

"No, but it was her office that released the information about your discoveries. I told them who I work for, and that I know you both personally. Sharma suggested I come with you to see what else you uncover in Dwarka," Dhara explains.

"Son of a bitch," Sarah mutters. "What happened to waiting until we get more facts on what's really happening? She let the press ambush us."

"Well, with seven signs already ticked off the list, it's opened a floodgate even Sharma can't guard for you anymore," Dhara says. "People are scared, especially after the Kumbh Mela stampede. That's probably why she suggested I come with you to do some proper investigative journalism. It'll help to counter the sensationalist stories going rampant out there."

Buri's posture is rigid, but he remains silent. Harshan looks around the van, and seeing no objections, he nods. "Okay, then."

Silence descends as they settle in for the three-hour drive ahead. Before long, Dhara and Buri start murmuring to each other, and Georgia strains to hear them but cannot make out their conversation. She tries to ignore the queasiness in her gut, looking out the window to distract herself.

The tide of traffic slows to relative calm as they travel away from the town of Jamnagar. Other than the chaotic confusion of determining who has the right of way at intersections, the drive is uneventful compared to Georgia's previous visits to India. Tall, verdant trees give way to sandy soil and small shrubs as they journey further. And as they near the coast, even those sparse patches of greenery disappear altogether, replaced by an arid expanse that spreads out for miles. The roads themselves begin to deteriorate too, their once smooth surfaces now pocked with fissures that jostle the van mercilessly with each passing mile.

Georgia contemplates their destination. Dwarka, an ancient coastal city in the state of Gujarat, carries a rich history that spans thousands of years and is entwined with Hindu epics like the *Mahabharata*. Once a bustling port, it is now a sacred Hindu pilgrimage site associated with Lord Krishna, a central figure in Hinduism.

Scriptures recount the magnificent grandeur of Krishna's 'Golden City' in Dwarka, a once glorious and advanced civilisation often equated to the Atlantis of the East. It is described as a utopian city of gold, resplendent with towering crystal palaces, ornate temples covered with jewels, vibrant marketplaces, and pleasure gardens filled with bird songs and fragrant flowers. The legends paint a picture of unmatched opulence, where riches overflowed the streets.

Just like Atlantis, the Golden City sank into the ocean after Lord Krishna's departure. As both a tangible ancient place and a mythical realm, Dwarka represents a fusion of history and mythology, inviting speculation about the magnificent past that may lie within the depths of the Arabian Sea. Many have attempted to find the lost Golden City of Dwarka, but it seems Dr. Khan's team has uncovered the legacy of its Harappan days instead.

As they finally pull up at the port, Harshan's excitement is contagious as he jumps out of the vehicle, dashing to the man waiting for them by a speedboat. The port is dusty and bustling with people, and various street vendors have set up shop nearby. The smells of fried food and the ocean greet Georgia as she exits the van, and when she joins the rest of the group, Dr. Faraaz Khan gives her a broad smile.

"Georgia. So happy you joined us." He greets her with palms pressed together.

"It's my pleasure." She returns the gesture. "Been a long time."

"It sure has. Let's get moving and I'll brief you on the way to the research vessel," he says, ushering everyone onto the boat before giving Georgia a wink. "I hope you like scuba diving."

9

SUNLIGHT GLINTS off the blue ocean, and the salt-tinged air fills Georgia's lungs as they leave the port. A flock of seagulls wheel overhead, their screeching sounds melding with the din of the motor and the wind.

Dr. Khan leads the group down to the small cabin, and they all squeeze into the wraparound seating. Buri has allowed Indi to stay above deck, where she is chasing and barking at the gulls.

"We've been working on this site for several years now, and thanks to Mallika Sharma's help, there's been a lot of progress," Dr. Khan tells them, bringing up a map on his tablet, displaying an incomplete sketch of the underwater ruins. "The layout is similar to that of Mohenjo-daro in Pakistan. It has all the characteristics typical of an Indus Valley city: uniform town planning with grid-based streets laid out in north–south and east–west orientation, multi-story buildings with private bathrooms connected to a centralised sewage system, standardised bricks, plenty of wells, and a lower and an upper town. The upper town is also known as the citadel. As you know, not only did the Indus people create the world's first toilet and underground drainage network, but the Great Bath in their citadel shows just how advanced they were as hydraulic engineers. We're still not certain what it was used for, but it's obvious that life in the Indus Valley centred around water. The Great Bath in Mohenjo-daro is twelve by seven metres, and almost two and a half metres deep—a swimming pool made watertight through gypsum, precision-cut bricks, and sealed with bitumen. Our Dwarka bath is twice that size, and we only finished excavating it last week."

Georgia notes the impressive scale of the site, unable to believe what she is seeing. Dr. Khan is right—this discovery is indeed one of the most monumental finds in South Asian archaeology in the past century.

"We found the inscriptions on the outer wall here," Dr. Khan continues, pointing to a large building next to the Great Bath labelled *Granary*, which contains a series of grid-like rooms. He brings up photographs of the Indus Valley script that have been etched onto the brick surface. Neat and tidy, the rows of text are laid out in a systematic fashion, just like the rest of the city. "It's now clear that we haven't uncovered all the writing yet, so today we'll be digging deeper into the sea floor to see what the rest of the message says."

"It's interesting you found the text at the Granary," Georgia points out.

"That's what I thought too," Dr. Khan agrees. "Scholars have called it the Granary by tradition, for lack of a better idea of what else it could be. It must have been an important place, being in the citadel and next to the Great Bath. But there's never been a single kernel found in there. Our discovery of what seems to be a religious message at the Granary might upend our previous assumption that the Harappans did not have a state religion."

"But… what if it isn't a temple, or a place to keep grain? What if it is somewhere to store knowledge?" Georgia says.

"Like an archive?"

"Or a library," she suggests.

"Mm." Dr. Khan cocks his head as he thinks on this. "It's a possibility. And given that this message was carved into the wall instead of written on a palm leaf manuscript, it likely held considerable significance to them. Important enough for the Harappans to make sure it stood the test of time."

The speedboat slows with the fading sound of the motor. The group emerges from the cabin, and Georgia gasps in awe as they pull up to the massive research vessel anchored off the coast of Dwarka. It is an impressive sight with its gleaming white hull, huge satellite domes, radars, and radio equipment. There are three visible levels and two inflatable tenders hanging over the starboard side. The sprawling research deck is a flurry of activity, with dozens of men and women operating winches, hoists, and air compressors. The smell of diesel is faint in the atmosphere, paired with the steady hum of machinery.

As they board, Dr. Khan rounds up his team and introduces everyone, and Georgia is more than a little envious as she meets the large crew of archaeologists, geophysicists, engineers, surveyors, dive masters, and many other experts. She can understand why Dr. Khan is so grateful for Sharma's support.

After some discussion, the team decides that Georgia and Buri will head down to the site with Dr. Khan and eight of his team. Dhara is unhappy about staying on the boat, but her recent injuries from the Kumbh Mela incident mean that she has no choice.

"It's an easy dive—only nine metres maximum depth," Dr. Khan says, giving them a briefing as he refers to the map of the submerged city. "We'll head straight to the Granary to find the missing text. Once we uncover it, let's take plenty of photographs, videos, and sketches, so that Buri and Harshan can decipher the rest of the message. While we are making the records"—he gestures to Buri and Georgia—"you two buddy up, check out the Great Bath, and see what we excavated last week. It's only a short swim from the Granary."

The dive master, Ramesh, walks up to Buri and Georgia with two wetsuits in his hands. He gives the smaller one to her, then holds up the other against Buri's huge frame. It's obvious that it won't fit.

Ramesh scratches his head. "Uh… this is the biggest one we have."

"I'll manage without it," Buri says.

Ramesh reviews their individual diving experiences, goes through the equipment they need, and provides them with extra information on the dive site. He then leaves them to get suited up. As the more experienced diver, Buri helps Georgia assemble her gear. She slips into her wetsuit, secures the weight belt around her waist, places her mask and snorkel on her head, then dons the buoyancy control device with the pressurised tank attached. Once Buri has kitted up, they go through all the safety checks together, and also the various hand signals they will use underwater.

One by one, Dr. Khan and his crew drop into the ocean from the platform. Georgia follows Buri to the edge with the heavy equipment on her back, her heart racing as it's been a while since her last dive. Closing her eyes and taking a deep inhale from her regulator, she takes a leap into the blue sea, relishing the cool embrace of the water as she plunges in.

Visibility is good as they descend to the bottom. Bubbles float upwards and envelop Georgia, her pulse decelerating to the resounding, hypnotic rhythm of her own breath. Below her, sand and seaweed still conceal most of the site, and there is not much evidence of aquatic life. Rather, there is accumulated trash mixed in with the kelp, an unfortunate and common sight these days.

The team locates the wall of the Granary and starts clearing the ocean floor to gain access. They bring down a dredge hose, which sucks up the seabed sediments like a giant vacuum cleaner. One of the divers records the entire process with videos and photographs, using powerful dive lights to illuminate the details.

Georgia's gaze sweeps over the structure before her. About a metre in height, the walls make up the multiple storage chambers of the Granary. Each is of uniform size and shape, connected by a long corridor down the middle. It is similar to the one at the Mohenjo-daro site, but to see it here in this setting is almost otherworldly, and the sense of weight-lessness in the underwater realm amplifies the magic of her experience. Sunlight streams down from above, filtering through the sea and reflecting off the brick surfaces to create a dreamlike aura. Outlines of more man-made construction stretch further from here and blend into the ocean floor beyond her line of sight.

Dr. Khan and his team have their work cut out, that's for sure.

Before long, she sees the familiar carvings on the wall: lines upon lines of Indus Valley script etched with precision. The team's pace quickens, excavating the marine sediment with care to reveal hidden ancient text.

As they labour away, Georgia turns her attention to exploring the surrounding area, delighting in the way her body glides through the ocean with effortless grace. This is the first time she has dived since she became immortal, and the difference is far more profound than she could have anticipated. In a moment of whimsy, she fancies herself a dolphin—powerful, agile, unbound. The image brings an unfamiliar lightness to her heart and incites a muffled giggle, her amusement rippling around her in a flurry of efferves-cent orbs.

She executes a somersault in the water with nimble fluid-ity, her long hair trailing behind her like a comet's tail, a manifestation of her buoyant spirit. The potent sense of freedom is intoxicating.

But her joyful exploration halts when she notices Buri studying her movements.

She freezes.

His face, obscured by his mask and the regulator, is impossible to read. What she does see is his eyes narrow at her. Then he looks away, swimming back to the team.

Over at the Granary wall, Dr. Khan makes a hand gesture, indicating that they have uncovered all of the message. They begin documenting the text with sketches and photographs, and Dr. Khan signals for Georgia and Buri to go to the Great Bath.

The two of them head east, encountering even more algal growth on the way. But the vegetation quickly thins out and the ground drops away. An enormous pit reveals itself before them. Multi-levelled and constructed out of bricks, it is about fifteen metres long and ten metres wide, with a set of stairs that lead down to the bottom on each of the four sides.

Enchanted by the magnificent sight, Georgia swims to the edge and follows the steps to the floor of the pool. She can imagine what it was like here over five thousand years ago, being the centre of activity for the city with every citizen visiting as part of their daily routine. She notes the north–south alignment of the structure, wondering at the significance of the design. If her memory is correct, the Great Bath in Mohenjo-daro has the same orientation.

Georgia makes her way around the perimeter, noting each detail of its brick construction. The wall looms above her at over two metres. Parts of it are crumbling, especially on the northern end, but all things considered it is in remarkably good condition.

She feels a tap on her leg. Buri is making the hand signal to indicate that he's running low on air, and that they should head back to the rest of the group. She nods reluctantly, sad to leave the site so soon.

Turning, she takes a last look at the bath.

That's when a glint catches her eye.

Georgia tilts left then right, trying to make out what it is. The thing glistens again, next to the stairs on the north side of the Great Bath, where the wall is in the worst condition. She turns back to see that Buri is several metres ahead, his fins kicking up sand as he swims away from her.

Deciding that it won't take long to investigate the source of the reflection, she makes a quick swim for it. She drops her depth to the floor and brings out her dive torch, removing a couple of fallen bricks and brushing off the sediment to discover an etching at the bottom of the pool.

Beside the carving, a stone as large as her palm is embedded into the brickwork. Smooth and rectangular, it is of a rich, deep green hue. She tries to remove it, but it refuses to budge.

Interesting.

From her knowledge of other Indus Valley sites, there aren't any other etchings or decorations of this kind. She marvels at the technology and workmanship the Harappan people must have possessed; the stone is so finely polished it sparkles in the soft, underwater light.

A sudden movement to her right catches her eye. She pivots, expecting to see Buri.

Nothing.

A fish, maybe? She dismisses the thought, turning her focus back to the stone. She grips it once more, and this time, it wiggles a little. It's enough encouragement for her to try prying it loose, careful not to damage it.

A shadow passes overhead.

She looks up, then whips around in a full rotation, but again sees nothing.

Her heartbeat quickens.

Goosebumps prickle her skin as a shiver of unease snakes down her spine. The dive master's warning of sharks in these waters swims into her thoughts, and fear anchors itself in her stomach.

She decides to leave the stone in place for now but pulls out the camera nestled in her vest, quickly capturing some images of the stone and its accompanying etching.

Something flashes by out of the corner of her eye. She looks up just as bricks tumble towards her like an avalanche. Air rushes from her regulator as she cries out, frantic to swim away. But it's too late. The rubble rains down upon her, trapping her beneath its weight.

Bubbles explode around her in a disorienting cloud. Gasping for breath, she wrestles to free herself from the debris. Her air comes in stuttered bursts, then cuts off completely.

No no no—

There's a sharp blow to her temple, and her vision tunnels to a pinprick.

Everything goes black.

10

"GEORGIA. GEORGIA! CAN YOU HEAR ME?"

When she finally recognises the deep cadence of Buri's voice, the violent reaction of her body takes over. Someone rolls her to her side as she heaves a stream of seawater from her lungs. She convulses as tears pour from her eyes, her throat burning as she gasps for air.

The torturous ordeal feels endless, and by the time it's over, she is utterly spent. Warm fingers smooth the hair away from her face, grasping her trembling hands.

The stench of doggy breath assaults her senses as Indi nudges her and offers her long licks to the cheeks.

"Indi, stop that!" Buri pulls the dog away.

Georgia blinks to clear her vision, realising she is lying on the floor of the research vessel. A dozen worried faces peer down at her.

"Jesus Christ. Are you okay?" Sarah shoves Buri aside and kneels next to Georgia.

Georgia tries to recall how she ended up here. She winces at the stabbing pain in her temple.

"I guess... ?" She gingerly touches the sore spot on her head, finding no open wounds there.

"What the fuck happened?" her assistant demands, glaring at Buri.

The man ignores Sarah as he crouches on the other side of Georgia, checking her pupils and her pulse.

"What happened, Buri?" Dr. Khan asks this time.

"I was halfway back to your group when I noticed Georgia wasn't behind me," Buri says in a low voice. The T-shirt he's wearing is still dripping with water and clings to his expansive chest. "I found her at the bottom of the Great Bath. Part of the wall had collapsed on her."

"You were supposed to be her dive buddy. How the hell did you manage to lose her?!" Sarah accuses.

"I saw something on the floor of the pool." Georgia's voice is raspy as she explains. Remembering her camera, she looks around, relieved when she sees it's still tethered to her wrist. Her brows knit when she realises that the housing and the screen are both cracked. She holds it up to Harshan, who's standing over Sarah.

"I took some photos," she says.

Harshan takes the device from her. "I'll see if one of our engineers can retrieve them."

"Give us some room," Buri says. "Can you walk, Georgia?"

"I think so," she replies as she studies his face, noticing the tension in his rigid jaw, the stoniness of his gaze, and the rigidity of his movements.

Something's off. Even for a taciturn man like him, he's too quiet, too controlled in his actions. And he hasn't made eye contact with her since she woke.

But his touch is gentle as he helps her to sit. "I need to get her warmed up and examine her wounds," he says to Dr. Khan. "Is there a room we can use?"

"Of course…" Dr. Khan gestures towards the cabins.

"Nah-uh." Sarah pushes Buri away. "You've done enough. *I'll* help her."

63

The pair glare at one another for a long moment, each waiting for the other to back down. Buri's stare is glacial, its iciness making Georgia recoil even though it's not directed at her.

"I'm fine, Buri. Thank you," Georgia says, shrugging off his arm and reaching for her assistant, who helps her to stand. "I'm not hurt. But I need to change and get warm. Sarah can help me."

She looks down, horrified when she sees how ripped up her wetsuit is. On the floor is what remains of her dive equipment, damaged beyond repair.

"You were bleeding in the water," Buri argues. "I have to clean and dress those wounds. We need to make sure you don't have a concussion, either."

"She said she's fine," Sarah snaps.

Dr. Khan guides them to one of the offices. Sarah ushers Georgia in, then turns to stop anyone else from entering.

"Women only," she declares, taking the first aid kit from Dr. Khan.

"Sarah? I can help." Dhara steps forward.

"I got this," Sarah says. When Buri doesn't move from the doorway, she yells at the top of her lungs, "Back off, trench monkey!"

She slams the door in his face.

"Sarah…" Georgia sighs.

"What?" Her assistant fumes as she rustles up bandages and supplies from the box Dr. Khan gave her. As if suddenly remembering something, she stops and turns to her boss. Concern is etched deep into her features. "Are you alright?"

"I am now."

"You got… any wounds?"

Sarah looks her over, and together they note all the torn spots on her wetsuit. There's a massive gash in the suit over her right arm. Left thigh, too. Thankfully, whatever injuries she sustained have already healed, and the blood she spilt was washed away when she was in the water.

"All the same, let's get you out of that and bandage you up, just in case anyone gets suspicious," Sarah suggests.

Georgia unzips and shrugs the wetsuit off her. She looks up to find Sarah staring at her with her mouth agape.

"What?"

Sarah closes her mouth. She opens it again. "I… I guess I didn't quite believe it… if you get what I mean. This is the first time…"

Georgia peers down at her body. Her swimsuit is torn down the side, but otherwise, every inch of her skin is unblemished.

"This is the first time you've seen me heal," Georgia finishes Sarah's sentence for her.

"Well, I didn't actually watch it happen, but I get the idea."

"Wait till you see it happen in real time." She gives her assistant a wry smile.

Sarah blanches. She swallows and looks away, muttering, "No thanks."

Georgia arches her brows. It's not like Sarah to be squeamish. She watches as her assistant stains a piece of gauze with iodine, then wraps it around her bicep with bandages. They do the same thing with the spots on Georgia's right side and left thigh where there would have been wounds.

"What happened down there?" Sarah asks as Georgia changes out of her swimsuit and into some dry clothes.

"I'm not sure," Georgia admits. "We were returning to the team when something on the floor of the Great Bath caught my eye, and I went back for a closer look without telling Buri. I guess I thought it wouldn't take long. I was taking photos of the design etched into the bottom of the pool when—"

"Do you reckon it was Buri?"

Georgia frowns at the idea. "You think he *pushed* the bricks on me? Why would he do that?"

"He might suspect something about your immortality. Maybe he wanted to see what would happen if you got hurt." Sarah snaps her fingers. "*That's* why he hung around Australia for eight months. I mean, who *does* that?"

The very notion makes Georgia ill, and she pushes it out of her mind. Sarah's right, she hasn't known the man for long. But she trusts Buri. She thinks of all that they've been through in Mongolia together: surviving hunger and fierce storms in the wilderness, fighting off the Russians, and even enduring attacks from the Mongolians. These experiences have cemented a deep bond between them, a silent and inherent understanding of each other. It seems impossible that he would ever want to harm her.

She shakes her head. "It was an accident. Buri would never do that."

"Why? Because he's your *friend?*"

"Yes."

"You're being naïve, Georgia," Sarah says, exasperated. "My God, we have to be so careful now. Even the way you move—the speed, the strength, the grace—it gives you away. *No one* moves like that, and when you forget, it makes you stand out. You hardly eat, and never sleep. And the worst thing is how you survive accidents like this without the slightest scratch or even a bruise."

"I know."

"And with that DIA arsehole hanging around, I'm worried that it's only a matter of time—"

"You don't have to tell me again. I'm the one who has to bear this cross."

Sarah's expression is a mixture of frustration and outrage. "But you're not in this fight alone, remember? How many times do I have to tell you that?"

When Georgia doesn't reply, Sarah exhales a heavy sigh.

Her tone is softer when she says, "Look, I've been wanting to call this whole thing off. Tell everyone that we're out so we can go back to our jobs at the uni and lay low. But the dust storm in Sydney changes things. It's too close to home. I can't help feeling that we need to figure out what's truly going on."

"Me too."

"When I saw them bring you out of the water, I—I thought…" Sarah pauses, staring at Georgia. "We still don't have a good understanding of your healing abilities—what you can survive, and what you can't. If Charlie and Wang Jian died in the cave in Taiwan, that means…"

She doesn't finish her thoughts, but Georgia senses it in her eyes. And what she detects there astonishes her, unnerves her more than anything she has been through today.

Sarah—who's usually a tempest of curses and bravado, who thrives in the throes of a good fight—is terrified.

Georgia pulls her close. "I know."

11

By the time Georgia and Sarah leave the room, the sun is getting low in the sky and the crew is packing up to head off for the day.

Buri is loading their belongings onto the speedboat. He pauses when he sees Georgia, his fierce gaze sweeping over her. Then he goes back to what he's doing without a word.

Dr. Khan and Dhara walk up to Georgia. The sense of relief is obvious in the Indian woman's features.

"You look much better," Dhara says. "Everything okay?"

"Yes, thank you."

Dr. Khan scrutinises her. "Maybe we should get you to the hospital, to make sure—"

"That's really not necessary," Georgia says.

"There should be an investigation into what happened," Sarah says to Dr. Khan.

Georgia puts her hand on Sarah's arm. "It was an accident."

"Bricks don't just fall. They were *pushed* on you," Sarah insists.

Dr. Khan furrows his brows. "Is this true, Georgia?"

"No, it was an accident. It must have been."

But the older man misses nothing as he gazes into her eyes. His frown deepens as he says, "I'm very sorry for what happened today. We'll investigate it, and also ask for tighter security around here. Our latest findings have the community on edge, and we've been getting all sorts of calls, day and night, from reporters to ordinary busybodies, to the downright mad."

"Speaking of which," Sarah says, staring at Dhara, "should we even have a reporter with us? How do we know that she's not leaking information to the press?"

Dhara is calm as she answers, "I can't speak for other journalists out there, but I only care about the truth. I suspect that's the same for you. We all have the same goal, so wouldn't you rather have someone who'll tell the world what's really happening, instead of the fear-mongering trash they are writing right now?"

"We are on the brink of something huge," Dr. Khan says. "End of the world or not, our discoveries could reveal so much more than what we've known about our heritage for the past six thousand years. And that can be threatening to those who already have their own set of ideas about who the Indian people are and where they came from. Let us work together, and not against each other on this. We have enough obstacles to overcome."

"I agree." Georgia turns to Dr. Khan. "I found something very interesting at the bottom of the bath. A decoration. One that I've not seen at any other Harappan site."

"Our engineers are trying to retrieve the photos you took as we speak." Dr. Khan places a hand on Georgia's shoulder. "You've been through a lot today. Get some rest. Harshan and Buri will work on those inscriptions tonight, and I'll come by your hotel in the morning to go through everything."

Sarah points to Buri at the back of the ship, who's helping Indi into the tender. "And what about him—" she begins, but Georgia pulls her away before she can say anything else.

They board the speedboat with the help of Buri, who refuses to look at Georgia for the entire trip to the port. In the van, Dhara sits next to him as they go through the photos on his underwater camera. His dark gaze flickers to Georgia as she gets in, and for a moment, she detects a hint of anger in his eyes. She blinks with confusion and looks away. When she glances back again, he's resumed his conversation with Dhara about the submerged archaeological site.

Georgia swallows against the lump in her throat. She moves to the rear of the van, where her assistant sits. Sarah seems exhausted. She's looking out the window while absent-mindedly petting Indi, whose chin rests on the woman's leg.

"That was fast," Georgia comments.

"What?" Sarah asks, still stroking Indi's luxuriant fur.

Georgia nods to the dog. "She's grown on you."

Sarah frowns down at the German shepherd.

Dropping into the seat beside them, Georgia closes her eyes as fatigue overcomes her. The journey to their hotel is a blur as she drifts in and out of sleep. When they arrive, she barely registers the check-in process before trudging to her lodgings.

"Let me inspect your room first." Buri's deep voice stops her before she walks in. "Make sure nothing's been tampered with."

She knits her eyebrows, looking up at him. "Why would—"

"Can't be too careful," is all he says before pushing past her. "Indi."

His dog trots inside, sniffing every inch of the space. Across the hall, Sarah stands in the doorway to her room, scowling as she mutters under her breath. Completing his inspection, Buri returns to take Georgia's bag, placing it on the luggage rack for her.

"How are you feeling?" He's still not meeting her gaze.

"Better now, thank you."

He straightens, brings out his phone and turns on the torch function. Tilting her head with a gentle hand, he shines the light in each of her eyes. He checks her pulse again.

"Headache?"

"No."

"Nausea? Dizziness?"

"No."

"Any sensitivity to light or sound? Trouble focusing?"

"I'm okay. I promise. Need a rest, that's all."

He ignores this last comment. "How are your wounds?"

"Fine." She pulls up the long, loose sleeve of her tunic, revealing the bandage Sarah wrapped around her arm. "Sore, but it's just a graze. It'll heal soon enough."

He finishes his examination and says as he turns away, "I'm next door. Call me if you get any of those symptoms I asked about. Or if you need anything."

"Thank you."

As he moves towards the door, Georgia says, "Hey... Are you okay? I mean... are *we* okay?"

He stops, his back to her as he remains there, his posture stiff, his fists clenched.

"What the hell happened?" His voice is low. "You were right behind me. Then when I looked around to check on you, you were gone."

"I saw something, and I thought..."

He turns and looks at her for the first time since their dive. The fury is now unmistakable in his eyes, but his tone is frighteningly calm. "That's not how this works, Georgia. You don't go off on your own like that. You're meant to communicate and watch out for your dive buddy."

"I know, I'm sorry—"

"We're supposed to be a team. How do I know if you've got *my* back?"

She flushes with shame as she realises he's right, and that he's not just talking about the dive.

He starts to say something else, then pauses.

"Moving on, Army Man," Sarah calls from across the hall.

Buri's jaw clenches. Without another word, he turns and walks out with Indi, closing the door behind him.

Georgia stares at the door for a long moment, the shock of their conversation rippling through her. Feeling defeated, she collapses on the bed, not even bothering to remove her shoes. Her mind gives in to sleep before she has a chance to pull the covers over her.

"Hey." Dhara hurries up to Buri as he opens his hotel room door. Indi greets her by licking her fingers, then pants with joy when Dhara strokes her on the head.

"How's Georgia?" she asks.

Buri grunts. "She's tired."

She studies him, taking in every detail of his rough features. It's been over a decade since she's seen him, and the years have not been kind. Her gaze traces the scar above his right eyebrow and the crooked bridge of his nose. The bags under his eyes and the speckles of white in his dark hair age him, and the sun-damaged skin is doing him no favours, either.

Harshan has shared snippets of Buri's capture in Syria, and the post-traumatic stress disorder it has left him with. She assumes this is why he's got Indi with him, most likely as a therapy dog.

And this is exactly the reason they broke up all those years ago, when he first joined the army. Dhara didn't believe in war. Still doesn't. Nothing can ever justify the violence and the cruelty, the shattered lives and the gruesome aftermath. And the man who's standing before her is a living, breathing example of that.

She tried everything to dissuade him from going, but Buri

comes from a military family, and they'd always been against his pursuit of an academic career. 9/11 was the perfect excuse for them to bring him into the fold, and Buri's sense of duty meant that no one could stop him.

"You're worried about her," she observes.

He doesn't reply.

"She's lovely, Buri," Dhara says. "Whatever is going on between you two, make sure you give it all you've got."

"Nothing is going on between us," he snaps. Then he softens his tone as he changes the topic. "You're calling me Buri, not Ben."

She shrugs. "It suits you. I'm glad you're finally embracing your Mongolian roots."

"How're your injuries?"

She grimaces. "A bit sore, but getting there."

Silence descends between them, and Dhara wonders what happened to the man she once loved. The Buri she remembers was brilliant, caring, adventurous, and fun. His smile was frequent, and his laughter infectious. Over the years, Dhara has often questioned if she made a mistake walking away from him, and wondered what she would do if their paths ever crossed again. In fact, the end of their relationship was one of the many regrets that ran through her mind as she fought for her life at the Kumbh Mela. But standing before him now, she's sad to realise that she's actually been right all along. The army has destroyed the man she knew, and the person she's speaking with is a complete stranger.

"I came to say goodbye," she says. "I have to cover another story."

He arches his brows.

"Looks like it might be another sign," she explains. "In Cambodia. I'll let you know when I find out more. Give this to Georgia for me." She presses her card into his palm. "Let's keep in touch. Tell me what the rest of the message says? Maybe I can help."

He nods. She raises to the tips of her toes and gives him a kiss on the cheek. Bending down to Indi, she ruffles the dog's thick coat.

"Take care of him," she murmurs to Indi. Then she straightens again and walks away.

"Dhara," Buri calls.

She turns.

"Be careful."

Her heart warms, taking it as a proof of his deeper affection. She flashes him a genuine smile. "Always."

12

GEORGIA WAKES at three in the morning, marvelling at the number of hours she has slept. She realises this is the longest her body has given into slumber since she became immortal. Feeling unusually famished, she leaves her room in search of food. She finds Buri and Harshan working on their laptops in the hotel foyer instead. Indi is lying on top of Buri's left foot, snoring softly.

"You guys been working all night?"

Harshan takes off his glasses and rubs his eyes. "Yeah. We've been fiddling with the software for hours now."

"Any luck?"

He shrugs. "We'll find out in about… two minutes."

On the screen, lines upon lines of white text flow across the black background as the program churns through algorithms. None of the code makes any sense to Georgia. The three of them watch with anticipation, and when the computer finally sounds a *Star Wars* chime, they all lean in to see the result.

"Oh… Wow," Harshan whispers.

DR. KHAN ARRIVES AT eight in the morning, meeting Buri and Georgia in the hotel restaurant where they are having some masala dosa and chai for breakfast. Harshan has gone back to his room for a few hours of sleep, and Sarah is still nowhere to be seen. As Dr. Khan looks over the rest of the translated message, he shakes his head with disbelief, mutters under his breath, and, turning to the last page, gasps with surprise. When he's finally done, he sits in silence, absorbing the new information.

His phone rings. Looking at the screen, he picks up the call. "Good morning, Madam-ji."

"Dr. Khan." Sharma's face appears on the device. She greets Georgia and Buri, then says, "I just read the translations you sent. Please explain what it all means?"

"It's an order to hunt down a stone," Georgia replies.

"A stone?" Sharma raises her eyebrows with surprise.

Dr. Khan explains, "The rest of the inscriptions gave us much more context to work with. We can now say with confidence that the message is partly historical record, partly divination. It describes how the Indus Valley was destroyed by a series of disasters over a short period. Strange things rained from the sky. The rivers became contaminated and the water undrinkable. Drought, famine, earthquakes, and so on —all happened one after another. Disease spread throughout the community, killing thousands."

"That sounds familiar," Sharma says. "Everything in the prophecy came true for them."

"Yes," Dr. Khan confirms. "And the Harappans thought it all came about because of a stone that went missing. They believed that if it was not found and put in its right place in time, then more and more disasters would come about, each sign happening in quicker succession until a final catastrophic event."

Georgia adds, "That event was a flood, which submerged the entire city of Dwarka."

"So they never found the stone in time," Sharma hypothesises. "What is this stone?"

Buri says, "The name they gave it is difficult to translate, so we've dubbed it the Indus Star."

"The Harappans claimed that the Indus Star was the source of all the successes of their culture," Dr. Khan says. "And its theft, the reason for the collapse of their society. They believed that disasters will occur whenever the stone is disturbed."

"And now it's all happening again. But this time, at a global scale," Sharma says. "Why?"

Georgia's inner sceptic kicks in. "Like Dr. Khan has said, the inscriptions are, in some parts, a factual account of what ended the Harappan culture, and in other parts, superstitious beliefs over a missing stone. I still think it's a coincidence, and that what's happening around the world is not connected to the message we've uncovered."

"That's what I hoped, too," Sharma says. "But there was another sign last night."

Baffled, Georgia looks to Dr. Khan, who shows her photos and video clips on multiple websites. Overnight, a category five hurricane hit Florida, with 180 mile per hour winds and catastrophic flash flooding—one of the strongest storms to ever strike the US mainland. The president of the United States has declared a state of emergency, and government agencies are scrambling to aid survivors and locate the thousands that are missing.

Every news article Georgia scrolls through links the storm to the 'Dwarka Prophecy,' igniting an internet firestorm of heated arguments between religious leaders, climate activists, deniers, conspiracy theorists, and politicians.

"I sincerely hope that Georgia is correct," Sharma says, "but with the entire world reacting like this, we must figure out what is really going on. Even if the prophecy is wrong, we have to prove that to the public."

Georgia bites her lower lip, realising that Sharma is right. She reveals, "I found a stone on the floor of the Great Bath yesterday."

Everyone is silent as they stare at her.

"I thought you said it was some kind of a decoration?" Dr. Khan asks.

"It was," she answers. "There was a carving, and next to it, a green stone lodged into the brickwork."

"Georgia took some photos during the dive," Dr. Khan says to Sharma. "Our engineers are still trying to retrieve them from the damaged camera."

"Could this be the Indus Star that the inscription is referring to?" Sharma asks.

"Maybe," Georgia replies. "But according to the message recovered from the Granary, the Indus Star was supposed to have been stolen."

"My team will head down there again today to investigate further," Dr. Khan says.

"One more thing: can someone please explain to me what the jumbled text is at the bottom of the translations?" Sharma asks.

"We're working on that," Buri says. "For some reason, none of the algorithms we've been using fit the text. There are still nine characters we can't decipher."

"Let me see those again." Georgia leans over to look at the laptop open in front of Buri, which shows a series of glyphs at the bottom.

She draws in a sharp breath, wondering how she could have missed it before. Pointing to the seventh character, she says, "I saw this etched into the brickwork, right next to the stone I found at the Great Bath."

"Are you sure?" Dr. Khan asks.

"Positive."

"I'll have a look later today, see if we can find more clues," Dr. Khan says. "At the same time, we should search for any historical or scriptural references to the Indus Star, and where it could have gone after being taken from Dwarka." He looks to Georgia.

Sharma says on cue, "Dr. Khan has his hands full with the excavation site right now. It would be helpful if your team takes over this side of the matter, Georgia."

Georgia nods.

"And it's about time we meet in person," Sharma adds, addressing both Georgia and Buri. "I'm tied up with business in Mumbai. Perhaps you can come here? I'll see to it that you have a comfortable space to conduct your research."

Buri and Georgia murmur their assent. They make arrangements for their meeting with Sharma before hanging up.

Just then, Sarah makes an appearance, her short-cropped hair a mess and her gaze still drowsy. She looks around the table and frowns. "What did I miss?"

13

Cambodia

THE SUN SITS LOW on the horizon, bathing the village in a dusky haze. Dhara Shah nods at the young man beside her, a local fixer named Kiri she picked up in Phnom Penh, and together they walk along the dusty track winding through the rows of elevated wooden huts with thatched roofs.

She has endured a long journey of three flights and a bumpy drive to arrive at this remote community nestled deep within the heart of Cambodia. Her arduous trek has cost her valuable time, which is confirmed by the pack of fellow journalists who have already descended upon the town.

The first thing that hits her is the smell. She wrinkles her nose at the scent which makes her think of rotten seafood, an odour that grows stronger as they progress further into the village.

Looking around her, she realises what is bothering her about this place. It's too quiet. The eerie stillness in the air heightens her senses. Even with all the reporters hanging about, there isn't the usual bustle she would expect. The villagers huddle outside their homes, whispering to each other with haunted expressions.

Dhara and Kiri walk on until they come to the town square, where men, women, and children are bringing in baskets full of trash, piling them into a massive mound almost eight feet high. The stink is heavy here, with swarms of flies buzzing about.

She stops one of the women walking past. There are bruises and scratches all over her face and arms.

"What happened here?"

Kiri translates for her, then replies in English for the woman: "Rubbish. It all rained from the sky, miss."

"Can you tell me more? How did it start?"

Kiri interprets for the Cambodian woman as she speaks. "Yesterday, after lunch… It was a sunny day. Most of the village was having a nap, and I was hanging up my laundry. Then out of nowhere, a plastic bag floated down and landed on top of my head. I thought it was one of the local children playing a prank. But when I looked up, I saw… I saw things falling." The woman's eyes widen with fear, and her voice is hoarse as she continues, "They hit my face, my body. It hurt. I screamed and ran for my house. But some of the trash broke through our roof. My kids and I hid under the table. When we finally came out again, the entire village was covered in this." The woman gestures to the stinking mound before them.

Dhara walks closer to the pile of garbage, covering her nose with the end of her cotton scarf. Inspecting the contents, she finds an odd amalgamation of discarded and worn objects: toothbrushes, plastic bottles, crushed cans, torn packaging mingled with broken glass and the occasional flip-flop. Sun-bleached plastics and crumpled wrappers create a patchwork of muted shades. The colours have faded, the vibrant hues of consumerism now dulled by exposure to the elements.

She kneels down and picks up a handful, repulsed by the damp, slimy texture between her fingertips. Some fragments crumble under the gentlest touch, disintegrating into fine particles that cling to her skin.

Her eyes water as she surveys the scene, her scarf doing nothing to block out the pungent stench of decay. The remnants of human consumption, once discarded and forgotten, are now insistently present once again, and she cannot help but recall the first sign from the Dwarka Prophecy:

The detritus of man from heavens fall...

14

Jamnagar, India

GEORGIA SHAKES her head as her assistant sprints up the stairs to the private jet. Indi bounds behind Sarah, her long canine legs taking two steps at a time.

"Is she always like this?" Buri asks, staring after the pair.

"You mean her enthusiasm?" Georgia gives him a sardonic smile. "Not for work, no."

The three of them are back at the airport in Jamnagar. Harshan is tied up with his work in Dwarka, so everyone agreed that he and Buri will keep in close contact while they both attempt to decipher the last of the inscriptions. Even though Georgia wants to dive the excavation site again, she knows no one will allow it given her recent incident in the water. She is also supposed to be covered in injuries, imaginary wounds that are still bandaged but have long since healed.

Buri's phone pings with a text. He looks down at the screen and slows his pace.

"What's wrong?" She stops beside him.

"It's Dhara, in Cambodia." He shows her photos of an

enormous pile of rubbish. "It's another sign, the one about trash raining from the sky."

The skin around his lips tightens as he slips the phone back into his pocket. It's the first time Georgia has ever seen him worried.

"Let's call her when we land in Mumbai." He resumes his path towards the plane.

Once on board, Buri dumps his backpack on the soft leather sofa and heads straight for the bathroom, locking the door behind him. Georgia chooses a seat at the rear and is about to turn on her laptop to resume her research when she notices Sarah picking the padlock on Buri's bag with a paperclip.

Next to Sarah, Indi starts a guttural growl.

Georgia walks quickly to her assistant, whispering, "What are you doing?!"

"Espionage."

Within seconds, Sarah unzips the front pouch and rummages through Buri's belongings. Georgia blinks in astonishment at the speed with which she has bypassed the lock. Then the memory of how Sarah outwitted her kidnapper last year using a clever MacGyver trick comes to mind, and Georgia makes a mental note to upgrade the security of her desk drawers at work.

Indi lets out a bark and shoves her snout between the rucksack and Sarah's searching hands.

"Stay out of it." Sarah nudges the dog aside with her leg.

"Stop that!" Georgia tugs on Sarah's arm, but the older woman's already found what she's looking for.

Sarah pulls out a passport and rifles through the pages. "What do we have here, Mr. Benjamin..." She stills. "What did you say his surname was again?"

"Myagmar. Buri Myagmar. It was his mother's maiden name."

Indi backs away from them and barks again. Twice.

Sarah narrows her eyes. "But he didn't tell you his father's name. His *actual* name."

"What the fuck are you doing?" Buri's voice is a low snarl behind them.

Georgia jumps, spinning around to find the burly man glaring down at them, his body taut with barely restrained anger. To her surprise, Sarah is even more enraged.

"No," Sarah fires back with more venom than Georgia has ever witnessed. "What the fuck are *you* doing? Why the hell did you lie about your name?"

Georgia touches her arm. "Sarah—"

"Look at this." Her assistant thrusts the passport at her.

Georgia's eyes focus on the document, and blood drains from her face as she registers what it says.

MILLER
BENJAMIN MATTHEW

Too stunned to speak, she lifts her gaze to meet Buri's. For the briefest moment, his composure drops, showing an array of emotions in the darkness of his irises that make her blood run cold. Fear and anger wrap around her heart like a vice, squeezing away any hope of keeping her fragile sanity intact.

"Miller? Your name is Benjamin *Miller*?" Her voice comes out as a hoarse whisper.

His nostrils flares, and his impervious mask slips back in place as he straightens his spine, making him seem impossibly taller. "Yes."

"So... you and Agent Brandon Miller are... ?"

All of a sudden, everything makes sense. Agent Miller infiltrated Anya Mihailovich's team in Russia when she was searching for *The Secret History of the Mongols*. Buri has mentioned his brother's military background and expertise in the Russian language, but Georgia never made the connection until now.

"Brothers," he admits, then adds, "half-brothers."

"You lied to me."

His stare is fierce. "No, I didn't. I told you my *mother's* maiden name was Myagmar."

"But you didn't tell me your *real* name, which is Miller! Are you spying for him? Do you work for the DIA?"

"What? No!" Buri's face twists with frustration.

"Yeah, you do." Sarah points an accusatory finger at him and steps into his personal space. "I knew there was something off with you coming to Sydney, then sticking around for eight months like a lovesick puppy, waiting for Georgia to trust you. This proves everything. You've been feeding information to Agent Miller."

"Why the hell would the DIA want to spy on Georgia?!" Buri's voice escalates, and Georgia takes an involuntary step back. Indi whines, licking her owner's hand.

"Because…" Sarah falters. She screws up her face, and Georgia knows she's almost blurted out her secret.

"Fuck this!" Sarah yells instead, throwing up her hands. "I want you off the bloody plane!"

A disquieting silence descends as Buri takes several deep breaths, his broad chest rising and falling. Within seconds, he regains his calm and purposeful demeanour.

Crossing his arms, his voice is quiet as he says, "I have every right to be here. Sharma and her team have contracted my involvement in this project. I can't say the same for you. In fact, what the hell are you even doing here?"

Sarah frowns. "I'm here for Georgia. She needs me."

"Does she, now?" He raises a brow, casting his gaze at Georgia, then back to Sarah again. "Let me remind you that Harshan came to Sydney for *my* help. As far as I'm concerned, you two are the tag-alongs. And I'm not accusing you of spying on me, even though you went through my shit. Honestly? I've been nothing but gracious throughout the entire trip. It'd be nice if I'm offered the same courtesy. If you don't like it, you're welcome to head back to Sydney."

Striding to the back of the plane, he sits down in one of the recliner seats and looks out the window. Indi follows, lying down beside his booted feet. Sarah continues to glare at him for a long minute, then gives up and pulls Georgia to the sofa as the captain announces their imminent take-off.

"See? I *knew* it. I always thought there was something fishy about him," Sarah whispers.

Georgia bites her lower lip. "He's right, though. Why would the DIA want to spy on me?"

"We've been over this already. They must suspect something. I have half a mind to pull the plug on this whole thing now, but it'll just make you look suspicious."

Georgia shakes her head, her thoughts going off on another tangent. She murmurs, "He *knows* something. About Anya, I mean. Something he's not telling me. He'll be able to help me find her."

"Are you insane?" Sarah widens her eyes. "You've got enough on your plate right now. Don't even talk to him unless you absolutely need to."

Georgia sighs. "Look, Sarah, you don't have to protect me. I don't want you to be burdened by this, too."

"I made you a promise, didn't I? As long as I've got a breath left in my body, you'll never have to go through this by yourself. Remember what Charlie said. You gotta keep your friends close. You cannot fight this on your own."

Georgia doesn't argue. In her mind, though, she knows how alone she really is.

Because she will always outlive those around her.

And that is her worst fear of all.

15

Mumbai, India

As they land at Mumbai airport after a long, tension-filled flight, Georgia looks out the window and her heart sinks at the mob of journalists on the runway. She searches the crowd for Dhara's face but doesn't find her.

"Roaches," Sarah spits out. "How the hell do they know where we are all the time?"

Buri is quiet, his eyes fixed on the view outside, his jaw clenched. He has not spoken since they left Jamnagar.

"Keep your heads down. Walk fast. Do not answer questions until we've talked to Mallika Sharma." He shoots Georgia a look, a silent warning to not engage with the media.

The flight attendant opens the door, flooding the cabin with humid air, and the team descends the stairs. Georgia cringes as the crowd erupts.

"Professor Lee! What can you tell us about the missing gem of Dwarka?"

"Does the Indus Star have anything to do with what's happening around the globe now?"

"Is the world going to end the way the Indus Valley Civilisation did?"

Georgia grasps Sarah's hand as they push through the crowd. Rivulets of sweat run down her back as she struggles to remain calm, but the frenetic flashes of light are like shards of glass plunging into her brain.

There's a tug on her sleeve, and fingers wrap around her wrist in a steely trap.

"What's your opinion on the latest omen manifesting itself in Cambodia—"

She turns, feverish to break free. Out of nowhere, Buri appears from behind the sea of faces, his vice-like hold on her arm towing her away as he effortlessly carves a path through the throng.

Relief floods through her when they finally make it into the black van waiting by the gate, but that doesn't stop the mob from smacking their palms against the windows, demanding answers.

"Jesus Christ, they're getting aggressive," Sarah comments.

"Desperate," Georgia corrects, watching the sea of animated faces fade as they pull away from the airport. "They're scared." She wonders if this is a reflection of how the rest of the world is reacting to the 'Dwarka Prophecies'.

The rising sun paints the cityscape a golden hue as they sink into the chaos of Mumbai. There is noise everywhere: horns honking, vendors shouting, and the ceaseless clatter of commerce. Soaring skyscrapers reach towards the heavens, standing tall amidst the sprawling slums of tin-roofed shanties and makeshift dwellings. Ornate colonial structures whisper tales of a bygone era. The chaotic streets weave together a complex and vibrant urban tapestry, where contrasting worlds collide and stories of resilience and the relentless pursuit of dreams echo through the air.

There is a heavy silence in the van as it crawls through the hubbub of the congested roads. In the front, Buri sits stock still, his back rigid and tense. Georgia shares the rear seat with Sarah and Indi, each of them transfixed by something outside the window. When they pull up to the renowned Taj Mahal Palace Hotel, though, Georgia's mood lifts in spite of herself.

"This is where we're staying?" she asks the driver.

"Yes, madam."

They climb out of the vehicle and Georgia looks up, admiring the architecture of the building. She has wanted to visit this place for so long. Built in the Indo-Saracenic style and often referred to simply as 'the Taj', it has been a symbol of prestige and refinement since its opening in 1903, hosting royalty, dignitaries, and luminaries from around the world. The hotel is intertwined with the story of the city itself; it witnessed the rise and fall of an empire and the birth of a nation, and even endured the tragic events of the Mumbai 2008 attacks.

But Georgia is most interested in the exquisite art collection within the hallowed halls of the Taj. Over two thousand works by modern Indian artists grace its walls, many of which are museum-worthy. There are also some paintings by her favourite Indian artist here, the late Vasudeo S. Gaitonde, whose works have been auctioned for record prices by Sotheby's.

The foyer is abuzz with patrons as she clears the hotel security and steps inside, spotting a surprising number of sheikhs dressed in white robes and traditional headdress. Towering vases hold extravagant displays of blossoms that burst forth in a riot of colours and fragrances. Polished marble floors inlaid with semi-precious stones reflect the opulence of her surroundings, and elaborate lighting fixtures illuminate the space with a soft, warm glow. To the right, there is a man seated with poised grace on a blue velvet platform, entertaining guests with the melodious strains of his sitar. His long fingers glide effortlessly across the strings, coaxing soul-stirring classical Indian tunes from the instrument.

Several bellmen take care of their luggage as the hotel manager, Ishaan, greets them. "Welcome to the Taj," he says with a warm smile and his palms pressed together. "Madam Sharma is expecting you. She's out at the moment but will return to meet with you in the afternoon. I do apologise, but housekeeping is still getting your accommodation ready. Would you like to relax by the pool with some refreshments while you wait?"

Buri's phone pings with a message. He looks at the screen and says, "Not now. Is there a place we can teleconference with our team in private?"

"Of course. You may use one of our guest rooms." Ishaan pauses and frowns when he sees Indi.

"She's a service dog," Buri says.

"Ah. Apologies." Ishaan inclines his head. "We are a pet-free hotel, but of course we'll make an exception in this case, especially for friends of Ms. Sharma. Come with me, please."

Georgia gives Buri a questioning glance, to which he says without elaborating, "Dr. Khan has found something."

They take the elevator to the top floor of the Tower Wing, the modern expansion constructed in 1972. Ishaan guides them down the narrow corridor, then stops to open one of the doors.

"Does this suit your needs?" he asks.

Warm hues of cream and gold envelop the large space, which is furnished with an elegant fusion of historic charm and contemporary luxury. A king-size bed dominates the centre of the room, but there's also a sitting area and a huge desk next to the floor-to-ceiling windows framed by Moorish archways.

"Yes, thank you," Buri says, already moving to the table and bringing out his tablet.

"I will be back in a few hours to escort you to Ms. Sharma," Ishaan says, then bows and leaves the room.

Buri connects the call before Georgia has a chance to sit down.

"Harshan. Dr. Khan," he greets the men on the screen.

"Hey, guys," Harshan says, his excitement unmistakable. "You won't believe what Dr. Khan found at the bottom of the Great Bath."

In Dr. Khan's hand is a large rectangular stone. Smooth and translucent with sharp edges, its rich viridian hue glistens in the light.

"Is this what you saw during your dive, Georgia?" he asks.

She nods, breathless as she takes in the beauty of the object.

"This wasn't the only one in the Great Bath. We found eight in total, scattered in random spots over the floor. Each was embedded into the brickwork, and each had a carving of an Indus script sign beside it."

Dr. Khan holds up a few to show them, presenting a collection as diverse as it is magnificent. There's a cube which captivates with its deep sapphire blue, its surface reflecting the light in a dazzling display. Another, a pyramid, is a fiery ruby red colour that sparkles with an internal flame. An oblong shape, smooth and finely polished like the rest, radiates a warm, luminous yellow, reminiscent of the midday sun captured in crystalline form.

"The characters are the same as the remaining text we couldn't translate," Harshan adds.

There's a long silence as they absorb this revelation. Then, Buri asks, "You said you found eight stones and glyphs. But there are nine characters on the inscription that we couldn't decipher?"

"Yes. The ninth was next to an empty hole, located on the west side of the bath. Its stone was missing," Dr. Khan says.

"That must be the Indus Star," Sarah says, her eyes round.

"We think so too," Dr. Khan says. "The hole was much bigger than the other stones we found. The Indus Star must be the largest of them all."

"Can you send us the shape and dimensions of the cavity?" Georgia asks.

"Sure. I'll have to dive down again tomorrow to measure that. I'll email photographs and details of the eight stones to you now. We're sending them for analysis today. Hopefully, the information from that will help us decipher the rest of the text."

16

ISHAAN, the hotel manager, returns just after lunch to take them to their meeting with Mallika Sharma. He guides them through the corridors of the Palace Wing, the heritage part of the Taj, which emanates a captivating old-world charm. Georgia is transported to a vintage era of elegance as she walks through the graceful archways, marvelling at the pillars wrought with fine details, panels carved with intricate patterns, and walls adorned with stunning artworks. They walk up a small set of white marble steps, past a couple of stone elephants, and through a door made of rich, polished wood decorated with golden motifs.

Entering the spacious living area of the famed, presidential 'Tata' suite, Georgia smiles at the blend of modern sophistication with timeless Indian aesthetics. Above them, a crystal chandelier bathes the space in shimmering light, and all around are priceless paintings, exotic artefacts, lush carpets, and plush seating arrangements with sumptuous fabrics and cushions. She spies a private dining area in the next room, its long glossy table large enough to seat ten.

Sarah's mouth is hanging open as she gazes around the room.

Ishaan introduces them to the butler, then takes his leave. In the corner is another man: tall, muscular, wearing a dark suit and an earpiece tucked behind one ear. He approaches them without a word, patting each of them down for weapons. Once done, he returns to his spot and clasps his hands together before him in a statuesque stance, keeping his vigilant gaze on them.

The butler bows. "Ms. Sharma is just finishing a conference meeting in the office. Please, take a seat and make yourselves comfortable. May I get you a drink? Tea, coffee, wine?"

Georgia requests a glass of water, while Buri asks for a cappuccino. Sarah deliberates for a long moment before ordering an espresso martini.

Buri's gaze sweeps the room, looking ill at ease as he lowers himself onto the expensive-looking sofa across from the women. Another fifteen minutes of awkward silence goes by before Mallika Sharma joins them, followed by two more bodyguards. Dressed in a cream pantsuit with a string of lustrous pearls around her neck, she greets each of them with a pleasant smile and a firm handshake.

"Thank you all for coming. It's a pleasure to meet you in person at last." Sharma sits down in one of the leather armchairs and gets straight to the point: "Well, this is some predicament we find ourselves in. I trust you've heard of the incident in Cambodia?"

"Yes," Georgia says.

"That makes it nine signs. After our last conversation, I thought more about what happened to the Indus Valley people. That series of catastrophes ended their civilisation. And now, the same things are taking place again, but on a much larger scale. Are we looking at a global apocalyptic event here?" She doesn't wait for their input before continuing, "I think it's imperative we find the current location of the Indus Star. The Dwarka inscriptions said disasters will occur whenever the stone is disturbed, and the only way to prevent more from happening is to put the stone back in its rightful place. Maybe there's a way to stop all of this before it's too late. Have you made any progress in your research?"

"I've been combing through scriptures and historical records for any mention of the Indus Star. So far, nothing has come up," Georgia says, even though it's not entirely true.

Mallika Sharma stares at her with a sharp and astute gaze, long enough for Georgia's cheeks to colour from her lie.

"You've spoken to Dr. Khan about his latest discoveries?" Sharma asks.

"Yes, we talked earlier this morning."

"The stones they found are… intriguing. It's obvious they're not just any ordinary rocks." Sharma thinks on this as she steeples her fingers before her. "What if the Indus Star was called something else in the literature? Like, for example, the Syamantaka gem?"

Georgia frowns.

"What's that?" Sarah asks, draining her drink and putting it on the coffee table.

"It's a jewel mentioned in Hindu scriptures," Georgia explains.

"The stone we're looking for… is a gem?" Sarah asks. "They looked like some kind of crystals to me."

Sharma purses her lips as her gaze lingers on Sarah's empty martini glass. After a moment, she says, "Syamantaka is not just any jewel. According to the ancient Purana scriptures, it once belonged to Surya, the Sun God. It was said that the Syamantaka gem glistened with such brilliance, it gave Surya his blinding appearance. And any land in possession of it would be blessed with prosperity and spared from droughts, floods, earthquakes, and famine. Not only that, but the gem would also produce gold for its keeper every day."

Buri raises his brows. "The Indus people believed their stone was responsible for all of their wealth and fortune."

Sharma smiles. "The story goes on to say that Surya gifted it to one of his devotees, Satrajita, who returned to Dwarka with the jewel. When he entered the city, he was shining so bright, everyone mistook him for the Sun God. The stone was then passed on to his brother, who was attacked by a lion, which was in turn mauled by Jambavan, the king of bears. Then Krishna tracked down the stone—"

"Krishna, the blue-skinned god?" Sarah interrupts.

"Yes. The story is a long one, but in the end, Lord Krishna retrieved the jewel and allowed his uncle Akrura to keep it, on the condition that it never leave Dwarka." Sharma pauses, looking out the window. "There's no mention of what happened to the Syamantaka gem after Krishna left the Earthly realm. But it is said that his city, Dwarka, sank into the Arabian Sea upon his death."

"So according to the inscriptions Dr. Khan found, that was when the gem was stolen from Dwarka," Buri hypothesises.

"We don't know that," Georgia says. "And we're also talking about the Bronze Age Harappan city, which was different from the scriptural version of Krishna's Dwarka."

"But you must admit, the parallels between the narratives are compelling," Sharma argues. "And don't forget, the best legends are often inspired by truths."

Georgia does not dispute this as she leans back in her seat. Her grandmother said something similar to her once.

"Okay, let's say we go down this rabbit hole," Sarah suggests. "First, we need to figure out what the Syamantaka gem is."

"Yes," Sharma agrees. "And I have read a little on this over the years. Some scholars speculate it could be the Koh-i-Noor."

Georgia's frown deepens. She is impressed with Sharma's knowledge, but the direction this conversation is taking makes her uneasy. The Koh-i-Noor is a highly controversial diamond, and given the media hype already surrounding their search, she does not want to risk fanning the flames. In her research, the Syamantaka gem has come up as a possible clue, but she's been reluctant to discuss it before she finds out more because she knows where it would lead.

"The Koh-i-Noor?" Buri asks.

Sharma crosses her legs and leans forward. "It's one of the largest cut diamonds in the world—"

"Wait." Sarah's mouth drops open. "The stone we're looking for is a *diamond*?"

"We don't know that," Georgia stresses again.

Sharma explains, "Koh-i-Noor means 'Mountain of Light' in Persian. No one knows where the diamond came from, and its true origin is shrouded in conflicting legends and mysteries. The earliest written record of it was in the 1740s, in which it was described as the centrepiece of the Mughal emperor Shah Jahan's Peacock Throne.

"The Peacock Throne was the most magnificent and expensive piece of furniture ever made. It cost twice as much as the construction of Taj Mahal," Sharma adds. "It was said to have been inspired by the fabled throne of Solomon, constructed in gold and studded with emeralds, diamonds, rubies, pearls, and many other priceless jewels."

"What happened to the throne?" Buri asks.

Georgia says, "Nader Shah of Persia invaded and sacked Delhi in 1739, massacring tens of thousands of people. When his troops finally left, they took with them the accumulated wealth of eight generations of Mughal conquest, part of which was the Peacock Throne."

Sharma nods, pursing her lips. "The Mughals' affluence was legendary, and they never recovered from this tremendous loss of fortune. It took seven hundred elephants, four thousand camels, and twelve hundred horses pulling wagons to carry all that loot back to Persia. This heinous crime robbed us of important cultural artefacts that could never be replaced."

"But the Koh-i-Noor wasn't the only well-known gem that was taken by Nader Shah," Georgia points out. "Embedded in the Peacock Throne alone were also the Timur Ruby and another famous diamond called the Darya-i-Noor, the Sea of Light. There were also the Great Mughal Diamond, the Great Table Diamond, and the Akbar Shah Diamond."

Sarah's eyes widen at the list of gems. She says, "I never knew there was so much wealth in India."

"Until the discovery of mines in Brazil in the eighteenth century, India was the sole producer of diamonds in the world." Sharma's smile is sardonic as she continues, "Speak of India these days, though, and people think of slums and open sewers and extreme poverty. Most forget that before the East India Company arrived, our share of the world economy was twenty-seven per cent. By the time the British left, it was reduced to a meagre three per cent."

"My point is," Georgia urges, "if we were to continue this path of investigation, there are many other contenders that could be the stone we are looking for. Or even those previously unknown. The speculation that the Syamantaka gem is the Koh-i-Noor has very little basis, and the descriptions of the two don't match at all. Syamantaka is rumoured to be a ruby, and the source of good luck and wealth. The Koh-i-Noor, on the other hand, is thought to be cursed."

"Cursed?" Sarah raises her brows.

"Throughout its known history, the diamond has caused bitter and bloody conflicts across several empires. Every male ruler who owned it ultimately lost his power or his life," Georgia says. "Because of its complex history, the governments of India, Iran, Pakistan, and Afghanistan all claim ownership of it."

"Where is it now?" Buri asks.

"It's part of the British Crown Jewels," Georgia says.

"Another piece of our heritage looted by the British," Sharma says. "Georgia has a valid argument, though, regarding other stones that should be considered. In any case, I think a good starting point is to examine the ones that have been misplaced. And we all know that countless gems have been taken from India."

Georgia considers this for a long moment, then replies, "We'll make a list and concentrate on those that have special spiritual significance."

"Excellent idea," Sharma says. "Now, I've business to attend to overseas, but please keep me updated on your progress—"

"Before we finish," Buri interjects, "we need to talk about security. The press is rabid everywhere we go. Someone is leaking our findings and movements to them."

"Of course," Sharma replies with casual nonchalance. "My staff has been transparent about everything regarding this project."

Buri doesn't seem surprised by Sharma's revelation. His nostrils flare as he takes a deep breath. Then he asks in a measured tone, "Why would you do that?"

"Media is my business. It's my job to keep the public updated on what's happening. They have a right to know."

"Even at the expense of your team?" he argues. "We were almost mobbed at the airport this morning. And Georgia was injured during the dive in Dwarka."

"I thought that was an accident?" Sharma frowns.

Georgia is quick to reply, "Yes—"

"*Not* an accident," Sarah says at the same time, glaring at Buri.

Sharma's discerning gaze travels around the room, assessing each of their faces. After a long pause, she says, "I'm sorry to hear that. I'll get my people to work on it. We'll make sure there's a security detail everywhere you go."

She exchanges a look with one of her bodyguards, who nods and exits the room.

"We also need to keep a lid on our findings, at least until we can actually confirm them," Buri suggests.

Sharma shakes her head. "Like I said, it's my responsibility to ensure people are informed. We'll take care of the security side of things to ensure your safety, but let's not compromise the public's right to knowledge. Censorship has never helped anyone."

A palpable veil of tension envelops Buri. His knuckles whiten as he clenches his fists.

"You must understand," Sharma continues, "this discovery has a huge implication for my people. Our recent colonial past has left a lasting and damaging impact on the nation's social, cultural, and economic fabric. The British Raj exploited India's wealth of resources, dismantled local industries, and perpetuated deep-rooted inequalities. When their archaeologists first discovered the Indus Valley Civilisation, the idea that the 'backward, primitive people of India' might be heirs to a civilisation far older than that described in the bible, and light years ahead of the Europeans at the time, astounded them. Our work in Dwarka will uncover a forgotten piece of our past. It is something I'm very proud of, and I'll never keep any of it hidden."

She gestures to the other man who followed her into the room. "This is Vijay Patel, one of my personal bodyguards. He and his team will take care of you, follow you wherever you go, and see to your every need."

Georgia watches Buri's piercing stare assess the young man standing behind Sharma. Vijay isn't tall, but his imposing physique reflects his fitness and training, and he exudes an aura of calm confidence that is rare in people of his age. He wears a suit that shows off his powerful frame, his black hair is curly and cropped short, his eyes alert and calculating.

With a begrudging twist of his lips, Buri says to Vijay, "I want to discuss strategies and protocols in detail."

"Good." Sharma flashes them a smile as she pushes to her feet. "Let's keep in touch. I'm sure you'll have a comfortable stay at the Taj. They're accustomed to high-profile guests here and have the best security measures. Vijay will take you to your rooms now."

17

DHARA SHAH WINCES as the jeep jolts violently. Nursing her broken arm in a sling, she attempts to redistribute her weight, seeking a modicum of relief for her fractured ribs. It's an impossible task, considering the constant upheaval of the vehicle along the fissure-ridden road.

After some fussing about, she gives up and accepts her fate, leaning back against the headrest and squeezing her eyes shut as she battles waves of nausea from seven hours of non-stop travel through punishing, mountainous terrain. Her personal discomfort feels trivial, though—an indulgence even —given the scale of calamity at her destination.

When the devastating 8.5 magnitude earthquake struck Lima, she was halfway across the world, in the bustling streets of Phnom Penh. She bought a ticket for the first flight out and made her way to Jauja, the nearest functioning airport, as the disaster had levelled the one in Lima. From there, her local fixer, Pedro, has been driving the long, arduous road to the capital.

As they come around a sharp bend, the full extent of the

earthquake's impact on Lima unfolds before them. Pedro curses in a low voice and slows to a stop, his shock mirroring her own at the devastation left in the earthquake's wake. Having just left behind the magnificent peaks of the Andes, the timeless grandeur of the mountains is a stark contrast to the carnage scattered across the valley below. The panorama of destruction takes Dhara's breath away, and she clings to the vehicle's frame as the car begins moving again, every bone-jarring bump of the journey underscoring the sheer magnitude of the disaster.

The city is a complete ruin. The collapsed remains of buildings lie at odd angles, their jagged edges sticking out like bones of animal carcasses. The air is thick with dust, and the sky dark with billowing smoke as fires burn throughout the city.

Dhara and Pedro shield their faces with scarves from the acrid atmosphere as they approach the nightmarish vision. They drive as far as they can over cracked and contorted roads, then abandon the vehicle and continue on foot, climbing over rubble and debris. What she remembers as a lively, vibrant neighbourhood is now a graveyard of twisted metal and crumbled concrete. There is an eerie stillness in the air, accentuated by the occasional groaning of metal and crunching of broken concrete. In the distance, there are sounds of people shouting and crying, sirens wailing, and helicopters buzzing overhead.

She spots an arm, pale and slender, sticking out through the wreckage. Rushing towards it, she scans for any signs of life. Her breath comes in stutters as she grasps the limb, her fingers searching for a pulse beneath the cold skin.

She finds none.

The ground under her suddenly shakes with a deep, resounding rumble. The few remaining buildings tremble around her, windows rattling in their frames. Pedro pulls her away just as a huge pane of glass falls, crashing to the fractured asphalt in an explosion of splintering shards. Dhara's heart thunders as she crouches low, clasping onto the edges of cracked concrete for support.

The tremor ends as quickly as it started, and the city awakens with a renewed cacophony of terror. Frightened cries, screams, and blaring car alarms resound throughout the streets. As Dhara walks further into the metropolis, haunted faces of the survivors stare at her from amid the rubble, their dusty features reflecting a surreal blend of horror and despair. Their affliction seizes Dhara by the throat, leaving her gasping for air.

Years of threading her path through conflict zones, natural disaster sites, and political uprisings have given her a thick skin. But days like this show her that there is always another level of desolation to encounter.

In the midst of this harrowing scene, Dhara's mind flicks back to the unnerving sights she witnessed in Cambodia: the terrified faces, the presage whispered with hushed paranoia.

Until now, she has regarded the Dwarka Prophecies with a healthy dose of scepticism. But standing within this landscape of unimaginable death and destruction, her heart skips a beat as she wonders if the omens foretelling the end times might indeed be unfurling before her very eyes.

18

ENGROSSED IN HER RESEARCH, Georgia sits on the lounge chair in her room, the soft hum of her laptop the only sound cutting through the deep silence of the night. Scattered around her on the soft carpeting, a chaotic ensemble of papers and books reflects her state of mind. She's been diving into the depths of Hindu literature and immersing herself in historical and mythical accounts of legendary gems. Meanwhile, Sarah has taken up the task of making a list of jewels stolen from India during ages of conquest, and Harshan and Buri are still working together to translate the remaining inscriptions from Dwarka.

Their lodgings, courtesy of Sharma, are no less luxurious than the billionaire's own accommodations. Dubbed the "Ravi Shankar Suite", it is a loving homage to the sitar maestro, who once taught George Harrison of the Beatles within these very walls. Bathed in warm hues reminiscent of a sitar, the high-ceilinged lounge houses an extensive library of concert recordings from the two music legends and a collection of memorabilia from the Ravi Shankar Foundation.

There are original artworks by eminent artists like Jamini Roy, Raja Ravi Varma, and Raza on the walls, and a stunning view of the Gateway of India against the backdrop of the Arabian Sea.

To Sarah, though, who possesses a marked predilection for luxury, the suite's most captivating allure appears to be the round-the-clock butler service. She rapped on Georgia's door hours ago, her excitement barely contained as she bounced on her toes in her fluffy dressing gown, raving about the bath Kian, their butler, had prepared earlier. It'd been an indulgent soak featuring an aromatic blend of salts and essential oils, complemented by the scatter of delicate rose petals.

"I've always fancied myself a maharani in a previous life," Sarah said, then gushed about a late supper in the dining room—a gastronomic feast arranged by the ever-accommodating Kian. She reasoned they might as well make the most out of their stay if the world were to end soon.

Declining Sarah's invitation to the meal, Georgia instead plunged back into her work. Now, a gentle knock interrupts her.

"Come in," she calls, expecting to see Sarah on another dining expedition. "Oh." She rises to her feet, failing to hide her surprise as Buri appears in the doorway, holding a tray with a silver-domed plate.

"I saw your light on," he says. "Can't sleep?"

She glances at her watch, surprised that it's now four in the morning. Her untouched bed is a stark testament to her restless night. She responds to his question with a shake of her head.

His tone is reprimanding as he adds, "Kian said you haven't eaten."

"I'm not hungry. You go ahead."

Ignoring her suggestion, he strides further into the room, taking a moment to locate some space in the sea of research material. He finds it at the edge of the bed, where he places the tray, offering a small island of nourishment.

Not wanting to draw attention to her lack of need for food these days, Georgia murmurs, "Thank you."

Their shared silence since the incident on the plane hangs heavy between them. She knows this may be his attempt at reconciliation, but the wound from his betrayal is still raw, and she cannot bring herself to ask the questions that really matter to her. So she sits down instead, waiting for him to leave. But he just stands there and stares at her.

"You heard about what happened in Peru?" Buri finally asks, pinpointing the source of her insomnia.

She nods, the knot of anxiety heavy in her stomach.

"That's ten out of fifteen," he points out, referring to the omens in the Dwarka Prophecy.

She sighs. "Any progress on your end?"

"Some. You? Any leads?"

"Yeah, Vijay brought up some very good material earlier." She gestures to the bombshell of her room. "I'm just compiling it now. We can go over it at breakfast?"

His head dips in a nod, yet his feet are rooted to the spot.

Disconcerted by his presence, she rambles on: "I have to admit that ancient Hindu literature is not my forte. There's so much to sift through," she says, hoping that he'll get the hint and move on.

"Call Dhara," he suggests, bringing out a business card from his pocket and handing it to her. "She studied history and Eastern religions in college. Her dissertation was on ancient Indian scriptures."

"But she's a reporter," Georgia argues. "Didn't you say to Sharma that we shouldn't tell the press anything until we're certain of what's going on?"

"Dhara's not like the others. She's a well-respected investigative journalist. She won the Pulitzer last year, and she wouldn't write just sensationalist shit. I trust her."

Georgia ignores the pinch of envy in her chest at the vehement way he defends Dhara. She takes the card from him even though she knows she would never make the call. "Thanks. Well, I should get back to—"

"I've been going over security protocols with Vijay," he says. "We've got a plan in place, but really, there's no predicting what the mob will do. They're scared and emotional, and that's never a good combination. And with Sharma telling them every detail of our search…" He exhales a frustrated sigh. "The risks are just too high. So I think we should prepare you for the crowd."

"How?"

From the back of his cargo pants, he draws out a pistol.

"No." She shakes her head vehemently. "No way."

He raises a questioning eyebrow.

"I've told you before: I hate guns and everything they represent."

His jaw tightens, and she expects him to lash out with an insult about her being Australian, just like he did all those months ago in Mongolia. What he says instead surprises her.

"Well, the next best thing is to make sure you can protect yourself." He puts the weapon away.

She furrows her brows, then raises them with disbelief when she catches his meaning.

GEORGIA GRUNTS as she hits the floor. Defeated, she remains on her back as Buri frowns down at her with disapproval.

"Again." He walks away, wiping at the beads of perspiration on his forehead.

After a lengthy argument in her room earlier, Georgia caved in to his insistence on teaching her basic self-defence techniques. Her reluctant agreement only came after a blunt reminder of how her vulnerability was a burden on him and ultimately a threat to the team. He argued that he couldn't ensure her and Sarah's well-being if they both remained clueless about how to fend off an attack. Driven by a protective instinct for Sarah rather than a desire for personal safety, Georgia relented.

They've been at it for almost two hours now in the hotel gym, and throughout, she's been hyperaware of her movements: how little of her newfound strength to apply, how much to curb her unusual speed and agility. These considerations have made it impossible for her to concentrate on Buri's instructions, resulting in him repeatedly flooring her.

His proximity and physical contact don't help, either. It has her belly fluttering with unwelcome nerves, her skin tingling at every touch.

Gritting her teeth, she pushes herself up. Buri moves behind her, his muscular arm tight around her neck in a chokehold.

"Grip my wrist, pivot your hip, and drop," he instructs.

She tries to perform the manoeuvre, but her movements are too hesitant, her hold on him too loose, and she ends up with her face pressed against the padded floor. Again.

He sneers, offering her a hand. "Seriously? This isn't a choreographed dance. It's a fight."

"I'm trying," she retorts and swats him away, rising to her feet with irritation simmering in her gut.

"Not hard enough," he counters with a biting voice. "And if you learnt this when you should have, maybe I wouldn't have gotten shot by that Russian blockhead in Mongolia."

His words ringing in her ears, she charges at him, frustration lending her movements a desperate edge. This time, when his arm goes around her neck, she doesn't think. She reacts. Gripping his wrist, she pivots, drops, and with a burst of strength that astonishes her, she sends Buri sprawling on the floor.

For a moment, silence fills the room. She looks at Buri,

both of them panting to catch their breaths, and a flicker of something passes over his face.

"There she is," he mutters.

Georgia jerks back as if he's struck her.

Is he... *testing* her?

She jumps up, looking anywhere but at him. Grabbing her towel and belongings, she heads straight for the door, stopping short when he calls out.

"Agent Miller and I only share the same surname," he says. "That doesn't mean we have the same interests."

She sucks in a breath at his admission. Turning to face him, she asks, "Why didn't you tell me you were brothers?"

"Half-brothers," he clarifies again as he stands, his gaze never wavering from hers. "It's not something we talk about, especially when we were in the military. Our family ties tend to... complicate things. But the army was a long time ago, and I hardly speak to Brandon these days. I guess it's an old habit I haven't been able to kick." He rakes a hand through his short-cropped hair. "I'm sorry I didn't tell you. But I promise, I have nothing to do with the DIA."

Captivated by his dark, intense gaze, she finds herself giving in.

"Alright," she sighs, realising with dismay that her inexplicable desire to believe him is probably clouding her judgement. "But no more lies."

Pursing his lips, he nods.

Then she asks the one thing that has been on her mind: "What about Anya?"

The flash of relief in Buri's features is replaced with a scowl. "What about her?"

"Do you know where she is?"

"No."

"Is Brandon your source?"

He hesitates. "Yes."

"Can he help me find her?"

A rigid stillness takes over him. "You don't want to ask him for any favours."

"Why not?"

He looks as if he's about to say something, then stops himself. A ripple of tension passes over his features, moulding his lips into a taut, unyielding line.

"There you are." Sarah barges through the door with Vijay following close behind her. She halts as she takes in the charged atmosphere in the room, the sheen of sweat on their bodies. "What's going on here? What did I miss?"

"Nothing," they both say at the same time.

"Oh, yeah, sure." Sarah's tone is heavy with sarcasm as she shifts her gaze from Georgia to Buri, then back again. When neither of them offer an explanation, she rolls her eyes and huffs, "Dr. Khan called. He wants to have a meeting now."

They follow her and Vijay back to the suite, passing the security detail stationed outside the door. The aroma of richly spiced food envelops them as they walk into the living area, the dining table covered with a feast of parathas, masala omelette, puri, fragrant chai, and a smorgasbord of other dishes Georgia doesn't recognise.

"Kian made us breakfast," Sarah says, gesturing to the butler standing by the lounge room. She sits down at her open laptop and calls Dr. Khan back. While it's connecting, she yawns and fixes herself a plate, slipping Indi a piece of paratha when Buri isn't looking.

Dr. Khan's excited face appears on the screen. "Good morning," he greets them. "We got the lab results for the stones. I'm emailing it to you now."

Buri retrieves his tablet from the lounge and goes through the information with Georgia.

"Sharma was right," Buri says with undisguised incredulity. "They're gems."

Dr. Khan nods. "And the analysis has identified six of

them. Emerald, ruby, blue sapphire, yellow sapphire, hessonite, and cat's eye. The other two were too deteriorated to determine what they were, so we've sent them to another lab for testing."

"They must be worth a fortune," Sarah gasps, pointing at the listed dimensions of the jewels.

Dr. Khan continues, "We went for another dive at the site this morning, and I've measured the cavity of the missing gem. I'm sending you the information now. We used a mould to determine the form and curvature of the hole, which is also in the email. It's round and looks like part of a sphere. At least, that's the shape of the bottom of the stone which once was embedded in the brickwork."

Buri brings up the correspondence on his tablet, showing Georgia the details.

"According to this, the missing gem must be"—Georgia does a quick calculation on her phone—"at a minimum, almost a thousand carats in size."

Sarah gapes at her. "And they just, what, had all these priceless jewels lying around at the bottom of their bath? Why?"

"For ritualistic purposes?" Dr. Khan suggests.

"Perhaps," Georgia murmurs. "But the important thing is that we're now certain it isn't the Koh-i-Noor, which is only a hundred and five carats. We must ask Sharma to drop that theory. I can't stress this enough."

"I'll talk to her," Dr. Khan offers. After a pause, he asks, "How is your research progressing?"

"There's no shortage of material to go through," Georgia admits. "The ancient Indians were the first to write exhaustive discourses on gemmology, and the subject was a repeated theme in texts of history, literature, and mythology. In some historic Indian courts, jewellery was more important than clothing as a sign of rank and title, but it was also worn by men and women of all classes and backgrounds. And there are Hindu stories of demons being sacrificed and converted to seeds of jewels, dropping down to Earth as the source of deposits of precious stones possessing magical qualities."

Georgia leans forward. "From cross referencing historical records and religious manuscripts, I've made a catalogue of gems worth investigating, highlighting ones of spiritual and cultural significance." She pauses. "At that size, there's only one that stands out."

"My list of jewels stolen from India doesn't even go anywhere *near* a thousand carats." Sarah throws up her hands and looks at Georgia. "Well, what did you find?"

"It's known as the Cosmic Eye. And the rumour is that at one point, it was kept at the Kailasa Temple."

19

Aurangabad, India

TOUCHING DOWN AT AURANGABAD, the nearest city to the revered Kailasa Temple, Georgia and her team alight from their jet and step straight into a raging tempest of protesters. Her heart drums like a pulsing beat against her ribcage as she takes in the impressive scale of the diverse crowd stretching across the tarmac before them, much larger and more impassioned than she's encountered since arriving in India. Men, women, and even children are present, the atmosphere palpable with tension as their shouts fill the air, blending into an incomprehensible cry of human rage. Each sign held aloft by the demonstrators expresses their wrath, some inked in the swirling scripts of Hindi, others bearing bold English words:

Return Our Heritage—Give Back the Koh-i-Noor!

India's Pride Is Not Your Prize!

Britain, It's Time for Reparations!

Georgia's palms are slick with perspiration as she clutches Sarah's hand. Buri is behind them, with Indi on a tight leash by his side. Members of Sharma's security team surround them, nine in all, forming a defensive human barrier. Georgia keeps her head down, avoiding eye contact with anyone as she follows Vijay, who ruthlessly pushes through the crowd. The stench of sweat and fury taints every breath she takes, and she hears the questions yelled out by journalists within the tumult of angry outbursts:

"Professor Lee! Can you confirm if the Koh-i-Noor is the missing gem of Dwarka?"

"Do you know if anything is being done to recover the Koh-i-Noor from the British?"

Georgia wants to stop and address these outrageous questions, but Sarah now has her arm in a tight grip as she pulls them forward. And agitated as the crowd is, nothing would help to calm them. Georgia doubts they would even listen to her.

When they finally rush into their awaiting van, she drops into the seat next to Sarah to catch her breath. Indi nuzzles her palm and Sarah's leg, providing them little comfort. The irate throng beats a discordant rhythm of dissent against the windows and the panelling as their vehicle crawls towards the exit.

As they pull away from the mob, Buri says, "Sharma ratted us out again." His features are dark with fury as he turns to Vijay. "You have to talk to her about this. It's hard enough to keep everyone safe without having to deal with the raging crowd. She has to keep sensitive information secure until we can confirm it."

"Madam Sharma has made her position clear," Vijay replies, his face like stone.

"But we already know the missing gem isn't the Koh-i-Noor," Georgia argues. "Why hasn't she corrected them?"

"It's the media. They will go with whatever story sells best." Vijay shrugs. "It's fine. We have enough men to deal with the crowd."

Buri's jaw tightens, his gaze hard and his shoulders tense. He looks as if he's about to fly into a rage when Sarah holds up her phone and says, "Look at this."

She reads out loud, flicking through several tabs on the browser, each with a different news outlet reporting on the rising tension between the governments of India, Pakistan, Afghanistan, and Iran, all claiming rights to the Koh-i-Noor: the story of how the eleven-year-old Maharaja Duleep Singh was coerced to surrender the diamond to Queen Victoria during the hostile takeover of the Sikh Empire by the British East India Company; a public demand by the representative of India for the jewel to be returned to Dwarka, asserting that its theft must have caused all the disasters around the world; the response from Pakistan that since much of the Indus Valley Civilisation and Duleep Singh's domain lie in what is now Pakistan, the stone should be handed over to his country instead; the lack of any response from the British government.

"We need to make a public statement," Georgia says. "Tell the press that it's got nothing to do with the Koh-i-Noor."

"You think that mob will listen to you?" Sarah argues, flicking a thumb behind her. "Those reporters are rabid, feeding off all the drama. The damage is already done. Only thing we can do is find the real jewel and put an end to all this."

No one argues against this, and a sombre silence descends in the van. The debate over the Koh-i-Noor has reopened wounds inflicted during the days of colonisation and the 1947 Partition. Georgia anticipates that the added tension will only make their job harder.

She looks out the window, seeking distraction from the gnawing anxiety in her stomach. Traffic is a nightmare as they fight their way out of the city. Bicycles, tuk-tuks, rickshaws, cars, and buses all compete for passage on the roads. There are motorcycles everywhere, straining under the weight of goods in precarious piles reaching up to three metres high. Colourful, towering lorries with customised musical horns blare out tunes, many with signs on the rear encouraging everyone to 'BLOW HORN OK'. The relentless symphony of honking echoes like a sonar system, a resonating guide for each vehicle to steer clear of the next in the midst of the chaotic dance. Yet by some unfathomable logic, it all works. And amidst the anarchy, there exists an unwritten law, unanimously respected by all: cows indisputably own the right of way.

Almost an hour passes before Buri turns to Georgia and says, "Tell us more about the gem we're looking for."

She nods. "The Cosmic Eye was lost a long time ago, so it has become more of a legend, and it's hard to filter out reliable information. According to sources, it was a ruby, and it was so crimson, it mirrored the vibrancy of the setting sun. It was believed to embody the very essence of Shiva, the lord of destruction and transformation. Some claimed it was a tear shed by Shiva himself, crystallised over aeons into a potent gem. Others said it was a fragment of the cosmos, a piece of the universe's heart that fell to Earth during the dawn of creation."

"And you said it had adorned the idol at the Kailasa Temple?" Buri asks.

Georgia opens her laptop, searching for a file. "That is the rumour, yes. It's a common thing to do, decorating Hindu gods with gold and precious stones. And diamonds have always received pride of place as the eyes of the statues. But over the centuries, many of the well-known ones have been pilfered by foreign plunderers."

"I've read up on some of these," Sarah says, listing some

examples. "The Nassak and the Black Orlov diamonds, both famous and huge gems, were in the eyes of temple idols until they were taken as spoils of war."

"Just like these stones, the Cosmic Eye was believed to have been stolen from the Kailasa Temple. But there's no mention of who was responsible," Georgia says, bringing up images and a map of the compound on her screen. "The Kailasa is an architectural marvel, and the largest structure within a multi-religious complex called the Ellora Caves. Considered the most remarkable rock-cut temple in the world, it's a monolith hewn from a single basalt stone. Stonemasons excavated it out of the mountainside by removing hundreds of thousands of tons of rock, working vertically from the *top down*, an astronomical engineering feat in itself. And being a bedrock excavation, there was zero room for error. The technology required to do this is so sophisticated, it's inspired several myths and legends around how the temple was made. Some even claim that it was constructed by aliens."

"So no one knows who built it?" Sarah asks.

"Not for certain, no. But it's generally been attributed to the eighth-century Rashtrakuta king."

The van pulls up to the parking lot for the Ellora Caves. It is busy here, with hundreds of pilgrims milling about, enjoying the manicured lawn and gardens. There's not a cloud in the sky, and even though it is still early morning, the temperature is already soaring.

"I called the temple before we left," Vijay says. "They've agreed to postpone the opening time so we can have the place to ourselves for an hour. And they're also providing us with a local guide, as you've requested."

They decide to leave Indi in the van with the driver, and Vijay goes through the security protocol before they exit the vehicle. Their bodyguards, having arrived in a separate van, are already there with the guide. The group stays close together as they walk towards the Kailasa Temple, their appearance sparking a buzz of curious chatter amongst the other visitors waiting to enter.

Their guide is a tall, lanky man who looks older than Georgia's father. In a thick Indian accent, he introduces himself as Sundeep and gives them some background information. Dating back to the fifth century, this UNESCO World Heritage Site includes temples dedicated to Buddhism, Jainism, and Hinduism, demonstrating the religious tolerance and harmony of the time. Its location on an ancient trade route meant that as well as being a place of worship, it was also a rest stop for pilgrims and an important commercial centre in the Deccan region. Unfortunately, being close to the city of Aurangabad where Muslim invaders once settled, the temples have suffered considerable damage over the centuries.

The crown jewel of the Ellora Caves, of course, is the Kailasa Temple. Dedicated to Shiva, it is said to have been inspired by Mount Kailash, Shiva's abode.

As they enter the stone gateway and walk into the sprawling courtyard, Georgia is overcome with a sense of awe. Even though she has read countless descriptions of this place, nothing could prepare her for its sheer scale and magnificence. Edged by a columned arcade three storeys high, the superstructure in the centre of the quadrangle looms over them at over ten storeys tall, commanding their immediate reverence. The overall design of the construction resembles a chariot, with towering elephants flanking either side. Intricately carved sculptures and reliefs decorate the colossal basalt walls, recounting epics and ancient tales of celestial beings, each a breathtaking work of art in its own right.

As they tread across the grounds, the figures of gods and goddesses seem to watch them from their silent perches, their stone eyes imbued with a sense of divine wisdom. Georgia can hardly fathom the mathematics, the engineering, and the genius required to carve the entire structure out of the mountain from the top. As with the pyramids of Egypt, it would be impossible to recreate something like this with modern-day technology.

"This place is *massive*," Sarah whispers in veneration. "And there are so many gods here. Where do we start?"

Georgia uses her tablet to bring up the temple layout. "A gem of that size and importance must have been used to decorate the principal idol, which would be in the sanctum sanctorum." She points to the innermost part of the compound.

Sundeep guides them into the central building. They climb up the narrow stairwell, eventually finding themselves in the darkened hall of the main Shiva shrine. The play of light and shadow casts a soft, ethereal glow upon the sanctuary's interior, accentuating its mysterious ambiance. Tall, majestic pillars with intricate designs support the cavernous ceiling, creating an imposing pathway that leads to the sanctum sanctorum at the far end of the space.

Guiding her team forward, Georgia feels transported back through the centuries with each pillar they pass. She pauses at the ornately sculpted doorway, guarded by two defaced, headless female deities. Then she walks up the stone steps, crossing the threshold into the temple's inner sanctum, the area most hallowed by worshippers.

The room is small and plain compared to the extravagant, embellished designs of the rest of the compound. In the centre is a short column with a domed top sitting on a circular platform with a wide channel that allows liquid offerings of milk and honey to drain off to another chamber. Crude graffiti blemish the surface of the naked walls, and there are no other forms of decoration.

Sarah stands next to her with an expression of bewilderment. "Where's the god?"

"This *is* the idol," Georgia explains, pointing to the column and the platform. "It's a lingam-yoni, an abstract representation of Shiva. It represents the union of the feminine and the masculine, and the eternal process of creation of the cosmos."

"But where would the jewel have been kept?" Sarah asks.

Georgia walks a slow circle around the lingam, noting every part of the devotional object. There is evidence of desecration here, too, with chips covering the stone surface.

She shakes her head. "It's hard to be sure with all these damage marks on the lingam, but it doesn't seem like any of the indentations here would fit the gem from Dwarka."

"What are you saying?" Sarah frowns.

"I'm saying that if the Cosmic Eye was once mounted on the lingam, then it isn't the Indus Star," Georgia muses, her heart sinking at the realisation. The Cosmic Eye is the only gem from her research that could have been the elusive stone they are after.

"Here," Buri says from the corner of the room.

Georgia follows the direction of his pointed finger to find a rough engraving amongst all the other defacements on the wall, the glyph that's associated with the Indus Star:

Spinning around, she asks Sundeep about the etching. The man saunters over, his face a picture of concentration as he considers the drawing. After a long moment, recognition flitters across his dark features, and he smiles.

"I remember now. I've seen this before," he says. "Someone must have seen it too and made a copy here."

"Where?" everyone asks him at the same time.

Taken aback by the zeal of their enquiry, he blurts out, "The Ajanta Caves. It's not so far from here. I can take you."

20

"THE AJANTA CAVES is also an UNESCO World Heritage Site," Sundeep says as they pull up to the car park two hours later. "There are thirty monolithic Buddhist temples and monasteries here, and they were built earlier than the Ellora Caves—starting from second century BCE and over the span of eight hundred years."

Sundeep guides them along the tree-lined path, explaining the history of the area. Ajanta was home to a flourishing monastic community, and a resting place for pilgrims and merchants. After Buddhism declined in India, the site was abandoned and forgotten. It wasn't until 1819 that it was rediscovered by a British hunting party by accident.

Visitors roam about, though there are not as many here compared to the Ellora Caves. As they proceed down the path, a dramatic panorama unfolds before Georgia's eyes: a beautiful, verdant valley in the shape of a horseshoe, the basalt and granite cliffs sheltering a string of rock-cut sanctuaries, their entrances like yawning portals into a world that once was. With the only sounds being the soft rustle of leaves and the murmuring Waghora River below, the site emanates a tranquil aura of ancient mysticism.

"The Ellora Caves are known for the sculptures, and the Ajanta Caves for their paintings," Sundeep continues. "There are 1600-year-old tempera frescos decorating the Ajanta ceilings and walls, and beautiful narrative carvings telling the stories of the Buddha. Here, we can see the evolution of Buddhist art over the centuries. Most of the natural pigments used were harvested from these hills, and there is evidence of artistic influences from Persia and Greece."

They walk the winding path that lines the cliff, passing a multitude of cave retreats cut into the rock face, each unique in its own right. Some are decorated with ornate pillars, some guarded by stone deities and elephants, and others feature intricately carved archways. Waterfalls cascade down the rugged escarpment, fuelled by the recent monsoon rainwater seeping through the foliage above. The soft drizzle infuses the air with a cooling mist, adding an ethereal charm and a refreshing comfort from the scorching sun overhead. Georgia's team attracts a curious crowd, and soon there is a long trail of onlookers following them.

Sundeep pauses at an entrance, which is plain in design compared to those they have passed. Other than four embellished, round pillars supporting the entrance, there are no other decorations on the polished surface of the stone walls. A red, metal mesh door bars entry from the public.

"This one has been closed for some time now because the Archaeological Survey of India has been doing some restoration work to prevent the ceiling from collapsing," Sundeep says, unlocking the gate and pushing it open. "The writing I saw is in here."

Vijay and his security team stay outside, keeping the spectators at bay. As Georgia crosses the threshold into the cavernous interior, a sacred silence envelops her. Relishing the still and cool air within, she looks around. The spacious, square chamber is edged by a series of wide columns, and there are a few small meditation rooms off to the left and right. There is an alcove recessed into the wall at the far end of the hall, a shrine filled by a two-metre tall Buddha sculpted in stone. Bamboo scaffolding and construction equipment are scattered about the temple, and there are wooden posts supporting the ceiling in several places.

Sundeep turns on the lights, and the temple comes alive as a dramatic theatre of art under the soft illumination of the lamps. Georgia's breath escapes her as she takes in the sublime beauty of the murals that cover the walls and ceilings, which are some of the finest surviving examples of ancient Indian art she has ever witnessed. Sophisticated in their execution, the frescos demonstrate the use of perspective, a technique that wasn't employed in Western painting until the Italian Renaissance many centuries later. Glowing in the warm, dim light, the paintings depict scenes from the Jataka tales: stories about the previous lives of the Buddha. The vibrant colours, from cinnabar reds to lapis lazuli blues, still retain their intensity despite centuries of weathering.

She walks towards the shrine, marvelling at the intricate designs in the stonework, which showcase a remarkable sense of movement and expression.

Buri's phone rings, the sharp sound giving Georgia a jolt. He frowns at the screen and picks up the call. "Hello?"

His frown deepens.

"Who is it?" she asks.

"Don't know. Lost signal." Buri puts the phone back into his pocket. Turning to Sundeep, he inquires, "Where did you see the writing?"

The old man points up, and Georgia takes a sharp inhale as she tilts her head. Above the shrine is the most stunning mandala she has ever seen, decorated in brilliant hues of red, blue, and green. But what surprises her is not the art itself, but the series of characters worked into the design. She counts a total of nine, dotted across the artwork like a constellation.

"These are the glyphs Harshan and I have been trying to decipher," Buri says, astonished. "The same ones that Dr. Khan found at the bottom of the Great Bath in Dwarka."

"They must be a crucial part of the puzzle," Georgia guesses.

"Look at this." Sarah points at the paintings on the walls. "The murals seem to tell a story... of a gem?"

Georgia inspects the artwork and finds that her assistant is right. One of the deities is cradling an enormous glowing jewel within her palms, holding it high above her head. Men and women prostrate themselves around the goddess, and there appears to be a narrative spanning across the frieze, but the surface is too deteriorated for Georgia to make sense of the tale.

Excited, she turns to Buri. "We might be able to recover information from this. Call Harshan and Dr. Khan. Ask them to send over some multispectral imaging equipment."

He nods, bringing out his phone from his back pocket. "Signal is patchy in here. I'll try outside."

"I know a good spot. Let me show you," Sundeep says, following him.

Alone in the temple, Georgia and Sarah take their time exploring the interiors, snapping plenty of photographs with their phones. Their footsteps echo on the worn stone as they move about the large space, the sound reverberating against the granite walls.

"This place is phenomenal." Sarah shakes her head with awe. "Makes me think of Indian history and culture in an entirely different way."

Georgia barely listens as her assistant continues to effuse about the wonder of India. Her attention is instead captivated by the expansive mandala above the shrine. There's a lotus motif in the centre, its three layers of delicate petals carved out of stone. Within the stigma of the flower is a round cavity, decorated with an elaborate design of yellow and white.

A frisson of exhilaration rushes through Georgia—the familiar thrill of a breakthrough.

"Sarah," she calls, "look at this."

Sarah joins her, uttering an expletive when she follows the direction of Georgia's pointed finger. "That looks like—"

Noise erupts from outside. Georgia spins around and peers toward the entrance, alarmed by the sounds of objects smashing into the ground, each impact growing louder, more intense and more frequent. Men and women are shouting with panic as they try to force their way in, but Vijay's security team manages to hold them back.

"What the hell is going on?" Sarah yells, her voice barely audible over the bedlam.

Suddenly, a deep, ominous rumbling begins within the temple, a low vibration that sends an icy chill down Georgia's spine. The ground beneath them trembles, and a fine mist of dust descends from the ceiling.

Oh no.

She whirls around in a panicked daze. Sarah is frozen to the spot, her eyes round with fright. Adrenaline surges through Georgia as she sprints towards her assistant, but before she can reach her, the ear-splitting sound of fracturing stone fills the chamber. One of the towering columns gives way and crashes to the ground.

In the harrowing split second before the impact, Georgia dives towards Sarah, tackling her to the floor. Their bodies collide into the hard floor just as the pillar collapses with a thunderous explosion of dust and debris.

21

GEORGIA GROANS with agony as she stirs to consciousness. Every nerve is alight with pain, searing through her veins and blistering her flesh, immersing her in a noxious fog of dizzying confusion. Her bones ache as if shattered, and a white-hot dagger of a headache threatens to split her skull. Terror flutters in her chest like a trapped bird as she searches her mind to recall how she ended up here, sprawled on her front and trapped by an unbearable weight.

Then she remembers the cave temple. The commotion outside. The ground trembling beneath her and the ceiling crashing down.

Her eyes snap open, darting around in the dim light. She coughs and squints through the cloud of dust in a desperate attempt to make sense of her surroundings. Her heart throbs with a raw, primal fear that she fights to smother, forcing herself to focus despite her rising panic. She pushes against the heft crushing her, but it won't budge. Struggling to free herself, she cries out at shards digging into her back like claws of an unrelenting predator.

She stiffens as the ground stirs beneath her, panicked at

the thought of the structure caving in further. Then she hears a moan, and Georgia realises with relief that someone is trapped under her.

The person groans again, and a frisson of recollection hits her.

"Oh, shit. Sarah, wake up. Sarah!"

"Georgia? Why are you… ?" Sarah's voice is groggy and filled with confusion. She coughs, then curses. "Owww. Get off me. You're really heavy."

"The cave collapsed. We're stuck under something. I can't lift it."

Sarah is quiet for a long time. Then she says, "Oh, fuck."

"Yeah." Georgia strains her neck, looking around. Her movements cause Sarah to emit a string of expletives. "I think it's a pillar. Can you slide out from under me?"

"I don't know…?"

Sarah wiggles around, grunting as she puts more effort in. After several long minutes of straining and tugging, she finally manages to free herself. Pushing up to her knees, she grips Georgia's arm and pulls. Georgia hisses, the pain erupting over her back making her eyes water, and her shirt tears in the process as she struggles out from underneath the column. They both take some time leaning against the stone, panting from the exertion.

"Jesus," Sarah says as she looks around. "What the fuck happened?"

The temple, once a masterpiece of rock-cut architecture and Buddhist art, is now unrecognisable. Rubble and debris litter the floor, and stone pillars that once supported the ceiling now lie in crumbled chunks. Splintered wood and bamboo from the scaffolding are strewn over the ruins. By some miracle, one of the spotlights has survived, their only source of illumination in the dim cavern. Dust particles dance in its beam, stifling the air. Shadows pool in the corners of the space, expanding into dark voids where the light fails to reach. The temple is eerily quiet, and try as she might, Georgia cannot hear anything other than their breaths resounding in the gloom, and the whistle of air through a small crack in the ceiling.

"I don't know," Georgia replies. "All I remember is the noise outside. Then the entire temple started to rumble and cave in…" She stretches, testing the pain in her back. "You okay? Are you hurt?"

She scans Sarah from head to toe, relieved when she finds only minor cuts and bruises on her assistant's dust-covered body.

Sarah inspects her in the same way, gasping when she sees Georgia's back. "Jesus. You're bleeding real bad."

Georgia strains to look behind her, glimpsing a small part of her shredded, bloody T-shirt. The pain she experienced before has dulled into a familiar numbness, and she knows that her body is already recovering from her injuries.

Sarah lifts Georgia's shirt, uttering a sound of pure horror.

"What?"

"You're healing. I—I've never seen…"

Georgia winces as Sarah reaches out and removes a shard of stone wedged into her flesh. The colour drains from Sarah's face. Her stomach heaves and she spins around, retching onto the floor.

When she finishes vomiting, she wipes her mouth with the back of her hand, her countenance sheepish. "Sorry. I guess I just…"

"I had the same reaction when I first saw Charlie heal." Georgia shrugs.

They are quiet for a while, each lost in thought as they come to terms with what has happened. Tears suddenly swell in Sarah's eyes.

"You saved me," she says.

Georgia grips her hand. Unsure of what to say, she gives Sarah a wan smile.

Wiping at her reddened eyes, Sarah takes a deep breath and says, "We should find a way to get out of here."

They explore the ruined temple, trying to locate an exit. Georgia is relieved to find her phone undamaged in her pocket. There is no signal, though. Using the flashlight function, she recovers Sarah's soiled backpack from under some broken pieces of wood, but cannot find her own. Sarah fishes out a spare shirt from the bag and gives it to Georgia so she can change out of her shredded one. The top, which Sarah bought at the market in Mumbai, is too colourful for Georgia's taste and hangs loose over her petite frame.

It doesn't take long for them to discover that there's no way out.

"I think we came in through here," Sarah says, placing her hands over an enormous pile of rubble. "Hello?!" she yells. "We're in here! Help us! HELLO!"

Her plea is met with a deafening silence.

"Fuck!" Sarah's obscenity echoes through the chamber.

"Buri and Vijay will find us, I'm sure of it."

A sardonic laugh rips from Sarah's lips. "Are you kidding? We have no idea what went on outside. Everyone was trying to get *into* the temple, remember? For all we know, something bad happened and now everyone's dead and not a living soul knows we're in here. And even if they're alive, you *do* realise that we're halfway up the side of a cliff? There's no way they can get a digger or a crane out here."

Sarah's assessment of their predicament hits her like a tidal wave, and Georgia sits down, unable to accept that they are trapped. Her gaze roams over the cave once more as she stews on her assistant's words. Realising that Sarah is right, she rises to her feet again and walks over to the mound of crumbled stone blocking their exit.

Determination surges through her, and she starts dismantling it, piece by hefty piece.

"You're nuts. That'll take you forever," Sarah says.

"Do you want to get out, or not?"

Cussing under her breath, Sarah joins her. In no time at all, sweat begins to slick their bodies, soaking through their clothes as they gasp for breath. Georgia, fuelled by her immortal nature, feels an uncanny strength as she works, and for a while they appear to be making headway, carving a path to their escape.

Their progress grinds to a halt when they come to a huge boulder buried under the debris, one that even Georgia cannot move.

"Here." Sarah retrieves a long piece of timber. Using another stone as a fulcrum, she wedges the end of the post under the rock to lever it away.

Nudging Sarah aside, Georgia makes the attempt herself. She groans with effort, the wood straining under the load. It snaps suddenly and sends her sprawling on the floor.

"Ugh." Sarah drops to the ground next to Georgia, despondent and utterly spent. She puts her head in her hands. "We're gonna die in here. Oh, God. I never imagined this. I always thought I'd cark it when I'm old, in my sleep, with my family around me…"

Georgia tunes out Sarah's whiny voice, her gaze steadfast on the obstruction. "We need to find a way to break that up into smaller pieces."

Sarah raises her head. She stares at Georgia as if she has gone mad. "How?!"

"I don't know!" Georgia snaps, frustrated at her assistant's antagonistic demeanour. "You're the MacGyver fan. Didn't you pick the lock with a light bulb filament when Wang Jian kidnapped you? Think of something, dammit!"

The outburst shocks Sarah out of despondence. Narrowing her eyes, she takes an extended moment to contemplate the problem. She looks around, then rises to her feet to explore the temple ruins. Climbing up and down the heap of rubble and sifting through the wrecked construction equipment, she gathers pieces of shattered timber, a long wooden post, and a hammer.

Her grin is wide when, on the other side of the temple, she locates a fire extinguisher.

"Bingo," she says.

22

GEORGIA STARES at the hammer Sarah holds out to her with open scepticism. Ordinary in size, she doubts it would even make a chip on the stone.

"You want me to break the rock with *that*?"

"Can you?"

"I don't know. I'm still getting used to my strength, but..."

"It's not just about strength. The ancient Egyptians split granite boulders by cutting a series of holes with a hammer and chisel. They inserted wooden wedges in the holes and soaked the wood, which expanded with the water and cracked the rock. Then they'd use the chisel to break the rock apart along the crack."

"Okay. So we need a chisel, and we can make some wooden wedges."

Sarah purses her lips. "I couldn't find a chisel."

"So how—"

"Shh. I'm still thinking this through, okay? Don't be so negative."

Georgia frowns at the accusation but shuts her mouth. It takes her assistant another ten minutes of quiet concentration before she snaps her fingers and exclaims, "Yes!"

"What?"

"We'll heat up the rock, rapid-cool it with the fire extinguisher, and the thermal stress will weaken it. Then we'll use the hammer along any cracks that form to help it along." She jumps up, piling a collection of splintered wood and bamboo under the stone to fuel the fire. Grabbing her backpack, she rummages through the contents. "We need tinder, something flammable."

She takes out a bottle of nail polish, and Georgia raises a brow.

"Highly combustible," Sarah explains. "I got it from the basket of toiletries at the Taj Hotel." She beams with pride.

"But you don't wear nail polish. Why did you take it?"

"It was free."

Georgia sighs. "Have you done this before?"

"Of course not. I watched it on a YouTube video."

"Okay… I don't have a lighter. Do you?"

"No."

"So how do we start a fire?"

"Umm…"

Georgia sits down, watching Sarah as she thinks through the issue. It's not long before her eyes light up again.

"Batteries!"

"Batteries?"

"Gimme a piece of gum."

Thoroughly confused, Georgia reaches into her pocket and retrieves the packet. Sarah snatches it out of her hand and unwraps a piece, tossing the gum aside and tearing the foil wrapper into a small strip: thin in the middle and wide at the ends.

"You said batteries?" Georgia asks, peering into Sarah's backpack. "Did you nab some free ones from the Taj, too?"

"Ha ha, very funny," Sarah replies. Then she flashes Georgia a crooked grin as she pulls something big and purple out of the rucksack.

"Is that"—Georgia screws up her face in disbelief—"a *vibrator*?"

A gleeful cackle erupts from her assistant.

"Why the hell did you bring *that*?!"

Sarah shoots her a strange look. "Hey, a girl's got needs."

"But why would you carry that around with you, when we're meant to be working?"

"I was hiding it from our butler at the Taj when he packed my luggage."

"But—"

"Shh. Working here. Don't jinx the flow."

Sarah unscrews the end of the apparatus and two AA batteries fall out. "And FYI, I *did* get these batteries for free from the Taj. I took them out of the TV remote and replaced them with my dead ones."

Sarah crouches by the rock and pours a generous amount of nail polish over the heap of wood and bamboo. Then she touches the gum foil to the positive and the negative ends of the battery, and Georgia exhales with surprise as the thinned middle ignites. Sarah drops the flame onto the nail polish, and the mound lights up with a dramatic *poof!*

"Aha!" Sarah leaps to her feet with triumph.

The inferno builds swiftly in strength, and Georgia takes a step back from the intensity of its heat. Her belated realisation that they have built a fire in an enclosed space makes her panic for a second, until she sees the smoke rising and disappearing through the rift in the ceiling she spotted before.

Sarah turns and follows her gaze, then looks back and gives her a wink. "I thought of that already."

Georgia is impressed. "How long do we need to heat it up for?"

"Dunno." Sarah shrugs. "An hour or two?"

They distance themselves from the blaze as the temperature climbs. Sitting down, Sarah finds some snacks and a drink bottle in her bag. She offers the water to Georgia, who takes a small sip and passes it back to Sarah.

"Maybe we should save—" She stops when Sarah gulps down the rest of the bottle before inhaling a banana and a chocolate bar.

"What?" Sarah asks with her mouth full when she catches Georgia staring at her.

"We probably should have rationed the food and water."

"Oh. But I was starving." Sarah frowns, then changes the subject. "What do you think happened?"

"It sounded like… like there were things falling outside." Georgia shakes her head, anxiety knotting in her gut as her mind trails to Buri. "Whatever went on out there must have destabilised the structure."

For the next two hours they add more wood to keep the fire burning, their gazes transfixed by the hypnotic dance of the flames beneath the rock. The cynic in Georgia is sceptical about their audacious experiment, half-expecting it to fizzle out just like their hope. So when tiny fractures spider-web their way across the stony surface, a hearty laugh of sheer joy bubbles out of her. With the fire extinguisher at hand, Sarah douses the entire boulder in a thick cloud of cold, compressed gas. Georgia grabs the hammer and targets the fissures, her sharp strikes causing the brittle mass to shed sizeable fragments.

"Holy shit! It's working!" The triumph in Sarah's smirk is contagious, spurring Georgia on.

Within fifteen minutes, the once daunting obstruction is reduced to an array of chunks, each far more manageable than their predecessor. The following hours are a gruelling exercise of manual labour and perseverance as they heave and lever the debris away from the entrance.

Georgia grunts when Sarah suddenly lets go of the load they are sharing, leaving her to bear the heft of a large stone.

"You hear that?" Sarah says, pressing her ear up against the pile of wreckage.

"What?" Dropping the rock in her arms with a resounding thud, Georgia moves to where Sarah is standing.

The clang of metal against stone and distant shouts are muffled but distinct.

Georgia and Sarah stare at each other with wide eyes.

"HELP!" they yell in unison.

23

AFTER SEVERAL MORE GRUELLING hours excavating scree and rubble, a sliver of dappled light gradually penetrates the darkened temple interior. As the slim ray illuminates the enclosed space, Georgia at last feels the tightness in her chest release. All the strain and worry that built up over the arduous dig seems to whoosh out of her in a long exhalation.

Buri's worried face is the first thing that greets her when she crawls out of the hole after Sarah. He's quiet as he helps her to her feet, his dark eyes sweeping over her.

"You okay?" he asks in a soft voice, the relief stark in his usually inscrutable features.

She nods as she attempts to brush the dirt off her clothes without any luck. Indi pushes through the crowd, her tail thumping with joy as Sarah crouches down to scratch her behind the ears with brazen adoration. The sun is peeking over the ridge of the hill, and Georgia pauses for a moment to bask in its warm rays, grateful to be out in the open space at last.

Then the overwhelming stench of fish fills her senses, and she frowns at the lifeless lumps of bulbous flesh littering the ground. An octopus, its gelatinous form at odds with the rugged landscape, is draped over the branch of a nearby tree, its tentacles fluttering listlessly as the bough sways in the breeze. A profusion of aquatic remains festoon the emerald green foliage, their vibrant scales glinting under the emerging sun, as if the trees have all at once bloomed with strange, piscine flowers. Fragments of jellies, crabs, squids, and other mangled marine life litter the place. A briny tang lingers in the air, and beneath that, the insidious odour of bitter decay as the tropical heat begins its cruel work on the displaced ocean dwellers. It's a scent that makes her stomach churn.

"What happened?" she asks.

"It's the eleventh sign," Buri says with a heavy exhale. "The one about sea creatures raining from the sky. Started coming down just before the temple caved in." His uneasiness is clear as he says, "They were... frozen solid when they dropped from above. We've got three dead and many injured."

He scrubs a hand over his weary face. "Vijay brought in a crew, and we worked all night to dig you and Sarah out." He scans her again. "Are you sure you're alright?"

"I'm exhausted, that's all. We moved a lot of rocks on our end, too."

"Let's get you out of here and cleaned up." He places his hand at the small of her back, guiding her as they walk through the lingering crowd. The possessive gesture is so unlike him, it sends tingles of awareness through her, heating her skin.

As they reach the car park, a cluster of journalists springs to action, shouting a torrent of questions. Their jumbled words merge into a garbled roar, and their floodlights and camera flashes blind her. Vijay's men form a human barrier, keeping the press at bay as the team makes its way to the van.

As they pull away from the Ajanta Caves and drive towards their hotel, Buri turns to Vijay, demanding, "I want a full investigation into how the cave collapsed."

"I thought it was triggered by the falling sea creatures?" Georgia says, surprised at his request.

"Maybe." Buri looks doubtful. "But we should rule out the possibility that it wasn't. I heard… *something*, before it all came crashing down."

"What?"

A muscle flexes in Buri's jaw, and his eyes narrow. He shakes his head. "I can't say for certain."

Vijay brings out his phone, tapping at the screen. "I'll get someone to look into it."

As they drive on, Georgia tells Buri of how they cleared the pile of rubble blocking the entrance of the temple, and he raises his eyebrows with admiration.

Turning to Sarah, he says with a curious display of respect, "That's pretty impressive, what you thought up back there."

Sarah stares at him, her surprise at the compliment plain on her face.

"Where did you get the fire extinguisher from?" Buri asks Georgia.

"It was amongst the construction equipment," Georgia replies.

Buri tilts his head. "And the battery?"

"Uh…"

Sarah bursts out laughing. "I got it from B.O.B."

"Who's Bob?" Buri's brows knit together.

"Not Bob. B-O-B. A girl's best friend," Sarah says. "It's an acronym, muttonhead. It stands for—"

"You don't want to know," Georgia says to Buri.

"I'm sure I don't," Buri concedes. He looks Georgia over again. "And you didn't even get a scratch or a bruise from the whole ordeal?"

"I'm lucky. Sarah pushed me out of the way just in time. She's got some cuts on her shins, though."

Buri surprises Georgia by saying to her assistant, "I'll have a look at that for you once we arrive at the hotel."

Sarah's response is a twist of her lips and an indifferent shrug. She looks out the window again, her hand ruffling Indi's thick coat.

When they pull up to their accommodation two hours later, Georgia suggests to Buri, "Let's meet up in the afternoon. We should call Dr. Khan."

"You sure you're up for that?" Buri cocks an eyebrow.

"Yeah, this is important."

"Alright."

While Buri and Vijay check in for them at the hotel counter, Sarah pulls her aside.

"What's wrong?" Georgia asks, reading the scowl on her assistant's face.

"This is the second time you've been attacked while Buri's not around," Sarah says in a hushed tone.

"It wasn't an attack. The eleventh sign—"

"I don't buy that. Seems too convenient for Buri to always be elsewhere when this kind of thing happens."

"Why would he ask for an investigation if he's the one responsible?"

"To confuse you. To make you trust him. I'm telling you, he's involved somehow."

Georgia sighs. "It was just a coincidence, him stepping out before the cave collapsed."

"How can you be so sure?"

"I..." Georgia's gaze travels to Buri at the front desk. "I can't imagine he would do that. He looked relieved when we escaped. Let's not jump to conclusions, okay? Last thing we need right now is to get paranoid and turn on each other. We have to work together, otherwise we'll never figure this out."

"You met him, what, nine months ago? And you only spent two weeks with him in Mongolia. How can you say for certain—"

"I know him well enough."

"But not his surname," Sarah retorts before walking away in frustration.

Standing alone in the foyer, Georgia watches her go, a seed of doubt planted in her mind about Buri's true intentions.

24

THEY DECIDE to reconvene in Buri's room after a hot shower and a quick nap. When Georgia and Sarah arrive, Vijay is already there, arguing with Buri about security protocols as Mallika Sharma joins the conversation via video call. There's a trolley by the chaise covered with steaming food, and Sarah sits down, digging in with gusto. She hands Indi a couple of pieces of chapati. When she catches Buri watching her, she raises a challenging eyebrow at him as she shovels more rice into her mouth. Surprisingly, Buri says nothing.

"Georgia," Sharma greets her. "How are you feeling?"

"Better, thanks."

"That's great. I'm sorry to hear what happened. We've got a crew looking into the incident. And Vijay will bring in more men to ensure your safety."

"Not good enough." Buri tightens his fist, tension rippling off his posture. "This is the second time our team has been in danger within a week. Accident or not, we can't continue with the constant threat of angry crowds breathing down our necks. You need to stop feeding the press details of where we are and what we're doing, especially when it involves a sensitive subject, like the Koh-i-Noor."

"My stance is firm on this matter," Sharma says with a stern voice. "I stand by my principle of freedom of information."

Buri surges to his feet, his robust frame shaking with rage, his tightly coiled anger ready to snap. Georgia rushes over to grip his arm, urging him to calm down. His dog whines as she moves to his side, gazing up at him.

He looks down at Georgia's hand, then at her face. His chest expands as he takes a sharp, audible inhale.

Georgia turns to the screen and says to Sharma, "We're not asking you to lie or cover up anything. All we want is to be given some time before you release the information to the public. It's hard to control the situation if there's a mob following us everywhere we go. And they don't need to be told where our team is going so long as they're being kept up to date about our findings, right?"

Mallika Sharma leans back in her seat, considering this. "I guess we can work with that."

"Thank you," Georgia says.

Dr. Khan comes online, joining in the conference call and asking after Georgia and Sarah's well-being.

Then Sharma suggests, "Shall we talk about what you found at the Kailasa Temple and the Ajanta Caves?"

Georgia nods, and describes at length everything they uncovered at the two sites. With a twist of her lips, she concludes, "Sarah and I didn't get time to measure the cavity in the centre of the mandala to confirm its size and shape, but with the presence of the other glyphs, it seems likely that the Indus Star was once embedded there. There was also more information in the paintings around the shrine—they were too deteriorated to see with the naked eye, though. I was hoping to extract some clues with multispectral imaging, but the temple caved in before we had a chance to do that. So unfortunately, whatever information was in the murals is now lost to us."

Everyone is quiet as they ponder this. The cavern held the only substantial lead they've stumbled upon in their quest, and the excitement that bloomed in Georgia now lies crushed at the bottom of the temple's ruins.

Sharma suggests, "Perhaps we should revisit the list of jewels of interest you've compiled?"

Georgia shakes her head. "I've been thinking that our approach is wrong. What we're searching for seems more elusive than that, and it's probably unknown to modern scholars. Something about the paintings in the Ajanta Caves tells me that this gemstone is like no other. For it to be documented and kept at a Buddhist temple—a faith that emphasises the renunciation of worldly desires—suggests that its spiritual significance transcends the boundaries of any single religion or culture."

"What do you suggest, then?" Dr. Khan asks.

"I think we need to look at the nine jewels together rather than just at the missing one, along with their associated glyphs. Any additional information you can give us on the gems you found would be helpful. Has the lab identified the two remaining stones?"

Dr. Khan shakes his head. "They are still working on it."

"While we wait on that," Georgia says, "we need to revisit the Hindu scriptures and find out if there's anything else we've missed. We should also include Buddhist literature in our search. Maybe even cover the other two religions that originated in India—Jainism and Sikhism."

"That's a lot of material to go through," Sarah protests.

"Call Dhara," Buri suggests.

Georgia stares at him without agreeing, chafed by the idea.

"We need as much help as we can get," Buri continues. "Dhara is someone trustworthy who has extensive knowledge of what we are researching. She also has a network of contacts that may be useful to us."

Sharma agrees. "Sounds like a good idea."

"I'll go back to the Great Bath again, see if there's anything else I can find," Dr. Khan offers.

They conclude the call, and as Vijay and Sarah leave the room, Georgia asks Buri, "Are we training today?"

He looks up from his laptop, surprised. "Shouldn't you get some rest?"

"I'm feeling pretty restless. And I think you're right—I need to know how to protect myself."

He rises from his chair after a brief pause. "Let's go. We can use the garden."

She opens the door but comes to an abrupt stop, a startled gasp escaping her as she almost collides with the man standing outside. Pulling back, she looks up at his face, her own blanching when she recognises him.

"Agent Miller," she whispers.

25

"GEORGIA," DIA Agent Brandon Miller acknowledges her with a curt nod. Then, looking over her head at the man behind her, his solemn face breaks into a wide grin. "Doc!"

Georgia steps aside to allow the half-brothers to greet each other. Despite their relationship, they couldn't be more different physically. Buri is a head taller than Brandon, has dark hair and eyes, and an olive complexion. He definitely resembles his Mongolian mother's side. Brandon, though solidly built in his own right, has a slighter frame, fair skin, blond hair, and blue eyes.

Agent Miller wraps his arms around Buri, squeezing him with a vigour that would usually be met with laughter or reciprocation. But Buri stiffens in his embrace, and the shorter man either doesn't notice or is choosing to ignore it. Brandon crouches down, ruffling Indi's thick coat as the dog pants with joy.

"The fuck are you doing here?" Buri asks in a gruff tone.

Brandon laughs, unfazed by his sibling's reaction. He claps Buri on the back with affection. "Yeah. I missed you, too. Nice welcome, by the way, considering you haven't seen your own brother in months." He throws Georgia a glance.

Buri scowls. "You didn't answer my question."

The blond man raises his hands. "Hey, I'm just doing my job. We've been monitoring the situation since this case is right up DIA's alley. The deputy director needs to know for certain if the hurricane in Florida has anything to do with the Dwarka Prophecy. It's a shit show back home at the moment —as you've probably seen on the news—and Wall Street is in pandemonium. We also have to defuse the tension between India and Pakistan before a full-blown war breaks out. There's conflict happening along their disputed borders every day now. And with both countries in possession of nuclear warheads... well, the stakes are high—*very* high. If things aren't resolved soon, then even if the prophecies don't kill us, it'll be the nuke fallout instead. And the British... let's just say they're in hot water over this, too, and have asked us to help."

Brandon Miller rakes a hand through his short-cropped, prematurely greying hair. He throws Buri a pointed look. "But... it's a relief to see you out in the world, fighting the good fight for US of A again, bro."

Georgia tenses, searching Buri's face, only to find his features smoothed into an emotionless mask. A heavy, inescapable sense of dread makes her pulse pick up. Still, she refuses to believe that Sarah is right about him.

"So tell me," Agent Miller drawls in the Southern American accent not unlike Buri's, "what's the game plan?"

Halfway down the corridor, a door opens and Sarah pokes her head out. Spotting Buri and Agent Miller, she narrows her eyes, then marches down the hall to join them.

"Who are you?" she demands.

Brandon raises a brow. "Agent Brandon Miller from the Defence Intelligence Agency," he says. "And you are?"

Sarah's eyes widen with outrage. She glares at Buri. "You asked your brother to come?"

Georgia explains, "Agent Miller showed up himself minutes ago."

The older woman glowers at Brandon with disdain. "Why are you here?"

His arched brow lifts even higher. "The American government is as invested in this as anyone, should the prophecy prove to be true. Last I counted, eleven of the fifteen signs have manifested themselves, and they're coming to pass in quicker succession now. We're out of time, and according to the Dwarka Prophecy, the world is going to be scorched to oblivion at the end of all this. I, for one, really don't want to find out what that actually means. So I'm here to offer my assistance. And I've got resources at hand—military resources."

At this, Buri's energy shifts. It's a subtle change, but Georgia picks it up straight away.

Sarah crosses her arms over her chest. "We don't need your help. So you can take your resources and shove it up—"

"Brandon's right," Buri interrupts her. "We'll have better control over the security issues with him around. Mallika Sharma's men are okay, but not good enough."

"What's been going on?" Miller rolls his shoulders back, his entire posture transforming into his military persona.

"We don't have any proof of foul play, but there's been some incidents since we got here." Buri describes what happened in Dwarka and at the Ajanta Caves, and explains the confrontations with protesters and journalists.

Brandon frowns, grabbing a phone out of his back pocket. "I'll call my guy to look into it. We can't be solving the apocalypse problem and dealing with hostiles at the same time. In the meantime, let's sit down with Sharma's men and put a better plan in place for when we're anticipating crowds."

"Your 'guy'? You've got only *one* guy?" Sarah challenges. "I'm sure Mallika Sharma can give us ten more."

Agent Miller scoffs. "We're talking special ops here. One of us is worth over ten of Sharma's men. And that's all I can have on the ground until we've ascertained the situation. The political tension is too high right now, and we can't afford to tread on any toes."

Sarah shakes her head. "Nup. There's already too many people involved as it is. Go back to your DIA and tell them we've got it covered."

Brandon stares at the older woman at least a head shorter than him. He changes his stance and straightens his spine. "The way *I* see it? Georgia's the archaeologist leading this team. Ben is the linguistics expert. I'll take point on security, do whatever is necessary to neutralise any threat. Tell me, who are *you* and what are you doing here?"

Sarah glowers at him. "I'm Georgia's assistant. *Very* important assistant. I go where she goes. Right, Georgia?"

"Right," Georgia says on cue.

Agent Miller nods. "Okay then. I'm glad that's settled." He turns to Buri, walking further into the room. "Let's get Mallika Sharma on the line. Pretty sure she wouldn't object to our help on this." He kicks the door behind him, shutting the women out.

Sarah's eyes bulge as she flushes with rage. "What the fuck! It was already hard enough dealing with one brother. Now there are two?" She paces up and down the corridor. "This proves everything. Don't you see? They're working together."

"But Brandon turned up himself. Buri looked surprised."

Sarah throws up her hands, exasperated. "You can't be that naïve!"

Georgia sighs. "Agent Miller's got a point. We need more help. You could have been killed in the Ajanta Cave. What we're trying to do here is bigger than any of us, and whatever problems we may have with the DIA."

But Sarah's not listening. She storms back to her room, fuming, "I'm gonna talk to Mallika Sharma and shut it down now." She slams the door.

26

AGENT BRANDON MILLER leans back in his seat as he ends the conference call with Mallika Sharma, thoroughly pleased with himself. He anticipated more pushback about his inclusion on the team, especially from Ben. But so far, it has been a breeze. With Sharma on board with the plan, Brandon can already see the pieces of his operation falling into place.

Like he has told Georgia, the DIA's primary aim is to figure out what the heck is going on with the Dwarka Prophecy. At least, that is the official objective. To Brandon, though, there is an equally important reason for his presence in India: to bring his older brother back to the fold.

Ben has already strayed too far, and for too long. And it's high time somebody reminded him of his duties and where his loyalty lies.

"Harshan said you told him I was in Sydney." Ben scowls at him.

"We keep a close eye on our assets. You know this."

"And *you're* aware that I'm no longer part of the US army."

Brandon's response is a carefree shrug. "Still an asset, whether you like it or not. And this is the first time you've left that place in the middle of buttfuck nowhere—you didn't think I'd take an interest?"

Ben's face turns a shade deeper and his jaw tightens. "I changed my mind. Stay out of this. Let me handle it."

"Hey, I got no doubt in your skills, Doc. But this is coming from the top. The president wants to understand what the fuck is going on. He's worried about the economy collapsing."

Ben sneers. "The whole world might be ending, and the politicians are only thinking about one thing."

Knowing better than to argue, Agent Miller takes a breath and exhales it in a rush. "Look. I'm glad you left Mongolia. I was beginning to think that you'd locked yourself away for the rest of your life. And that would've been such a doggone shame. A tragic waste of talent. The world needs a hero like you, Doc. *America* needs you."

Ben scoffs, turning from him as if he's heard enough. He heads for the desk in the corner of the room and opens his laptop. Brandon leans back, observing his sibling as he types furiously away at the keyboard. The big man has made drastic changes to his appearance since Brandon last saw him. Gone is the long hair and the scruffy beard that the army would have disapproved of. The image is one that Agent Miller remembers well from their days in the Special Forces, and it transforms Ben from the growling Neanderthal into the intelligent, highly trained asset he once was.

Whatever the professor did, she managed to achieve what half a dozen shrinks couldn't. Brandon's relieved to see his brother finally back in action. And now that Ben's showing signs of recovery from what happened to him in Syria, Brandon has to remind his sibling that the military blood runs deep in him, and where he truly belongs.

Agent Miller is surprised that Ben has already told Georgia about their familial connection. When Brandon made the backhanded comment earlier, it was to test how much she knew, and to shake the obvious bond between the two. It was also a declaration of allegiance, a staking of his claim. Now that his brother has returned—both physically and mentally —Brandon can't bear to lose him again.

"Alright," Agent Miller says, knowing that it'll take some time for Ben to warm up to him. It has always been this way, since the first day they met. So he sticks to what his sibling will actually talk about. For now. Because Brandon understands him like no other, and he knows that Ben's greatest weakness is the fear of losing people on his watch. "Let's talk strategies. Give me a full briefing."

At last, the burly man looks up at him, and with a nod, they begin to go over their plan.

27

BURI ROLLS ONTO HIS BACK, the bed creaking beneath him, the sheets tangled around his legs. He glares at the ceiling in the darkened room, exhaling a frustrated breath. Then he glances at the clock on the bedside table, realising that he's been tossing and turning for three hours over the predicament he finds himself in.

Not for the first time, he wonders about the hold Brandon has over him. Yes, they are brothers, but they couldn't be more different, whether in the physical sense, in their divergent interests, or in the wide gap between their distinct personalities. Sometimes, Buri can't even decide if he likes the guy. But the inexplicable bond between them has been set in concrete since the day they met, and try as he might, Buri has never been able to deny his little brother anything.

Exasperation grips him, and he turns to his side, punching his pillow twice to get rid of an imaginary lump. Finding no comfort in this position, he moves onto his stomach, then again onto his back. But no matter how he contorts his body, the nagging thoughts persist. His mind races through a mental maze of memories, moments when he'd yielded to

Brandon's requests, regardless of how ridiculous they might have been.

Indi whimpers softly beside him, shifting to place her head on the centre of his chest, her fur tickling his skin. Darting out her long tongue, she laps at his chin.

"Yeah, girl, I know."

He sighs. He focuses on his respiration.

Four seconds in, four seconds out.

Four seconds in, four seconds out.

It's another ten minutes of this before sleep finally claims him. In the liminal zone between slumber and wakefulness, his mind trails back to his childhood, and the day he first set eyes on his half-sibling.

Thirty years earlier, South Carolina, USA

"Here we are," the man said as he turned the car onto a street lined with tall, verdant trees.

Buri looked around with wide eyes, taking in the colossal houses, the endless driveways, the immaculate lawns, and the strangely manicured gardens. He blinked a few times, struggling to reconcile this new reality with the one he had left behind. It seemed that everyone here had a car, and the vehicles lined the streets like a metallic herd.

But where were the horses? The sheep?

He sank lower into his seat, fear quaking through his little body.

Only days ago, he'd been on the vast plains of Mongolia, riding his mare alongside his cousins, playing ankle-bone dice and honing his horse racing skills for the annual Games. The steppe was all he knew. It was his entire universe.

Of course, his mother had taken him to the capital from time to time, so he wasn't ignorant of the modern way of life. But he'd always resented those visits to Ulaanbaatar. There were too many people, too much traffic, not enough horses, and concrete every-where. The buildings obstructed his view of the Eternal Blue Sky, and everything was filthy. The foulness made him want to wash in the river as soon as they returned home.

He preferred the serenity of living in a ger *camp with his mother and their extended family, travelling from one pasture to another every season with the herd of animals they tended. He found joy in their simple way of life.*

But then the man showed up and changed everything.

Buri would never forget the expression on his mother's face when she saw the man stepping out of his shiny black truck, a tall stranger with hair as golden as the sun and eyes as blue as the heavens. Fear was unmistakable in her features, but there was also something more complex and intangible Buri couldn't comprehend. Mounting her horse, she'd disappeared with the man for hours, and when they returned, she grabbed Buri by the shoulders and told him it was time for him to leave Mongolia, and that she wasn't coming with him.

Then she revealed something which overturned his world in the most profound and irrevocable manner. She said that the foreigner, someone who Buri had never set eyes on, was his father. She told him that the man was going to take him to America to live with his family so that he would have a proper education and a better life.

Buri had argued with his mother. He couldn't see how his life could be better than it already was. But her mind was made up. He watched with despair as she packed his belongings, which barely filled the satchel that now sat in his lap.

"I was saving this for your birthday," she'd said as she pressed a felt horse into his palm. It was brown, the same shade as his favourite horse. "You are eight now, Buri. Almost a man. Think of home whenever you hold this. Never forget your mother. Always remember who you are and where you come from."

She pulled him into a tight embrace. With a last instruction to 'be a good boy', she let him go abruptly and walked off. No amount of pleading or sobbing made her glance at him again. He was hauled

*away by the man and shoved into the truck, and Buri watched with
tears streaming down his cheeks as the ger camp became smaller and
smaller, until it disappeared altogether.*

*Throughout their voyage, there'd not been much said between
Buri and the strange man. His mother had taught him English, so
he understood what little was being communicated. Flying in the
aeroplane was a terrifying thing, and he'd vomited twice, his body
so exhausted and shocked by the experience that he'd drifted in and
out of sleep during the journey. When awake, he'd curled up and
buried his face between his knees, fighting back his tears, only to be
told to sit up straight again.*

*Now, as the man drove further into the alien neighbourhood, the
ordered rows of homes, each similar to the next, seemed to close in.
Their towering structures pressed down, blocking out the sky and
the distant horizon, suffocating his senses. When the man pulled
into the driveway of one of the biggest houses Buri had ever seen, he
clawed at his neck, wrestling with the unfamiliar constriction of his
throat.*

"Hey hey hey," the man said. "Take it easy. Breathe."

*Buri gulped. He took several deep breaths and tried to calm
himself. The man spoke to him in hushed, reassuring tones until air
came more naturally. They sat in silence, neither of them moving for
the longest time.*

*"Look," the man finally said. "I know it's all a bit much to take
in right now. But you'll settle in soon. You'll see. And you'll make
new friends in no time."*

*Buri looked out the window on his right, spotting a girl in a
pink dress standing in the neighbour's yard. She was the most beautiful vision he'd ever come across: porcelain skin, huge green eyes,
and white-golden ringlets. And she was staring straight at him.*

*With his heart racing in his chest, he conjured up a tentative
smile and raised his hand to wave at her.*

*She didn't reciprocate. Instead, she scrunched up her nose with
what can only be interpreted as disgust, and ran towards the door of
her house.*

"Never mind her, son. The Stevensons are good, patriotic people." The man paused, then sighed before murmuring to himself, "And they won't like you."

When Buri turned to him, the man said, "Now, before we go into the house..." He cleared his throat. "Well, look. Your step-mother is expecting us, but she ain't happy about it. Just stay out of her way for a while, give her some time to get used to the idea of you. Okay?"

Buri stared at him and nodded. The man adjusted the collar of Buri's polo shirt, something which had been bought for him as a last minute thought at the airport when it became clear that his tradi-tional Mongolian robe was drawing stares from those around them. The man had instructed him to get changed in the bathroom with gleaming white tiles, then stuffed Buri's best sky-blue deel in the trash can on their way out.

"Now there's also the issue with your name," the man said, his posture stiffening when a woman emerged from the door of the house.

"My name?" Buri's voice came out as a bare whisper.

"Yes. 'Buri' won't do. Not around here, in the Deep South. You need a good, Christian one... Yes. We'll call you Benjamin."

"Benjamin." Buri repeated the foreign sounds. They were as odd as everything else surrounding him.

The man smoothed Buri's hair and opened the car door. "Here goes. Follow my lead, son."

Buri opened his own door and trailed behind the man down the driveway. A tall, handsome woman with short-cropped, light brown hair stood at the open door, watching them with a stern expression. It was clear she didn't like Buri, along with everyone else he'd come across in this town, and he couldn't understand why.

"Susan," the man said, kissing her on the cheek. Her lips were pressed into a flat, thin line. "This is Benjamin." He paused before adding, "Benjamin Miller."

Her glacial stare sent a tremor up Buri's spine. He'd never seen *eyes the colour of hers before. It was a pale grey that reminded him of the sky in Mongolia during the worst months of winter.*

He looked down at his feet.

"C'mon, son," the man addressed him. "There's someone else you should meet."

Susan remained in the doorway, looking like she had no intention of letting them in. After a long, awkward silence between the two adults, she turned without a word and stepped into the house, disappearing down the corridor.

Buri followed the man and, beyond his towering figure, he noticed a little boy in the hallway who had the same blond hair and blue eyes. He was several years younger than Buri, and his smile was as radiant and magnificent as the sun. He bounced on the spot on the balls of his bare feet, bursting with palpable excitement.

"Daddy!" The kid raced over to the man, who crouched and scooped him up.

"Hey, son." His laughter was warm and infectious. He tickled the boy, who erupted in a fit of giggles. They exchanged a few words before he put the kid down and turned to Buri.

"What did you bring me?" the boy was asking, looking up at his father with open adoration. "What'd you bring me from your trip, Daddy?"

"Brandon." The man's voice became serious as he placed a hand on Buri's shoulder, who fought from recoiling at the contact. The man urged him forward. "I want you to meet Benjamin."

"Ben... Ben... ja..."

Buri knew how the boy felt as he frowned and struggled with the sounds.

"You can call him Ben."

"Ben." Brandon's face bloomed with another brilliant smile, and something shifted deep within Buri's chest.

The man bent down so he could gaze into Brandon's eyes. "Ben is your brother."

"My brother?" Brandon's eyes became round like double moons. "You brought me a brother from your trip?"

"Uh, well…"

Brandon threw his arms wide, his bellowing voice reverberating off the walls. "That's what I asked Santa for Christmas this year!" He pushed past the man and wrapped his chubby arms around Buri in a tight hug.

Astonished, Buri froze. He looked at the man, whose eyes had grown moist from watching them.

"This is the best present ever! Thanks, Dad!" Brandon was shouting at the top of his lungs. He released Buri and grabbed him by the hand. "You wanna come see my room? I'll show you all my toys! We can play soldiers! Or we can play with my trucks! And Momma got me…"

As Brandon chatted on and on, Buri found the first trace of a smile touch his own mouth. Hope unfurled its delicate petals within his chest.

Maybe—just maybe—this strange new place wouldn't be so bad after all?

28

Present day, Aurangabad, India

GEORGIA RUBS HER TIRED EYES, blinking a few times when her vision blurs. She stands and stretches, letting out a giant yawn as she looks around her room, seeing the chaotic mess of papers and books strewn across every flat surface. For hours, she has been poring over the research material, trying to unlock some kind of revelation about the gems and the Dwarka Prophecy. But so far, it has been fruitless.

The sheer volume of sacred Hindu texts is overwhelming. The Vedas, the Upanishads, the Puranas, and the Bhagavad Gita form the basis of her search, and these alone account for almost three thousand pages of content. Added to those is the *Mahabharata*, one of the two principal Sanskrit epics. As the longest poem ever penned, it comprises over 200,000 verses, an astounding length that is roughly ten times the length of Homer's *Iliad* and *Odyssey* combined.

And she hasn't even started on the Buddhist, Jain, or Sikh literature yet. Or the countless ancient treatises on gemmology.

She lets out a long exhale and starts sorting through the mess of her room. Her gaze falls on the business card Buri gave her last week, and his suggestion of asking Dhara Shah for help echoes in her mind. Curiosity overcomes her, and rather than continuing her study of the scriptures, she reads up on the journalist for the next half hour instead. What she finds online is pages upon pages of accolades, including the Pulitzer Prize that Dhara won a year ago for a fearless exposé on the concentration camps for the Muslim minority in China. Dhara's work gleams with dedication, integrity, and intelligence, and her articles are a blend of meticulous research, poignant storytelling, and an unapologetic pursuit of truth.

And all of it adds to Georgia's annoyance.

It would have been easy to dismiss the journalist outright, had her work lacked brilliance and evidence of an ethical compass. But her writings aren't just articles; they are catalysts for change. Her dedication to unearthing the untold stories, her knack for asking the right questions, and her relentless pursuit of the facts have made her a beacon in investigative journalism.

As much as it rankles, Georgia sees a kinship in their shared passion for uncovering buried facts. She also feels downright intimidated. But this quest is larger than her insecurities and her small-minded jealousies. There are nations in upheaval and lives at stake.

Her gaze drifts outside the window. The sun is rising, igniting the sky with a pink hue. How much time do they have left, now that the eleventh sign has manifested itself?

She reaches for her phone. It's not until she has dialled the number that she realises her hands are trembling.

"Dhara Shah," the familiar soft, husky voice comes through the line.

For a brief moment, Georgia panics, and she almost hangs up.

"Hello?"

"Dhara, it's Georgia Lee."

There's a short pause. "Hey," Dhara says, her surprise evident. "I'm glad you called. How's everything going over there?"

"Not great." She fiddles with her pen. "Are you still in Lima?"

"Yeah." Dhara sighs wearily. "It's pretty bad—the earthquake. And there are still aftershocks every day."

"I read some of your articles. I'm sorry about what's happening over there."

"The words hardly begin to describe it. I keep hoping that I'm going to wake up and realise it's all just a nightmare. God knows I dream about it all at night—buildings crumbling, people screaming, children crying…" Her voice cracks, and it's clear that the memories are not only vivid, but also deeply personal.

Georgia swallows the lump in her throat, at a complete loss about what to say.

"Anyway. Sorry." Dhara exhales a harsh breath. "You didn't call to listen to me whine about it. I saw on the news what happened at the Ajanta Caves. I'm so glad you and Sarah are okay."

"Thanks." Georgia drums her fingers on the desk.

"You said that things are not great… What's going on? Is there anything I can do to help?"

"Well, we're kind of stuck." Georgia lets out a nervous laugh. "And Buri suggested that I reach out to you. He said you are an expert on ancient Indian scriptures."

"Hardly an expert, but I'll assist where I can."

Georgia nods even though Dhara cannot see her. She takes a deep breath before divulging everything that has happened since she last saw the journalist.

Dhara's quiet for a long time when Georgia finishes. Then

she says, "I think you are right to consider the nine stones in Dwarka as a whole, rather than focusing on the missing one. Those glyphs… can you send them to me?"

"Sure, I'll email them to you now." She sends the file.

"Got it. Thanks." Dhara muses, "Gems are an almost obsessive theme in ancient India, appearing in plays, poetry, and literature on just about any subject. Even the Buddhist scriptures are filled with gemmological imagery, and there are similar metaphors used in Jainism, too. I don't envy what you're trying to do—it's like finding a single raindrop in an entire ocean."

There's rapid typing in the background before Dhara continues, "But I know someone who may be able to help. I'm going to put you in contact with a gemmologist in Surat. I once interviewed her—in confidence—for a story I wrote on blood diamonds."

"Thank you," Georgia says, startled at the strength of her gratitude.

"It's nothing. Hey, can I ask you something?"

Georgia's pulse picks up. "Of course."

"I know from reading your work that you are a woman of science—someone who relies on hard evidence rather than superstitious beliefs. With all that's been going on around the globe… what's your opinion on the Dwarka Prophecy?"

"Off the record?"

"Sure."

"Fortune-telling is not something I usually tolerate. Unfortunately, the subject comes up more often than I'd like in my line of work. But I have to say that I'm… concerned. Maybe more than a little spooked. The stakes are too high for us to just ignore the whole thing and pretend it'll all go away. So I'm committed to this until we can make sense of it."

Dhara murmurs her agreement. "Good luck, Georgia. Let's keep in touch. I think the more people we have working on this together, the better."

"I think so too," Georgia says, once again surprising herself. "Stay safe, okay?"

She can hear the smile in the journalist's voice when she says, "Always."

29

Surat, India

AFTER THEY TOUCH down in Surat, Georgia braces herself to face another crowd, but when the door of the private jet opens, they see only an empty runway. It seems Sharma has kept her word, and Georgia hopes this means that their journey will be smoother without the interference of the public.

The group now travels in a three-vehicle fleet, with Vijay's men in the armoured black SUVs leading and following their van. In the front row, Agent Brandon Miller sits shoulder to shoulder with his operative from the DIA, Agent Ricardo Reyes.

Reyes is a silent, imposing figure, his muscular six-foot frame filling much of the seat. Dark hazel eyes scan his surroundings, while tanned hands rest casually on the weapon concealed by his clothes. He wears a black suit, and doesn't seem to break a sweat despite the heat. His presence, combined with the armed escort, amplifies the already tense atmosphere.

All morning, Buri's mood has been like a stormy cloud,

his faithful dog a silent shadow by his side. In the rear seat, Georgia catches Sarah staring daggers at the American men in front. Her curses have been a constant backdrop since she discovered Sharma's agreement with the DIA.

Gazing out the window, Georgia takes in the sight of the sprawling port city. The second largest metropolis in the state of Gujarat, Surat is home to the world's biggest diamond cutting and polishing industry, with over ninety per cent of the world's diamonds being processed here. Nisha Mehta is the gemmologist the team is meeting today, and her family is one of the oldest in the gem trade in India.

It's a short drive to Mehta's factory. Within half an hour, they pull to a stop before an imposing gate set into white concrete fortifications over four metres high. Coiled barbed wire lining the top of the barrier glints in the bright sunlight. Three armed guards approach, one checking his register of expected visitors, and the other two scanning the bottom of the vehicles with mirrors. There are several cameras around the entrance area and further along the perimeter of the property.

After a brief exchange with Vijay in the front vehicle, the man with the list lifts his gaze to one of the surveillance CCTVs and nods, and the gate swings open in a slow revelation of the premises.

The grounds are meticulously paved, the neat gardens groomed with care. Taking up most of the modest-sized plot is a white, unassuming, two-storey construction devoid of windows. Its huge, polished mahogany door is a rich, dark contrast to the pale façade. Another uniformed guard with a weapon holstered at his hip stands to the right of the entrance.

As the convoy draws to a halt before the building, a short, middle-aged woman in long saffron tunic and matching pants steps out, approaching Georgia when she exits the van.

"You must be Professor Lee," the woman says. "I'm Nisha."

Georgia greets her with a smile and a handshake. Introductions are exchanged all round, and the security personnel are left outside. Only Georgia, Buri, and Sarah enter the building with Nisha, who gives them a quick tour.

Plush, dark carpets cushion Georgia's feet, and heavy drapes, opulent and graceful, frame the rooms, adding to the ambiance of luxury and exclusivity. The ground floor serves as a gallery that showcases priceless artisan and antique pieces, each work telling a story of history and craftsmanship. Soft lighting casts a warm glow, allowing visitors to become entranced by the collection.

A winding staircase leads to the second level, where the commercial heart of the business beats. Here, display cabinets and glass shelves glisten with gold and silver jewellery, the array of precious stones and intricate designs dazzling in the light. Patrons fill the store, discussing their purchases with the staff.

"This doesn't look like a gemstone factory at all," Georgia comments.

"Ah, all that happens right under our feet." Nisha winks.

She leads them to a tiny, two-person elevator at the end of the hallway. Georgia and Nisha go in first, descending to the basement. When the door opens, they walk into a small space confined by a metal-bar gate. Sarah and Buri join them minutes later, and Nisha unlocks the barricade by entering a code in the keypad on the wall.

"Tight security," Georgia comments.

"It's necessary, given the volume of diamonds we deal with," Nisha answers, then laughs. "I won't bore you with the details of what our employees have to go through when they enter and leave the premises every day."

She guides them down the corridor past a series of glass doorways. The fit-out is sparse and utilitarian, and more suitable for a workplace than the decor upstairs. Through one glass door, Georgia sees a woman seated at a desk, examining a diamond with a magnifying scope. Through another, she spots a man drawing up engagement ring designs on the computer.

Nisha pauses at an entrance at the end of the hall, and the group peers through the thick glazing. Beyond the threshold is a huge workshop. Dozens of men and women sit at stations lit with fluorescent desk lamps, hunched over polishing mills and tools.

"And this is where the magic happens," Nisha announces.

Sarah's eyes widen as she moves closer to the door. "They're all working on diamonds? There must be over a hundred of them," she whispers in awe.

"They don't call Surat the Diamond City for no reason," Nisha replies with evident pride in her features.

"Holy cow." Sarah gapes at the sight. Turning to Nisha, she adds, "The space down here seems bigger than the building upstairs."

Nisha smiles. "You're right. Our main operation is in the underground vault. The establishment you entered through is more of a shopfront. The setup allows us to keep a tight control on security."

Nisha moves on, guiding them down the hallway to the left. She opens another doorway by keying in the code, and they walk into a luxurious office with tasteful antique furnishings. Accent lighting illuminates artworks on elegant, timber-panelled walls. There's a huge, dark wood desk with a swivel chair across the room, and at the centre of the space is a Chesterfield couch and several armchairs around a coffee table.

They each choose a seat, and the door next to the desk opens. A young woman enters with a tray, serving them steaming chai and lotus seed popcorn.

"Thank you for taking the time to see us," Georgia begins once everyone is settled.

"The honour is mine," Nisha replies. "I've been following the stories on the Dwarka Prophecy, and I hope to be of help."

"Can you tell me what you know of our search?" Georgia asks, wondering how much Dhara has revealed to the gemmologist.

"Just what's in the news: that the world might end, and somehow, it has something to do with the Koh-i-Noor. Is this true?"

Georgia shakes her head. "The press has been misleading. This is not about the Koh-i-Noor at all."

"Oh?"

Over the next half hour, Georgia describes their findings. She shows Nisha photographs of the gems at the Great Bath in Dwarka, the associated glyphs, and the murals at the Ajanta Caves. They also go through the translated inscriptions uncovered by Dr. Khan.

Nisha says, "And you suspect that the missing stone might have triggered what's happening around the world, just like the events that ended the Indus Valley Civilisation?"

"To be honest," Georgia answers, "I don't know what to think. But we believe that all nine stones are significant and connected somehow. We are hoping you could shed some light on this, given your understanding of gems. None of my readings on the subject has come up with a helpful lead."

Nisha is quiet for a long moment. A myriad of emotions pass over her face, fear being the most dominant. She is cautious when she says, "That's because some things are never written down in India. We have a strong oral tradition here, where knowledge is transmitted verbally from generation to generation."

Georgia leans forward, knowing this to be true. "Any information you have that might be related to this would be appreciated."

Nisha cups her hands around her chai. "I'm not sure how much Dhara has told you, but my ancestors have been trading gems for longer than anyone can remember. Our business dates back to the sixteenth century, and probably further. Jewels run deep in our blood, and our reputation has been built upon this history. Of course, there are stories that have been passed down within the family—ones that I have always dismissed as bedtime fairy tales. I've kept up the tradition by sharing with my daughters the inherited lore of our kin, but they are not things we usually repeat outside of the household."

Georgia remains quiet, waiting for her to go on.

Nisha shifts in her seat. "This particular one is the story of a legendary gemstone. Not just *any* stone, but *the* stone. The one that gave birth to all others—one as primordial as time itself. It's said that Vishnu held it in His hands while the universe was being made. Known as the Original Star, it was the first light that lit up our skies, bringing life to this world. With pristine clarity and no discolorations, it's perfect in every way, and reflects all hues of the rainbow."

"So it's a diamond," Sarah guesses, "if it reflects all the colours?"

Nisha murmurs her agreement. "But Georgia is right—this has nothing to do with the Koh-i-Noor, which is no comparison for the Original Star. What we're talking about is the mother of all diamonds. According to the stories, it's the size of a small coconut."

Sarah's mouth drops open.

Nisha continues, "Ancient treatises and scriptures have all claimed that possessing such a flawless gem would grant prosperity, progeny, and power to rule over others. Once the world was created, the gods placed the Original Star in a sacred city, where life began on the subcontinent. Wherever the diamond was, it brought forth great dynasties and empires, gifting an abundance of wealth and the flourishing of cultures. The location in which it was kept was important, of course. Astrologists had to be consulted, for the nature of the stone was intertwined with the constellations. During the Golden Age of India, a king had it mounted on his greatest tribute to Vishnu."

She pauses, then exhales. "But the thing about the diamond is that it's the very embodiment of God. It brings life and enormous fortune, but it also takes it back. Every time the gem is disturbed, great calamity and destruction is left in its wake."

"Just like how the Indus Valley Civilisation fell to ruins after the stone was removed from Dwarka," Buri says.

Nisha bobs her head, adding, "And other great empires also rose and fell as the diamond was taken from place to place, before arriving back in its initial and final resting place, in the sacred city where it all began."

"Do you know where this city is?" Georgia asks, knowing it cannot be Dwarka, because the Indus Valley Civilisation never revived itself.

Nisha shakes her head and takes a sip of her tea before continuing, "That's not the extent of it, though. You have to understand the bigger picture, which is far more important. The Original Star, being a vital part of the creation of the world, holds the balance of the yugas."

"Yugas?" Sarah asks.

Nisha seems at a loss as to how to explain the concept. She looks to Georgia, who says, "In Hindu cosmology, time is eternal, and the universe undergoes an infinite series of cyclic creations and destructions known as the yuga cycle, which is divided into four main epochs: Satya Yuga, Treta Yuga, Dvapara Yuga, and Kali Yuga. The first, Satya Yuga, is known as the Golden Age—a utopia of truth and purity. As the cycle progresses, the length of each yuga decreases in time, and every stage is a gradual degradation in the physical, spiritual, and moral state of humanity. By the time Kali

Yuga comes along, the world is full of chaos, conflict, and sin."

"Let me guess: we're now in the age of Kali Yuga," Sarah mutters.

Georgia confirms this with a nod. "Some of its characteristics include unreasonable rulers who become a danger to their people, the emergence of false prophets, spiritual apathy among the masses, rampant drug and alcohol addiction, volatile weather patterns, and degradation of the environment."

"Sounds about right." Sarah says wryly. "And what happens at the end of this phase?"

Georgia frowns. "The complete dissolution of the universe, followed by its re-creation. With this, a new yuga cycle begins."

"So we're at the end of Kali Yuga?" Sarah asks with alarm. "Is that what's happening to the world right now?"

"Scriptures say that it's supposed to finish much later," Georgia replies, searching for the figure in her memory. "Some time around four hundred thousand CE."

"As I said before, though," Nisha says, "the Original Star preserves the stability of the yugas. Just like jewel bearings that ensure the accuracy and longevity of a watch, the mother of diamonds is the gem in the sacred clock of time, its vibrational energy designed to maintain the equilibrium of the divine forces of the Holy Trinity in Hinduism: creation, preservation, and destruction. The diamond's destiny is intricately linked to the fate of the world. The first relocation of the stone only marked the beginning of Kali Yuga—this, I believe, is what the Dwarka inscriptions describe."

Nisha places her elbows on her thighs as she leans forward. The gesture seems to emphasise her next point as she looks into Georgia's eyes. "The same omens would mark the end, but at a greater scale. Legend says that the Original Star, having travelled the subcontinent during the age of Kali

Yuga, has to stay in its final resting place. And it must never leave India, or the balance of nature would be disrupted, speeding up its divine clock. Then the devastation that happens afterwards would not be localised like what occurred in Dwarka."

"Which means the diamond must have been taken out of India," Sarah concludes.

"And it needs to return to the sacred city before the last sign manifests itself, or…" Nisha shakes her head.

"Or it'll be the end of everything as we know it," Buri finishes for her.

Nisha purses her lips before adding, "And Lord Kalki, the last incarnation of Vishnu, will take the gem and wield it to destroy the world, wiping the slate clean for a new cycle."

30

THE TEAM'S journey back to Surat airport is a blur as Georgia's mind races with the implications of what Nisha has revealed to them, her inner sceptic—as always—warring against the fantastical nature of the story. She doesn't even realise that Agent Miller has sat down beside her on the plane until he speaks up.

"You okay, Georgia?"

She flinches, startled by his presence. At the other end of the jet, Buri is tending to Indi, grooming her thick, fluffy coat with a brush and getting the knots out of her fur. Sarah seems lost on her phone, engrossed in whatever she is looking at. In the cockpit, Agent Ricardo Reyes and Vijay are speaking with the pilot as the group decides on its next destination.

"I'm fine," Georgia finally answers.

"Pretty crazy stuff, huh?" He runs a large hand over his close-trimmed hair. "Ben gave me the rundown on the drive over. What do you make of it all?"

"I... don't know."

"So let me get this straight. What we are looking for is a diamond. Not just *any* diamond, but one that's probably over two, three thousand carats, is completely flawless, and reflects all colours of the rainbow."

"That just means it's colourless."

"Right. And if we don't find it and put it back where it belongs, then all the disasters around the globe will escalate until the entire prophecy has unfolded... after which, the world will burn to hell."

"Or we'll have a nuclear war on our hands, with what's going on between Pakistan and India at the moment."

"Same thing." Agent Miller uses his palms to mimic a scale. "Nuclear war. Earth on fire."

Georgia takes a deep inhale and lets it out in a rush.

"And how many signs have we got before this happens, exactly?" He looks up as Sarah, Vijay, and Buri join them.

"Four," Georgia answers, grimacing at the low number. She recounts the omens from the Dwarka inscriptions, ticking them off with her fingers. "*And men feast upon the flesh of their kin... And the Earth swells with warts and tumours, which burst and rupture to create portals to hell... A disease so foul spreads its wings through our realm... And bones of the dead rise from their graves.*"

"Jesus." Sarah mutters.

The group is quiet, and Georgia can tell everyone is doing their own mental calculations of how long they have left.

"Do you believe the gemmologist?" Agent Miller looks at Georgia.

"The legend she describes has uncanny parallels with the Dwarka Prophecy," Georgia admits.

"My opinion? It's the best lead we've got," Sarah says. "We really have nothing else to go on at the moment."

"So, where to from here?" Agent Miller asks.

"We need to find the Original Star's final resting place. The sacred city that Nisha talked about." Georgia ponders on this, then says, "And we do that by tracking where the diamond went after it left Dwarka."

Agent Miller tilts his head to the side. "How?"

"Nisha said that the stone travelled from city to city, giving rise to great dynasties and empires. That's where we can start. There must be official records in the courts, of astrologists being consulted for locations to place the gem."

Sarah nods with enthusiasm at this. "Nisha also said something about the Original Star being mounted on a king's greatest tribute to Vishnu during the Golden Age of India."

"Any idea what that means?" asks Agent Miller. "When was the Golden Age?"

"It was the Gupta Empire, spanning from the fourth to the early sixth century CE," Georgia answers, noticing the glimmer of recognition in Buri's eyes. "That was when India saw incredible strides in cultural and intellectual pursuits, with groundbreaking advancements in the fields of arts, sciences, mathematics, and philosophy. It was during this time that some of the most important works of Indian literature were written—the Puranas, the Mahabharata, the Ramayana, and even the Kama Sutra. Games such as chess, snakes and ladders, and ludo were invented. And it was also under the patronage of the Gupta kings that the world's first residential university, Nalanda, was established."

Buri nods. "I've read about this too. Indian mathematicians were pioneers, introducing the world to the concept of zero and the Hindu-Arabic numeral system, the very foundation of the mathematics we use today. During the Gupta period, they set the stage for modern trigonometry and made significant contributions to algebra, calculus, and geometry. Gupta astronomers demonstrated accurate predictions of solar and lunar eclipses, and the observation of Earth's rotation on its axis."

Agent Miller looks impressed. "Okay. Any idea what the 'greatest tribute to Vishnu' could be?"

"Another temple? An idol?" Sarah hypothesises.

Georgia's gaze meets Buri's. She can tell he is thinking the same thing.

"It's the Iron Pillar in Delhi," he says, and Georgia bobs her head in agreement. "It has to be. I saw it on my last visit to India years ago."

"Delhi it is." Vijay gets up, starting towards the cockpit. "I'll let the pilot know."

Georgia turns to Buri. "Any progress on figuring out the significance of the characters at the end of the Dwarka inscriptions?"

"No, but I've been thinking more about how they're so different from the rest of the text that Harshan and I can't decipher them with the same algorithm. Maybe the glyphs are not from the same writing system."

"What could they be, then?" Agent Miller asks.

"Beats me." Buri cocks his head. "But I'll have a chat with Harshan, bounce some ideas around. And I'll update Dr. Khan at the same time about our meeting with Nisha."

He pushes to his feet and walks to the back of the jet with Indi scurrying after him.

"Why don't you help him, Sarah?" Georgia suggests.

Her assistant stares at her, not moving.

"You can also get started on the notable empires and dynasties. See if you can find court records that relate to what we're looking for."

Sarah's left eyebrow twitches. She turns to glare at Agent Miller. Then she gets up without a word and grabs her laptop, joining Buri and Indi at the rear of the cabin.

"You know…" Agent Miller's gaze is on his brother, his expression unreadable. "I think you're a good influence on him. I haven't seen him like this in years." He flashes her a rare smile.

"Buri told me that Anya Mihailovich is alive."

His smile fades. "That's what my sources in Russia have informed us, yes."

"Do you know where she is now? Or how she managed to escape the Mongolian prison?"

He shakes his head. "Sorry. I couldn't get any more information. The DIA has other priorities, ones more important than searching for Anya Mihailovich right now. But I imagine she's lying low so that her ex-associates don't catch up to her. They're not happy that she failed her mission in Mongolia, given how much they'd invested."

Georgia frowns, twisting her hands in her lap.

"I'll keep asking around for you, though, okay?" He stands and places a hand on her shoulder.

She gives him a weak nod.

31

ENSCONCED within the sleek confines of her New York office, Mallika Sharma reclines in her chair, the supple leather cradling her form. Her gaze remains fixed on the barrage of news reports spread across the wall before her. An array of screens illuminates the room, forming a gruesome mosaic narrating the endless tale of human despair from all corners of the globe.

Nations consumed by war. Governments tainted by corruption. Murders and fraud fuelled by avarice and wrath. The relentless chaos is amplified by a haunting soundtrack of disasters, both natural and man-made.

This is her canvas, her daily vista—a tableau of tumult that could harden any heart.

When Dr. Khan unearthed a prophecy foretelling imminent cataclysm last year, Mallika didn't dismiss it as mere superstition or myth. Instead, it resonated with an eerie familiarity. Haven't the scriptures of her own culture, and those of many others, pointed at the twilight of civilisation?

Now, as she watches humanity's tale unfold before her,

each news report is like a herald, a harbinger of this prophesied end.

Her thoughts circle back to Professor Lee and her team, pondering their latest discoveries. Nisha Mehta's story falls into place like a key into a lock, the jigsaw pieces aligning to reveal an undeniable truth, making sense of the jumbled narrative thus far. The team's breakthrough, however, fails to quell the unease that has gripped her since meeting with Professor Lee at the Taj.

There is no doubt that Mallika has recruited some of the brightest minds for this project—this, of course, has never been her concern. But the human element is a delicate variable, which was why she'd summoned the group to Mumbai to assess them in person.

During that meeting, she'd observed the dynamics of the team, noting the obvious undercurrents of tension. The open antagonism between Buri Myagmar and Sarah Wu was troubling. And Georgia Lee, for all her brilliance, seemed to be guarding her findings from her own crew members, who were clueless about the details of her research.

All of this, without a doubt, has been contributing to their frustratingly slow progress. And Mallika wonders what else Professor Lee might be hiding.

Her personal phone buzzes on the frosted glass surface of the desk. Seeing the caller ID, she picks up.

"Vijay," she says.

"Madam-ji," her bodyguard addresses her. In rapid-fire Hindi, he tells her, "We have the investigation results of how the cave collapsed at Ajanta."

"Yes?"

"They found traces of explosives, ma'am. It was sabotage."

She leans forward in her seat, taking a moment to process this. "Any information on possible culprits?"

"Not at this point."

"Do we know if it was related to the diving incident in Dwarka?"

"We're still looking into that, but it's difficult to say if what happened to Professor Lee was an accident or not."

Mallika taps her finger on the desk. She frowns, considering her options.

"Madam-ji?"

"Tell no one. Keep up the investigation. I want to find the people responsible."

32

Delhi, India

THE MORNING SUN beats down mercilessly from a cloudless sky, its intense heat causing the air to shimmer and distort the view. A sultry breeze offers little relief, stirring the dry grasses and kicking up loose dust which swirls around Georgia's legs. Sweat beads on her skin and she wipes her forehead, gazing up at the Iron Pillar looming over her. Rising from a stone platform to a height of 7.21 metres, it is tall and slender, surrounded by a low metal fence, and has a bell-shaped capital on the top. Having read about its construction, Georgia cannot help but feel awe for the craftsmen who built it. Buri appears to share the same sense of wonder, looking at the column in silence beside her.

"This is it?" Agent Miller says with obvious disappointment.

Georgia explains, "You have to understand that it was created in the fifth century, over a millennium before the Industrial Revolution. The entire pillar is made of wrought iron crafted through forge welding, and it weighs more than six metric tonnes. Scientists from around the world have studied it because of its astonishing resistance to corrosion despite being unprotected against the elements for centuries. It's a marvellous engineering feat and a metallurgical wonder of its time."

"But…" Agent Miller gestures to the much larger, more impressive monument behind him, which casts a shadow over the comparatively humble Iron Pillar. Ten times as high and over thirty times wider, the tower of Qutb Minar is the one of the tallest minarets in the world and a majestic sight. Its red and buff sandstone exterior is illuminated by the sun's rays, highlighting each intricate band of Islamic calligraphic script engraved into its surface. Its powerful presence renders the Iron Pillar insignificant.

"Qutb Minar was made much later by the Delhi Sultanates," Georgia explains, "a Muslim empire that ruled over most of the Indian subcontinent in the thirteenth century. In fact, they built the complex in which we are standing now."

Spread out around the Iron Pillar are the extensive ruins that make up the UNESCO World Heritage Site of the Qutb Complex. Weathered sandstone arches, domes, and minarets in various states of disrepair loom over Georgia on all sides. Columned walkways lead between towering walls and the remnants of elaborate buildings, the polished floors now overtaken by creeping vines and grasses. Intricate carvings cover the architectural masterpieces, sporting both Islamic calligraphic scripts and Hindu iconography and designs. The mosque, having been constructed from torn-down temples, is a unique blend of Islamic, Hindu, and Jain architecture.

"So what was the Iron Pillar used for?" Agent Miller asks.

"According to some scholars, it was a flagstaff," Georgia replies, staring at the capital at the top of the column, which consists of a series of round discs and bands decorated with geometric and floral motifs. At the highest point is a square abacus, something that seems to be the ideal platform for a crowning object.

She murmurs almost to herself, "Looking at it now, though... makes me think it would be the perfect seat for a large gem."

Miller raises his eyebrows, inspecting the monument with fresh appreciation. "What's it doing in the courtyard of a mosque, then? I thought you said it was commissioned by a Hindu king—his tribute to Vishnu?"

"That's because this wasn't the original location of the Iron Pillar." Sarah points to the sign beside the stone platform at its base. "Look. Says it was brought here from somewhere else."

Agent Miller frowns. "Where?"

"No one knows for sure," Georgia says. She points to the remarkably well-preserved carvings at the middle of the pole, a location too high for her to make out the writing. "The inscription attributes this to Chandragupta the Second, recording the erection of the pillar on a hill called Visnupada-giri." She looks to Buri. "Can you find any other information on there?"

Buri is already studying the text through his binoculars. "I can't read it since it's in Gupta script. But my research confirms yours. It's a eulogy for the king." He continues scanning the entire surface of the shaft.

"Are you looking for the glyphs we found at Dwarka and Ajanta Caves?" Georgia asks.

"Yes."

"Anything?"

He shakes his head, lowering the binoculars.

"What does that mean?" Agent Miller asks.

"Probably that the Original Star wasn't mounted on it," Buri hypothesises.

"Or maybe the glyphs were carved nearby at Visnupadagiri, where the pillar was originally," Georgia adds, not willing to give up on the theory.

Sarah is looking up information on her phone, saying, "Some scholars have speculated that the original location of the Iron Pillar was in Mathura. Others say it was the Udayagiri Caves."

Georgia considers this, thinking out loud as she murmurs, "Visnupadagiri means 'hill of the footprint of Vishnu'. Mathura doesn't have any hills; it is mostly plains. Also, it was a major centre of Buddhism, not Hinduism, during the Gupta period." She brings up the map on her smartphone, locating the Udayagiri Caves instead.

An idea forms in her mind as she contemplates on its location. She does a few more searches online, finding the information she's seeking.

She looks up and says to Vijay, "How quickly can we get to the Udayagiri Caves?"

33

Northern Siberia, Russia

DHARA LOOKS out the small window of the helicopter as the tundra wilderness of Siberia drifts by thousands of feet below. The sun casts its rays over miles upon miles of grassy plains, dotted with sporadic bodies of water and meandering rivers. There are no visible signs of human life in this vast expanse, and not a single tree in sight.

"Almost there. Just another thirty, forty kilometres," the pilot's voice, thick with a Russian accent, crackles in her earpiece.

Even with her headphones on, the drone of the rotor blades is deafening. Dhara pulls her coat tighter, feeling tiny and isolated in the immense vacuum of the alien landscape.

It's been an arduous few weeks. Her body aches with the punishing journeys she's made around the globe. The injuries she sustained at the Kumbh Mela incident are still bothering her, and lately, it has become a struggle to remember where she is when she wakes up in the morning. But the anxiety in her gut pushes her forward, spurring her on with her investigations.

Having witnessed the devastation of the Lima earth-quakes firsthand, Dhara cannot help but wonder if there might be some truth to the Dwarka Prophecies after all. She is determined, however, to not give in to the hysteria that has overtaken much of the coverage by the press. It seems that every time she checks her phone, there are new reports of disasters around the world, whether apparently connected to the ancient inscriptions or not.

Journalists have moved beyond simply reporting current affairs and are now scouring history for any incidents that can be recast as 'evidence' of the impending doom. Stories of extreme weather—such as the hailstorm in Canada that injured thousands earlier this year, or the unprecedented drought in Taiwan that disrupted semiconductor production eighteen months ago—are being presented as possible fulfil-ments of the prophecy. Even events from decades past, like the flash floods in China or the devastating famine in Soma-lia, are now seen through an apocalyptic lens. Strange phenomena too are highlighted: the milky white rain in Paris, the frog storms in New Zealand, and the tens of thousands of spiders descending upon the city of Melbourne from the sky.

The press claims the Dwarka Prophecies began unfolding long before Dr. Khan's discovery, publishing sensationalist stories stoking worldwide panic. Headlines scream, '*Clock Ticking on the Apocalypse: Is It Too Late To Stop the End,*' '*Doomsday Cult Stockpiles Guns, Food in Bunkers,*' '*Dwarka Prophecy Sends Markets Plunging,*' and '*Mass Suicides Reported as Dwarka Fever Takes Dark Turn*'.

A swell of frustration and anger fills Dhara as she thinks of the fear-mongering and shameless clickbait flooding the internet, symptomatic of a media landscape that cares little for truth or factual reporting. These journalists and publica-tions are solely focused on riling up their readers in the pursuit of profits, heedless of real human consequences. En-tire populations are worked into a frenzy, scrambling as basic essentials vanish from store shelves. Lifetime savings evaporate overnight as economies collapse. Tensions between India and Pakistan now reach a boiling point over the disputed diamond, with many speculating that an all-out war will soon break out between the two nations.

Dhara can't help but feel disgusted by her professional colleagues, who seem to have abandoned responsible journalism altogether. Not one article bothers to substantiate outrageous allegations or ease public anxiety.

"There it is," the pilot says, breaking her away from her thoughts.

She looks in the direction of his pointed finger and is astonished at the sight of an enormous crater. A raw, gaping wound in the earth, it is at least three hundred feet across. Its edges are raised, jutting upward like ragged stitches failing to hold closed a massive surgical laceration. Dhara peers over the lip into its depths, the inky abyss threatening to swallow her whole. Darkness as dense as crude oil conceals whatever lies stewing at the base of the brutally formed chasm.

A shockwave of disbelief and unease quakes through her. Her pulse quickens as an icy prickle raises the hairs on her neck.

"This wasn't here last week? You're sure?" she speaks into the mouthpiece of her headset.

The pilot shakes his head emphatically. "I make trips through here every week for the oil and gas fields in Yamal. The local reindeer herders said they felt tremors, saw the ground rise into a mound several metres high, and then there was a huge explosion. Some of them said there were flames and smoke."

"How deep is it?"

"Don't know. We've had some scientists out here. They abseiled down the hole but ran out of rope after thirty metres."

"And you said there are more like this?"

The pilot nods. "Three others. About fifty kilometres from here."

Dhara snaps a series of photographs with her phone. Her mind reels with unanswerable questions about what violent forces could have produced such cataclysmic damage. Though every rational fibre in her tries to dismiss illogical panic, she is left quaking with unspoken dread as one of the omens in the Dwarka Prophecies repeats itself in her head over and over again.

And the Earth swells with warts and tumours,
Which rupture and burst to create portals into hell…

34

THE TEAM SETS off for their destination in a three-van convoy as dawn unfolds on a new day. On the way, Georgia explains, "Udayagiri was another tribute Chandragupta the Second made to Vishnu. Its twenty rock-cut caves contain some of the oldest surviving Hindu temples. The location is close to traditional mining and iron forging areas in India, so it would make sense that the Iron Pillar was constructed near here. But what I like the most about this site is its association with the sun."

"The sun?" Buri asks.

She nods. "There's a common theme here. In ancient Vedic text, there is a strong link between Vishnu and the sun. Some hymns even describe him creating it—the source of all energy and light."

"The Original Star… 'the first light that lit up our skies,'" Sarah murmurs, repeating the words of Nisha, the gemmologist in Surat, as she makes the connection.

"Exactly," Georgia says. "Given the advances made in astronomy during the Gupta era, I believe that Chandragupta the Second would have chosen a specific location that was symbolic of the sun. This was meant to be his greatest tribute to Vishnu, after all."

She brings up a map of India on Buri's tablet, locating the Udayagiri Caves. Overlapping it with the lines of the Equator, the Northern and the Southern Tropics, she says, "Udayagiri is positioned slightly north of the Tropic of Cancer."

The team stare at her, unsure of the significance. "Tropic of Cancer is where the sun travels directly overhead every June solstice," she explains.

Buri raises his brows, catching onto the direction of her thoughts. "You think that the Iron Pillar was used for some kind of ritualistic purpose?"

"I think it's a strong possibility."

"Maybe it was a sun dial," Buri muses. "If the Original Star was mounted on the top of the Iron Pillar, the stone would have concentrated or directed the sun's ray in a specific way."

"Perhaps. And the idea couldn't be more apt, since Nisha said that the Original Star was the gem in the sacred clock of the universe's life cycle." Georgia smiles, exhilaration buzzing through her at the thought.

"But the caves aren't *on* the line," Sarah points out, tracing her finger over the Tropic of Cancer on the map. "They're north of it."

Buri thinks on this, then says, "That's because there's a slight wobble in the Earth's axis."

"So the position shifts over time?" Agent Miller asks.

"Yes, and back in the Gupta period, Udayagiri would have been right on the Tropic of Cancer," Georgia replies, barely able to contain her excitement as the pieces fall into place.

"Looks like we're here," Agent Reyes announces from the front passenger seat as the vehicle slows to a stop.

Heat engulfs Georgia as she steps out of the van, making her skin prickle with perspiration in an instant. Enclosed within a long line of steel fencing are horizontal layers of weathered sandstone making up a hillock. The site is much smaller than the Ajanta Caves, and Georgia is relieved to see the place is deserted. Dotted along the bluff are archways opening into rock-cut sanctuaries, revealing an ancient world of artistry and devotion.

"What are we looking for?" Sarah asks.

"Clues as to where the Iron Pillar could have been placed. And hopefully, where the Original Star went after this."

The team spreads out, wandering through the compound. Vijay's men stand guard outside the fenced enclosure, while Agent Miller and Agent Reyes climb up the hillock, searching the grounds above the caves. The rest of them concentrate on the area around the shrines.

Georgia climbs the rocky path, peering into the rustic, ancient places of worship. Some are tiny spaces with only a simple lingam on the floor: a smooth, rounded, cylindrical emblem representing the Hindu god Shiva. Others contain eroded carvings of Hindu iconography and inscriptions. Despite the shade of the few nearby trees, there's no escaping the unrelenting heat, and it serves as a stark reminder of the unforgiving climate of this region.

A few hours pass, and they find nothing.

"It's been too long since the Iron Pillar was here," Sarah comments. "That's if it was ever here at all. The grounds would have changed over the centuries."

Georgia's phone rings. She looks at the screen and picks up.

"Dr. Khan," she says.

"Georgia," Dr. Khan greets her. "The lab results are finally back for the last two gems we found at the Great Bath."

"Oh?"

"The reason they were too deteriorated for us to identify at first is because they aren't really stones. One is a pearl—a huge one, I have to say. And the other is coral."

"That's unexpected." She wonders what Nisha would say about that.

"We've been back to the dive site as well, and found faint lines etched into the bottom of the Bath. The carvings form a decorative wave pattern. It makes sense, given how important water was to the Harappans. What's peculiar though, is that the stones intersect these lines. We're not sure yet of the significance. Also, we found the glyph for the Indus Star repeated on the southern end of the Bath. This one doesn't have a stone or cavity next to it though."

Georgia's eyebrows lift at this information. "Do you have a picture of the whole layout? Can you send it to me?"

"Doing that now."

Her phone pings with his email as she updates him on their latest theories about the Iron Pillar.

"Georgia!" Sarah calls from around the corner.

She says a quick goodbye to Dr. Khan and ends the call, walking over to find her assistant. "What is it?"

They're standing in a shallow cavity, not much more than a slight overhang of the sandstone. In this humble indentation of the cliff face is the most well-known part of the Udayagiri Caves. Spread before them across the flat rock wall is an enormous bas relief panel depicting Vishnu in his man-boar avatar, rescuing the earth goddess from her time of crisis. The refined detail of the deity's celestial and animal features are all the more arresting within the cramped confines of the natural shelter.

Sarah points to the bottom of the artwork. "Look."

Georgia crouches down, reaching out to brush off the dirt obscuring the area. The sight of the nine glyphs revealed takes her breath away.

35

THE TEAM CLIMBS BACK into the van, all of them keen to escape the punishing heat of the midday sun. Georgia dials Nisha's number, and she answers on the second ring.

Putting the call on speakerphone, Georgia tells Nisha about the two remaining gems identified in Dwarka.

"Can you name all the stones that were found in the Great Bath for me, please?" Nisha says.

"Emerald, ruby, blue sapphire, yellow sapphire, cat's eye, hessonite, red coral, and pearl."

Nisha hums on the other end of the line. "That's interesting. Add diamond to the list, and we've got *Navaratna*. Have you heard of it?"

"No," Georgia admits.

"Navaratna means 'nine gems' in Sanskrit, and it has special spiritual significance in Vedic astrology," Nisha explains. "Each gemstone represents a different celestial body or god: pearl for the Moon, red coral for Mars, ruby for the Sun, emerald for Mercury, yellow sapphire for Jupiter, diamond for Venus, blue sapphire for Saturn, hessonite for the ascending lunar node, and cat's eye for the descending lunar node."

"So it's not just the Indus Star that is important. All nine gems are connected." Georgia confirms her earlier theory.

"As the legend goes, the Original Star is the one that gave birth to all others. It makes sense that it was found at the Dwarka Bath with other stones," Nisha says. "Navaratna is considered sacred across almost all cultures and faiths in Asia, and its historical origin extends so far back in time, it's impossible to trace. There are links between the Navaratna and cosmology, Hinduism, Buddhism, and Jainism. According to ancient beliefs, these gems change the energies of the planets in a person's astrological chart and bring divine powers when combined. Each gem in the collection signifies a different virtue, and topping the list is the diamond, symbolising strength and invincibility. Together, they are said to give fortune, influence, and protection from evil. For centuries, jewellers have created Navaratna pieces for royalties and deities. And even today, they're seen as symbols of wealth and status."

"We also seem to find the nine associated glyphs in every place where we think the Indus Star used to be: Dwarka, the Ajanta Cave, the Udayagiri Caves," Georgia murmurs, wondering at the significance. "Thank you for this information, Nisha. You have been so helpful."

As Georgia hangs up, an idea forms in her mind. She grabs her notebook and pen and scribbles the names of the celestial bodies next to each of the gems, as well as the corresponding glyphs found at the sites.

She turns to Buri. "I think you were right. You and Harshan couldn't decipher the remaining texts in Dwarka because they weren't from the same writing system."

His eyes brighten as he catches onto her meaning. "That's because they are symbols."

"Symbols?" Agent Miller asks.

Buri nods. "There are similar examples in our culture. Mathematical ones, like plus and minus signs. Logos and icons. Things that communicate distinct messages that are common knowledge within a specific tradition, even though together, they don't make up a language."

"So what do these represent?" Agent Miller points to the glyphs that Georgia wrote down.

Georgia says, "I believe they're astronomical signs of celestial bodies. And I have a feeling they are linked to the positions of the stones in the Great Bath."

"Their positions?" Sarah cocks her head.

Georgia brings up the email that Dr. Khan sent her earlier and opens the image depicting the etchings at the bottom of the Great Bath.

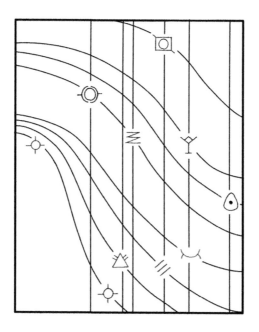

"It's a wavelike pattern," Sarah observes.

"Yes, but look at the lines," Georgia points out. "Each of

them connects to a gem. And we've seen this design before, remember?"

Sarah stares at her blankly.

Bringing out her phone and scrolling through the photographs, Georgia taps into the one she snapped right before the ceiling collapsed on them at the Ajanta Caves.

"It was incorporated into the design of the mandala above the shrine," Georgia says.

Sarah raises her brows. "That means the location of the gems is also important." She points to the southernmost point of the Great Bath. "The symbol for the Indus Star is repeated here, but this has no stone or hole beside it. Why?"

Staring at the layout of the jewels and glyphs, Georgia says, "I'm not sure."

Her phone rings, jolting her out of her reverie. She picks up the call when she sees who it is. "Dhara?"

At the mention of the journalist's name, there's a subtle yet telling shift in Buri's posture: a slight straightening of his frame, and a tension in his broad shoulders. He exchanges a glance with Agent Miller, who seems amused.

"Hey," Dhara says, but Georgia can barely make out her voice amid all the background noise. "We're running out of time."

"What do you mean? Where are you?"

"Just landed in Thailand. I was in Russia yesterday, investigating another omen—the one about the portals into hell."

Georgia frowns.

"I'm sending you photos now. I… I can't believe it." The aircraft noise fades, and the distress in Dhara's voice becomes clear. "That means we've only got three signs left."

36

GEORGIA PUTS Dhara on the speakerphone, and the journalist tells the team of her latest discovery in Siberia.

"How do you think the craters were formed?" Buri asks as he flicks through the photos.

"I have no idea. Not from explosives or meteorites. The shapes are wrong, and the holes too deep. Honestly? I've never seen anything like it in my entire career as a reporter. The sight of them made my skin crawl. I'm getting goose-bumps just thinking about it." She is quiet for a long moment, and when she speaks again, there's a profound weariness in her voice. "I'm going to interview some scientists, get their opinions on it. How are you guys doing over there? Did you speak with Nisha Mehta?"

Georgia fills her in on all of their findings so far, and emails Dhara the picture of the markings in the Great Bath.

"Huh," Dhara mutters, "They look like…"

"What?" Georgia asks.

"Well, they remind me of astrocartography lines, that's all. I think you might be onto something when you said the glyphs could be symbols of cosmic bodies." Dhara pauses, then says, "I need to take another call, but let's keep in touch about this."

As Georgia hangs up, Sarah finds an example of an astro-cartography chart on her laptop. Laid out over the map of the world is a web of colour-coded lines denoted with a myriad of symbols. Some traverse linearly from north to south, inter-secting with others crossing over continents in swooping curves. Dhara was right—the markings in Dwarka are remarkably similar to what is displayed on the screen.

"I don't know why I didn't see it before," Sarah says. "I've consulted a few astrologers over the years. All my kids have had their charts drawn up like this—each is different according to the person's exact time of birth. These lines, with their associated symbols, correspond to different planets and lunar nodes, just like the gems at the Great Bath."

"What are the charts used for?" Georgia asks, knowing that this is a field her assistant is well versed in.

"The places that fall on the lines or the intersections hold special planetary energies for the person," Sarah explains. "Based on the chart, you can choose to spend time in loca-tions that are more lucky for you."

Buri's countenance is thoughtful as he says, "When we were in Surat, Nisha said that astrologists had to be consulted as to where to place the Original Star… What if the positions of the gems in the Great Bath actually correspond to—"

"Locations on the ground," Georgia finishes for him, staring at the etchings with fresh eyes. "It's a map."

"But the lines aren't laid out over geographical locations like the astrocartography charts," Sarah points out. "How would anyone know what areas the points correspond to?"

"A map could have been painted on the floor surface. Maybe it eroded over time," Georgia theorises. "Nisha said that the Original Star must never leave India, so we know these must lie within the subcontinent."

Buri's gaze travels between the astrocartography chart

and the Dwarka engravings. "She also said that the gem was taken from place to place, before returning to its initial and final resting place, 'the city where it all began'." He looks up. "What do we know about ancient, sacred cities in India?"

"There are a lot of them," Georgia replies. "Probably hundreds. And many of them go back thousands of years."

"Let's list a few," Buri suggests.

"Well, there's the Char Dham," she starts, "which is a set of four sites: Badrinath, Dwarka, Jagannath, and Rameswaram."

"Dwarka," Buri repeats with emphasis as Sarah marks the cities on a map of India in red.

Georgia continues, "Then there's Chota Char Dham, which is another pilgrimage circuit made up of Gangotri, Yamunotri, Kedarnath, and Badrinath."

Over the next hour, they map out the towns until the subcontinent is covered with coloured dots. Not seeing a discernible pattern, Georgia returns to the gems in the Great Bath.

"This is where the Indus Star was over five thousand years ago." She points at the hole where the missing diamond used to be. "And there are ten points here, nine of them with gems and different symbols. The tenth is at the southernmost part of the bath. It's the only one without an accompanying stone. *And* it has the same glyph as the Indus Star."

"You're thinking that if it really is a map, then this southern point is the sacred city that Nisha was talking about," Buri muses, reading her thoughts once again.

"And this," she continues, pointing to the hole where the Indus Star once was, "must be Dwarka."

On the laptop, Buri overlays the etched lines of the Great Bath onto the map of India that Sarah has marked on, playing with the images in different rotations and sizes, trying to fit the points of the gems to the cities on the map.

"No, it must be a north–south alignment, just like how the

Great Bath was constructed in Dwarka," Georgia says. "The configuration can't be a coincidence. They designed it that way for a reason."

Nodding, Buri realigns the map with the dots, then plays with the sizes of the layers until he gets a match.

"Holy shit," Sarah exclaims at the resulting image.

"It's the perfect fit," says Georgia. "We've got Dwarka, the Udayagiri Caves, and the Ajanta Caves on here."

Buri puts his finger on the tenth location. "And the sacred city we are looking for is in Thiruvananthapuram."

Georgia eyes widen, and she whispers, "Of course... That must be it."

37

Chiang Rai, Thailand

DHARA SETTLES into the passenger seat as her driver, Krit, navigates the small car away from Chiang Rai Airport. She switches her phone on, and the device begins an incessant buzzing as the deluge of messages and emails come flooding in. Scanning through them, her attention is captured by a particular communication from a university lab in Delhi. Her eyebrows knit together at the information, and she dials the number at the bottom of the correspondence.

"Dr. Chowdhury," she says in Hindi when the man answers the phone. "It's Dhara Shah from the *Washington Sentinel*. I'm having trouble understanding your results. Can you please explain them to me?"

"Sure. Our lab analysed the two water samples you gave us. One was black, the other red. The black one settled and separated into a layer of very fine powder at the bottom. We found that it was activated charcoal."

"What is that?"

"It's a form of carbon that has been treated to make it

highly porous. Commonly used in water purification, gas filtration, precious metal recovery, and so on."

She scribbles on her notepad. "So it's man-made?"

"Yes."

Dhara chews the end of her pen, thinking on this. "What about the red sample?" she asks.

"Ah, that's *Haematococcus pluvialis.*"

"Meaning?"

"It's a type of freshwater algae known for its high content of astaxanthin, a strong antioxidant. It's used mostly in aqua-culture and cosmetics."

She raises her eyebrows in surprise. "So it's not blood?"

"Blood? God, no. What made you think that?"

"I guess the colour made it look like..." She stops herself before revealing too much. "Listen, I'm going to send you some more vials. Can you please analyse them as soon as you can?"

"Of course."

She hangs up, frowning down at her notebook filled with scribbled information, maps, and timelines. Frantically flipping through the pages, she searches for some clue that has eluded her. Ideas race too fast to grasp, jumbled theories and half-formed connections colliding in her head without coherence. She rubs her bleary eyes, struggling to corral the chaotic speculations zooming through her mind.

Nothing fits, and nothing makes logical sense.

Before she can formulate a rational theory, the vehicle slows, and she looks up with surprise.

"We're here already?"

"Yes, madam," Krit says.

"That was quick." Dhara glances at her watch, realising with disbelief that two hours has passed since she got in the car. Then unease settles in as she takes in her surroundings.

Cresting the steep, verdant hill is a cluster of bamboo huts surrounded by lush jungle. The dirt road narrows and splits off into three small, almost-hidden tracks. The dappled light of dusk filters through the dense canopy of trees overhead, and tall grass lines the edges of the footpaths, swaying gently in the breeze. In the valley below is a patchwork of farm fields amid palm trees.

It's so quiet, she can almost hear the hum of the mosquitoes.

Dhara asks, "Where's everyone?"

"Don't know, madam."

The only sign of life around are the *soi* dogs—ownerless, free-ranging creatures that lay motionless on the muddy trails, undisturbed by their presence.

Dhara turns to Krit. "Show me the clinic that was set up by the NGO."

They exit the car and walk further into the tribal settlement, neither of them speaking another word, as if fearful of disturbing the gloomy silence. Tall fig trees press in from all sides, their thick foliage blocking much of the light and creating a shaded, green-hued world. Birdsong trills from hidden perches high in the branches. The air is still and humid, filled with rich earthy scents of vegetation.

Navigating along the narrow pathway between homes, Dhara glimpses flashes of village life amid the encroaching rainforest. Chickens peck in dirt yards. Laundry hangs on lines strung between buildings. There is a distinct struggle between civilisation and wilderness here, where vines as thick as her wrist crawl up crumbling walls, their roots burrowing deep into every tiny fissure and crack.

They pass a sign: a simple post in the ground with scribbles made in chalk. Krit points to it, then in the direction of the arrow. "This way."

As they approach the clinic, Dhara's pulse quickens with trepidation and dread. The structure comes into view—a simple house raised on stilts, with a roof of densely woven grass thatch like the other dwellings. But outside this building, the entire town has congregated. Men and women cluster together, some weeping openly while others stand mute with pale, drawn faces. Their traditionally woven hill tribe clothing is worn and soiled.

Even from thirty feet away, Dhara catches the thick stench in the air: the ripe scent of vomit, rot, and faeces. Sounds of anguished suffering echo from within the clinic. Wracking coughs overlap with screams of torment, a chorus of misery that cuts through the eerie stillness hanging over the village.

Exchanging a glance with Krit, she sees her own grave apprehension mirrored in his eyes. Dhara steels herself, acutely aware of the immense crisis she is about to confront. From the depth of her backpack, she retrieves two N95 masks, handing one to Krit and putting another on herself.

They try speaking to some of the people gathered outside, hoping to get an idea of what has transpired. But the villagers just shake their heads, too overcome with grief and despair to respond.

When Dhara finally peers through the door of the clinic, a sense of terror overwhelms her. At first, all she sees are shadows and shifting forms lurking within the dim interior. But as her eyes adjust to the low light, the horrifying scene that emerges makes her blood run cold.

38

India

THE NEXT DAY, as they fly over the length of India towards the southwest coast, Georgia tells the team a little about Thiruvananthapuram.

Formerly known as Trivandrum, it is the capital and largest city of Kerala, and has a long and rich history dating back thousands of years. In fact, geneticists have identified the first human migration from Africa in these regions some seventy millennia ago, and the research also shows strong evidence that the rest of the world may have been populated from here.

"The 'sacred city where life began on the subcontinent.' Just like what Nisha said," Buri murmurs.

Georgia nods, smiling. "And there's something else. I spoke to Dhara before we took off. When I told her we are heading to Thiruvananthapuram, she suggested we look into the Sri Padmanabhaswamy Temple."

She brings up an image on her laptop. Showcasing an intricate fusion of Kerala and Dravidian architecture, the most distinctive aspect of the compound is its gopuram: a monumental, elaborately ornate, seven-storey entrance tower which appears golden in the photograph.

Georgia shows the team several news articles on her screen. "It's also known as 'The Golden Temple'—thought to be the richest in the world, and also one of the most secretive in India. Dhara wrote a story on it back in 2011, when hidden treasure worth over twenty billion US dollars was uncovered in its secret underground chamber. Priceless gold coins, artefacts, and jewels were found in the vault after a lawyer filed a court petition to make an inventory of the unknown treasury. He accused the Travancore royal family—who have traditionally presided over the temple as spiritual leaders and custodians of its wealth—of being negligent of their duties. The collection far exceeds some of the most famous troves unearthed, including those found in the Egyptian tombs."

"Ooh! I've read about this." Sarah's eyes light up. "The papers described it like a scene out of an Indiana Jones movie. When they opened the subterranean enclosure, all the gems sparkled like stars on a moonless night. There were idols sculpted from pure gold, encrusted with hundreds of precious stones, heavy gold belts, and chains the same height as me, solid gold thrones, ivory ornaments, thousands of gold coins scattered all over the floor, and sacks full of huge diamonds, emeralds, and rubies."

"So you think that the Indus Star was kept in there?" Buri asks Georgia.

"I'm wondering if it was stolen when the vault was opened in 2011," Georgia says. "According to the royal family, it hadn't been opened for centuries. And like Nisha said, if the diamond was smuggled out of India, then it would have triggered the end of Kali Yuga."

"Sounds like the best people to ask about this is the royal family of Travancore," Buri suggests. "They should know what was kept in the vaults."

He looks at Vijay sitting beside him, who nods and says,

"I'll speak with Madam Sharma." He walks to the front of the plane, speaking on the phone in low tones.

Agent Miller asks, "Where did all that wealth come from? And who owns it? The temple? The royal family? "

Georgia shakes her head. "It's hundreds of years of accumulated offerings from royalties and devotees. There were also ritual donations made by generations of maharajahs, who were weighed against an equivalent amount in gold which was then donated to the shrine as a tribute. And all of it belongs to Vishnu, the main deity of the temple."

At Agent Miller's bewildered expression, she explains further, "Long before British colonisation in the eighteenth century, Trivandrum had established itself as a strategic hub along prominent eastern trade networks, accruing vast riches over hundreds of years."

"I get that," Agent Miller says, rubbing a hand over his buzz cut, "but not the bit about how it all belongs to Vishnu?"

"Under Indian law, gods can own physical assets," Georgia replies. "Devout Hindus believe that the temple's deity actually resides within the compound. Believers commit to promissory offerings with the gods, and if their wishes come true, they pay up. The trove is regarded primarily from a spiritual, rather than monetary, perspective. It embodies many centuries of vows and wishes."

Agent Miller's frown deepens as if he's even more confused by her answer. Before he can ask more, though, Vijay returns, shaking his head as he says, "The royal family won't speak with us."

"Why not?" Buri asks.

Vijay shrugs.

"I'm not surprised." Georgia purses her lips. "With the media hype around the treasure and the criticism of the royal family as custodians of all that wealth, anyone would be wary of speaking to outsiders about it."

Vijay's phone rings, and he takes the call, walking away

just as the pilot announces their imminent arrival in Thiruvananthapuram. Once landed, the team alights from the jet, and Vijay's men quickly usher them to the three-vehicle convoy waiting for them.

When they're settled in the van, Vijay turns around in the front passenger seat and tells them, "Madam Sharma has secured a meeting for you with the temple executive, Arun Nair. We will take you there now."

———

ARUN NAIR'S office is just outside the gates of Sri Padmanabhaswamy Temple. As the team squeezes into the small room, a clerk appears with a tray of hot tea, serving the guests.

Introductions are exchanged all round, and Agent Miller gets straight to the point by saying, "We'd like to have a look inside your temple vault."

Nair's expression is a stony mask as he leans back in his chair. Dressed in a blue button-down shirt and a white dhoti —a traditional, long loincloth—he's a scrawny, balding man with a thick moustache above his grimly set lips. There is an intensity about him, an air of seriousness that permeates beyond his physical presence.

"What Agent Miller is trying to say," Georgia intervenes with a conciliatory smile, "is that we appreciate you taking the time to see us."

Nair turns his gaze to Georgia. "You have powerful friends," he says as a way of explanation. "I suspect there's not many who can say no to Mallika Sharma."

"Did she explain why we are here?" Georgia asks, and at the shake of Nair's head, she says, "I assume you are aware of the Dwarka Prophecy?"

"Of course. It's all over the news. And all because of the Koh-i-Noor."

"This isn't about the Koh-i-Noor," Georgia says. Seeing that the temple executive is dubious, she tells him everything the team has uncovered so far. She speaks about the stones in the Great Bath of Dwarka, the eerie prophecy in the inscriptions, the legends told by Nisha, and all the clues that have led them to Thiruvananthapuram.

She finishes by adding, "Trust me when I say that we're only here because we need to stop the rest of the prophecy by understanding what happened to the Indus Star. We are running out of time, since we've only got three signs left."

A long silence stretches out as Nair processes the information. With a look of determination, he nods at last, saying, "I will help where I can, but the vaults are off limits. What do you need to know?"

Buri says, "We believe the Indus Star may have been inside the temple's treasury, and that it was taken when the chamber was opened in 2011."

Nair frowns. "What does the stone look like?"

"We're not sure," Georgia answers. "All we know is that it's round on the bottom, so it could be a sphere. It's completely flawless, and around the size of a small coconut."

Nair shakes his head. "Something like that would have stood out. The contents were carefully catalogued—that was the point of the petition. I oversaw the entire process with the maharajah and several others appointed by the court. There were many large diamonds—some the size of my thumb—but nothing as big as what you're describing. I would've noticed if it was in there."

"How many people were present when you documented the treasury?" Buri asks.

"There were a lot of things in there," Nair replies. "It took fifteen men all day to haul everything upstairs from just one vault for inspection."

"So it's possible that the gem was whisked away before anyone noticed it?" Buri suggests.

Nair's frown deepens. "That is a serious allegation."

"You said the men took everything upstairs from *one* vault," Sarah says. "There are others?"

"There are six," Nair replies, "labelled from A to F. C and D contain ritual items used every day by the priests. E and F store the ornaments for festivals. We catalogued Vault A in 2011, but never went into Vault B."

"Why not?" Sarah asks.

"We couldn't get in because one of the locks was broken," Nair explains. "Then the royal family petitioned the Supreme Court to rule against opening it, as we believe that doing so would compromise the spiritual integrity of the temple. The Hindu community of Kerala was also outraged that our spiritual sanctuary was being violated, and some threatened protests and mass suicide if any of the items were removed. Such an abhorrent act would incite the wrath of our god. There's also the curse."

Agent Miller arches an eyebrow. "Curse?"

"Vault B remained shut because a catastrophe would be unleashed on Kerala if we opened the door. The room is guarded by cobras and celestial entities, and disturbing their peace would unleash evil upon the world. The lawyer who led the case to investigate the chambers died for no reason two weeks after Vault A was opened, which is further proof that the curse of the cobra exists. After his death, no one wanted to push the issue."

"Do you know what's in Vault B?" Agent Miller asks.

Nair twists his thin lips. "The only person who has that information is the last maharajah, who died a few years ago. When he was interviewed about it in 2011, he said that there is *something* in there, but not what everyone is talking about, and that speculations of an enormous fortune were just tall tales. He also warned that going into the room would be a sure path to ruin."

Buri throws Georgia a glance, and she can tell he is thinking the same thing.

"It sounds like the Indus Star could have been stored in Vault B," Georgia suggests.

Nair thinks on this, then shakes his head. "You said that the prophecy was triggered by the theft of the diamond, but that room hasn't been opened for centuries. Ergo, it can't have been taken from Vault B. So it was never there in the first place."

"How can you be sure that no one has accessed the chamber?" Sarah challenges.

"It's impenetrable. We couldn't open the vault when we tried in 2011, unless we forced the locks or destroyed the door. And last I checked, everything was intact."

"There could be another way in?" Georgia suggests. "I read of a rumour of passageways connecting the temple to the Arabian Sea, which is just two miles away."

"That's hearsay. In all of my years as the temple executive, I've never come across such secret tunnels. I can show you the plans. What you are searching for is not there."

"Look"—Agent Miller leans forward—"there's no point arguing over it. We can easily settle this by opening that chamber. And if the Indus Star *was* taken from there, we can gather clues as to who did it and where they went."

An eerie calm settles over Nair. He says, "After the lengths we went through to stop anyone from gaining access, what you are asking for requires nothing short of a miracle. Even myself and the high priests have been kept away. The temple has tried to keep a low profile since 2011. You can't imagine what a nightmare the publicity has been. As long as no one knew about it, the treasure was safe. But now the security protocol for entering the premises is tighter than in airports, and we need armed guards at every entrance."

"I'm guessing that you, like the priests, haven't checked that vault since 2011?" Agent Miller challenges.

At this, Nair falters. His nostrils flare. The subtle movement is the only indication of annoyance on his otherwise inscrutable, gaunt face.

"I thought so," Agent Miller says. "If that's the case, how can you be sure that the door hasn't been tampered with? All the disasters started happening over the last month. That would imply that the theft happened very recently."

When it seems like Nair is still unconvinced, Georgia says, "We respect the temple's wishes to keep the vault closed. May I suggest, though, that we go down there to make sure that there hasn't been a break-in?"

Nair's lips are pressed into a firm line as he thinks on this. After a few moments, he gives her a grudging nod. "Let me speak with the board."

39

BURI STANDS at the window of Arun Nair's office, muttering an expletive at the sight of the crowd swarming outside. Late afternoon heat hangs heavy as scores of people mill about—men bare-chested in white dhotis, colourful saree-clad women strolling down the stone-paved promenade towards the gopuram, the magnificent entrance tower of the temple. Its pale granite façade is a canvas for a vibrant spiritual panorama, intricately carved with ornate images of deities, nymphs, and demons, depicting episodes from the Puranas and Hindu epics.

The door bursts open, and in marches Arun Nair, saying, "It's done. The board gave their consent for me to take you down there." Before anyone speaks, he adds, "But only to check that the vault door is intact. We've asked the guards to close the temple early, since your presence would surely stir up a strong reaction."

Brandon pushes to his feet. "Let's move then."

"What do we do about that?" Buri points out the window. "Looks like the entire city is out there."

"Heads down, walk fast," Brandon says, exchanging a glance with Agent Reyes. "Reyes, take point with Nair. Tell

Vijay's men to flank the women. Weapons stowed. Ben and I will follow up the rear. With any luck, we'll be halfway to the gates before anyone notices us."

Nair shakes his head. "No guns inside the temple. No shoes, either."

Buri and Brandon swivel around and stare at Nair.

"You're kidding, right?" Brandon exclaims.

"Those are the rules."

"If all hell breaks loose, we need to be able to defend ourselves." Brandon's exasperation is met with a stony silence.

Georgia suggests to Nair, "What if the security team hands over their weapons once we're safe inside the gates?"

The older man appears to think on this, then gives her a begrudging nod. "Fine."

Buri's assessing gaze sweeps over the restless horde outside, which seems to be growing by the minute. He clenches his jaw as he considers the situation. Something gnaws at him in the seat of his gut. "It's too risky. We should wait. I don't like it."

"You don't like a lot of things, Doc. You know what *I* don't like? The thought of everyone out there dying when the world ends because we didn't do our job right." Brandon places a hand on Buri's shoulder. "We just have to make it to the gates. A short stroll away. Hell, I can see the armed guards from here."

Buri tightens his jaw, then looks over to give a terse nod to Agent Reyes, who starts giving instructions over the radio to Vijay in the van outside. Brandon launches into action, checking his earpiece and his weapons.

Buri's eyes fall on Georgia, who is peering out the window with her bottom lip caught between her teeth.

"I'll be right behind you," he says.

Her dark brown eyes rise to meet his, and her gaze is so

trusting, it sends guilt lancing through his chest. All the air leaves his lungs, and he struggles to draw in another breath.

He clears his throat and shakes his head, then leans over to attach Indi's leash, giving her a stern order: "Guard." Even though his voice comes out as a hoarse whisper, the German shepherd huffs, acknowledging his command.

Agent Reyes opens the door and steps outside with Nair. Vijay's team is with them in a flash and surrounds Georgia and Sarah, with Buri and Brandon sticking to their heels.

But they stand out too much as the only foreigners in the local crowd. It takes mere seconds for someone to recognise the group, and a few more for the situation to spiral out of control.

All eyes turn to them, and within moments, the mob has closed in. Questions fly thick and fast in Hindi, English, Malayalam. Angry voices demand answers about their purpose at the temple, and the long-lost Koh-i-Noor.

Indi's threatening barks are drowned out amid the commotion, and Buri keeps a tight hold on her leash, his gaze darting about the throng, his breath coming in short bursts.

They plunge into the roaring crowd, bodies jostling on all sides. When they finally make it to the steps before the gate, Buri realises Brandon is no longer beside him. He swivels around, eyes searching, and something flashes by at the edge of his vision.

"Get down!" he yells, lunging for Georgia.

A brick hurls past and scrapes the side of her head, landing on her right shoulder with a sickening crunch. She cries out, her left hand cupping her wounded ear.

Shoving through, Buri hauls her and Sarah towards the gates even as the mob surges after them.

"Reyes! Move your ass!" he yells.

Stumbling through the temple entrance, Buri whirls around to run back for his brother, only to find the man right at his heels just as the gate slams shut on the enraged swarm. Relief floods him, followed swiftly by anger.

Heart still racing, Buri turns his focus to Georgia. Her pale face is screwed up in pain, her left hand clamped over her injury. Blood seeps between her fingers, dripping down her skin and staining her white top. Buri's stomach drops at the sight of her right arm dangling unnaturally by her side, with no sign of support or movement.

"Let me see," he demands, striding towards her and swinging his rucksack to the front, unzipping it to retrieve the first aid kit.

She steps away from him, and his anger escalates.

"I'm okay," she says, panicked.

"The hell you are," he says with a growl, unable to keep the frustration from his voice as he sorts through the medical supplies. "Your shoulder looks broken."

Sarah snatches the kit out of his hand. "*I'll* help Georgia. You and Miller sort out this fucked-up security issue." She glares at them both.

Buri narrows his eyes, and it takes every ounce of self-restraint to stay put when the women walk away with Nair, who guides them to a private bathroom.

Outside, the mob continues to rally, shouting through the metal gates. His anger turns to Brandon. "What the fuck happened to you?"

"I got shoved behind." Brandon meets his challenging gaze. "Had to punch my way through."

"Some plan that was. We should have waited."

"No, we shouldn't have. Georgia's alright. Just a graze."

Except it isn't. Buri knows what he saw when that brick fragment landed on her shoulder. She'll probably have to go to the hospital.

"Someone could have been killed." He takes a step towards his brother, speaking through gritted teeth, "*Never* underestimate an angry mob in India."

"Well, no one died. We weighed the risks, and it all turned out okay." Brandon turns away, already dismissing the incident.

Fury erupts, and before he can contain it, he's grabbed a fistful of Brandon's shirt. "We're not done."

Brandon's gaze zeroes in on him, and with calculated calm, he says, "Georgia is *fine*, Doc. Isn't she, Sarah?"

The woman appears beside him, surprise flittering across her features as she witnesses their confrontation, but she locks down her expression in an instant.

With a curt nod, she says, "Yep. Just a scrape on her ear and a nasty bruise on her shoulder." She grabs Georgia's abandoned backpack on the floor and leaves without another word.

"See?" Brandon turns his gaze back to him. "You gonna let go of me now?"

Buri frowns but releases his hold, and Brandon straightens his shirt.

"Look, I get it, okay? You like her," Brandon says. "But don't let your feelings get in the way of your duty. Remember which side you're on."

"What the hell is that supposed to mean?"

"What I mean is, you need to get your priorities straight. Remember your training. Remember what Dad would say."

Buri clenches his fists. This time, he keeps them glued to his sides as Brandon saunters off.

Twenty-six years earlier, South Carolina, USA

"HEY! MONGREL!"

As the last school bell chimed, an exuberant flood of children poured out of the classrooms. Their voices filled the air with animated conversations about their holiday plans. Ben picked up his pace, kept his eyes down and his grip tight on the strap of his back-pack as he hurried out of the grounds.

"Hey! I'm talking to you."

Within moments, three boys surrounded him. Christopher, the biggest of the bunch, stood in his way with a smug smile on his pudgy face.

"Where're you off to, mutt?"

Ben averted his gaze. Instinct told him to run, but experience rooted his feet to the ground. Things would only be worse if they caught up to him. And they always hunted him down, no matter what.

At twelve, Ben was a head shorter than most in his class. Some boys had even broken their voices and begun to shave, while Ben still spoke like a girl. His dad called him a late bloomer, promising that one of these days he'd sprout up overnight and overtake everyone else, but Ben knew better.

"I asked you a question," Christopher said, circling him like prey. "Are you deaf? Or dumb?"

The others grinned, closing in on him. It was now or never. Ben made a sprint for it in the gap between the two smaller boys. His breath rushed out of him when a fist flew into his gut.

He fell face-first onto the asphalt. Grabbing his head and curling up into a ball, he braced himself for the kicks that would surely follow.

But the assault never came. He looked up with surprise at Christopher's screech of pain, quickly followed by the screams of his friends. The thud of pebbles raining down around Ben made him tuck his head in again until rapid footfalls receded into the distance.

Silence.

Then, "Yeah! Bring it!" shouted his brother's voice.

He unfurled himself just as Brandon ran up to him. "Are you okay?"

Ben nodded, an odd mixture of relief, gratitude, and shame washing over him. Rescued by his little brother. He could imagine what the kids in his class would say about this.

He pushed himself up, and pain shot through his limbs. Scrapes and cuts criss-crossed his arms and legs. The beginnings of bruises swelled on his knees, covering the skin with a mottled blue-purple hue, radiating a dull throbbing that seemed to intensify with each passing moment.

Wincing, he dusted off his shorts and looked over to Brandon, saying, "How did you—"

Brandon answered his unspoken question by holding up a sling-shot with a triumphant grin. "I'll make you one, too. You won't have to worry about those assholes anymore."

But as soon as they got home, one glance at his stepmother's face told Ben that he was in bigger trouble than he'd been in with the bullies from school. Her icy glare pierced him as he walked through the door, and an unnerving chill ran up his spine.

"You can't fight your own battles," she seethed, "so you get my son involved?"

"Momma—" Brandon started, coming to Ben's rescue as always.

She cut him off with a pointed finger. Dad walked in, stopping in his tracks as he picked up the tension in the room. Before he could speak, Susan rattled off the news—Ben started a schoolyard brawl and dragged Brandon in.

"Ben had a slingshot," Susan accused. "He damn near took out one boy's eye. Both Ben and Brandon are now suspended for a week."

"It wasn't—" Brandon started again.

"You're grounded," Susan said to him, then turned to Ben. "And you. I knew I should have sent you to military school."

Dad took a step forward. "Susan," he said in a placating tone, "let me handle this."

She gave him a hard glare. Seconds passed, then she pivoted on her heel and marched down the corridor, slamming the door on her way out.

Dad turned to them, his fists planted on either sides of his waist.

"It wasn't Ben's fault, Dad," Brandon blurted out. "Honest to God, it wasn't."

"Tell me what happened."

Brandon wrung his hands, then spilled the truth. Admitting to using the slingshot earned Brandon a lengthy scolding, but eventually Dad's stern expression melted into a smile.

He rubbed his chin. "It worked like a beauty, huh?"

Laughter broke the tension, and even Ben's own lips curled up, remembering the slingshot's efficacy and precision.

Then Dad grew serious. "I know your mother is upset, but what's important is that you two had each other's backs out there." He looked between them with obvious pride. "Family is everything. You boys stick together. Never forget you're brothers, and that your bond is stronger than any trouble that could ever come your way."

His eyes lingered on Ben's cuts and bruises. "Time I taught you to defend yourself. Go change—you've got a training session outside in five."

40

Present day, Thiruvananthapuram, India

BAREFOOT, Georgia trails behind Arun Nair as he guides her and Buri through the temple. The rest of the team have been instructed to wait by the gate, since an exception has already been made by allowing two non-Hindus to pass within the sanctified walls, a place usually exclusive to devotees alone.

Georgia purses her lips as she imagines the complaints she's going to get from her assistant later for having been told to stay behind with the 'grunts'. Earlier, it took almost twenty minutes of patient reassurance to calm the older woman down over the incident with the brick. And only half that time for Georgia's shoulder to heal from the fracture.

Passing the main shrine, she draws in a breath as she glimpses the six-metre-long reclining idol in the sanctum sanctorum. Sri Padmanabhaswamy, one of Vishnu's many incarnations, lies atop a giant five-headed serpent, with a lotus emerging from the deity's navel. According to her research, this breathtaking sculpture contains some twelve thousand fossils collected centuries ago from the sacred Gandaki River in Nepal.

Nair circles the exterior of the shrine and stops outside an unassuming metal gate, barely high enough to admit Georgia. He draws out a hefty set of keys and unlocks the door, revealing a shadowy corridor beyond.

Peering into the dim passage, he instructs them to wait, then vanishes for a few minutes before returning with an oil canister and a lamp.

The lamp illuminates their way as they enter, with Buri stooping low to avoid the ceiling. Several paces in, they encounter some saffron-coloured drapes.

Nair pulls back the curtain and reveals two diverging paths: to the left, a hallway bathed in the flickering light of flaming torches, and to the right, a wooden door secured with heavy bolts.

Pointing to the open corridor, he explains, "That leads to Vaults C to F. Vault A and B are through this door." Facing them, his tone is grave as he says, "Again, I must stress the utmost secrecy of what you are about to witness."

Georgia nods in earnest, both her and Buri murmuring their agreement. Nair's keys jangle as he works through the five complex locking mechanisms, disengaging them one by one. A rush of anticipation and excitement fills Georgia as the door groans open onto a narrow, pitch-black stairwell.

"There's no electricity down here and the light from the oil lamp won't be bright enough," he explains. "Use the lights on your phones. Be careful on the steps," he instructs.

Georgia's senses are alert as she follows him down the rock-hewn stairs, the rustle of their footsteps echoing eerily off the masonry walls. The cool, stagnant air has lain undisturbed for years. She can hear Buri's soft breathing behind her, but what little illumination comes from her phone barely penetrates the dense shadows a few steps ahead.

The bottom of the staircase opens into a large antechamber, where two massive doors stand opposite each other. Georgia sweeps her light across the one on the right, which possesses a simple, unadorned wooden face. Ancient and worn with time, its weighty brass handles and hinges are green and pitted with age. Thick spiderwebs extend in every direction, and moss festoons every nook and cranny. She wonders at the relics and treasures hidden beyond.

Nair pauses methodically before each vault, lighting a series of oil lamps that gradually illuminate their surroundings.

Georgia turns to her left, and her breath catches in her throat. In stark contrast to the simplicity of its companion, this portal is adorned with an elaborate archway of twisting stone bodies carved with chilling precision. Two cobras snake up the pillars on either side, joining at the top to sprout five heads with gemstone eyes, glistening with multiple hues of fire in the wavering light. Among the sinuous forms are terrifying demons and celestial beings glaring down at them with uncanny menace. One of them Georgia recognises as the Kanjirottu Yakshi, a female deity who waylays men with her beauty and drinks their blood.

"This is Vault B?" she asks Nair, though she already knows the answer.

He nods, looking satisfied as he says, "You see? The door is in the same condition as when I came down here last. Obviously no one has been through it for at least decades, or even centuries. I'm sorry, but you've wasted your time. Your theory of the Indus Star being in there must be false."

"Should we not open it, just to be sure?" Buri suggests.

"And what would be the point of that?" Nair frowns.

"Just because the door is intact doesn't mean the chamber hasn't been accessed," says Buri.

"That's impossible. Like I told you before, we couldn't open it in 2011. The vault is impenetrable."

The two men's voices fade into the background as Georgia ignores their argument, examining the intricate design of the entrance. Her fingers trace the stone carvings, awed by the craftsmanship. Cobwebs forming thick veils of white mesh spread across the entryway, concealing much of the iron grille gate. Intrigued by what lays beyond, she tears through the layers of webbing with her hands.

Leaning in, Georgia sweeps her light through the rusty metal bars to find even more ornate engravings of serpents and goddesses gracing the dark wood surface of the inner door.

Then she freezes.

"What is it?" Buri asks, stepping closer.

She holds up a hand, gesturing for him to be quiet, and presses her face tight against the cool iron bars, straining to detect what she noticed before.

"I hear water," Georgia says when she catches the trickling sound again. She steps aside for Buri and Nair to verify her claim.

When Buri moves away from the door, he says, "This confirms the legends. There must be a tunnel connecting the vault and the Arabian Sea, which means that there's another way to access the chamber. We have to open the door to find out what happened to the Indus Star, and look for hints of the identities of the thieves and where they went."

For the first time since their meeting, Nair's face is an open display of conflict. He's silent for a long time, then he shakes his head, saying, "On the off chance that you're right, we still won't be able to get in. No one—not even the royal family—knows how to access the vault. There are multiple doors to it. In 2011, we opened the metal gate and the wooden door that you see now. But then we came across a third, made of solid iron. We tried all the keys, but none of them engaged with the lock. The only alternative was to destroy the door. And I can tell you right now with absolute certainty that the board will never agree to that, under *any* circumstances."

"Destroying the door isn't an option," Buri agrees. "We'll

risk messing up any evidence the thieves left behind, and that's the whole point of getting in there."

"Perhaps there are other clues, or ideas you may have, about how we could unlock it?" Georgia asks. "Maybe something that was passed down over time—a legend, or a rumour?"

Nair thinks about this. He's a little hesitant when he reveals, "There's a longstanding belief that a mantra needs to be chanted in order to activate the key in the locking mechanism."

"A mantra?" Buri asks.

"It's said that during the reign of King Marthanda Varma, his highest priest sealed the portal with an incantation that harnessed the powerful, primordial forces of the universe. Only a sage of similar calibre is able to reopen the door with the same chant. But those words have been lost over time. All that remains is an inscription written in a long-forgotten language on the door itself."

"Where's the writing?" Georgia asks, already searching with her light.

Nair clears the remaining webs from the gate, then takes her phone and points at the top of the doorway. "See?"

She looks up, going completely still when she spots the engravings. Inlaid with gold and embedded within the elaborate designs of nymphs and vipers, are the series of nine glyphs she has committed to memory.

41

***

Delhi, India

Mallika Sharma rises from the sofa and drifts over to the towering windows. Beyond the glass confines of her apartment, Delhi sprawls out like a vast, undulating ocean of lights, its nocturnal pulse humming with an energy that mirrors its restless spirit.

She lets out a slow, weary exhale. From this lofty perch, it would be easy to imagine oneself atop the world, gazing down at all those myriad souls below. But her lavish apartment and breathtaking views are a hollow comfort. For all the envy her privileged life attracts, she would trade it without hesitation for what she yearns for most.

Overcome by sudden nostalgia, she swipes on the screen of her smartphone, tapping on the folder where she keeps her most treasured possession. Dozens of photographs fill the album, all capturing the same subject. She selects one, and Amrita's enchanting face fills the screen: a demure smile, warm and kind eyes, and ebony, luminous hair flowing over her shoulders. Mallika scrolls through the images, each frame unveiling a different facet of their shared life. Most are candid; some focus solely on Amrita, while others portray them both wearing carefree smiles. One snapshot shows Amrita standing on the balcony of her home, beaming as the sun sets in a blaze of orange and pink behind her. Another captures them engrossed in animated conversation at a bustling café, their eyes locked in a magnetic connection that required no words. A picture of their first day of school show-cases them, both in pigtails and dowdy uniforms, holding hands and wearing face-splitting grins. Mallika's thumb pauses over a photograph from a rain-soaked day when they were barely teenagers, their clothes clinging to their gangly forms as they danced with abandon, the sheer delight of the moment encapsulated in their shared laughter.

Gazing at that image, Mallika's mind floods with vivid memories: the joy of their friendship, the whispered promises shared in tender intimacy. She can almost hear echoes of their conversations, sense the passion in their stolen embraces, and feel the love that blossomed in the depths of their connection. These photographs embody more than mere recollections; they hold the essence of a love that is indelibly etched in her heart.

Decades of cherished memories, reduced to one private album on her phone.

Her childhood confidante. Her soulmate.

Her beloved.

Naturally, no one knew of their relationship. Both from traditional, respectable families, what was between them was not only considered inappropriate, it was something that would have brought disgrace to all those around them.

So they kept it a secret, and being young and naïve, they thought their discreet love would last a lifetime. But a year after Mallika graduated from Cambridge University and returned home to India to join her father in his business, Amrita was kidnapped.

In her panic and desperation to rescue her love, Mallika

did something stupid: she complied with every demand on the ransom note against the advice of the police and her security staff. Two million US dollars in duffel bags, deposited at a remote location on the outskirts of Delhi. Mallika went alone; she came back alone.

But the perpetrators never delivered their promise, and Mallika never heard from them again.

For days, she teetered on the edge of sanity. Every noise made her startle, each ring of the phone had her lunging in hope, and her heart pined endlessly for her beloved to walk through the door. She prayed to all the deities in her faith, vowing to be the epitome of a devout Hindu if only Amrita came back safely. But two weeks later, Amrita's body was found in a nearby slum, her clothes in tatters, her bloated, lifeless face resembling nothing of what Mallika had remembered of her.

Mallika's life crumbled to ruins. To the outside world, she was the powerhouse at the helm of a global media empire. Behind closed doors, she was unravelling, sustained only by a steady stream of alcohol and drugs. For years, she navigated her daily routine in a haze, her mind foggy, her actions mechanical, her heart heavy with guilt and grief. She turned her back on her religion, and under her father's persistent urging, she even entered an arranged marriage—a match which lasted three embarrassingly short years.

It was another decade after her acrimonious divorce before she managed to quit her vices and clawed her way back to some semblance of a life. During this time, something snapped within her, and there's been a steady procession of lovers ever since. It's all very clichéd, she knows, but these days, she has a particular weakness for tall, leggy blonds.

The women never last long. A few weeks or months at most, and the sight of her latest paramour would grip her with revulsion.

Her current lover has proven to be an exception, though.

Like the others, she's breathtakingly beautiful, but this woman possesses an unusual intellect and conversational prowess that sets her apart from Mallika's circle of friends. On several occasions, she's even managed to coax genuine laughter from Mallika—a rare feat indeed.

The object of her contemplation strides into her office now, oozing confidence and sex. Dressed in a classy, long-sleeved, black cocktail dress, her silver stilettos and matching clutch add a touch of elegance and sophistication. Her luxuriant locks, a shade of blonde that owes its hue more to a skilled stylist than genetics, cascades over one shoulder in luminous waves. A subtle, delicate scent of jasmine graces the air.

At the sight of her sultry, red-lipped smile, something stirs within the core of Mallika's being. She appreciates every detail of Anastasia's alluring appearance, artificial or not.

"Ready to go?" Anastasia asks in the Russian accent Mallika has come to adore.

Mallika nods, finding herself smiling back.

42

Thiruvananthapuram, India

"WHAT?" Nair asks with confusion when Georgia and Buri both take an audible inhale at the inscriptions above the vault door.

"We've seen these symbols before," Georgia says. "They are etched into the floor of the Great Bath in Dwarka, on the relief panel at the Udayagiri Caves, and within the mandala at the Ajanta Caves. These nine symbols only appear in locations where we believe the Indus Star has been kept."

Searching through the photo album on her phone, she shows Nair pictures of the etchings at each site.

"That means the Indus Star was once kept inside this vault," Buri urges. "You must let us access it."

Nair examines the images, his face betraying his shock. Then, releasing a deep sigh, he says, "This is not a decision I can make myself, and like I said, we don't have any means to get the door open."

Georgia says, "We would like to at least try. Will you speak to the board for us?"

The temple executive's gaze darts between Georgia and Buri. After a long silence, he gives a slight nod of his head.

They head back up the stairs, and as they walk towards to the rest of the team near the temple entrance, Sarah runs up to them.

"I've been trying to call you," she complains.

Georgia looks at her phone as it beeps with multiple messages. "I don't think there was any signal down at the vaults." She frowns at the distress on Sarah's face. "What's wrong?"

"It's the thirteenth sign." Sarah thrusts her tablet at them.

On the screen, a news anchor stands with her microphone, her calm and professional expression belying the tension in her eyes. Behind her, people are running and screaming in a fit of panic. Fire and smoke billow out of broken storefronts, and glass shards litter the street. Car alarms and sirens blare through the din of chaos, and citizens clamber over one another, trying to escape the mayhem.

"The city of Bangkok has descended into calamity. Riots have broken out in the neighbourhoods, and gangs are looting businesses and setting buildings on fire. The outbreak of this strange new virus has sent the population into panic as yet another sign from the Dwarka Prophecies manifests itself. Thai officials estimate that thousands have been infected over a number of days, though that number may be grossly under-estimated…"

The footage switches to the inside of a hospital, where countless patients lie on beds in the hallways, and even more sit slumped against the walls. Some have collapsed on the floor, and one child convulses, foam frothing at her mouth, though no one comes to her aid. The men and women are sweating and delirious, their skin pale and beaded with sweat, and many have the same patches of scab-like lesions on their bodies. Sounds of racking coughs and struggling breaths fill the air, moans of pain and anguish echo through the corridor, and as the camera zooms in on the people's faces, Georgia realises with horror that blood is oozing from their orifices.

"Oh, my God," she whispers.

Nair blanches as he takes in the story, his bony hands trembling. Walking away in a hurry, he says, "I'm going to talk to the board now."

Georgia's phone buzzes in her hand and she looks down at the screen: *Dhara*. She fumbles to connect the call.

"Hey."

"Oh thank God," Dhara says. "I've been leaving you messages. Have you seen the news?"

"I'm watching it now. What do you know about the virus?"

"There was a rumour of an illness affecting the hill tribe villages in northern Thailand. I went to investigate, and only just got back to Bangkok now. I didn't realise it's already spread to the city. It's… it's bad, Georgia. I'm at the airport waiting for the last flight to India. Governments are shutting down borders to try and contain this thing."

Georgia swallows thickly as the gruesome images play out on Sarah's tablet. Unable to watch anymore, she squeezes her eyes shut and tells Dhara what they've found at the vaults of the Sri Padmanabhaswamy Temple.

"Will you be able to get access?" Dhara asks.

"The temple executive is speaking to the board about it. Then we need to figure out how to get the door open."

"Good luck. Let me know if I can help."

"Thanks. Please be careful."

"Always."

As Georgia hangs up, Agent Miller turns to Buri, saying, "The virus changes things. Home office called a few minutes ago, giving us the full go ahead. We've offered the Indian government our official support. This means we should be able to bring more men in, get equipment and tech on the ground."

Nair returns with his phone in hand, his expression grim. "In the light of the circumstances that we now face, and the seriousness of the situation, the board and the royal family have given their consent."

"That leaves us the problem of how to open the door," Brandon says. "Can't we just blow the damn thing up?"

"Absolutely not." Nair glares at him.

Georgia asks Nair, "Perhaps there are temple archives we can search through that might give us some information?"

"The Mathilakom Records." Nair nods. "They document the daily affairs of the temple. Every donation received, every event, festival, and miracle, are all written in there."

"Let's start there," Georgia says.

43

ANYA MIHAILOVICH AMBLES around the foyer of one of the most prestigious venues in Delhi, head high as she scans the room. Her all-black attire stands out in stark contrast against the pristine white decor, and she straightens her spine, the knowledge sending pride and satisfaction rippling through her.

Vaulted ceilings soar high above, and golden light from an ornate chandelier washes over polished marble surfaces, reflecting her image. The floors sweep outward in a starburst pattern from a central mosaic, inlaid with fragments of carnelian and jade. To her left, four neat rows of plush velveteen chairs face the podium, where the auctioneer waits patiently for guests to arrive.

Anya accepts a catalogue and the flute of champagne offered by the staff, casually surveying the small gathering with a practised eye. Only a handful of patrons mill about within the venue, but each radiates affluence and influence. Silk and brocade garments in rich hues swish about elegantly manicured forms. Jewels and gold glitter at throats and wrists, and light dances at fingers adorned with gem-encrusted rings.

She recognises several influential industrialists—no surprise, given the controversial lots coming under the gavel this evening. A smattering of celebrities from the Bollywood world add frivolity, their ostentatious outfits belying keen business minds.

She commits each face to rigorous analysis and cross-referencing, assessing and filing away every minute detail.

"Anastasia. There you are." Mallika approaches her, wearing an indigo silk saree that shimmers like a moonlit lake against her creamy skin. "They're about to start."

Anya flashes her most sultry smile. She purrs, "I do so love a good auction."

And it's truly at its best when accompanied by someone with the resources to indulge her proclivities, for what is an auction without the thrill of the chase, the pulse-quickening anticipation as prices climb ever higher, the exquisite pleasure of a hard-fought victory, and the exhilaration of watching others squirm at their defeat?

Anya pulls her lover by the arm and slides into the front row with lithe grace, an unspoken claim to prominence. She has her heart set on a Chola Empire amulet tonight.

But as the auctioneer begins, her focus is already drifting, as it does so often of late. That fateful week in Mongolia nine months ago refuses to relinquish its tenacious hold on her thoughts, and the memories intrude her mind like an unwelcome houseguest.

Nine months earlier

ANYA WOKE WITH A JOLT. *The howl ripping from her throat startled her, but that shock was quickly forgotten as an intense wave of agony tore through her body. Her breath came in short, rapid bursts, and she blinked at the darkness, panicked as she realised she'd lost her sight. Reaching up to feel her face, she screamed. Her left hand was on fire, and her right arm lay uselessly against her stomach.*

Long moments passed before she could form a coherent thought. Turning her head, Anya was overcome with relief when she found a thin sliver of muted light through the base of a door.

Not blind. Thank God.

Then dismay filled her when she realised that her left eye was swollen shut, and for some ungodly reason, she could not breathe through her nose. White-hot pincers clamped around her jaw, tightening with every excruciating heartbeat.

With a grunt, she rolled to her side, her cheek pressed against the floor. She winced as she pushed herself up with her burning left hand. It was then she realised it'd been bandaged, and that her right arm was in a cast. When she struggled to her knees, she cried out as her left ankle shot sparks of agony up her leg.

Unable to see in the dark, Anya reached out with her hand, assessing the dim space with her touch. Roughly two-by-two metres, the room was barely large enough for her to stretch out in. To her horror, every inch of every surface was lined with soft padding.

She listened.

Absolute silence.

She called out, her jaw searing with pain, her voice a bare whisper. She pounded on the cushioned lining of the door.

Nothing.

She was in a soundproof cell.

No.

Rage erupted in her chest as she screamed and thumped on the door until her hand could take no more. The fatigue in her body finally took over, and she slumped against the wall, panting with exertion.

It took her a while to compose herself and to fully assess her situation.

There was no toilet and no wash basin, only an empty bucket in the far corner of the room. The indignity of her position sent her reeling. And fuming.

With her left hand, she investigated the cast over her right arm, which she now remembered had been crushed under a tree during a freakish storm in Mongolia. The repair was a rough job, and she knew for sure it would leave unearthly scars all over her limb.

The idea of disfigurement disgusted her. Mortified her. Tormented her.

She searched through her mind for recollections of how she ended up here and who was responsible. It was a long time before she recalled her last conscious moments, which came in fragmented bursts.

The Mongolian mountains. The hidden tomb of Chinggis Khan. The shock of Georgia's punch.

Her jaw and her swollen eye ached from the memory.

She had no idea how long it had been since the events at the Mongolian royal tomb. Had the Americans captured her? Or did they leave her fate to the Mongol authorities?

Worse, did they pass her off to her Russian investors?

The thought stilled Anya, causing goosebumps to break out all over her skin.

No, she finally decided. If that were the case, she would have been tortured—or dead—by now. Her associates were not people you fucked with. She'd convinced them to fork out an exorbitant amount of resources for the expedition in Mongolia, promising insane riches within Chinggis Khan's burial site, and the possibility of a military weapon so potent it would obliterate all of Russia's enemies and restore Her former glory once more.

For Anya to return with nothing would be the utmost betrayal. She would gladly take this padded, dark cell in exchange for what her investors would do to her, which would make her current state seem like a tropical beach vacation.

Her mind circled back to Mongolia, and more recollections came flooding into her mind: images of her struggling up the mountain to the ancient tomb, where she found Georgia speaking with two women dressed as Mongolian royalties. In the elderly woman's hands was a book with covers forged in gold. It was something Anya had coveted since a little girl, and her true reason for the mission: The Secret History of the Mongols.

Then Anya gasped as she recalled the incineration of the priceless tome, feeling again the scorch of flames on her hand as she'd attempted to rescue it.

The cry that escaped her lips belonged to a wounded animal— raw, primal, filled with anguish.

In that moment, all those endless nights poring over dusty archives and obscure texts came rushing back. The months and years dedicated to building her career through diligent research and forming the right influential connections. The patience and cunning required to methodically manoeuvre the intricate pieces of her puzzles into precise alignment.

All of it had facilitated, and hinged upon, obtaining that singular lost volume. She'd been so close to securing everything she'd ever striven for in her life. And then, in one unrelenting fraction of a second, she'd watched her dreams and ambitions disintegrate before her eyes.

Immortality.

Eternal youth.

Absolute power.

All gone, in an inferno of writhing orange flames.

Anya froze, every muscle rigid as a shadow fell across the narrow sliver of light spilling into the room. It was the sole illumination in the impenetrable darkness, her only link to the exterior world.

Someone was outside.

She scrambled to her knees and banged on the door again.

"Who's there? Let me out!" she croaked.

No response. With all of her energy she mustered more volume than before, yelling and pounding until her throat was raw and her fist bruised.

The shadow moved out of sight.

The idea of being trapped in this room forever finally struck with its full, terrifying force. Her throat suddenly constricted as her blood roared in her ears. Gasping for breath, she clawed at her neck, unable to get enough air into her strained lungs.

No.

Her heart pounded violently, and she struggled against the frenzied tightening of her chest. Darkness encroached on the edges of her vision.

She was having a heart attack.

Before she could yell for help, she collapsed on the floor, and the second her head thudded against the soft, padded surface, she was certain that this moment would be her last.

44

Present day, Thiruvananthapuram, India

THE NEXT MORNING, Nair leads Georgia, Sarah, and Buri into
the Kerala State Archives, a white, two-storey building with a
terracotta-tiled roof. The serenity found here is a welcome
change after another narrow escape from the raucous crowd
at the temple last night. Indi stays outside with Vijay's team
and the two DIA agents, who are on their phones arranging
more agency support—something Sarah is very unhappy
about.

As they walk into the foyer, a petite, bespectacled woman
approaches. In her early thirties, she wears a modest yellow
dress with her shiny dark hair plaited down her back. Sharp
intelligence glints within her large, kohl-lined eyes, and her
poised yet understated manner conveys a confidence beyond
her years. For a fleeting moment, recognition and shock cross
her round face upon seeing Georgia and the others. But
composure quickly returns, and she presses her palms
together, lifting her hands to her forehead in a gesture of
respectful welcome.

Nair says a few words to her in Malayalam, the official

language of Kerala. With a nod of understanding, the woman ushers them down the hallway to her office, closing the door for privacy.

"This is Seema Menon, the manager of the archives," Nair says in English once he has introduced everyone. He turns to Seema and gets straight to the point. "Professor Lee believes the Indus Star may be in one of the vaults at Sri Padmanabhaswamy Temple."

The young woman's eyes widen. "Here? In Kerala? But the Koh-i-Noor—"

Nair waves a dismissive hand. "This has nothing to do with the Koh-i-Noor. The press has been misleading. Professor Lee is here because her team wants to open the vault to find out who has taken the gem. Unfortunately, we have no idea how to unlock the door. We thought there may be some information in the Mathilakom Records that could help us. Have you come across anything of the sort?"

Seema shakes her head. "Not myself, no. We've been digitising the contents for several years now to preserve the archives, but it's a Herculean task since there are over three million documented entries. We've barely made it through half of the scrolls."

Georgia asks, "How far do the records go back?"

"Since the very beginning of the temple. But most of it was lost in a big fire. The earliest entry we have now is from the fourteenth century." Seema walks over to the door. "But I think you'll understand the scope better if I show you."

Exiting the office, Seema guides them down a long corridor. At the end, they pass five workstations outside a double door, which opens up to a cavernous warehouse. Row upon towering row of sturdy wooden shelves disappear into unfathomable, shadowy distance. As Georgia's eyes adjust to the dim light, she realises that the racks are crammed full with long bundles of scrolls stacked from floor to ceiling.

Seema explains, "The Mathilakom contains more than just

temple records; it's also a detailed history of the erstwhile Kingdom of Travancore. These traditional palm leaf manuscripts were made with dried fronds, then inscribed and rubbed over with ink. As you can imagine, the task of conserving them has been challenging, especially in the hot and humid climate of South Asia."

Sarah lets out a low whistle as she gazes up at the looming shelves. "Where do we even begin?"

Georgia chews on her lower lip. "If the vault hasn't been touched for centuries, then any clues to unlocking it would likely be in the earliest records."

Seema nods. "The good news is that we've been working chronologically, starting with the oldest manuscripts, which are deteriorating the fastest. I can show you those on the computers."

She walks out the door to the five monitors they passed earlier. On the screen is a simple interface with a search box in the centre. Everything is written in Malayalam.

"Let's look for any mention of the vaults," Georgia suggests.

Seema's slender fingers fly across the keyboard, and the computer churns for half a second before returning with a single line.

"Nothing," Seema says, frowning. "We can't ignore the possibility that the information may have been destroyed during the fire in the fourteenth century."

"Yes, but let's not dwell on that for now," Buri says. After a brief pause, he says, "They must have done major repair work after the damage. Are there any records of that?"

As Seema enters the search on the screen, Buri gestures to the workstation beside her.

"This is connected to the same network?" he asks.

Seema raises her eyebrows. "You know Malayalam?"

"Some," Buri says as he sits down at the desk.

Visibly impressed and delighted by this, Seema's about to ask more when her own screen lights up with the results. She scans the page, clicking into a few items and reading through them.

After a few minutes, she says, "Looks like the fire didn't affect the subterranean structures of the temple. None of the reconstructions mention any work underground."

"Buri may be onto something, though," Georgia says. "There must have been some restorations in the last few hundred years. We should concentrate on all the maintenance and major procurement records."

"This will take some time." Seema pushes herself up. "Let me ask my colleagues for help. And I'll also start looking through the undigitised part of the collection."

Nair gazes down at his watch. "I'm late for an important appointment, so I'll leave you here. We'll catch up afterwards, but please keep me updated on your progress," he says before leaving them.

When Seema returns with two women and a man, Sarah takes the last remaining computer, and Georgia and Buri stare at her.

"What are you doing?" Buri asks.

"Helping," Sarah answers as she wakes up the screen.

"You don't read Malayalam," he points out.

"But there's Google Translate." She pushes her keyboard towards him. "Now type in what I should look for and I'll flag things you need to go through in more detail."

Buri considers this for a beat, then nods. The five of them delve into discussing their search strategy, and for the first time since graduate school, Georgia feels left out of her own team.

As if reading her mind, Seema says with a beckoning smile, "Come. We've still got manuscripts from the seventeenth century to cover."

Taking a last look at Buri and Sarah, who are deep in

conversation, Georgia heads back through the double doors with the archive manager.

"This section isn't on the database yet." Seema makes a sweeping gesture with her hand, covering almost half of the room visible to them.

Instant overwhelm inundates Georgia. "It's going to take a lifetime to go through it all."

"Ah, but most of the work has already been done." Seema winks. "My colleagues and I have been sorting through them, marking the entries according to subject matter."

She leads Georgia down a seemingly endless aisle, deep into the looming stacks. Ahead, four women pore over bundles of parchments at a spacious worktable. Georgia's focus is captured by one unfurled across the surface, and she notes the delicate nature of its construction. Each tan-coloured palm leaf, cut neatly to the same size—about one metre long and two fingers wide—is stitched to another to make up the scroll.

Raising her eyes, Georgia's gaze roams across the never-ending shelves. Tiny bursts of colour amidst the browns and tans catch her attention. Peering closer, she realises they are tags affixed to each leaf of every manuscript, coded by hue. Her imagination runs wild, pondering the untold volumes of hidden stories, knowledge, and wisdom contained within this teeming archive.

Seema speaks in Malayalam to the women, who nod and make room at the table, each gathering more documents from the archive to sift through. Turning her attention to Georgia, the archive manager shows her how to assist with the search for particular phrases in the records, and with organising the manuscripts based on dates.

Hours go by, the sun tracing its arc across the sky outside the archive's windows. The hum of discussion and diligent work fills the room, yet despite their efforts, the day wanes without the breakthrough they hoped for. Georgia, now adept at recognizing the dates and key phrases she's been taught to look for, can't help but feel a twinge of disappointment each time Seema shakes her head at the contents of a document. The pile of reviewed manuscripts grows, but so does the stack of those yet to be examined.

One by one, the women go home for the night, until only Georgia and Seema remain at the table, unwilling to give up their search.

"Do you think the Indus Star is really in the temple vault?" Seema's sudden question jolts Georgia out of concentration.

Stretching her back, Georgia says, "Everything we've uncovered so far seems to suggest so."

"What if what you're searching for isn't there, though? Has Nair-ji told you about the curse?"

"Yes. But with this latest outbreak in Thailand—I think it's a risk worth taking, don't you?" Since the media has been inaccurate on many accounts regarding her team's search, she fills Seema in on Nisha's story of the Indus Star, and how its disappearance has triggered a premature ending of Kali Yuga.

A tiny crease appears between Seema's dark eyebrows as she contemplates the information. "But what if the Indus Star isn't really missing, and we just got the Kali Yuga dates wrong? It's not the first time someone came up with a new prediction for the end of the world. What if this yuga cycle is supposed to finish in our lifetime, and everything that's happening around the world now is meant to be?"

"Then we still need to stop it."

"Do we? Is it really our place, or even within our power, to change what is divinely planned?"

Georgia frowns. "I don't understand."

Seema drops her gaze, rubbing her right palm. "I'm sorry. You're a scientist with a Western background, and though I'm also a scholar, I consider myself—first and foremost—a

Hindu. I guess we would obviously see the world in different ways."

"How do you view it?"

Seema considers this. "Are you familiar with the Hindu creation story?"

"I've heard a few versions, each very different from the other. One says that a lotus flower grew from Vishnu's navel with Brahma sitting on it, who then created the sun, the moon, and all living beings. Another speaks of the world originating from a golden, cosmic egg that cracked open. And another, about how Brahma split himself into two, forming a male and a female."

Seema nods. "There are many accounts, because we believe our universe is not the only one ever created. According to our faith, there's an unending cycle of multi-verses that are constantly going through the process of creation, existence, and death."

Georgia leans forward in her seat, intrigued by the explanation.

"You may have heard some talk about the 33 million, or 330 million, gods in Hinduism, but essentially they all represent the Hindu Trinity: Brahma, the creator; Vishnu, the preserver; and Shiva, the destroyer. And all three are aspects of a single source: *brahman*, the highest universal principle, and the ultimate reality in the cosmos. It is the pervasive, infinite, eternal truth, and the supreme consciousness that does not change, and yet is the cause of all changes."

Tilting her head, Seema continues, "All of this is to say that impermanence is the fundamental essence of the cosmos, where transformation happens at each and every moment. And time does not progress in a straight line, but in an eternal loop. There is no beginning and no end. When you view it from this perspective, the rise and fall of civilisations becomes but one small turning of the great wheel. And destruction plays its natural role within an ongoing process of renewal and rebirth. Would you lament at the daily setting of the sun? Or despair at the turn of the seasons? In the same way, death makes way for new life to sprout once more from fertile ashes."

She pauses, and Georgia is reminded of the similarities of this cosmological view to present-day physicists' version. Some scientists now believe that the Big Bang was not the beginning, but that there was a pre-existing universe before that.

But while she marvels at the inherent wisdom of ancient cultures, the sceptic within her compels her to ask, "But isn't that a little... fatalistic? If our purpose is solely to encounter what's already predetermined, with no room for choice, what incentive is there to endeavour or achieve? Why bother having ambitions or putting in any effort?"

Seema smiles, and once again Georgia notes the shine of insight in her eyes. "You misunderstand me, Professor Lee. Of course, we're all here to live our best lives and to strive for our fullest potential. All faiths originating from India, whether Hindu, Buddhist, Jain, or Sikh, share the highest goal of moksha—the realisation of one's true self, and liberation from our endless rebirth into a realm that is full of suffering. Time and again, our souls return to this world, repeating histories and lessons until we understand life's deeper truths. Like this, we are to learn from our mistakes, purify our spirit, and ultimately return to brahman—the supreme reality from which we all came. At the same time, we are also to live in accordance with dharma and karma—to accept the conditions that we are dealt with and to make the best of it. Control is an illusion. There is wisdom in knowing when to let go."

Seema's words resonate profoundly with Georgia, and even though it wars against her tenacious and driven nature, she finds herself asking, "How do you know when to strive and when to let go?"

"I guess that's the eternal human struggle," Seema says

with a smile, which fades as she continues. "But when it comes to something as momentous as this—the natural life cycle of the universe—we must come to terms with the truth of our insignificant, mortal existence against the grandeur of time itself. As much as change and loss are troubling to our limited perspective, from the vantage of eternal dharma, they represent nature maintaining her equilibrium. Wouldn't you agree?"

Seema's calm acceptance of the world's end unsettles Georgia's very foundations. Yet within the young woman's words is an elevated consciousness that belies her years, and Georgia glimpses a depth rarely found in one so young. In that strange moment, she is struck by a surreal sensation: it is as though her friend Charlie is present in the room, his thoughtful spirit echoing Seema's insights.

Seizing the opportunity, Georgia steers their discussion to ask something else that has been ever-present in her mind.

"But what if there *is* a way to carry on, to stop the cycle of reincarnation? What if we could keep going in this life rather than moving on to the next, and remember each lesson we must learn? Isn't that a more effective way of evolving, rather than spending years fumbling through life, figuring out what we're here to achieve?"

She wishes she could voice the real question that has been nagging at her since she saw the news about the virus in Thailand: should she share her immortality to prevent lives from being lost, especially now that the world seems to be coming to an end?

Taking a long inhale, Georgia continues, "I guess what I'm trying to ask is this: is death really necessary? Must we have an ending? If our scientists found a way to prolong life indefinitely, would that not be a more efficient way of achieving moksha?"

"Ah, well, that may be the case for another level of existence," Seema says.

"How do you mean?"

"The yugas, as you know, exist in four stages. We're currently in the last: Kali Yuga. People of this time are characterised by negativity, doubts, despair, and violence. And for us, death is almost like a reset button, a break from the toils of this existence. To live too long without that interlude... well, it requires a strong soul, one that is rare in the present world."

Georgia is reminded of something similar Charlie once said to her, and the reason he thought the world was not ready for immortality. His mentor, Naaya, had first discovered the elixir of life and shared it with her people. Instead of bringing happiness and freedom from misery, eternal life had resulted in madness and self-destruction in her tribe.

"Do you think that humanity will ever evolve to the stage of being able to tolerate a longer life?" Georgia asks.

"Oh yes," Seema says with bright eyes. "However slow we appear to be evolving, it's our destiny and the greater fate of the universe to return to brahman, the ultimate truth and bliss. That day will come, and it is up to every single one of us to persevere so that we are ready."

Georgia takes momentary comfort in the strength of Seema's assurance. Cocking her head to the side, she smiles with wonder. "How do you know all this?"

Seema gestures to the sea of manuscripts around her. "In my culture, it's not unheard of for kings and princes to renounce their lives of opulence and luxury in pursuit of spiritual answers. For millennia, India has pondered these questions. But the same ideas can also be gleaned from nature if we pay enough attention. It's in the whisper of the wind through autumn leaves, the surge of life after the monsoon, and the shifting phases of the moon. All you have to do is to stand still and listen to what the world is telling you."

"And what's it saying?"

"That in the midst of life, suffering, and death, there is one thing that is constant. One truth to hold onto in the flux of change."

"What's that?"

"Love." Seema smiles.

The one-word answer is uttered with such conviction, the force of it takes Georgia's breath away. She opens her mouth to ask more, only to be interrupted by Buri striding down the corridor.

"There you are," he says. "Come, quick. I think we've found something."

45

As GEORGIA, Buri, and Seema arrive back at the workstations, Sarah stands with visible excitement, gesturing for the archive manager to take her spot.

Sitting down, Seema reads through the text on the screen and tells Georgia, "This is from the early fifteenth century. They had extensive flooding from the monsoon rain that year. But even though it happened in July, they had to wait until the September equinox to carry out 'underground repairs.'"

"Why so long? And why the equinox?" Georgia wonders aloud.

"Those were our questions, too," Buri says. "So we searched for other mentions of that. Two entries came up." He points to his screen, and moves aside to allow Seema to read the file.

Scanning through the record, Seema says, "This is earlier, from the fourteenth century. The temple commissioned a new door, but there's no mention of where it's for. All it says is that they had to wait for the March equinox to install it, so they had to find a temporary location for storage."

Buri leans over to bring up another log. "Here's the one on the day of the equinox."

Seema's forehead creases, and she pushes her glasses up on the bridge of her nose. "It just says that they opened the door to replace the old one before sealing it shut again."

"It doesn't say where?" Georgia asks.

"No. And that's unusual. The Mathilakom is a meticulous record of everything that went on. Each minute detail of daily affairs was written down, no matter how trivial."

"Which means the information was deliberately left out for a reason. The specific timing is curious. Does the equinox hold special meaning in Hinduism? Is it regarded as an auspicious day?"

"Not that I can think of." Seema looks it up on her phone. "The equinox happens twice a year, on March 20th, and around September 23rd. Holi—also known as the Festival of Colours—is the closest, but there's usually a few days' or weeks' gap. The Hindu calendar follows the lunar one, not the solar, you see…" She falls quiet, her eyebrows pinching together.

Then her entire body stills.

"What is it?" Georgia asks.

"I just remembered…" Seema's frown deepens. "There *is* something special that happens at the Sri Padmanabhaswamy Temple during this time. But it's not to do with any of the religious ceremonies."

"What?" Sarah and Buri say in unison.

Clicking out of the database, Seema opens a browser and types a few words into the search engine. She selects one of the several videos that pop up. It's of the gopuram, the seven-tier entrance tower adorned with ornate stucco reliefs and sculptures. There are a pair of openings at the centre of each level on opposite sides, so that one may see through the structure when facing it head-on.

"The gopuram is a later addition, completed in the eighteenth century during the reign of King Marthanda Varma,"

Seema says. "It was built perfectly aligned in the east–west direction."

"Which means," Sarah murmurs, already understanding the implication of the design, "the sun would pass directly through its windows during the equinox."

Georgia's breath catches in her throat as she watches the phenomenon play out on the screen. On the right side of the video, a timer is ticking away as the sun sets in the fast-forwarded footage. The blazing orange orb begins its descent, disappearing behind the top of the gopuram. After five sped up minutes, it appears through the top opening, spilling its golden light through the aperture before disappearing once more. Like this, each successive opening is lit up in roughly five-minute intervals until the sky dims to a deep purple hue.

"Holy shit," Sarah whispers. "That's the stuff of movies."

Georgia paces the corridor, thinking out loud as she rambles on, "There's a pattern here. We believe that the Indus Star was once atop the Iron Pillar, the greatest tribute to Vishnu by Chandragupta the Second. And the Iron Pillar was erected at the Udayagiri Caves, where the sun travelled directly overhead every June solstice. Sri Padmanabhaswamy is also an avatar of Vishnu. In the Vedic texts, Vishnu is associated with the light and the sun, and many consider the sun god, Surya, to be an incarnation of Vishnu. This display during equinox, an engineering feat, would have taken extensive planning and resources. It's obviously a tribute to the deity. And the fact that they only ever accessed the vault during the equinox means…"

She trails off as she slows to a stop, and Buri completes the sentence for her: "It means that the gopuram is the key to opening the door."

46

Mumbai, India

DHARA CLICKS into the video conference software on her laptop and waits for the other party to join the online meeting. She leans back in her chair, exhaling a long sigh.

Having landed in an eerily empty Mumbai airport an hour ago, she has endured exhaustive health screenings, rushed through immigration, retrieved her baggage, and sat down on the nearest seat in the arrival hall to make her pre-arranged call. It's a meeting that has taken her days to set up, for the subject of her interview is some kind of recluse, and it was no simple task tracking him down. She had to beg one of her colleagues to drive all the way to the author's house in the middle of the Australian desert to assist with the call.

Her screen lights up with a series of alerts and emails, and she scrolls through them to read the latest news: Pakistan has been hit by freakish weather, causing extensive flooding throughout the country. Thousands are injured, missing, or killed. Even more are displaced.

Meanwhile, the press continues to churn the global frenzy to a feverish pitch by exhuming stories from years ago. The latest is almost a decade old, of an ancient hunger stone revealed at the banks of a dried-up river in Central Europe—a famine memorial marking the water levels during historic droughts. Carvings warn: "Woe to those who find me bared to view."

Fatigue dragging at frayed nerves, Dhara shuts down the windows one by one. She takes her first look around since landing, and a chill seizes her. Never in her life would she have imagined being the only soul in the once bustling, vast terminal of Mumbai. Apocalyptic scenes from films flash unbidden to her mind, and she shakes her head to banish them, hoping that beyond the glass doors, some remnant of normalcy remains.

The screen blinks, and relief floods her at the sight of two faces popping up, as if she is somehow no longer alone. Darren Lang smiles at her, his boyish features pixelated from the poor connection.

"Ah. Here we go," Darren says in his soft accent. "Got ya now."

"Thanks for setting us up today," Dhara says.

"You owe me one." He flashes her a dimpled smile. "Hell of a drive. It took some time getting the satellite phone to work, too, since there's no reception out here... Let's just say I'm expecting that beer when we catch up. That's if... we survive the apocalypse." Darren grimaces, and an awkward silence settles over them.

He clears his throat. "Anyway, wouldn't want the boss to complain about me hiking up the satellite phone bill with idle chitchat. This," he says, gesturing to the man to his right, "is the person you should be speaking with."

"Dr. Scott," Dhara says in greeting.

Possessing a shock of stark white hair, a snowy beard, and blue eyes as piercing as the summer sky in Australia, Dr. Scott is a burly man in his sixties. Wrinkles line his ruddy skin, tanned and wind-worn from years of exposure.

"Call me Mike," he intones in a deep, sonorous voice, giving her a nod without a smile.

"Thank you for speaking with us today," she says. "Your publisher has probably told you I wanted to interview you about your book, *Strange Nature*. It's a fascinating read. I saw somewhere that you have a PhD in Environmental Science. Is that correct?"

"Yep." He straightens in his chair. "Did my dissertation on the effects of climate change on the Great Barrier Reef. The book you mentioned was more for fun, a break from the scientific papers I was writing. I'm surprised you know it. It was published over five years ago, and tanked within weeks. Barely sold five hundred copies. Why are they only setting up an interview now? Seems a little late for that."

"Oh, this isn't a promotional interview. I'm interested in the chapters where you describe odd objects falling out of the sky. I'm sure you're aware of the events around the world right now?"

"Some. I don't keep up with the news much out here. There's a reason for that." He scratches his scruffy beard, but doesn't elaborate.

"In the past month, there have been... troubling things happening, some of which you've described in your book."

"What sorts of things?"

"Frozen sea creatures dropping out of the sky. Rivers running red. Black rain. And others."

"Oh, yeah." His head bobs up and down. "Happens more often than you think."

"How often, would you say?"

"I don't think there's been any proper studies done on that."

"If you were to guess?"

He gives a casual shrug. "On average, maybe every few months? Hard to tell, really. Usually it's somewhere remote. But when it's at a more populous place, people'll freak out, and there'll be talk of the apocalypse. Most of the time, though, there's a perfectly scientific explanation for it."

"Like what?"

"Raining fish is probably from a tornado out in the ocean, sucking up a whole lot of water and whatever's in it, then dumping it elsewhere on land. There are also records of snakes, golf balls, toads, and even shredded meat dropping out of the sky—all with similar causes. Rivers can turn red when nutrients are too high and there's an algal bloom. Of course, people mistake it for blood and scream for God and forgiveness."

"*Red* algae?" Darren seems puzzled.

"*Haematococcus pluvialis*," Mike confirms. "It's a freshwater species."

Dhara nods. "I got a lab to test water samples from the Ganges, the Yangtze, the Nile, and the Tigris–Euphrates. All tested positive for the algae you're speaking of."

"What do you mean, *all* of them?" Mike's bushy brows knit together.

Dhara pauses, momentarily stunned by the man's ignorance of the world's events. She explains, "Last month, these rivers became red—"

"Wait," Mike interrupts. "All at the same time?"

"Yes. And it happened during Kumbh Mela in India. That's the largest religious gathering on Earth, where millions of Hindus make the pilgrimage to the Ganges to cleanse themselves of their sins. At the same time, black rain started falling from the sky." Dhara takes a stuttering breath, the memory of the event still fresh on her mind. Gesturing to her arm in the sling, she gives him a sardonic smile. "I was there. You can imagine the carnage when everyone thought there was blood in the river."

She rubs at the lingering pain in her lower chest, where she's still nursing two cracked ribs. "Since then, there've been more freak occurrences around the world. Dust storms, devastating floods, massive fires, giant craters erupting in Siberia."

"Craters?" Mike's eyebrows rise.

Dhara nods, then describes what she witnessed in Russia.

"That *is* strange."

"This coincides with a major archaeological discovery in India: a prophecy for the end of the world. Everything in the list of omens is being manifested. It's creating panic across the globe. The media hasn't helped, and I'm trying to undo that by finding the truth of what's going on. I'm hoping that you could somehow put a logical spin on the phenomena."

Mike's lips press together. "I'll do my best. Send me all the information you have." He pauses, then adds, "But for it all to happen over a short period seems highly unusual. I'm an atheist, but listening to your descriptions just now is giving me the creeps."

"Is it possible... that it's all a coincidence?"

"Maybe. A very big one, though, if it is."

Her phone vibrates beside her, and she glances at the caller ID.

Blocked.

She says, "I'll email everything to you through Darren."

Thanking the men, she exits the teleconference software, reaching for her phone just as it stops buzzing.

Then, almost immediately, it starts again.

Swiping at the screen, she says, "Dhara Shah."

There's a long silence on the line.

"Hello?"

A man's timid voice says in Hindi, "Miss Shah?"

"Who is this?" she asks in the same language, impatient.

"I—uh—I got your number from... Never mind. Sorry. I—I have some important information for you."

She's about to hang up, thinking it's another prank, when he says, "It's about the virus in Thailand."

47

Thiruvananthapuram, India

GEORGIA FROWNS in concentration as her eyes sweep over the architectural drawings of the gopuram once more, hoping something new might jump out at her. But just as the previous times she's studied them, the blueprints reveal no obvious clues. She looks up at the construction soaring high before her, trying to think despite the din of the raging crowd outside the gates.

Beside her, Nair says, "Like I told you, there's nothing. I know the designs well, and I would have let you know if there was a connection."

Sarah says, "No offence, but whoever made the documents had a habit of leaving out information whenever the vault is involved."

Georgia nods in agreement. "Seema mentioned that the gopuram was only completed during the reign of King Marthanda Varma. Didn't you also say that it was his highest priest who sealed the door of the vault?"

"That's the rumour, yes," Nair says.

"And look," Buri adds, pointing to the plans, "the tower

itself is about ten stories high above ground, and its foundation is almost half that underneath. That's quite a subterranean structure, if you ask me."

"The gopuram windows must have a role in opening the vault," Georgia says. "I think the only way we'll know for sure is to go up there and investigate."

Nair shakes his head. "We're carrying out extensive refurbishment to the stairs and passageways right now. It's all blocked off. You can't go up the steps."

Buri points towards the tower. "But we can use that."

Georgia follows his gaze, eyeing the long, flimsy bamboo ladder leaning against the façade and reaching to the lowest window. The blood drains from her face.

"What's wrong?" Buri frowns.

"She's scared of heights," Sarah answers for her.

"Oh. Well, that's fine, I'll go up," he offers.

Georgia shakes her head. "No—"

Sarah cackles at Buri. "Have you looked in the mirror lately? No way that thing will hold your weight."

Buri scowls. "Bamboo is stronger than you think."

"That may be so," Sarah taunts, "and as much as I'd love to see you fall on your arse, if you die we'll have to deal with your meathead brother by ourselves. And no one wants *that*."

Georgia throws a glance at Agent Miller, who's observing the conversation with his arms crossed over his chest. One corner of his lips tips up with mirth.

"Nope," Sarah continues, "*I'll* go."

SARAH GAZES UP, scrutinising the length of the ladder for any defects. She grasps the bamboo rods, steeling her nerves as she tests the first rung with a few taps of her foot.

"Let me go instead," Georgia says beside her.

"Shut up." Sarah gives her a sideways glance. "A few

metres up and you'll be shaking so much you'll have to come back down anyway. You stay here and make sure the gorilla keeps the ladder steady."

Turning to lock eyes with the burly Mongolian-American behind her—who she now refers to as Buri-Ben to remind Georgia of his duplicity—Sarah musters all the authority she can into her glare, ordering, "Hold on to the bottom. Don't you *dare* let me fall."

The big man nods, silent as he grips the base. Taking a deep breath, Sarah begins her slow ascent. It's still early morning, yet the sun is already beaming down at her without mercy. Sweat breaks out across her brow and slithers down her spine. Pausing, she wipes damp, trembling palms on the legs of her trousers.

"Okay, Sarah?" Georgia calls from below.

"Yup," she shouts, resisting the urge to look down.

She grits her teeth and pushes onward, focusing on the action of pulling herself up one step at a time, and all the while distracting herself by admiring the beautiful stucco carvings on the gopuram. Before long, she reaches the ledge of the first window.

"What do you see?" trench monkey Miller hollers.

She ignores him. With a final heave, she pulls herself up through the opening, sagging briefly against the wall as relief sweeps through her strained muscles. Her eyes sweep across the interior. At initial glance, there seems little of note. Bare white walls and ceiling meet her searching gaze. Corridors stretch left and right but are blocked by construction materials as Nair has warned. She crawls to the window opposite to the one she entered from, and her stomach drops at the crowds swelling below, buzzing like an angry horde. Someone catches sight of her, points and yells out.

The ensuing roar of the enraged mob prompts Sarah to duck her head back in. She takes a steadying breath. Squaring her shoulders, she turns away from the troubling scene outside the temple gates and resumes her search. She rises to her feet and paces from one window to the other, scrutinising the entire surface of the left wall. Then she makes the trip back as she scans the right wall.

"Sarah?" Georgia calls out, the sound of her voice barely audible above the commotion of the crowd.

"Yeah yeah, give the woman a minute," Sarah mutters under her breath, looking over the floor this time.

She comes to an abrupt stop. Frowning, she crouches for a closer look. There, nestled in the corner where wall meets floor, she finds a small circular indentation, obscured by dust and debris. Gently she brushes at the surface, then blows away the clinging particles, coughing as they swirl into the air.

Squinting through watering eyes, Sarah examines her discovery. About three fingers wide, the circular disc is smooth and cool to the touch, and has a bulge in the centre.

Another gem? She wonders at its clear, dark colour.

She lifts her gaze and stands, looking for similar objects in the space. After ten minutes, she finds a total of five other discs distributed around the area. Instead of bulging out in the middle, though, some of these objects are flat, others with slight curvatures. She uses the edge of her shirt to wipe the surfaces clean, discovering that they are mirrors.

"What the—?" Sarah frowns with confusion.

Then her eyes widen as an idea hits her. She quickly retrieves her phone and takes a few snaps.

Scumbag Miller yells again, "Hey, Sarah—"

This time, she sticks her head out the window and grins at the faces peering up at her. Waving her hand wildly, she shrieks, "Bingo!"

48

THE MUGGY AIR embraces Anya as she steps onto the tarmac, her stiletto heels clicking a rhythmic beat against the hard surface. Beside her, Mallika's commanding presence draws all eyes, much like the sleek private jet awaiting them.

Anya's gaze sweeps over the aircraft with appreciation, taking in its polished black exterior and tinted windows. The plane is a tangible symbol of the lavish life now afforded to her through Mallika's wealth and status.

Stepping aboard, she bites back a smile when she realises Mallika has taken care to fill the space with jasmine floral arrangements—Anya's favourite. The subtle scent permeates the plush cabin, and she sighs in contentment as she sinks into the soft leather seat.

The attendant offers them chilled champagne alongside caviar and oysters, presenting the first indulgences of their journey. Anya exchanges a smile with Mallika, and a comfortable tranquillity fills the air between them as they settle into the luxurious confines of the plane.

But as the aircraft taxis onto the runway, Anya finds her

thoughts straying to her recent past again, a stark contrast to her current extravagance. She recalls the gnawing pangs of starvation, a ruthless spectre shadowing her every step. The jet engines blast them skyward towards obscured horizons, and her mind floods with vivid recollections of her imprisonment, every detail painfully clear and suffocating in its intensity.

Eight months earlier

ANYA'S EYES SNAPPED OPEN. *She gasped for air, chest heaving as her eyes darted around the murky chamber. Horror surged through her body, electrifying every nerve and sending tremors down her spine. The memories flooded back, each more harrowing than the last, as she struggled to come to terms with her new, nightmarish reality.*

She curled in on herself, unsure if she had been imprisoned for days or weeks. All she knew was the endless cramps of hunger in her stomach. Her captors seemed to feed her at irregular, unpredictable intervals. Whether it was once a day or twice a week, she never knew. Time had no meaning in this place.

Some days she would weep with gratitude when the bowl of cold, unidentifiable gruel was pushed through the slot at the bottom of the door. It was the one thing that brought her comfort, for the food that arrived would reek of mutton. Always mutton. That was how she knew she was in Mongolia, and the relief from the knowledge made whatever tortuous conditions she was in surmountable, because any fate was infinitely better than being at the mercy of her own Russian comrades.

Anya wondered how her investors would react to her disappearance. In their eyes, she must have fled with the sizable funds entrusted to her. The image of their wrath made her shudder. Should she somehow escape this hell, she would have to keep running, always hiding, and forever remaining one step ahead of those who sought retribution. And she would need a complete change of identity.

Trapped with her fears and imaginings, the oppressive stillness of her cell began to take its toll. The boredom was nothing she'd ever experienced. She'd cry out just to hear a sound—anything to stimulate her stifled senses—but the noise was soaked up by the padding of the walls surrounding her, and over time it was as if her very being was swallowed by the void. The eerie silence had such a disconcerting effect, it warped her sense of reality.

Over days, weeks, months—she had no way of telling how long —she began to have the strange idea that her life and her work never happened. That her very existence had been a mere dream or fantasy, an apparition conjured up by the universe, bursting like a bubble in the thin air. Memories of her past life became fuzzy and fragmented. She struggled to recall simple details like names, places, and events as her sense of self faded.

Time ceased.

The world disconnected itself from her.

She was no more. In fact, she never was.

The concept absolutely terrified Anya. It had her pulling her hair out by the fistful, sobbing and screaming into the dark, only to have nothingness echo back at her.

Sometimes, when she was lucid and not clawing at herself, her mind would inevitably play over the last moments of her past life:

The Mongolian royal tomb.

The Secret History of the Mongols. Its gold covers studded with gems of every conceivable colour, glistening in the dim light of the flames.

Georgia. Her big brown eyes, her long black hair in tiny plaits down her slender back. The shock and pain in her expression when Anya shot her in the stomach.

To Anya's utter surprise, the last image was what haunted her most.

Over and over again, she wondered if Georgia had survived the *bullet wound. She did not like the odds. Up in the remote mountains of Mongolia, it would have been impossible to get her to a hospital in time for the critical surgery necessary to save her life. The professor very likely bled out in the tomb.*

The thought sent a strange, startling regret radiating from deep within Anya's chest—an emotion she'd never experienced before. What an utter waste. She had never admired many people in her life, but Georgia had been one.

And what of the two women who Georgia was speaking with at the tomb? Dressed as they were, Anya wondered if they were descendants of the Mongol royalty clan, and if they knew about the contents of The Secret History. *Were they privy to how Chinggis Khan had attained his immortality?*

Did they tell Georgia?

Anya cycled endlessly between fits of madness and moments of lucid torment. Then, one day without warning, the heavy door groaned open. Blinding light rushed in, searing her sensitive eyes. She shielded her face as two men dragged her weak body from the cell.

By that point, Anya could hardly walk on legs rendered feeble from disuse. Her muscles had wasted away during the prolonged isolation. Every minuscule movement caused agony.

The men unceremoniously dumped her into a chair, fastening metal cuffs around her thin wrists. As her vision adjusted to the glare, a dreadful realisation took hold.

She was in an interrogation room.

Bare concrete walls surrounded her. A lone spotlight beam blazed down, making her wince. In the far corner, a burly Mongol stood tall, looking dead ahead. To her left sat a long wooden table, upon which various instruments had been methodically arranged. Her frail mind recognised them all too well.

Torture devices.

Things she had once used herself to elicit confessions.

Anya broke out in a cold sweat.

Had her Russian investors found her and brokered a deal with the Mongolians?

Terror clawed up her chest, strangling her throat. With what little voice remained in her infirm state, she rasped out a plea towards the young guard.

The man did not stir, continuing to stand as silent and stock still as before. His dark eyes saw nothing, staring straight forward with hands clasped rigidly behind his back. It was as though Anya had not uttered a sound at all.

Summoning all her strength, Anya attempted to stagger to her feet, desperate to capture the guard's attention through any means. But her emaciated legs betrayed her, buckling under her weight. Uncontrollable shivers racked her body, rattling her steel handcuffs.

Then the door to the room opened, and a shadowy figure appeared before the harsh floodlight. Anya squinted against the glare, but the silhouette gave away no identifying features.

"Hello, Anya."

The sound of her name uttered in her native tongue sent a chill up Anya's spine, and it took every cell of her body to rein in the scream barrelling from the depths of her stomach.

49

Present day, Thiruvananthapuram, India

GEORGIA'S HEART pounds a frantic staccato against her breastbone as she watches Sarah clamber down the rickety ladder. When Sarah's feet finally touch solid ground, she releases a lungful of air in a long, shaky exhale. Only then do the strangling bands of anxiety begin to loosen their grip around her ribs.

Sarah's excitement is unmistakable as she immediately fishes out her phone, asking Nair, "Have you seen these before? Do you know what they're for?"

Peering over her shoulder, Georgia watches as Sarah flicks through photographs of round, silvery discs embedded in the white surfaces. Nair narrows his eyes as he scrutinises the images.

"I'm not sure what I'm even looking at," the temple executive admits. "Like I mentioned, not many people go up there."

"What did you find?" Agent Miller joins them, poking his head in to get a glimpse of the pictures.

Sarah steps away from him and ignores his question. Turning to Georgia, she says, "I found a series of mirrors."

"Mirrors… ?"

"Yeah, they were distributed around the space. There was also a transparent disc wedged into the corner of the floor." Sarah shows her the corresponding image. "I thought it was another gem at first."

Georgia studies the object, observing its peculiar bulging shape. "What do you reckon it is?"

Sarah gives her a pointed look. "I think it might be some sort of lens."

"A lens?" Georgia's mind works faster now as she makes the connection. She turns to Nair. "Where is Vault B in relation to the gopuram?"

He thinks about this. "Well—"

"It's directly under us, isn't it?" Sarah says.

"I think so… At least, it's in the near vicinity," Nair speculates.

"That must be it," Georgia says as a tingle of exhilaration courses through her. "This is why they had to wait for the equinox."

Buri nods, thoughtful as he seems to catch on to what she is thinking.

"Okay, what am I missing here?" Agent Miller looks around. "What does the equinox have to do with the mirrors and the lens?"

Buri explains, "It's the only time the light would pass directly through all the windows."

"Yeah, I got that much." Agent Miller crosses his arms, impatient.

"The sun is positioned elsewhere at all other times of the year, so the windows would be lit from different angles, with shadows falling on certain parts… you get the idea," Buri continues, "which would imply that the mirrors were deliberately placed to manipulate the light in a specific way during the equinox, to somehow facilitate the opening of the vault under the gopuram."

"It's a working theory," Georgia says.

"And there's only one way to find out if it's true," Sarah adds, gazing up at the gate tower. "We need to see if the other windows have the same setup."

Nair nods, already walking away as he says, "I'll arrange for a longer ladder. Once you get up to the second level, the stairwell should be accessible to the others."

"So we have to wait for the equinox to open the vault?" Agent Miller asks. "When's the next one?"

Buri looks it up on his phone. "Three months away."

Agent Miller frowns. "We don't *have* three months. Home office called earlier. The news hasn't broke yet, but word is that the virus has now spread to Kolkata. And if the epidemic has crossed one border already, it'll most likely be in other countries as well."

"I'LL GO UP with you this time," Buri-Ben offers.

Sarah laughs and is about to issue another wisecrack before she thinks better of it. Depending on what she finds up there, Buri-Ben may come in handy. Certainly, he has a few more brain cells than his dim-witted brute of a brother. He can also haul all the heavy gear.

Plus, she'll have a chance to grill him.

And maybe push him out the window.

"Fine," she snaps, noticing how Georgia falters in her step at the response.

Her boss quickly regains her composure, walking away to speak with Nair, who is supervising the setup of the equipment. Thankfully, the new ladder is much steadier and made of aluminium.

It takes another hour to prepare everything for their

experiment, and as Sarah and Buri-Ben make their way over to the gopuram, the big man says to her, "Ladies first."

Sarah snorts, for no one in their right mind has ever called her a 'lady'. The idea is as ludicrous as their mission in India, working with these DIA numbnuts.

Gripping the metal rung and gazing up at the blazing midday sun, she begins her ascent. Keen to get into the shade, Sarah makes a direct path for the second opening of the gate tower. She moves as fast as she can manage, ignoring the slight wobble in her legs and not bothering to pause and look down to check on Buri-Ben.

She heaves herself through the window once she reaches the second floor. At first glance, the space is much the same as the level below. Sarah scans every surface for objects similar to what she has found before. By the time Buri-Ben pulls himself up to the opening, she's already located three of the mirrors—all of them at different locations than those downstairs.

The two of them work without exchanging a word. While Sarah tracks down more of the silvery items, cleaning them of dust and debris, Buri-Ben sets up a portable pulley system on a tripod. He drops the hook at the end of the rope to the ground, waits for the crew to attach the large spotlight, then operates the winch to lift the cargo to their elevation.

Cries of indignation continue outside the temple walls, the crowd's unrest showing no signs of abating. The chants of protest set Sarah on edge, each impassioned shout sending unease skittering across her skin.

She finds another five mirrors and a prism wedged in the corner between the wall and the floor. Polishing each of them with a soft cloth, she brings out a laser pen pointer and shines it into the mirror closest to the window.

To her utter fascination and delight, the red pinprick of light bounces off each reflective surface in a magical display of ingenious design, traversing through the space in a luminous showcase of a mirror-maze before entering the prism.

"Holy shit," she whispers with wonder. Turning to Buri-Ben, she instructs, "Go on, turn it on."

He positions the enormous floodlight and flips the switch. An intense beam fills the space, making Sarah squint and scramble for her sunglasses.

She moves to crouch before the prism on the floor, which is now glowing a glittering red in the bright, illuminating glare.

"Where does it go?" Buri-Ben wonders beside her. He, too, has put on his shades.

"I'm betting downward. Maybe there are even more mirrors and lenses inside the walls and floors to concentrate the light and direct it all the way to the vault."

"I guess it's possible, given the kind of creative engineering that was common back then."

Sarah nods. "I've seen it done before."

"You have?"

"All the time."

"Where?"

"In the movies."

She has to give the man credit when he doesn't bat an eyelid at her response. Instead, he gives a solemn nod, as if the whole thing makes sense.

Shutting off the spotlight and removing his dark glasses, he wonders, "So how does that open the vault?"

"Nair said they managed to access the first and second door, but not the third one made of solid iron. None of the keys would engage with the lock. I think the light somehow triggers a mechanism."

"We've still got the problem of the equinox being three months away, though," Buri-Ben points out.

Rising to her feet, Sarah's mind whirls with possibilities as she paces slowly towards the opening facing the street. She examines each piece of the mirror-maze, tracing their angled placements.

"Yes, but maybe we can make our own equinox," she muses out loud.

"Sarah, stay away from that window, please," Buri-Ben cautions, "The crowd below can see—"

His voice is drowned out as a deafening boom rips through the space. A flash of blinding red overwhelms her senses, and panic takes over as Sarah throws her arms up to shield her face.

Disoriented, her footing falters. Empty air meets her grasping hands. For a split second, time stands still as horror overcomes her.

The floor vanishes beneath her completely. Her stomach lurches into her throat as a sickening freefall seizes her body.

Sarah screams as she plummets into the abyss.

50

Lucknow, India

As THE TAXI comes to a screeching halt, Dhara peers out at the ramshackle chai shop, her suspicion growing with each passing moment. Tucked away between two towering warehouses, it is almost hidden, as if evading attention.

Her anonymous caller refused to give her any information other than this address, and even though she would normally have ignored the request to meet, something in his voice compelled her to see where this would lead.

Experience has shown her that high-stakes stories tend to draw wack jobs spouting conspiracy theories out of the woodwork. Nowadays, though, these individuals like to unleash their unhinged rants on her Twitter feed. Rarely does someone actually go to the extent of tracking down her number and calling her directly.

She jumps when her phone rings. Seeing an Australian number, she picks up.

"Dhara Shah."

"It's Mike Scott," says the author in his deep voice and rich accent. "I've had a look at everything you sent me."

The dilapidated upholstery of the car creaks as Dhara scrambles for her notepad and pen.

"At first glance," he continues, "it seems very alarming, especially given that everything has happened within a two-month window. It made even a sceptic like me almost believe in the prophecy."

"Almost," Dhara repeats the word, sensing that he has more to say about that.

"Yes. *Almost*. Look, with anything, my approach is always this: I look at the data, isolate the correlated events from ones that are likely unrelated, then assess each for possible causes. At first, the information you gave seemed to all be connected, especially within the context of the prophecy."

"I'm sensing there's a 'but' in there."

"Well, let's separate the incidents into two categories. There are the random phenomena I've described in my book that have logical reasons behind them—strange objects dropping out of the sky, rivers running red, that sort of thing. Then there are the fires, floods, sandstorms, and droughts—all of which have been happening more frequently around the world anyway because of climate change."

Dhara frowns. "What about the earthquakes, the volcanic eruptions, and the black rain?"

"Again, the first two are natural events that happen all the time around the world. And black rain isn't an unprecedented phenomenon. Rain clouds can pick up ash from a nearby volcano, then deposit it elsewhere. After the Hiroshima bombing, the intense fires sent a huge amount of char and radioactive fallout into the atmosphere, which ended up 'seeding' the clouds. A couple of hours after the nuclear explosion, the rain that fell in Hiroshima had the colour and consistency of tar."

A shiver travels up Dhara's spine as she imagines the terror the survivors would have experienced at the sight of tar descending from the sky in the aftermath of the bombing. It would have eclipsed everything she felt at Kumbh Mela.

Taking a deep breath to steady her emotions, she asks, "Can you explain the seeding?"

"Cloud seeding is the process of injecting clouds with particles of silver iodide crystals from a plane or a rocket. Under the right conditions, it can induce rain. The technique has been around for decades, and is widely practised in China and dozens of countries, including the US. It can also happen naturally under the right conditions—like the tar rain in Hiroshima. For Kumbh Mela, the clouds must have picked up the activated carbon from somewhere else. I would search for a factory or a supplier warehouse that has been destroyed by a cyclone recently."

Dhara makes a note of this. "I still don't understand why all the major rivers from the old world became red at the same time. What are the chances of that occurring?"

"You're right—that does seem pretty unlikely. And it'll need some further investigation. But I wouldn't be surprised if the more extreme weather has been washing nutrients into the rivers to cause the algae blooms."

Dhara purses her lips, unconvinced. She presses on. "And what about the craters in Siberia?"

"I don't have an explanation for that yet, and I have to say this one really threw me. I'm still working on it and waiting to speak to a few other scientists about it."

"And the pandemic?"

Mike sighs. "Well, to be perfectly honest, we've not had a serious one of global scale since the Spanish flu. Add over-population to the mix, and I'd say we've been quite overdue for some time."

Dhara scratches her head. Something doesn't fit. Climate change or not, all of these events cannot be unrelated to the prophecy.

She says, "Thanks, Mike, I appreciate this. Please let me know once you've got more answers."

"Sure."

Ending the call, she glances at her watch and at the chai shop again. Tapping the end of her pen on the notepad, she makes a snap decision.

"Might as well go in, since I'm here already," she mutters to herself.

She sends her location and the limited information about the man she's meeting to her editor via text.

Just in case.

Giving the taxi driver a generous tip, she tells him in Hindi, "I'll triple that if you stay here and wait until I come back. Keep the meter running, too."

The driver waggles his head, flashing her a wide smile. "Very good, ma'am."

51

Thiruvananthapuram, India

Buri slams against the floor, the impact jarring through his body. With no time to recover, he makes a desperate lunge for Sarah, his fingers closing around her wrist just as she plummets out the window.

"Gotcha!" he growls, fighting to tighten his grip. "Hold on!"

But Sarah's not listening. Shrieking like a mad banshee, the unearthly, blood-curdling sound coming out of her mouth pierces through Buri's brain, striking an instinctive chord of panic within him. For an instant, his clutch on her wavers.

"Sarah! Sarah!" Her name tears from his throat as she thrashes in his grasp. Each violent spasm sends fresh agony shooting up his arm.

A primal roar rips free and he bellows, "Shut the fuck up!"

The woman stills, blinking at him in shock. Recognition comes flooding back into her features. With a strangled cry, she flings her other hand up to grip his forearm.

"Don't you dare let go," Sarah threatens with a trembling voice, her eyes wide with fear.

Not bothering to reassure her, Buri spreads his legs and pushes against opposite walls, mustering all his strength to lift her. The woman is heavier than she appears. Straining with a grunt, he pulls until she gains purchase on the floor, then grabs her by the armpits to help her in.

They both collapse on their backs, gasping for breath. Before he can even recover, Sarah demands, "What the *fuck* was that?"

He shakes his head, unable to find words as adrenaline courses through his body.

After several seconds, he utters, "I think it was a flare."

"Somebody shot a flare at us?" The look on her face is one of disbelief, then undisguised fury.

As the wild thudding of his heart slows, Buri registers the commotion coming from below. Crawling to the window facing the temple, he thrusts his head out. Georgia is yelling, the fear on her delicate features visible even at this distance.

"You guys okay?!" shouts Georgia over Indi's frenzied barks.

Beside him, Sarah lets loose a string of curses, screaming, "Who the hell is shooting flares at us?!" She then glares at Brandon, who is halfway up the ladder. "And why the fuck isn't the *security* guy doing his bloody job?!"

"Come back down here, please," Georgia begs.

"Yeah, give us a minute," Sarah says, retreating from the opening and lying down again.

Buri stares at her, but the woman seems to have no intention of budging from her spot. Shock will be coming over her body soon, and he needs to get her to a safe and warm place.

Pushing up, he says, "Let's get out of here."

Eyes closed, she waves him off. "Let me catch my breath, will ya."

He sits down, keeping a watchful eye on her. After a while, her breathing slows. Buri's about to suggest they move on when she mutters something inaudible.

"What?" he asks.

Meeting his gaze, she repeats begrudgingly, "I said thanks. For saving me. You didn't have to do that."

He frowns. "It's not like I'd just let you fall."

She looks away, and for a brief moment he wonders if she would have returned the favour if roles were reversed.

"And it's not like we've got on since you showed up," Sarah says. "Plus, you're DIA."

"How many times do I have to tell you—"

"Yeah, yeah. You're not working with your brother," she says, mimicking his tone. "You really expect me to believe that?"

"It's the truth."

Sarah stares at him, long enough for it to become awkward. "Then why *are* you here?"

"Harshan—"

"Spare me the Harshan excuse. You turned up at the university before he came. Why?"

"To let Georgia know that Anya—"

"But that wasn't the real reason, was it? You could have told her over the phone or sent her an email if she didn't answer."

"I—" Buri clamps his mouth shut. He scrubs a hand down his face, fighting to rein in his flaring temper.

What can he say? That he doesn't quite understand it himself? That since the night of the storm in Mongolia, Georgia has burrowed deep under his skin in ways even he can't explain?

That night, he was in the midst of a full-blown episode over the disappearance of his PTSD service dog. The incident was so distressing, he was one moment from snapping completely. Then Georgia sat beside him, her calm voice and steady hand slowly pulling him back from the ledge when no one else ever could, other than Indi.

And since then, Buri's not had a single panic attack.

That strange, soothing effect Georgia has over him... he needs to understand it. Needs to know why her presence alone can chase away the demons that have plagued him for years.

But it's more than that.

There's also another reason he showed up at her workplace nine months ago, then stubbornly stuck around Australia even after she turned him away.

A reason he'll never admit, especially to the woman staring him down right now.

Sarah narrows her eyes as his silence stretches on, suspicion creeping back into her features. Before she launches into another interrogation, he cuts her off gruffly.

"What do you want me to say?"

She sits up, jabbing her finger at his chest as she punctuates every word. "Tell. Me. What. You. Want. With. Georgia."

Thoughts flash through his mind, of all the things he wants but can never have—fantasies he only allows in the dark hours when sleep won't come. Buri grits his teeth, shutting them down one by one.

Sarah fires off questions too fast to follow, her incessant needling striking nerves already raw.

"Why did you stay in Australia for eight months, even after she told you to fuck off? What are you and your brother planning? What does he know?..."

She rants on, accusations pouring from her tongue. Buri's anger surges, fingers curling into fists by his sides. For a brief moment, he considers telling her the truth just to shut her up. But before he gets the chance, Brandon appears at the window.

"Dude, you alright?" his brother asks, eyes darting between them.

Sarah levels Brandon with a hardened glare before fixing her wrath back on Buri.

"Yeah," Buri grinds out.

Brandon climbs through the opening. "Good. Let's get you both down to solid ground, yeah?"

Brandon offers a hand to Sarah, but she ignores it, shouldering past him. She doesn't look back as her feet clatter down the ladder rungs.

52

THE AFTERNOON LIGHT wanes as Georgia observes the frenetic work unfolding before her. What began as a few bamboo poles has transformed into an intricate web scaling the lofty heights of the gopuram tower. The team Nair hired constructs the scaffolding with unmatched efficiency, their skilful hands weaving together an aerial access at a startling pace. It was the only option available, given it would have been impossible to drive a crane through the temple grounds.

Within mere hours, lithe forms occupy each window, clinging onto the bamboo rods like agile arachnids. The technicians secure enormous floodlights, positioning them to illuminate every opening.

"Think it'll work?" Georgia asks Sarah, who is crouched beside her, grooming Indi with a loving caress. The German shepherd rolls onto her back, tongue lolling out with a languid yawn as she luxuriates in the attention.

Sarah looks up at Georgia and shrugs. "Guess we'll find out. Bathing the windows in direct, intense light is the best we can do to simulate an actual equinox. Hopefully, it'll create the same effect and trick the mirror mazes into doing whatever is needed to unlock the door."

"Seems pretty farfetched," Georgia comments. "Like you said—the stuff of movies."

Sarah grins. "Actually, Hollywood stole their ideas from cultures like this. You know that."

Beyond the gates, the shouts of protesters have dulled to a faraway rumble. Agent Miller wasted no time bolstering security after the incident with the flare, calling in additional DIA reinforcements who are working with local police to establish a substantial perimeter. The streets surrounding the temple grounds have been cleared and a wide no-go zone set up, extending six hundred yards from the property limits. Armed temple guards patrol the area, letting no one in.

All of which, Sarah has complained, should have been their top priority from the moment they arrived.

Georgia straightens as Buri emerges from the second-floor window. Her breath catches in her throat as she watches his descent, every graceful movement on the bamboo scaffolding sending spikes of anxiety through her. Only once his feet firmly touch the ground does she release the breath she's been holding.

He strides over to them, wiping the palms of his hands on his cargo pants.

"Done," he says. "I checked the other floors. All had similar setups with the mirrors and lenses, or prisms. Slight variations, but essentially the same. I've cleaned and polished them, so we're good to go."

Nair joins them. "We're ready with the lights, too."

Georgia glances at Miller and Reyes, who have just returned from outside, suggesting, "Sarah and I will go down to the vault with Nair. Buri, why don't you and Agent Miller stay up here to direct the technicians with the lights? We'll communicate through the earpieces."

Buri's expression tightens. Glancing at the two DIA operatives walking towards them, he says with reluctance, "Take

Reyes with you." He hands a large, baton-like flashlight to the agent.

Nair's gaze falls on Reyes. After a long pause, he gives his consent with the slightest inclination of his head. He guides them towards the vault entrance once more, his bare feet silent on the worn paving stones. He retrieves an oil lamp, and Georgia follows him as they descend the stairwell, her senses on high alert, absorbing every detail that might prove significant.

Seeing the underground structure for the first time, Sarah's mouth is agape when they stop before Vault B, her eager eyes drinking up every line of the intricate carvings on the archway. The keys in Nair's hands jangle as he inserts one into the metal gate. To Georgia's surprise, it swings open without any fuss.

Nair steps deeper into the doorway, unlocking the ornate wooden door with the same key. Wrapping his hands around the large metal ring, he tugs outward but manages only the barest creak of movement before resistance halts further progress. Leaning his full body weight into the pull accomplishes nothing.

"We had trouble with this last time, too. The wood has swollen up." He points to the floor where it's grinding against the stone.

"Let me try," Agent Reyes says, joining Nair within the tight space. Wriggling his fingers into the minuscule gap, he braces himself, then pulls with a grunt of exertion.

Georgia exchanges an anxious glance with Sarah as Reyes wrestles with the stubborn door. After a few attempts, it grants a sliver more space before coming to a stop again, emitting a screeching groan from its long-frozen hinges. Reyes heaves again, pouring all his might into loosening its grip.

Slowly, the heavy wood scrapes further outward, until at last the DIA agent manages to expose what lies beyond.

Georgia peers into the gloom and finds a third barrier guarding whatever secrets lay within the vault.

Unlike the wooden door Reyes just opened, this one is devoid of any decoration. Made of solid iron, its bare surface is covered by layers of rust accumulated over the centuries. On one side is a single keyhole and metal ring, marked by flecks of oxidation.

"We couldn't get this one to open, back in 2011," Nair says.

"You tried all the keys?" Georgia asks.

"Yes, but they all just turned freely. It's like there's no locking mechanisms inside." He demonstrates by putting a key in and spinning it all the way around.

"Let's see what happens when we turn on the lights," Georgia suggests. She speaks into her transmitter: "Buri, we're ready for you now."

"Copy. Do I switch all of them on?" his voice crackles through the line.

Georgia considers this. "Let's start with the top window first."

"Gimme a moment. And... it's on."

As if by some silent agreement, everyone takes a step back simultaneously from the entrance.

Nothing happens.

Frowning, Georgia moves forward and places her palm on the door. She presses her ear against the cool surface. The sound of trickling water is clearer than before, but this time, there's a distinct whirring noise.

"Sarah, listen," she whispers to her assistant.

By the time Sarah joins her, the whirring stops.

Something drops with a clonk.

An electric thrill rushes through Georgia. She widens her eyes at Sarah, whose expression is one of astonishment and awe.

Sarah turns to Nair. "Quick, try the key now. No, not

those. The one you opened the other two doors with."

Nair does as she asks, and this time, the unmistakable click of an opening lock echoes through the chamber.

"Oh, my God." Sarah's mouth drops open. "The light must trigger the locking mechanism to engage."

Nair pulls on the circular metal handle, and the door creaks open with a shuddering groan.

A tremor of exhilaration courses through Georgia's body as she switches on her flashlight. Its beam washes over the dark portal, illuminating a delicate lacework of cobwebs lining the narrow passageway. Their shimmering threads resemble a gossamer curtain stretched across the opening.

She takes cautious steps forward, parting the sticky strands. Only a few paces in, and she comes to an abrupt halt.

"What is it?" Sarah asks from behind her.

"There's another door."

"Seriously?"

"Let me see." Nair squeezes over to her side. He examines the construction before them, identical to the one they've just opened. When he tries the key again, it rotates freely as before in the lock.

"Buri, can you hear me?" Georgia says.

"Loud and clear," comes his faint reply through the crackle of static.

"It worked, but we've found a fourth door inside."

A brief silence, then, "Yeah, I expected as much. We've got five windows up here, so there must be the same number of doors down there."

Georgia murmurs her agreement. "The key won't engage with the lock, just like before. Can you turn on the light in the second window?"

"On it." There's muffled conversation on Buri's end, then his voice again, "One second... There, the light is on now. Let me know if that works."

Georgia nods at Nair, who tries the key again to no avail.

Cursing, Sarah glares at the metal barrier with obvious frustration, then presses her ear flush against its iron surface.

Her body stills, and her eyes grow round.

"Holy… Come listen to this, Georgia." She beckons, excitement edging her voice.

Georgia mirrors Sarah's stance. She frowns. "It's the same trickling water sound, but without the whirring this time."

"No, there's something else. Listen again."

Georgia closes her eyes and holds her breath, straining her ears. Then she hears it—a faint rhythm beneath the dripping.

"It's… ticking."

"Yes!"

Realisation washes over Georgia. "A timing mechanism?"

"Must be." Sarah's expression brightens with wonder and reverence. She looks down at her watch. "What time did we open the first metal door… two minutes ago?"

"I think so. I didn't keep an eye on the time," Georgia says, feeling frustrated with herself.

"Dammit," Sarah says. "We need to simulate the equinox properly. Each window has to be illuminated at around five-minute intervals, just like in the video we saw."

Georgia brings the comm-link to her lips, striving to explain their discovery to Buri amid her rushing thoughts.

"We started the top light at 21:46," Buri informs her. "I made a note of it. That's just over three minutes ago."

"Oh, good." Georgia exhales with relief. "Shut the second one off for now and turn it on again at the five-minute mark. We need to time it like how it would be during the equinox."

"Copy."

The four of them fall into a hushed anticipation, each occupied with their own watch. Suddenly Buri's voice rings through Georgia's earpiece, counting down: "Turning on in ten… five… three, two, one."

Georgia presses her ear flush to the metal barrier once more. At first: only the faint trickling of water. Then the faint, familiar whirring and dropping sounds emerge from deep within. Her pulse quickens.

"May I?" Georgia asks Nair. He passes over the key and she slides it into the lock. The mechanism yields as she turns, and a satisfying click rings out as the tumblers fall into place. Gripping the iron handle in both hands, Georgia steadies herself and pulls with all her might. Bit by painstaking bit, the heavy door shifts.

Finally, a sliver of an opening emerges, just wide enough to admit her frame.

"Buri?" she says into her mouthpiece as she looks into the doorway.

"Let me guess, another one?"

"Yeah."

"Counting down." After roughly five minutes, he says, "Coming on in five… three, two, one."

Inserting the key once more, she turns the lock and pulls on the handle. This one opens with relative ease compared to the others.

She peers into the pitch-black passage. Her pulse thuds in her ear as she advances with trepidation, the cobwebs growing thicker as she progresses. Strand after silken strand seems to materialise out of the darkness, clinging to her clothing and skin as if tiny spider legs are scrabbling to drag her into their clutches. Overcome with repulsion, she fights the urge to brush and flap wildly.

Forcing herself to move at a steady pace, she half expects to encounter another doorway. When she finds none, she pauses, furrowing her brows with confusion.

"Georgia," Buri's voice comes online in her earpiece. "What's going on down there? Did you find another door?"

Pacing forward some more, she comes to a stop at the top of a stairway. Weathered stone steps plunge into blackness, vanishing into an inky abyss that swallows up the beam from her torch. An unwelcoming chill seeps from the bottomless depths, making her shiver.

"I'm not sure." Pausing, she explains to Buri what she has found.

"But we've only lit up three windows so far. What about the other two?" Buri asks.

Considering this, she suggests, "Keep counting down. Maybe there are more doors we have to open at the bottom of the stairs."

"Copy. Keep me updated. You've got… two minutes and fifty seconds before the next light is on."

Despite the time constraint, she remains rooted in her position.

"Let me go down first." Agent Reyes pushes past and shines his powerful flashlight down the stairwell, descending the smooth stone steps with measured efficiency.

Georgia follows at a slower pace, her torch beam dancing along the walls, revealing elaborately carved figures emerging from the shadows. Coiled cobras stretch the length of the stairwell, their raised hoods and flaring tongues ready to strike. Interspersed among the serpents are demonic faces, with sharp fangs protruding from twisted mouths and claws. Menacing eyes follow her movement as if guarding long-held secrets.

Buri comes online again. "Window three lighting up in fifteen… ten… five… three, two, one."

Something whirrs within the walls. Rattled by the sudden noise, Georgia stops, unsure of what it all means. Ahead, Agent Reyes has reached the bottom of the stairs, his light illuminating another doorway.

He turns. "Quick, give me the ke—" but his words are cut short.

The floor gives way beneath him with a booming crack. Reyes yells as he plunges through the opening. Georgia rushes forward, shining her light into the pit, her blood running cold at the sight below.

Rushing water fills the chamber, its roar drowning out Reyes's screams as the current sweeps him away. His arms flail as the torrent drags him deeper into the murky depths. For a moment his face, contorted with terror, appears in her beam before he's engulfed by the merciless tide.

"Reyes!" Georgia screams, horror-struck by how fast the agent vanishes from view.

"Buri! Get down here now!" Sarah yells into the comms.

No sooner have the echoes of his name faded than the floor begins to shudder beneath Georgia's feet. With a clamorous tremor, the stone trapdoor moves back into place to seal off the cavity below.

Georgia lunges forward and claws at the edges of the slab, but it keeps moving with inexorable force. Her fingers scrape against the smooth surface as the gap shrinks with dizzying speed. Within a fraction of a moment, the door seals shut, plunging the space into utter silence once more.

53

"HELLO?" Dhara calls out in Hindi as she peers into the chai shop.

The blood-red metal sliding gate is shut, and there's no one in sight. Her gaze sweeps over the cramped interior, painted bright blue and sheltered by the corrugated tin roof. Two wooden tables and a few white plastic chairs are scattered around the space. Large steel pots sit over portable gas burners behind the counter, with an array of glass jars containing spices and tea nearby. There's a door in the far wall, its bright green colour clashing with the bold red and blue. A faint glow peeks through the crack under the entrance. There's someone inside.

"Hello?"

No one answers.

A cockroach scurries over Dhara's shoe, and she shakes it off with disgust. She checks her watch and the address again. Time ticks by, and she starts to second guess herself. Was this just a prank call? Did she waste her time coming here?

She quickly dismisses the idea. Years of working as a journalist have sharpened her ability to discern credible leads from dead ends. The man on the phone was genuine, and his words sent shivers down her spine. Even though he didn't divulge much, something tells her it's worth meeting him face-to-face.

Dhara rattles the rusty gate. Narrowing her gaze, she sees a shadow move across the thin line of light under the door.

Straightening, she says in Hindi, "It's Dhara Shah from the *Washington Sentinel*. We spoke on the phone."

At last, the sound of locks disengaging breaks the stillness. The door inches open, its movement hampered by the chain latch still attached. A man's face peeks out, his gaze darting around nervously.

"Are you alone?" he asks.

She nods, then adds, "My taxi's waiting for me, though. The sooner we get this done, the quicker I'll be on my way."

His gaze moves beyond her, assessing the taxi driver in the car. Seemingly satisfied, he shuts the door, and Dhara hears the telltale sound of the chain being removed. When it opens again, she assesses him with a quick glance.

More boy than man, he appears to be barely twenty. A blue button-down shirt and black slacks cling to his slight frame. Jet black hair sticks out in all directions, and thick eyebrows arch high on his face, giving him the appearance of perpetual astonishment. Behind glasses that magnify his round eyes, keen intelligence shines through.

Dhara peers into the dark brown irises, trying to gauge his character. She decides within an instant that he's harmless. As he pulls the door open, her gaze sweeps through the room behind him, checking that there's no one else inside.

"I'm Dhara," she introduces herself again as he walks a few hesitant steps towards her.

"Vikram," he replies, putting a hand on his chest.

When he shows no signs of opening the gate, she offers, "We can talk inside, or right here. Completely up to you."

Vikram purses his lips, scanning the street behind her. Darkened skin underlines his eyes, lending him a gaunt, haunted look. Then he fishes a key out of his pocket and opens the rusty door, closing and locking it just as quickly once she moves inside.

He leads her into the small, windowless room, dimly lit by a naked bulb dangling from the ceiling. A colourful plastic sleeping mat is spread out in one corner, while piles of paper litter the rest of the floor. The scent of unwashed skin lingers.

"Sorry, it's a bit of a mess here." Vikram wrings his hands. "I arrived a few days ago. This is my cousin's place. They're away."

He ducks out to the shop area, grabbing a couple of chairs for them. She thanks him, bringing out her notepad and pen as she sits.

"I'd rather not go on the record for this," Vikram says quickly. "Sorry."

She looks up. "That's okay. These notes are just for me."

He nods and apologises again. "It's just that... well, I'm still not quite sure... But there's something weird going on, you know? I read your articles and thought you'd be the best person to call. I guess I don't know what to do."

"Okay, slow down," Dhara says, offering him a reassuring smile. "Just sit and take a deep breath."

He follows her suggestion, lowering himself into the white plastic chair.

"Sorry," he says as he rubs his palms up and down his trousers. "Did... did you bring it?"

"Oh. Yes."

She fishes out the wrapped chapati in her bag and offers it to him, watching him wolf it down like he hasn't eaten for days. When he finishes, he wipes his mouth with the back of his hand, giving her an apologetic smile.

"It's okay." Sensing his unease, she tucks away her notes.

"There. Now it's just a friendly conversation. Why don't you start by telling me why you reached out?"

Vikram's chest expands as he sucks in a breath. "A few days ago, my lab went up in flames."

Lines of exhaustion deepen on his boyish face. She nods, letting him continue at his own pace.

"I was there, working late as usual—crashing in my office rather than making the long commute home."

Keeping her tone gentle, Dhara prompts, "Which lab was this?"

"HealthPrime."

Dhara raises her eyebrows. HealthPrime is one of the biggest pharmaceutical players in India. She recalls seeing headlines about the devastating fire. The incident made national news. Police are still investigating the cause, determined to find answers. One of the security guards died, and damage estimates put the losses in the hundreds of millions.

"I barely made it out alive." Wincing, Vikram gingerly rolls up his right sleeve to reveal the burns up his arm.

Angry red blotches of raw, inflamed skin merge together in mottled patterns. Large blisters have formed, filled with clear fluid to protect the damaged tissues underneath. Some have burst open, leaving weeping red abrasions edged in yellow.

Dhara takes a stuttering inhale. "We need to get you to the hospital."

"I can't risk it."

"Risk what?"

"The fire was no accident. I'm pretty sure of it. I can't have anyone knowing where I am."

"Who?" she presses.

Vikram rakes a hand through his hair, making it even more messy than before. He blows out a weary sigh.

Dhara shifts forward. "Hey. It's alright. This is off the

record, remember? Start from the beginning. What is your role at HealthPrime?"

"I'm the leading researcher in the vaccines department."

Dhara sits back in surprise. "But you're so young."

"I finished my PhD at fifteen. I've been working at Health-Prime ever since," he says with a note of defiance, and Dhara can imagine that Vikram struggles to be taken seriously because of his age.

She nods, encouraging him to go on.

Vikram says, "About three years ago, my boss proposed a new project. We had discussed how, statistically, a serious pandemic has been overdue since the Spanish flu. It started out as a theoretical exercise—finding a way to minimise the death toll once it hits."

Dhara frowns, recalling similar discussions with Mike Scott. Unease churns in her gut, but she remains silent, letting Vikram speak at his pace.

"I brainstormed some pathogen ideas and conditions for a 'super virus' to wipe out a decent percentage of Earth's population. My boss encouraged deeper research—vaccine synthesis timelines, mass production simulations, delivery plans, and so on. The goal was to have a strategy in place so that we could deal with a viral outbreak as quickly and efficiently as possible."

Pushing his glasses up the bridge of his nose, he continues, "I was given a private lab in the basement and all the funding I needed. It was a researcher's dream. At first the work was mostly computer simulations modelling viral mutations in humans and animals. I came up with some of the deadliest and most contagious strains. But to truly test the methodology, experiments had to be done."

Dhara's stomach drops. "So you created a virus in order to test your approach?"

Vikram swallows, bobbing his head up and down. "The lab had the best security in the world, and only my boss, his boss, and I knew about the project, so I assumed it was safe. None of my colleagues were aware of what I was doing in the basement—it was something I researched on the side. And I was careful, following every safety protocol to the letter to make sure the contagion was safely contained."

"But it got out, anyway."

Vikram clears his throat, his right leg jiggling up and down. He shifts in his seat, then confirms her guess with a single nod of his head. "I was studying the virus and developing its vaccine at the same time, testing them on mice. Then, ten days ago, I arrived at the lab to find a few of the vials missing. I turned over the whole place, searching for them. When I finally gathered the courage to talk to my boss about it, my calls just kept ringing through. And I never got a reply. A week later, the Thailand outbreak happened."

Sweat beads on his forehead. He cracks the joints of his fingers. "I freaked out. I went back to the lab, thinking this was what I was preparing for—to produce a cure in case something like this happens. I worked through the night and fell asleep on the couch. When I woke up, my lab was on fire."

Dhara closes her eyes, taking a long exhale. "How close were you to getting a vaccine on this thing?"

"Close. I mean, I already had samples in the lab that I was working on, and they just needed some minor tweaks. But everything was destroyed in the fire—all my notes, the research..." He leans forward, his head sinking into his hands.

"How much of it do you remember? Can you replicate it?"

Vikram gestures to the papers strewn all over the floor. "That's what I've been trying to do in here for the last few days, writing down everything I can remember. But I need a lab and equipment to finish my work."

Dhara chews on her bottom lip, her mind straying to

Georgia and her DIA contacts. She says, "I think I can get you to a research facility."

Vikram looks up, and for the first time since their meeting, a glimmer of hope shines in his eyes.

"But first, I need you to tell me a few things," she says, bringing out her notepad again.

———————

HOURS LATER, as their meeting draws to a close, Dhara promises to devise a plan. Vikram will remain here safely hidden while she coordinates with the DIA agents.

Stepping through the chai shop's gate, Dhara glances back as Vikram secures the lock once more. Beyond the metal bars, hopelessness has fled from his features.

"I'll send food and provisions," she says. "In the meantime, work on that vaccine."

Wide eyes fill with gratitude, and he gives her an enthusiastic nod.

She walks towards her taxi, knocking on the driver's window. He jolts awake, then grins at her as he lets her in.

"To the airport," she tells him in Hindi.

Dhara takes out her phone as soon as she settles in the car. The call goes straight to voicemail without ringing: "Hello, this is Georgia. Sorry I missed your call. Please—"

Cursing under her breath, Dhara hangs up and tries Buri instead.

"Leave a message." Buri's brusque recording is short and to the point.

"It's Dhara. Call me as soon as you can, please. It's urgent."

54

Thiruvananthapuram, India

OMINOUS SILENCE ECHOES through the chamber as Georgia stares at the unyielding slab in the floor.

"Fuck," Sarah whispers. "What do we do?"

Having no answers for her, Georgia rises to her feet even as dread anchors her limbs.

The clamour of Buri's footsteps thunders down the steps. "What happened?" he demands, swinging his torch around. "Where's Reyes?"

Nair points to the ground and explains the recent events. He concludes with, "The fourth opening in the gopuram must have triggered it."

"And the fifth must open that." Buri gestures to the door at the other end of the landing and speaks into the transmitter. "Brandon, make sure you light up the last window on time. Reyes has fallen down a trapdoor. It's connected to an underground water channel. He may still be alive. Get your men on that."

A muffled curse from Agent Miller. "Roger that. I'll put Vijay in charge of the lights and join you downstairs."

Georgia's gaze lingers on the iron doorway, noticeably smaller than its predecessors. The beam from her torch skims across its surface, revealing swirling intricate patterns around a dominant cobra figure wrought in gleaming metal. Its eyes are studded with shimmering rubies that shine like droplets of blood. She searches for the keyhole, and locates it within the serpent's open, fanged mouth.

Vijay's accented voice comes online. "Last window lighting up in five… three, two, one."

Georgia slips in the key and twists it twice. Finding no handle, she pushes against the iron slab. With far more ease than expected, the door emits a piercing shriek as it swings slowly inwards to reveal impenetrable darkness within.

As she moves to enter, Buri's hand falls upon her shoulder. "I'll go first. There might be another trap waiting for us."

"No, I—" she protests, but a sharp pinch on the arm from Sarah cuts her short.

"Don't even think about it," her assistant hisses.

Buri snorts. "For once, I'm with Sarah on this."

Georgia searches her mind for a convincing argument. Whatever dangers might be in the vault, she has a better chance of surviving them than Buri. But Sarah's silent glare forbids her to risk exposing her healing abilities, in the event she is injured.

The sound of Agent Miller's approach reverberates down the steps.

"Jesus Christ." He pauses halfway down the stairwell, taking in his surroundings.

Sarah ignores him. "Now that I think about it… Buri-Ben is the only trained medic here. If any of us gets hurt, he's the one we need." Looking at Miller, she says, "This one should go first."

Miller's lips press together. "Fine by me."

Borrowing Buri's large flashlight, Miller sweeps the beam through the portal. A narrow tunnel stretches deep into the shadows. The team inches forward one by one, alert and cautious as their flashlights cut through the pitch-black surroundings. A creeping sense of claustrophobia rises up Georgia's spine and tightens her chest as the sloping path gradually descends, her heartbeat echoing loudly with each step into the unknown.

After what feels like an eternity, Sarah breaks the silence from behind Georgia. "How long have we been walking for?"

"About ten minutes," Buri answers.

"Jesus, where the hell is this taking us?" Sarah asks with a subtle tremble in her voice.

"West," is Buri's simple reply.

Nair adds, "We must be beyond the temple grounds by now, moving towards the sea."

The air grows heavier and more humid, and Georgia's hand comes away slick with moisture when she touches the tunnel wall. Distracted, she walks straight into Buri's back when he comes to an abrupt halt.

"What is it?" she asks.

Brandon calls from the front, "This is the end."

Georgia tries in vain to peer past Buri's bulky frame. "What do you mean, the end?"

"I mean, there's a room at the end of the tunnel. No door."

There's a brief pause, then Sarah says, "Well, what you waiting for? Keep moving."

With Sarah and Nair following closely behind, Georgia trails Buri into the chamber, peering into the darkness. Then Nair's oil lamp illuminates the space with a diffused, golden glow, and the scene comes into focus through the lamplight.

The rectangular vault is far smaller than Georgia imagined. Yet the cool air within feels fresh, hinting at airflow or another means of access. Both the walls and the floor are constructed of unadorned panels of smooth grey stone, much of the surfaces covered with dewy moss.

She furrows her brows, confused at what she is seeing.

No treasure. No boundless riches as described in the other vaults.

"There's nothing here," Agent Miller says, his shock echoing her sentiments.

Then she stubs her toe against something on the ground, almost tripping over the bulk. Crouching, she frowns and scrapes away the lichen covering the small mound.

Georgia gasps as the large oblong stone comes into view, reflecting a warm, luminous golden hue in the dim light, just like the yellow sapphire Dr. Khan found in Dwarka.

"Holy shit," Sarah whispers beside her. "Guys, look at this."

Motivated by Georgia's find, the others spring into action, scouring the area for more gems. As they work on clearing the green growth, Georgia rises to her feet, seeing a distinct, familiar pattern in the way the clumps of moss have accumulated along every crack of the floor.

"It's a wave pattern," Georgia murmurs, dropping to her knees and unveiling the lines etched on the stone surface. Realisation dawns. "It's the exact same layout as the Great Bath."

She orients herself, recalling that the chamber lies due west of the passage they have just come through. Locating the southern wall, she moves towards the unmistakable protrusion on the floor. The rush of blood resonates in her ears and she makes quick work of clearing away the mossy growth. All the air leaves her lungs as she struggles to process the confounding sight.

Atop a lotus motif carved in stone is a magnificent, colossal diamond. Its shape and size reminds her of an ostrich egg, and it possesses a purity and clarity unlike anything she has seen. Surrounding this colourless, flawlessly cut gem are eight smaller stones, each embedded in the petals of the lotus: emerald, ruby, blue sapphire, yellow sapphire, cat's eye, hessonite, red coral, and pearl. Together, they form a stunning ensemble that catches the light and scatters a mesmerising, kaleidoscopic array of multicoloured sparks throughout the room.

"The Indus Star," she whispers with reverence.

55

Lucknow, India

AS THE TAXI hurtles down the road towards Lucknow airport, Dhara calls Georgia's phone once more. Chewing her nails, she listens to the familiar voicemail message with escalating unease. Cursing under her breath, she hangs up.

Her leg jiggles restlessly, agitating the bag nestled in her lap. Contemplating a call to Buri next, Dhara jumps when her phone shrieks. She fumbles at the device, answering without checking the caller ID.

"Dhara, it's Mike Scott." His calm baritone does little to soothe her frayed nerves.

Foregoing pleasantries, Dhara cuts straight to the heart of her turmoil. "Do you think it's possible any of these phenomena could be man-made?"

There's a long pause on the line. Just as she's beginning to think that there's a connection problem, Mike says, "Well, sure... I guess some of them."

"Which ones?" she presses.

"Strange things falling out of the sky—the trash, the frozen sea creatures. You'll have to check the flight patterns on the day, but that kind of stuff could be dumped from a plane. And cloud seeding with activated carbon could cause black rains. Did you look for any factories producing the material that have been destroyed by a cyclone?"

"I did. There were none reported within the last six months. No warehouses, either."

"Hm. Red algae could have been introduced into the rivers, and with the nutrient-rich waters, an algal bloom would have been inevitable. Obviously, the fires in Europe could have been due to arson—not that the extreme weather patterns have helped with that." He pauses, then adds, "And we wouldn't know until studies are done, but the virus could have been man-made, too."

Dhara checks her list of the fifteen signs from the Dwarka Prophecy, ticking off each as Mike speaks. The hairs on the back of her neck stand on their ends. "You've just accounted for six out of the thirteen omens that have occurred so far. Most of the others, like you have said, are natural events that happen from time to time, many of which are exacerbated by climate change: drought, sandstorm, hurricane, earthquake, and the volcanic eruption which also produced the ashes that eclipsed the sun. I'm just wondering why it's all happening at once—it seems like too much of a coincidence?"

"It's not," Mike says. "I looked back through years of records, and to be honest, this is the new normal with all the climate-related disasters. They've just been given more emphasis in the media in the last month, and the press has been reporting older events again, making it seem like every-thing is related rather than being separate incidents. Really, none of these phenomena are anomalies. They've just been sensationalised by the news outlets."

Dhara considers this, then says, "The only thing that we can't explain are the giant craters in Siberia."

"Yes, that's why I was calling. I've spoken with several old colleagues about this. Russian scientists have examined the sites. They discovered methane emission from the craters."

"Methane?"

"Further investigations are to be carried out, of course, but given this information, we believe the events were caused by climate change."

"How?"

"Siberia has huge gas deposits beneath permafrost, which are very sensitive and vulnerable to climate change. As the earth gradually warms, it makes the ground layers unstable. Methane gas pockets begin to build up in the thawing ice, and when the pressure of these accumulations increases, a mound forms—which was described by the eyewitnesses. Eventually, as pressure reaches a critical point, a huge explosion happens. And *voila*, a massive crater is formed."

Dhara's mind races, analysing the complex puzzle from a new angle. What if these events aren't linked to the prophecy, as everyone has assumed? What if, instead, some are natural phenomena, while others are caused by an individual?

Add to the volatile mix a lethal pandemic, frenetic media attention, and international political tension, and the conditions are ripe for mass hysteria and worldwide panic.

Mike seems to have deduced her line of thinking, saying, "You think someone has deliberately manipulated these crises? But who would do that? It would take a hell of a lot of resources and influence to engineer this on a global scale."

"Precisely," she mutters under her breath, heart pounding as fears crystallise in her mind. "Listen, Mike, I have to go. Thank you. You've been more than helpful."

"Sure, but—"

She doesn't wait for him to finish before she hangs up and dials Buri's number with trembling hands.

"Leave a message," says the recording in his curt voice.

Dhara hangs up, trying Georgia once more. It goes to voicemail for the tenth time.

"Dammit. Where the hell are you guys?"

56

Thiruvananthapuram, India

GEORGIA'S BREATH catches in her throat as she grapples with
the scene before her. A silence, thick and unsettling, falls over
the team, as if the very air has vanished from the room.

As usual, Sarah is the first to break the stillness. "What the
hell does this mean? If the Indus Star is here... what triggered
the end of Kali Yuga?"

Georgia's phone startles her with its shrill ring, its echoing
clamour amplified by the vault's stone walls. Her pulse
quickens as she peers down at the device, and she swipes to
accept the call.

"Hey, Dhara. What's—Hello?"

The line goes dead.

She checks the bars on the screen. Nothing. Then she sees
the twelve missed calls from the journalist. A sense of unease
coils tight in her gut, and she moves towards the exit to see if
she can get a better signal.

Just as she steps out, she hears Nair addressing the room:
"Okay. I've done my part in helping you access the vault. But
now we can see the diamond is safe and where it should be,

please respect our wishes and leave this place. Let me remind you that you've all sworn to keep our secrets—"

The icy press of steel against Georgia's forehead rips her gaze from her phone. Blood rushes in her ears as she locks eyes with the man pointing the gun at her skull, his dark gaze piercing through the shadows of the tunnel.

"Inside. Slowly," he hisses.

The pistol digs deeper into her skin, and Georgia stumbles backwards into the vault. Vijay's features emerge from the gloom as he follows her into the room. Behind him, five armed men rush in, frisking each of them and stripping them of their comms.

Sarah glares at Vijay. "What is the meaning of this?"

Ignoring her, Vijay calls out to the doorway, "All clear!"

Moments later, Mallika Sharma strides into the vault with two guards in her wake. Dressed in an emerald silk saree that shimmers with her every movement, her focus is immediately drawn to the Indus Star. She drifts towards the glittering diamond as if mesmerised, ignoring everyone else.

Nair intercepts her. "How did you and your men get in here with your weapons?"

Sharma tears her gaze away from the jewel and meets Nair's stare with a look of pure disdain. "You're not the only contact I have in Kerala who owes me favours."

She surveys the room, her gaze finally settling on Georgia. "Well done, team. I didn't think you'd actually find the stone. I'm happy to be proven wrong."

"How predictable," Sarah scoffs, crossing her arms over her chest. "You're in it for the diamond. All that talk about wanting to preserve your people's legacy, to save the world from destruction... What a load of sh—"

Sharma's chuckle echoes through the room. "Oh, I'm in it for the greater good, alright. I didn't even know about the Indus Star before Georgia joined us. Hell, I wasn't even sure if it was real!"

"Drop the cryptic bullshit," Buri threatens.

Sharma's gaze flicks to him, and her smile fades. Straightening her spine, she says, "Very well. I suppose I could afford you an explanation. This, my friends, is what the English would call a 'wild goose chase'. You've been misled. But trust me, the world will have much to thank you for."

Georgia's mind is a whirlwind of thoughts, but one resonates above the rest. "You started all this. Not the diamond."

Sharma gives her a faint smile. "Not entirely. What I did was… add a touch of drama, an embellishment here and there. After all, my family's roots are in Bollywood, and theatrics are in our blood. I know how to sell a story, to captivate an audience, and to make them believe in fiction. "

"How?… *Why?*"

"It was surprisingly easy." Sharma shrugs. "As for why… well, as I said, it is for the greater good. I abandoned religion long ago, but the way our scriptures describe this Age of Darkness is unerringly accurate. Our society is a cesspool of evil, corruption, violence, and injustice. Despicable crimes are committed against the innocent every day. We're in the midst of global extinction and climate crises, and still, we fail to change because of our greed and ignorance. Do you really think such a world is worth saving? I don't." Mallika shakes her head. "I believe it's time to turn the page, to end the Kali Yuga and begin anew. I'm simply accelerating the inevitable by stepping in. Frankly, I see it as an act of mercy for humanity. Why would anyone with a sane mind choose to endure this disgusting world of constant suffering and depravity? I'm ending our pain, our vile existence. And in the process, I'm saving the natural world from our destruction."

"You're not God," Sarah says. "Who are you to decide when Kali Yuga should end?"

Sharma's response is unsettlingly calm. "I think it speaks volumes about humankind that I hardly had to do anything to spark global chaos and turn nations against each other. Sure, I've long envisioned the end of Kali Yuga. I've fantasised about it for years, even went as far as developing a virus capable of decimating half our population—something which can thin the herd and bring the human population back into equilibrium with the planet. It's a perfectly natural process, especially when a species overruns its habitat and exhausts its resources."

She smiles, continuing, "But as you pointed out, I'm no god. I can't dictate the end of an age. Sometimes, though, a clear sign from life points you in the right direction, and that's what happened when Dr. Khan uncovered the Dwarka Prophecy. A divine nudge, if you will. All I did was answer that call. My actions were simple, yet effective. Dropping objects from cargo planes, contaminating rivers with red algae, igniting fires. I played on the press's appetite for sensation. The rabid media frenzy, climate change events, and the longstanding controversy around the Koh-i-Noor diamond did the rest. Honestly, it was frighteningly straightforward. And now the human race, with its own hatred, greed, and stupidity, is on the brink of self-destruction, especially with nuclear weapons in the mix. There's a certain irony and symmetry to that, don't you think?"

The weight of her words hangs in the air, but Georgia can't parry them. For a moment, it's almost as if the outside world is irrelevant—a chessboard on which Sharma has rearranged the pieces at will.

With her eyes fixed on the stone, Sharma muses, "Finding this diamond feels like fate—as if the universe itself is aligning with my plan. Maybe there's something to religion after all?"

Stepping forward and crouching down, she wriggles the diamond free from its lotus seat and carefully lifts it with both hands. A look of surprise, then awe, crosses her face.

"It's heavier than it looks."

Moving towards the oil lamp, Sharma examines the Indus Star under the warm glow. The diamond casts an entrancing dance of glittering light around the room.

"The legends were right," she murmurs, almost to herself. "The Koh-i-Noor is nothing compared to this."

Desperate to stall her, Georgia asks, "What are you planning to do?"

"Isn't it obvious? I'll take the diamond, claim it was never here, and say that your team fell victim to the vault's infamous curse. Then I'll get the press back on the story of the Koh-i-Noor. With any luck—and I've been having plenty—there'll be a nuclear war before we know it. That'll finish off whatever little population there is left after my virus is done with the world." Sharma's lips curl into a self-satisfied smile. "And if there's any truth to the Dwarka Prophecy... well, taking the Indus Star with me will only solidify my success."

She wraps the gem in a silk scarf and tucks it into her bag. Nair protests with a shout, lunging towards Sharma. But one of her guards is quick to react, striking him on the back of his head with the butt of his pistol.

Collapsing to the ground, Nair's head strikes the cold stone floor with a sickening thud. Blood, thick and dark, begins to pool beneath him. As Georgia rushes to him, another guard grabs her from behind. She struggles against his grip, her eyes on Nair's unmoving body.

With a powerful surge, Buri and Agent Miller use the momentary distraction to take down the nearest guards with relentless strikes. But even with their ferocity, they are outnumbered and soon overwhelmed, their limbs pinned to the ground by the weight of their captors.

Georgia launches herself at one of the men, and her attack is met with a brutal blow to the face. She stumbles back, blood trickling from her split lip, while Sarah lets out a hoarse cry and charges headfirst at the guard. In the chaos, Buri seizes the opportunity to break free.

A booming gunshot shatters the chaos.

Georgia's heart stops, fearing for Sarah. She whirls around, expecting the worst, and finds Buri crumpled over her assistant.

"Oh God," she whispers.

Buri groans and rolls onto his back, blood seeping through his fingers clamped over his left arm.

Sharma's face twists with disgust. "Make it look like an accident," she orders Vijay as she turns towards the door. "No loose ends."

She marches out of the vault with two bodyguards.

57

HALF DEAF, with an incessant ringing in his ears, Buri stares up the barrel of the pistol, his eyes flickering between the cold steel and the man's dark gaze. The pungent scent of gunpowder lingers in the air, intermingling with the metallic tang of blood from his wounded arm. Sweat beads on his temple, each drop tracing a slow path down his skin as his mind spins over iterations of a possible escape. Six against two, with him injured and helpless on his back—the odds are slim.

A quick glance at Brandon confirms his fears, who seems to share the same grim realisation.

They're screwed.

The sudden sound of rapid gunfire shatters the air, sending Buri's heart into a frantic beat. Adrenaline courses through his veins as he scans his surroundings, checking on Brandon, Georgia, then Sarah to ensure their safety. His relief is short-lived when he realises the three distinct shots came from outside in the tunnel, followed by the shocking sight of Mallika Sharma bursting through the door. Blood gushes from her chest as she clutches it with both hands, her body writhing in agony as she struggles to breathe. She stumbles towards the group with red foam gurgling at her mouth and collapses onto the ground with violent convulsions. The Indus Star tumbles out of her bag and rolls across the floor, forgotten amidst the pandemonium that erupts.

In a wild burst of raw fury, Buri wrenches at his captor's ankle, slamming him onto the cold floor. Gunshot rings out and, despite the searing pain in his arm, Buri launches himself onto the guard and delivers a vicious elbow strike to his face. The man's eyes roll back into his skull. In his peripheral vision, Buri catches glimpses of Brandon taking on two assailants at once. Grasping for the fallen guard's weapon, Buri crouches low as bullets ricochet off the stone walls. He rolls and returns fire with deadly accuracy, dropping two more enemies before aiming at the last one standing.

Vijay holds Georgia captive, his arm wrapped tightly around her throat, his Glock pressed against her temple.

"Let her go," Buri commands in a low growl, the pistol in his hand steady despite the tension that ripples through him.

His finger hovers over the trigger, itching to act. He's confident in his marksmanship, sure he can take Vijay out. But the risk is high—there's no telling if Vijay might fire on Georgia in response.

As if reading his thoughts, the Indian man's sneer widens. Tightening his grip on Georgia, he says, "Drop it. Or she dies."

Buri's gaze cuts to his brother, who's still grappling with the two guards.

"I mean it!" Vijay's voice escalates, jerking Georgia backward. She lets out a yelp, her hands clawing at his arm.

Georgia's expression shifts to one of resolve. Buri, with a stab of panic, realises what she's about to do. She's going to try the self-defence manoeuvre he taught her, something too risky for this circumstance.

"Alright, alright." Still crouching, Buri places the gun on the floor in front of him and raises his hands in a gesture of surrender. "Easy."

"No!" Georgia's protest is cut short as Vijay drives his knee into her back. She cries out, her legs buckling.

Enraged, Buri makes a move to rise, but Vijay's threat stops him. "Stay where you are." He tightens his arm around Georgia's neck, pressing the pistol harder against her temple.

Buri's jaw clenches, his breathing rapid and shallow. He watches with growing agitation as Vijay drags Georgia across the room, stopping near the diamond that lies discarded on the floor.

"Pick it up," he commands her. "Slowly."

She obeys him, hands trembling as she lifts the large stone.

"Put it in the bag and give it to me," Vijay says, eyes never leaving her as she complies.

That's when Buri notices a flicker of movement in the corridor. It's quick and fleeting, but he's sure he saw it. Whoever shot Sharma is still outside.

In an instant, a deafening gunshot echoes through the room and the left side of Vijay's head explodes, spraying blood and brain matter across the room as he crumples to the ground. Georgia screams, dropping the diamond on the floor.

Buri rushes to Georgia's side, his heart pounding at the sight of gore pouring down the side of her head. Frantic, he checks her injuries. Blood gushes out of the graze wound where the bullet narrowly missed her skull, staining her skin and clothes.

But there's no time to stop the bleeding as he grabs Vijay's weapon and spins around to aim at the figure stepping into the vault.

Tall, blond, with startling blue eyes, the woman is dressed in black linen pants and a matching blouse. She has her gun trained on Brandon, who has just managed to knock out his opponents on the floor.

Recognition flickers in Buri's mind, but he can't quite place her.

"Who are you?" he demands.

58

Trembling with shock, Georgia grabs the hem of her shirt to staunch the warm blood streaming from her head. Sarah is at her side in an instant, wrapping her wound with a scarf, but they both freeze as a woman appears in the doorway.

The woman aims her gun at Agent Miller and ignores Buri's questions. She throws a glance at Georgia with an eerily serene smile.

"Professor Lee. We meet again."

Her voice, laced with a thick Russian accent, sparks memories too painful for Georgia to handle and sends her heart into a frenzied gallop. Confusion overwhelms her as she studies the woman's unfamiliar face. Then she notices all the details she missed before: the rough nose job, the fuller lips, the auburn roots peeking through the bleached mane, and the unnatural blue of the eyes.

Realisation dawns, sharp and clear. She draws in a stuttering breath. "Anya Mihailovich."

Beside her, Buri stiffens. He adjusts his stance, tightening his grip around the gun.

Georgia breaks out in a cold sweat at Anya's broadened smile, momentarily stunned by the transformation of the woman before her. The subtle alterations in the Russian archaeologist's features have completely changed her appearance. In any other context, Georgia wouldn't have recognised her.

"You look… different," Georgia says. "Your eyes are—"

"Coloured lenses." Anya's smile drops. She steps further into the room, her pistol still trained on Agent Miller. Bending down with calculated grace, she reaches for the Indus Star.

"I wouldn't do that if I were you." Agent Miller pushes up to his feet.

For a fleeting moment, Georgia catches a glimpse of something dark twisting Anya's features.

"Oh, you wouldn't, would you?" Anya taunts, rising to her full height with the diamond in hand.

"What are you doing here?" Georgia asks.

"Why," Anya purrs, her gaze fixed on Miller as she answers, "I'm saving you from Mallika, of course."

"You know Mallika Sharma?" asks Sarah.

"Intimately." Anya's smile returns, and she tilts her head to the side. "Did you really believe it was a coincidence that she specifically chose you all for this project? I've been feeding her information all along, guiding her with subtle nudges behind the scenes. For months, I've been trying to sabotage her plans, especially with the virus. But in the end, she still managed to release it."

Every hair on Georgia's neck stands at attention. "Why—?"

"What's my interest in this? I did it all because of *you*, Georgia."

Georgia's frown deepens, her mind racing to make sense of the Russian woman's cryptic response.

Anger contorts Anya's face. "They tortured me in that Mongolian hellhole for months, did you know that? The only thing that kept me alive was the hope of seeing you again.

But I had no easy way of getting to you. I couldn't just turn up at your doorstep; I knew they'd be watching."

"Who—?"

Anya raises a silencing hand, her expression becoming urgent as she locks eyes with Georgia. "I'm so relieved that you survived your injuries. I need to know what happened in that tomb. Who were those Mongolian women? What did they say to you? Did they show you the contents of that book?"

Georgia's eyes dart to Buri. His expression is locked down, his gaze intensely fixed on Anya. He has no idea of the true events that unfolded at the Mongolian royal tomb after he was shot by Lev Ivanov. Georgia has lied to him and Agent Miller, claiming that the authorities prevented her from opening the door. Neither of them knows about her encounter with the Mongolian princesses, or about Anya shooting her inside the tomb, or her miraculous recovery minutes later— secrets that Georgia has fiercely protected to conceal her immortality. It appears that Anya, too, remains unaware of Georgia's rapid healing abilities, as the Russian woman was knocked out immediately after shooting Georgia in the stomach.

Beads of sweat break out over Georgia's skin as she makes a weak attempt to redirect the topic. "How did you meet Sharma? How did you know of her plans?"

Sarah interjects with a pressing question of her own: "And how the hell did you get out of jail?"

Anya scowls and points her gun at Agent Miller. "You can thank *him* for that."

Miller glares back at her. "Oh, no, you don't."

Anya's snigger sends a chill slithering down Georgia's spine. "Why don't you tell them how I got out and how I ended up here?" Anya taunts, her voice dripping with smug superiority. "I've got the vaccine, just so you know. I stole the vials and the research, and I burnt Sharma's lab to the ground

—along with her scientist, the only one who knows how to contain the outbreak."

Agent Miller freezes. His entire demeanour shifts. "What do you want?"

"Two hundred million US dollars. And I want every one of my former associates eliminated, so I'll finally be free. No one is telling me what to do anymore, especially—"

She doesn't get to finish her sentence. Agent Miller's movements are a blur as he lashes out, disarming her in an instant and striking her across the temple with the butt of her pistol. The blow is savage, efficient, and Anya crumples to the floor without a sound.

Miller spits on her motionless form, seething with palpable anger. "I've had it with that woman's damn lies."

"Lies, were they?" Sarah challenges. "What was she about to say before you knocked her out?"

"Fuck if I know," Miller fumes. His gaze shifts to Buri, addressing him instead. "I told you how she is. She's a liar, a master manipulator. Probably trying to drive a wedge between us because she's holding a grudge against me for infiltrating her team in Russia."

"Bullshit," Sarah says, pressing for answers. "What's this about a vaccine?"

Miller meets her questioning with a hardened glare. "I'm a US government agent. Exactly what are you accusing me of?"

In the midst of their heated exchange, Anya stirs. Georgia is taken aback by Miller's ruthless brutality as he drops to his knees and delivers a few more vicious blows across her face.

Anya's body goes limp once more.

"For fuck's sake." Sarah shakes her head. "You're really trying to shut her up, huh?"

Bristling with hostility, Miller advances towards her with menace, causing Sarah to stumble back.

Buri, who has been observing the unfolding drama with unsettling composure, intervenes. He steps between them, and in a single fluid motion wrests Miller's weapon out of his grasp.

"You better start talking, bro," Buri says, tucking the gun into his belt. Blood drips down his left arm, and Georgia tears up her shawl, wrapping the piece around his wound.

The DIA agent's eyes lock with his brother's, burning with fury. His tone is almost dismissive. "I'll debrief you later."

"No. You'll explain everything now."

Miller's nostrils flare in a mix of outrage and disbelief. His gaze flickers between his sibling's face and the pistol in Buri's hand by his side. "Are you serious? You're taking their side against me? Your own brother?" Every word is churning with betrayal and frustration, punctuated by the rapid rise and fall of his chest. "Remember your oath, soldier. Remember where your loyalties lie."

His outburst is met with a steely, fierce stare. Tension curdles in the air, an impasse at the brink of violence.

After a long, drawn-out moment, Miller exhales with frustration, his stance shifting from fight to concession. He shakes his head, exasperated. "I can't believe this," he mutters through gritted teeth. "Fine. But by the time I'm done explaining, you'll be seeing things my way."

59

Eight months earlier, Mongolia

"*HELLO, ANYA,*" *Agent Brandon Miller said in smooth Russian.*

Anya's dirt-smeared face contorted in pure terror, twisting into a grotesque mask of fear. She struggled against the metal cuffs binding her to the chair, wild-eyed and on the brink of a blood-curdling scream. But then, with an astounding show of restraint, Anya visibly reined in her distress, clamping her trembling lips shut and squinting against the blinding glare that silhouetted Brandon's form.

Brandon took a moment to survey the interrogation room, appreciating the meticulous preparations that had gone into setting the stage for his interview. The space was stark and intimidating, with its bare concrete walls and floor, a long wooden table arrayed with an assortment of torture devices, and a harsh spotlight beam directed squarely into Anya's eyes, blinding her to her surroundings.

A smirk played on Brandon's lips. Anya had to be absolutely terrified.

He moved towards her and she flinched, eyes darting around the room for an escape. Freezing in alarm as he settled into the chair across from her, Anya's eyes scanned his now visible face. Recognition flickered across her features, quickly giving way to a mixture of relief, loathing, and utter disdain.

"Don't worry. It's only me." Brandon flashed her a smile.

He observed her for a moment, noting her tousled red hair, her frail, skeletal frame. The once-beautiful Russian archaeologist was unrecognisable, a mere shadow of her former self. Her captors had really done a number on her.

Reaching for the mirror on the table, he held it up to her, and she drew in a horrified breath at her own reflection.

"Poor Anya. Prison hasn't been too kind to you, has it?" Brandon put the mirror back where it belonged. "Now, why don't we get down to business? Be a good girl and tell me what happened at Burkhan Khaldun, when you were searching for the tomb of Genghis Khan."

Her response was to spit in his face. But in her weakened state, the spittle landed on his shoe instead. Brandon laughed, relishing in the stark shift in power dynamics—a complete role reversal from their last encounter when he had been undercover, posing as part of Anya's security team.

He leaned forward in his chair. Switching to English, he said, "C'mon. All I want to know is what happened. You can tell me, or you can go back to that cell of yours. Do you really want to die alone down there?"

As the silence stretched on, Brandon began to question the value of his visit. He'd already interviewed Ben and Georgia separately, receiving the same tale from both. And even though he had compiled his findings and reported back to his superiors, something nagged at him. He was certain Georgia hadn't told him the whole story, and he suspected she was withholding information about the secret military weapon buried with Genghis Khan.

When Anya showed no signs of giving in, Brandon decided to try a different tactic. He stood up, pretending to leave the room. It wasn't until he was at the door that Anya asked in a cracked, raw voice, "Is Georgia okay?"

Brandon frowned, his hand hovering over the door handle. He had never known Anya to be concerned about anyone else. Keeping his expression composed even as suspicion reared its head, he turned back to her. "Why don't you tell me what I want to know first, and then I'll answer your questions?"

She seemed to think on this, so he nudged her along. "This is a one-time offer, Anya. Mother Russia has washed her hands clean of you. After the shit show you left behind in Australia and Mongolia, they claim not to know you at all. Now, I haven't told your investors where you are—yet—but just think of what will happen to you when they find out."

Fear returned to Anya's face, and she tried in vain to hide it.

Sitting back down, Brandon sweetened the deal. "If I think you're telling the truth, I might consider helping you get out of here."

She narrowed her gaze. "So... I'll get some kind of... witness protection?" She struggled with the English phrasing.

"Not quite the same, but something like that."

The proposition seemed to sway her, and with a reluctant, gradual start, Anya began to unravel her tale. Brandon recorded every word on his phone, each disclosure further confirming his suspicions about Georgia's deceit.

Anya recounted how a tree had crushed her arm during a storm, and her subsequent search for Georgia after regaining consciousness. Her description of the Mongolian royal tomb was detailed, including the unexpected death of her head of security, Lev Ivanov. As she spoke about the encounter with Georgia and two Mongolian women inside the tomb, her frustration was evident, her brows furrowing with each revelation.

"What were they doing?" Brandon asked.

Anya shrugged. "Just talking."

"About?"

"I couldn't hear."

"And what was inside the tomb?"

"Nothing that I could see," was her smooth answer. "They were inside a circular chamber with eight doorways spread evenly around. I didn't get to find out what was beyond those passages."

Brandon nodded, allowing her to go on. When Anya revealed that she had shot Georgia in the stomach, he struggled to conceal his surprise. His initial reaction was to dismiss her admission as false, but then he thought—why would she make up such a lie? It made no sense. Anya must have expected Brandon to recognise her attempt at deception, since Georgia had clearly come away unscathed from the ordeal. In fact, when he'd met the Australian professor just days after the incident, she hadn't had a single scratch on her—surprising given the amount of time she spent exploring the Mongolian wilderness.

All of this, added with Anya's earlier unexpected concern about Georgia's well-being, set his mind into overdrive.

Even as the Russian woman continued her story, Brandon's thoughts took off like a sprinter down the track, leaving her voice a distant murmur in the background. His mind looped around the persistent unease he'd always felt around Georgia. There was just something off about her. He thought of the way she moved in an almost unearthly manner when deep in thought, as if she had no weight and was made of air. Brandon also couldn't help but recall how little she ate and slept.

Then he remembered Georgia's file, and the details of her last expedition in Taiwan. It was the one where the billionaire Mark Lambert had hired her to find the elixir of life—

He sucked in a quiet breath.

No way. It couldn't possibly be.

Could it?

His head spun over what a discovery like this could mean for his career. Working in the DIA's specialised division for supernatural and unexplained phenomena, he had always hoped for precisely this kind of breakthrough. The mere thought of what could be achieved, particularly the creation of super soldiers—the ultimate objective of his department—sent a thrilling chill down his spine.

As Brandon grasped the full weight of the implications, a jolt of *electrifying anticipation surged through him. But nothing was certain until he had solid, irrefutable proof—something tangible and undeniable. He would have to bring Georgia in for interrogation and arrange for DIA scientists to examine her.*

But how could Brandon convince his superiors to green-light the plan? Their tolerance for his pursuits was already wearing thin, especially after the fruitless outcome of the Mongolia expedition. Having already shelved Georgia's case, they were pushing him to focus on more urgent issues. For Brandon to propose a new mission based solely on the testimony of an unhinged Russian archaeologist would be tantamount to career suicide. Just being here speaking to Anya was a risk, one that could land him in hot water with his boss.

And if, by some stroke of luck, he managed to persuade his boss to sanction this, Brandon's obstacles were still challenging. He'd been ousted from Australia by its intelligence agencies following the disaster of his undercover mission. That meant that even if the investigation proceeded, his superiors would likely assign it to someone else, sidelining him despite the fact that he was the originator of the lead. Complicating matters further was his brother, who seemed smitten with Georgia and was now in Sydney, chasing fanciful dreams. The thought of having to go up against Ben filled Brandon with dread.

The stakes were too high to ignore. And the prospect of uncovering something monumental, too enticing.

He had to be strategic, crafting an intricate strategy that would not only reveal Georgia's secrets but also protect his professional standing. A delicate balance was required with careful plotting and execution, but the potential rewards were too significant to dismiss.

That was when he remembered the new case on his desk involving Mallika Sharma, and he thought, Maybe I could kill two birds with one stone?

The Indian media mogul had been identified as a potential threat due to the secretive biotechnology experiments being conducted under the guise of her pharmaceutical company. Sources revealed she had been pouring funds into dangerous virus research, but details about her motivations were hazy.

Sharma had also been bankrolling some major discoveries in the Indus Valley archaeological site of Dwarka.

"What?" Anya had stopped talking and was studying him.

"Nothing. Continue."

Anya's pale hazel eyes searched his face. Despite her haggard appearance, her gaze remained shrewd and calculating.

Meeting Anya's probing stare, a particular detail of Mallika Sharma's file suddenly surfaced in Brandon's mind. He realised that with a little makeover, Anya could easily fit Sharma's type.

Adrenaline rushed through Brandon's veins as an idea blossomed in his head. He wove together a ploy that even he would later admire for its brilliance.

Anya asked again, "How is Georgia? Did she... survive?"

He kept his expression strictly in check as he gave her the single-word answer, "Yes."

The relief on the Russian woman's face was stark. Sensing his advantage, Brandon leaned forward.

"Anya, how would you like to see the professor again?"

60

Present day, Thiruvananthapuram, India

As Agent Miller delves deeper into his story, every detail sends a wave of nausea churning through Georgia's stomach. Her throat is parched, tightening to the point of pain as she throws glances at Buri, whose expression remains—as always—inscrutably controlled and unreadable.

"So you sent Anya to spy on Mallika Sharma," Buri summarises.

"I didn't want to use DIA resources," Agent Miller admits. "And Anya's knowledge of archaeology put her in an ideal position to sway Sharma's choices on the Dwarka discoveries. That's how she got you and Georgia involved. Like I said before, Anya has a knack for manipulation and seduction."

"And you promised Anya… what?" Buri asks.

"That she'd eventually get to speak with Georgia in person. She knew she couldn't approach Georgia herself since the Russians were watching everyone she'd been in contact with. Anya also wanted some work done on her face to make sure she wouldn't be easily recognised—which suited me fine, because it made sure Sharma would fall for her charms.

While Anya was under during the surgery, I planted a tracking device in her. I also made it clear that if she made one wrong move, I'd feed her to the people she feared most."

"But she went rogue, anyway," Buri points out, glancing at Anya's limp body on the floor.

"She still served her purpose." Miller shrugs. "To the DIA, I was investigating Mallika Sharma. But my real focus was on Georgia. When the Dwarka Prophecy blew up, I realised Sharma's plans, but I let it unfold. I needed the whole thing to escalate until Georgia exposed herself. I knew you have a soft spot for her, which was why I tried to make you see her for what she is."

Tension grips Buri's frame. "What do you mean by that?"

Agent Miller hesitates, as if deciding how much to reveal. Then his face hardens with resolve and he says, "You can be a stubborn fuck sometimes. I couldn't just tell you what I suspected. I needed you to see for yourself, and to come to your own conclusions."

Georgia's heart pounds, the implication hitting her like a physical blow.

Buri's eyes narrow, his broad chest lifting as he takes a sharp inhale. "You're the one who's been sabotaging us."

"No." Miller points at Georgia. "I've been sabotaging her."

"So the dive in Dwarka, the Ajanta Caves, and the attack outside the temple… that was all you?"

Miller's lips press into a thin, flat line. He confirms with a single nod.

"And what about the flare?" Rage colours Sarah's face as she demands an explanation. "The one that almost killed *me*?"

"You came out of the Ajanta Caves unharmed, just like Georgia. I had to know if you were the same as her… something I'm still trying to find out," Miller says.

"You arsehole—"

Georgia is quick to intervene, grasping Sarah around the

waist just as she lunges at Miller in fury. In the ensuing chaos, Miller seizes the opportunity to grab Georgia, pulling her forcefully against him. He yanks off the scarf that Sarah tied around Georgia's head, revealing her gunshot wound.

Sarah screams and charges at them, desperate to pry Miller's grip off Georgia. He strikes her across the face, sending her sprawling across the floor.

Buri brings up his weapon and aims it at his brother. "Let Georgia go."

But the DIA agent ignores him, his focus fixed on examining Georgia's wound. She tenses as he parts her blood-matted hair, his sudden gasp betraying his shock.

"Damn. I knew it," he murmurs. Twisting her head to show Buri, he says, "Do you see now? She's completely healed."

Georgia's breath hitches as she looks to Buri, searching his face for any hint of what he might be thinking. But his expression remains a mask of impenetrable calm as he stands there, gun pointed at Miller. Her heart thuds against her ribcage, each beat echoing her rising panic. In Buri's stoic presence, she finds no comfort, no hint of understanding or judgement, only an enigmatic stillness that leaves her feeling more isolated and exposed under Miller's scrutiny.

Miller's voice is full of condemnation as he says, "I've been acting in the best interests of our nation, and of humanity itself. That's more than what can be said for the professor. "

Before she can protest, Agent Miller leans in. "Think about it, Georgia. This secret you've been harbouring can save millions. If you had come forward, those deaths from the virus could have been prevented. How can you be so selfish, keeping this all to yourself?"

His words sting, sending a rush of heat across Georgia's cheeks. Deep down, she feels the weight of truth in his accusation.

"You can't be serious." Sarah staggers to her feet and wipes the blood from her split lip. "You're the one who let Sharma release that virus when you knew exactly what she was up to."

"Anya was meant to stop her."

"And you actually trusted her to come through. What a joke," Sarah spits out with palpable scorn. "Also, spare us that bullshit about the greater good. We all know that the DIA will be keeping this to itself and weaponising it against its enemies."

Miller's body stiffens, his grip tightening around Georgia's neck as he launches into an argument with Sarah. But Georgia's attention is riveted to Buri's stony face, trying in vain to read his response. His piercing gaze meets hers, and she gulps at the lump in her throat.

"Enough!" Buri's deep voice booms in the chamber, and the room falls silent under his command. He keeps his pistol aimed at Brandon, levelling him with a stern look. "Let Georgia go."

"But—"

"I knew about her all along."

"What?" Miller and Sarah exclaim in unison.

A whirlwind of astonishment and fear sweeps through Georgia. "How?"

Buri's gaze is unflinching as it settles on her. "You think I didn't notice when you came out of the Ajanta Caves with Sarah's shirt on instead of your own? And how you stopped bleeding as soon as you came out of the water in Dwarka?" A brief flicker of emotion passes over his features, too quick for Georgia to decipher. "After you left Ulaanbaatar, Brandon told me about your last expedition in Taiwan. That's when it all clicked for me. I thought of all the times you'd been injured in Mongolia—how I never actually saw the wounds, and how quickly you seemed to recover when it would have taken weeks for a normal person."

"I knew it." Sarah wags an accusatory finger at Buri. "That's why you came to Sydney."

Buri shakes his head, keeping his eyes on Georgia. "I had my suspicions back then, but I wasn't sure. Brandon wasn't satisfied with my briefing about what had happened in Mongolia. He said that the DIA was going to keep a close eye on you. So I came to Sydney, worried about what might happen if they found out about your secret. Then the Dwarka Prophecy happened, and throughout our time in India, I watched you. That's when I knew for certain."

"You suspected all this time, and said nothing to me." Miller's voice is tinged with a sense of betrayal.

"You never asked me," Georgia says to Buri, her voice weak.

Remorse flickers across Buri's features, gone in an instant. "At first, I thought it'd be absurd to even mention it. I thought you'd laugh in my face and I'd look like a fool. Then Brandon showed up, and you and Sarah got more suspicious of me, making it even harder to approach you. And"—he exhales with impatience—"I wanted you to tell me yourself. I hoped you'd trust me enough because trust is a two-way street, Georgia."

Overwhelmed by his words, a tumult of guilt and a flicker of hope pierces her heart.

"You should have told me, bro," Miller says, pulling Georgia closer. "We could have brought her in earlier. Could have saved time. And lives."

"No." Buri's tone is unwavering.

Infuriated, Agent Miller raises his voice. "You're a medic. Can't you see what this means? Think of the brothers in the army we could save."

"You're not doing anything against her will."

Agent Miller scoffs. "She's not exactly cooperative, is she? *And* she let all those people die of the virus in Bangkok. What makes you think she'll offer herself up now?"

"That's not how it works, you idiot," Sarah snaps, her voice dripping with venom. "We don't know that whatever Georgia has can work against the virus. All we know is that she heals faster than normal people."

"Well, I guess there's only one way to find out."

Miller's fist slams into Georgia's kidneys with a vicious force, causing her to let out a gut-wrenching cry as she drops to the floor. In a flash of movement, he snatches the pistol from Buri's grip. But Buri is not unarmed, drawing another gun from his belt as the two brothers engage in a tense stand-off, their eyes locked in a deadly stare and their chests heaving with rapid breaths.

It takes Georgia several agonising moments to recover from Miller's savage attack. She struggles back to her feet, her voice trembling as she pleads, "You don't understand. There's a reason I've kept this all a secret. The last time the elixir was shared—"

Before she can finish, Miller's gun swings towards her. With a deafening crack, he fires directly into her chest, sending a searing bolt of pain through her body. She gasps for air, her hand reaching to grasp at the wound as she stumbles backwards in shock. Buri's gaze meets hers, his eyes filled with disbelief, before Miller charges forward and punches him on his wounded arm. Roaring with pain, his grip on his gun loosens, and Brandon grabs the weapon out of his hand and strikes it against his temple. With a nauseating thump, Buri crumples to the ground.

Falling to her knees beside him, Georgia's world spins into darkness.

61

BRANDON LOOMS over Georgia's unmoving body, baffled when Sarah scrambles to her side in a panic. She clamps her hands over the gaping wound in the middle of Georgia's chest, her hands slick with warm blood as she tries to stem the relentless flow.

"No no no no no," Sarah chants, frantic. She throws a fiery glare at Brandon. "What the fuck have you done?"

"She can heal, can't she?"

"Not from everything, dickhead. She's never been shot in the heart before."

Icy dread washes over Brandon. He drops to his knees, reaching out to check Georgia's pulse. But before his fingers can make contact, Sarah belts him across the head.

"Keep your hands off her, you prick!"

Brandon rears up just as Sarah's claws narrowly miss his face. He stumbles back, heart racing as he watches Sarah fret over her boss's lifeless form.

Shit. What does he do now? Brandon's plan, which seemed foolproof at the time, now teeters on the brink of disaster. He thought he was being clever by shooting the professor and knocking out Ben, so he'd have no problem extracting Georgia. Exhausted from fighting Sharma's men, he just couldn't take the chance with Georgia's enhanced abilities and Ben being on her side. But now he realises he's acted without truly understanding the limits of her healing abilities.

A cold knot of fear forms in his stomach.

What if she's dead?

Then he tells himself that it doesn't matter. He can still bring her body back to the headquarters, where DIA scientists will examine her remains. Surely, they'll be able to learn something valuable from her DNA, dead or alive.

Brandon steels himself with a fortifying breath. He reminds himself what he's doing this for.

For the USA. For the stars and stripes forever. For freedom.

He raises his gun at Sarah.

She looks up and glares at him. "What, you gonna shoot me too?"

He pushes down the remorse creeping up his chest, trying not to feel bad about what he has to do, even if Sarah happens to be the most annoying woman he's ever met. "Sorry, Sarah. I can't have you telling everyone about this."

What catches him off guard is her complete lack of fear. Instead, her face twists in fury. "Well, fuck you very much. Have you forgotten that I might be just like Georgia?"

He hesitates. Before he can decide what to do, a searing pain explodes at the back of his head, sending him to his knees. Dazed and disorientated, he struggles to stand but his limbs feel like lead, moving in slow motion.

With a groan, he turns to face his assailant. Anya stands over him, clutching the blood-stained Indus Star in her hands. Her left cheek is swollen and bruised from his previous assault, but her eyes gleam with a calculating resolve. "What did I say? No one is telling me what to do anymore. Especially not you."

She raises the diamond high above her head and brings it crashing down onto his face.

62

SARAH IS FROZEN with abject horror as Anya bashes Agent Miller on the head with the stone over and over again, each crunching blow turning his face into unrecognisable, bloody pulp. Bile rises to her throat at the gruesome sight, but even more frightening is the eerie calm with which Anya executes the murder, as if she is simply tenderising a piece of steak.

Then the woman stands over the carnage of Miller's brutalised body, a mixture of fascination and satisfaction on her face as she examines her handiwork. Looking up suddenly, she sweeps her gaze across the room, and her eyes lock onto Sarah, who is crouched over Georgia's unmoving form. In a panic, Sarah scrambles to her feet, but as Anya prowls towards her, she finds herself backing up until she's pressed flat against the wall.

Anya's menacing approach is intercepted by a swift sweep of Buri's leg. She goes down hard, and the blood-stained diamond drops onto the floor with a resounding thud.

Buri launches himself at Anya, landing a solid punch on her face just as she drives her knee into his groin. He howls with agony, collapsing to the side as Anya rolls over and scrambles towards Brandon's discarded pistol. Sarah also dives for the gun, but Anya beats her to it, snatching the weapon before aiming it at her.

Their ragged breaths fill the air as Anya slowly rises to a standing position. Buri lies on the floor, incapacitated by his injury, unable to stop what is about to unfold.

Adrenaline heightening Sarah's senses, she catches a glimpse of movement in the far corner of the room. She shoots a quick glance at Georgia, who's still lying on the ground with her eyes shut.

Was it her imagination?

Anya tilts her head to follow Sarah's gaze, her icy blue eyes narrowing into slits as she takes in the sight of Georgia's lifeless body. Sarah is taken aback to see a flicker of despair on the Russian woman's face.

Returning her attention to Sarah, Anya takes a quick scan of her. "You're Georgia's assistant."

Sarah remains silent, refusing to confirm or deny.

"Georgia must have told you what happened in Mongolia."

Sarah swallows against the lump in her throat. "Not really... She doesn't actually tell me much."

"You're lying," Anya hisses, closing the gap between them and pressing the gun against Sarah's forehead. "Tell me what you know."

"Okay. Okay," Sarah concedes, her hands raised in a gesture of surrender.

Out of the corner of her eye, she detects movement again. Her heart soars, but she resists the urge to glance in that direction.

Keeping her gaze firmly on Anya, she says, "I would tell you, but..." She takes a long, deliberate pause. It's only then that she allows her eyes to shift, just in time to see Georgia rising to her feet with formidable calm. "Maybe you should ask Georgia yourself?"

In a heartbeat, Anya's face transforms from a puzzled

frown to a look of sudden realisation, then morphs into pure shock as the impact of the truth hits. She spins around and is met with Georgia's fist delivering a swift, powerful jab to her face. Staggering to her left, she falls within Buri's reach. He grasps at her ankle, but Anya manages to wrench free, struggling to maintain her balance. In her disoriented state, she steps on the bloodied diamond.

Her foot slips on the slick surface of the gemstone, catapulting her backwards. With a harrowing crack that reverberates through the room, her skull slams against the lotus seat of the diamond.

Anya's body lies motionless, contorted in an unnatural position. Blood oozes from her wound, staining the ground in a pool of crimson.

Grunting with palpable pain, his limbs trembling and his breaths shallow, Buri drags himself towards Agent Miller. He collapses as he reaches his brother's lifeless form, an animalistic, primal sound of despair ripping from his throat as he takes in the atrocity of Anya's assault.

Frantically, his shaking hands roam over Miller's torso, lingering on the neck as if seeking a pulse that isn't there. With a ragged gasp, he cradles his brother's head, his entire frame racked with uncontrollable sobs.

Sarah stands frozen, witnessing the heart-wrenching scene as Buri unleashes the raw intensity of his grief with a guttural howl that echoes through the subterranean vault.

63

Two days later, Delhi, India

GEORGIA STANDS at the microphone in the press conference hall. Packed to the brim, the room is full of journalists elbowing for space. The barrage of camera flashes blind her as she delivers her address. And as soon as she is finished, the room bursts into an uproarious cacophony of questions.

After answering a few of them, Georgia points to a familiar face in the front row, calling out, "Ms. Shah."

Dhara stands. "Professor Lee, are you saying that this entire situation has been a ruse, and that everyone has panicked over nothing?"

Georgia nods. "In terms of it being a hoax—yes, that's correct. But we're still facing a serious threat. The virus has now spread to India and China, as you're all aware. On that note, I'll pass the floor to Dr. Vikram Kumar."

A hush comes over the crowd as all eyes turn to the young scientist. He clears his throat and smooths out the notes on the podium with trembling hands. Pushing the thick glasses up the bridge of his nose, he begins.

Georgia's thoughts drift back to the tumultuous events of

the past few days. After Anya slipped on the diamond and smashed her head against the floor, she was rushed to the hospital along with two surviving members of Sharma's security team. Now she lies in a coma, suffering from severe brain swelling, and doctors are sceptical about her chances of making it through the week.

The police discovered a vial of Vikram's vaccine in Anya's belongings. This has prompted an unprecedented global cooperation, with governments worldwide joining forces with Vikram to expedite the production of the vaccine. With India scrambling to contain the virus's spread and Pakistan grappling with the aftermath of its devastating floods, the focus of both nations has shifted away from the contentious Koh-i-Noor dispute, allowing a brief respite from their longstanding rivalry.

Vikram finishes his statement and answers a few more questions with Georgia. As the press conference concludes, Georgia's gaze lifts and finds Dhara's across the room. The journalist offers her a warm, acknowledging smile.

Returning the smile, Georgia reflects on their conversation from the day before as they caught up on each other's stories. Dhara has really grown on her over the past few weeks, and she looks forward to their future interactions.

She exits the conference hall and is soon joined by Sarah, Buri, and Indi.

Sarah says, "I'm surprised Dhara didn't point out that while Sharma was behind certain parts of the Dwarka Prophecies, the natural disasters and climate events are very much real."

Georgia purses her lips. "True, but Dhara probably understands the importance of keeping everyone calm right now, especially after everything that has happened."

She lets out a deep sigh, then stoops to ruffle Indi's soft fur. The German shepherd returns the affection with big, wet licks on her hand.

Glancing up at Buri, Georgia finally musters the courage to ask the question that's been weighing on her mind for the last couple of days. "Will you be coming back to Australia with us?"

Buri shakes his head. "I need to go back to the States for a while."

"Oh." Georgia can't hide the note of disappointment in her voice.

"I talked to my father this morning. We're planning Brandon's funeral for the end of the week. The DIA also wants a debrief." His dark brown eyes betray his deep sorrow.

She tenses. "Again, I'm so sorry." She reaches for his hand, wanting to offer comfort, yet she knows no words could ever bridge the chasm of his loss.

He maintains his intense gaze on her, adding with quiet assurance, "Don't worry. Your secret is safe with me." His attention briefly shifts to Indi, who looks up at him, her tongue hanging out in a display of canine adoration.

A wave of relief washes over her, more potent than she expected. "Thank you," she murmurs. In a hesitant voice, she ventures, "Once you've handled everything you need to, will you... come back to Sydney?"

Buri's eyes snap back to hers, clearly taken aback. He searches her face as if gauging the sincerity of her inquiry.

"I—uh—I'll give you guys a moment." Sarah saunters off, barely concealing a smirk.

Left alone with Buri, Georgia's nerves intensify. "I want to share my story with you. The entire thing... which I haven't had the opportunity to. That's if—if you come back. I mean—when you come back."

She clamps her mouth shut and berates herself for the ramble, but Buri doesn't seem to mind.

"You do?"

"Yeah, I do. And, um, I was thinking about the self-defence training too. Maybe we could continue that? Also, didn't we talk about getting you a job at the university?"

"We did."

She drops her gaze, recalling her callousness when she rejected him nine months earlier. "About the last time... I'm really sorry. I was dealing with a lot, but that's no excuse for how I treated you."

His eyes stay on her for a prolonged, agonising moment, making her even more anxious. Her heart galloping like a wild horse, Georgia gathers her courage to ask once more, "So... what do you say?"

"I say... yes." Buri rewards her with one of his rare smiles.

The sight hits her squarely in the chest, taking her breath away. She finds herself beaming back at him, a rush of youthful exuberance flooding through her.

In that moment, a new world of possibilities opens up. A burden is lifted from her spirit, replaced by a rush of exhilaration.

Ever since discovering her immortality, Georgia has resigned herself to a solitary life. After all, Charlie—for all of his wisdom and knowledge—chose to live as an ascetic. Convinced that isolation was her only option, she shut herself away, fearing the inevitable pain of outliving anyone she grew close to. But now, a realisation dawns on her: This isn't the only way to live. Life is offering her a different path, one filled with connection and hope.

Seema's words echo in her mind, revealing their true depth: amidst life's turmoil, suffering, and the certainty of death, there remains one enduring constant.

Love.

She has Sarah, Buri, and Indi—a circle of companions that promises a richer, more fulfilling life than she has ever dared to hope for.

Is humanity ready to embrace eternal life?

Maybe not right now. But perhaps one day it will be.

And when that day comes, she'll be right here, waiting.

EPILOGUE

Six months later, somewhere in Australia

"Are you sure this is the right location?" Georgia asks Buri, her voice tinged with doubt.

"It's what the coordinates point to," Buri says.

"Well, whatever this place is, Charlie made sure no one else will find it," Sarah chimes in, mopping the sweat from her brow. "No one in their right mind would ever come out here. Except maybe kangaroos. And snakes." She shudders and walks off with Indi trailing behind her.

Georgia stares at the envelope in her hands, given to her by Charlie's lawyer at Ethan's funeral. It contains nothing but a set of coordinates scrawled on a card, and a mysterious string of six numbers she has been unable to decipher. There are no explanations, and no instructions.

It has taken her over a year to work up the courage for this journey, and she is glad that Buri, Indi, and Sarah are with her. But the purpose of this far-flung, desolate location, deep in the Australian outback, eludes her.

"Hey, you okay?" Buri asks, lifting her chin to meet his gaze.

Her stomach aflutter with nerves, every inch of her skin buzzing from his touch, she gives him a wan smile. These intimate, stolen moments between them—albeit brief—have become a frequent occurrence ever since Buri returned from the States two months ago.

"Just say the word, and we'll be out of here," he offers.

"No, let's keep looking for a bit longer." She swallows. "We'll have you back at work in no time, I promise."

He searches her eyes. Finally he nods, but doesn't let go of her chin. "You *do* realise… that I didn't come back to Australia just for a job at the university, right?"

Georgia's heart skips a beat. "You didn't?" she squeaks.

His features soften with a ghost of a smile. He leans in, his breath hovering over her lips, his earthy, masculine scent overwhelming her senses.

"Gross." Sarah reappears with Indi. "Get a room, you two."

Letting her go with a sigh and a shake of his head, Buri brushes past Sarah and saunters off with Indi to continue their search. Georgia scans the area, looking everywhere but in the direction of Sarah's inquisitive stare, squinting against the intense glare of the sun blaring from above. The relentless heat, the endless ochre sand, and the incessant buzz of flies make for an inhospitable environment. Every time she opens her mouth, there's a risk she might swallow an insect. As she surveys her surroundings, all she sees are three rows of towering solar panels, standing stark against the red, barren landscape.

"Those must generate electricity for something," Georgia observes.

"Yeah, but we've been here for almost an hour, and we haven't found *anything*," Sarah whines. "I'm *melting*. Can we go? This is exactly why I should stick to being the research assistant back at the university while you two gallivant

around the world, solving mysteries. I'm too old for this shi
—" Sarah splutters and chokes as she inhales a fly.

"I found it!" Buri shouts from a distance. Beside him, Indi
digs into the sand with enthusiasm.

Georgia hurries over to join them just as Buri kneels down
to help Indi. Together, they uncover a concealed metal hatch,
painted black and with a digital keypad next to its handle.

"Holy shit," Sarah says.

Dropping to her knees, Georgia retrieves the card from the
envelope, keying in the six-digit code.

With a hiss, the hatch swings open, releasing a wave of
cool air. Lights flicker to life, illuminating a set of stairs
descending into the depths. Peering through the hatch,
Georgia discovers an enormous room below.

Sarah is the first to bound down the steps. "Oh thank God,
it's so much cooler down here," she exclaims.

Dozens of fluorescent lights flicker on in succession as
Georgia follows, revealing a large underground warehouse
lined with extensive metal shelving.

Large battery cells line the walls, presumably storing power
from the solar panels. Near the stairs, a console catches Georgia's attention. She examines it, realising that the entire space is
equipped with state-of-the-art temperature and humidity
control systems—the kind that one would find in a museum.

"What *is* this place?" Sarah's voice echoes in the
cavernous space.

"It's a vault," Georgia murmurs.

"For what?"

Moving down the first row of shelves, Georgia peeks
inside one of the crates to find what appears to be ancient
bronzeware from China's Shang Dynasty. Several rows down,
she discovers a collection of Viking swords.

"Charlie had a passion for collecting artefacts," Georgia
explains. "He said he held onto things as a legacy of the times

he lived through. When his collection grew too large, he'd donate pieces to museums. It was his way of preserving history."

She takes a deep, quivering breath. The possibility of what this immense trove might contain begins to dawn on her, and a rush of excitement surges through her veins.

"And now he's left it all to you," Sarah says. "Jesus, Georgia, you're *rich*!"

Buri's voice reverberates through the expansive chamber, and Georgia and Sarah make their way towards the end of the aisle, where they find him and Indi beside a large table. On it, conservation tools are meticulously arranged on small desktop trays. But what catches Georgia's eye is the crate marked with her name.

With trembling hands, Georgia lifts the lid of the box. Inside, she discovers a multitude of objects, copies of official documents and papers, and photographs. Atop it all is a memo in Charlie's handwriting.

A mystery for you to solve, the note says.

Sarah rummages through the contents, bringing out a large, rolled-up piece of paper. She unfurls it across the work-table, her body tensing as she takes in what it reveals.

Picking up on her sudden anxiety, Georgia asks, "Sarah?"

"I've seen this before," Sarah says in an eerie whisper.

"Where?" Georgia scans the detailed infographic, which appears to be some kind of vast family tree. Her heart skips a beat when she spots Charlie's name at the top and recognises several names at the bottom.

"In Wang Jian's basement," Sarah murmurs. "He had something similar on the wall when he kidnapped me." Sarah shakes her head as if to dispel the memory, then lifts her eyes to meet Georgia's gaze. "This is your family tree, Georgia. Yours and Charlie's."

Georgia is unable to speak. Before he died, Charlie had told her that she was the last of the Hsu clan, his only remaining descendent. Her eyes sweep over the page, pausing on her grandmother's name and the three children listed under it.

"Wait. Amah had *three* kids?"

"I thought your mum is an only child?" Sarah asks.

Georgia shakes her head. "Amah told me recently about a son who died during the Nanjing Massacre. But she never spoke of another daughter. It says here"—she leans closer, scrutinising the fine print beside the unfamiliar name—"'Unable to locate'?"

"I think Charlie wants you to find your aunt," Sarah says in a soft voice.

Straightening, Georgia draws in a deep, steadying breath. Growing up as an only child with no cousins or extended family, her childhood was marked by solitude. Now, the possibility of finding new family members makes her heart ready to burst.

Three sets of eyes stare at her, all waiting for her to speak.

Georgia grins.

"What are we waiting for? Let's get to work."

ACKNOWLEDGMENTS

Creating the Georgia Lee Adventure Series has been nothing short of a wild adventure, and while writing is mostly a solitary pursuit, bringing a book to life is undoubtedly a team effort. I am deeply grateful to the following people for their invaluable assistance and generosity:

Firstly, to my readers out there, for cheering me on every step of the way. Getting to know some of you and hearing your thoughts has been one of the most rewarding aspects of this journey, and has encouraged me to keep going when the going gets tough.

To my family, especially Mum and Dad, for their unwavering love and support.

When I decided to write a book about India, I didn't realise just how big a project it would become. I'm so thankful to Nicola Smith, Manohar Thyagaraj, Trupty Vora, Priya Mehta, Tejas Mehta, Dr. Steven M. Vose, and Roma Mehta for their guidance and their help with my research.

To Vanessa Lawless and Anthea Blaikie, for their valuable feedback and support in my work as always.

To my friends at Taipei Writers Group, for their sage advice and for being such an inspiration to me: Jenny Green, Claire Lohan, Pat Woods, and Mark Will.

To Michelle Chan, Tee Yen Ng, and Tee Ken Ng, for their amazing generosity in providing me with such a beautiful studio to work in.

To the brilliant Kristen Tate at The Blue Garret—the editor of this book.

Lastly and most importantly, to my husband, Mark: as ever, you have been the muse, the fellow adventurer, the cheerleader, the sounding board, the marketing guru, the nurse, the chef, and the one to wipe away the tears when things go wrong. Your patient tolerance and your selfless love and kindness continue to dazzle and inspire me. Without you, none of this would have been possible.

ABOUT THE AUTHOR

A. H. Wang is a contemporary visual artist and author with a fascination for history and a passion for adventure. Born in Taiwan and raised in Australia, her travels have taken her across five continents and dozens of countries. Throughout her journey, she has developed a sincere appreciation for local cultures and the lore of ancient civilisations.

As well as making art and writing, you will find her deeply involved with her meditation practice. In a previous life, she was also a scientist, an engineer, a holistic counsellor, and a Reiki Master. She now lives in Perth, Western Australia, with her husband.

www.AHWangAuthor.com

facebook.com/ahwangauthor
instagram.com/ahwangauthor
goodreads.com/ahwangauthor
bookbub.com/authors/a-h-wang

Join A. H. Wang's Readers' Group to be notified of new releases, giveaways, and pre-release specials:

www.AHWangAuthor.com/#sign-up

Printed in Great Britain
by Amazon